"I WON!" SHE CRIED OUT ~~~ ~~~
YOU MY MARE WAS FASTER."

Evan looked at Fire Dancer. With her face flushed from the excitement of the race and her green eyes dancing with exhilaration, she looked beautiful. He dismounted, ducked beneath his mount's neck, and without a word lifted her from the saddle. As he set her on her feet just inches from him, he said, "Yes, you won. I concede your victory. And now I'm going to collect my consolation prize."

"What consolation prize?"

"A kiss."

"But that's what you wanted for your reward if you won—for me to kiss you," Fire Dancer objected. "Well, you didn't win. I did!"

"Yes, I know. And for that reason, I kiss you."

Fire Dancer's heart raced at the prospect, but perversely she said, "No! I won't allow it."

Evan's blue eyes darkened to an indigo as he said in a husky voice, "I'm afraid you have no choice in the matter. I have it coming to me, and I'm a man who always claims his prize. . . ."

JOANNE REDD

DANCE WITH FIRE

A DELL BOOK

Published by
Dell Publishing
a division of
Bantam Doubleday Dell Publishing Group, Inc.
666 Fifth Avenue
New York, New York 10103

The trademark Dell® is registered in the U.S. Patent and Trademark Office.

ISBN: 0-440-20826-2

Printed in the United States of America

Published simultaneously in Canada

April 1992

10 9 8 7 6 5 4 3 2 1

OPM

To Monica, with love, Mom.

1

The hair rose on the nape of Evan Trevor's neck, and a cold chill ran up his spine. He knew the savages were lurking in the forest all around him, even though he could distinguish no sign of them in the dark shadows cast by the thick woods. But he didn't have to see them. He could feel their eyes on him, boring into his back, watching every movement he made. God, he wished he knew if they were friend or foe, if they were simply being cautious before revealing their presence or waiting for the right moment to spring, like a panther stalking its prey. It wasn't that he was particularly afraid of death. He had come face to face with the dark angel many times in the past without the slightest trepidation. But torture was an entirely different matter. He didn't relish the prospect of being slowly burned to death while his skin was sliced from his body and eaten before his very eyes.

Evan risked a quick sideways glance at his guide, Josh McDougal. The lanky, long-limbed Scot didn't look in the least concerned as he led his horse down the narrow trail, although Evan felt sure that he, too, was aware of the eyes watching from the depths of the forest. The Indians' presence was so powerful, it was almost palpable. Still, if Josh wasn't worried, then Evan supposed he shouldn't be. After all, Josh was the Indian expert. But the eerie silence of the forest and knowing the savages were there, crouching in the darkness waiting for God knew what, was unnerving.

Evan looked about, hoping to catch at least a fleeting glimpse of a feather, but he saw nothing unusual. All around him massive tree trunks, some as thick as ten feet in diameter, cast dark purple shadows. There was no underbrush, for no light penetrated the dense canopy of leaves hundreds of feet overhead. For that reason, there were no songbirds—there was nothing for them to eat here in this deep forest. Only woodpeckers visited, their steady drumming on the trunks seeming inordinately loud as it echoed through the woods, an irritating noise that wrought even more havoc on his nerves.

Evan had never seen forests like those here in America. There were certainly none like them in England. Here, in this new land, a person could travel for days through one without seeing a glimmer of sunlight, and he'd had no earthly idea that trees could grow to be so huge. But then, woodlands like the one they were passing through were true virgin forests, untouched by man. The only place he had ever heard such silence was at sea, in the dead of night, when there was no wind. Even the sound of the horses' hoofbeats was so muted that he had to strain his ears to hear it, as the ground was cushioned with thick layers of rotted leaves that had accumulated over hundreds of years. There was no beaten trail on the ground to show the way. Instead, the two men made their way by following the deep axe marks that had been made at eye level on the tree trunks. Without them, they would have been hopelessly lost.

Evan heard a noise, so slight that it was little more than a whispered rustle. He tensed, half expecting to feel the blade of a tomahawk in his back. When nothing happened and he could hear no further sounds, his nerves got the better of him and he demanded irritably of his guide, "If they're not going to attack us, why in the devil don't they show themselves?"

Without breaking his stride or even bothering to look at Evan, the Scot asked lazily, "Are ye talkin' about the Indians?"

"Of course I'm talking about the Indians!" Evan answered. "I assume they're friendly, or we'd be dead or taken captive by now. You could have told me that, you know, and saved me the worry."

"Now, don't get yer dander up," Josh replied soothingly. "I thought ye'd figure it out on yer own, which ye did. And ye're right about 'em bein' friendly. I figure they're Chickasaw, since we're on their huntin' ground and the town we're headin' for is nearby. As for 'em not showin' 'emselves, I assume they just ain't ready to yet. Ye've got a lot to learn about Indians, Major. They take their time doin' things, and out here, we have to play by their rules."

Evan ignored the rugged guide's remark about him having a lot to learn about Indians. That was something he had no intention of doing. As soon as the present mission was completed, he planned to leave this blasted country and go back to England, even if he had to conjure up a mysterious illness to get shipped back. He'd had quite enough of fighting Frenchmen and their brutal ·Indian allies in the wilderness, quite enough of America and its independent, hard-headed rangers, quite enough of fighting beside savages who might turn on him at any moment and scalp him. If he had to fight for a living—something that didn't sit well with him to begin with—then he'd do so in Europe, where they fought sane wars with well-disciplined masses of uniformed soldiers out in the wide open. At least there was never any doubt about who or where the enemy was.

Evan did take note, however, of the Scot's announcement that their destination was near. That news came as a welcome surprise. He had begun to fear that they would never reach the place or, despite Josh's reassurances, that they were lost. They had been on the trail for over a month, and it had been ten days since they had seen another human being. The sooner he reached his destination, the sooner he could finish the job and get back to civilization. Civilization was not the colonies, with their backward standard of living. Civilization was England.

"There's a clearin' up ahead," Josh informed him. "Figure we'll stop there, so ye can don yer uniform."

Evan saw several bright beams of sunlight cutting at an angle through the deep shadows ahead. As the wind moved the branches of the trees above, the rays too seemed to move, first here, then there, as if they were dancing. Where the light was reflected on the fine mist that hugged the forest floor, a fleeting rainbow appeared, disappeared, then appeared again. For a moment, Evan watched the display in mute fascination, then asked, "Why would I want to change into my uniform? You said it was a ridiculous garment for a soldier to wear."

"Aye, that it is, particularly that scarlet jacket of yers. Stands out like a sore thumb, even in these dark forests. Wearin' that, ye're a sittin' duck just beggin' to be shot. But these are our allies, and the Chickasaw dearly love pomp and pageantry and anythin' red. That uniform may be ridiculous to wear in battle, but it's impressive-looking, and ye do want to impress 'em, don't ye?"

"They've already seen me," Evan pointed out.

"Just their scouts, not Chief Promingo and his council. Why, the entire town'll probably turn out to welcome ye."

Evan fervently hoped he received a welcome. Despite Josh's assurances that the Chickasaw were in total agreement with his mission and were Great Britain's most steadfast Indian allies, he was still uneasy about just how he would be met. The Chickasaw were also renowned for being the fiercest and most warlike tribe in North America. Even the aggressive Mingoes—as the British called the Iroquois—had a healthy respect for the Chickasaw and gave them a wide berth.

Evan glanced around as they entered the sun-splashed clearing, shading his eyes against the bright light with his hand as he did so. All along the way, they had passed through clearings similar to this one: sudden treeless meadows varying in size from a few acres to several hundred, surrounded by thick forests. Josh had explained that they were either abandoned Indian farmlands or areas where the Indians had set fire to the forest to smoke out game. These meadows were prized and much sought after by the colonists, who were steadily moving westward and pushing the Indians back, since it saved the frontiersmen from having to clear the land themselves—an awesome chore considering the size of the trees.

Josh brought his horse to a standstill, turned to face Evan, and leaned casually on his long Pennsylvania rifle as if it were a post. The lanky Scot's fiery red hair was so bright in the glaring sunlight that it almost hurt Evan's eyes to look at it. He wondered how the guide had had the audacity to criticize the color of his jacket. Seeing the expectant look on Josh's face, Evan reined in and dismounted with disgust, knowing what was required of him. Personally, he couldn't care less if he impressed the Chickasaw or not, but as an officer of the Crown, he had a duty to perform, and Major Evan Trevor was a man who took his responsibilities very seriously, despite his distaste for his job. Laying the long rifle he had been holding on the ground, he slipped his uniform and boots from his saddlebags and began to remove the frontiersman's clothing that his guide had insisted he wear.

First he slipped off the leather hunting bag that hung at his side. The bag contained his balls, patches, bullet mold, flint and steel, and an awl to repair his moccasins; his powder horn was strapped to its side. Then he removed the tomahawk and scalping knife that hung from the sash of his linsey hunting shirt, which was tied around his narrow waist. Next Evan stripped off the loose, wraparound shirt, baring his magnificent chest with its light furring of golden hair, followed by the knee-high moccasins and the dark green trousers.

As the Englishman stripped, then donned his uniform, Josh watched idly. The guide had to admit that the major was a fine specimen of manhood. Unusually broad shouldered, lean hipped, and taut bellied, there wasn't an ounce of fat on him, as Josh would have expected of a nobleman. Rather, his tall frame was covered with hard, powerful muscles and sleek tendons that bespoke a physically active life. Even his features had a strong masculinity about them—the square jaw, piercing blue gaze, and firm set of his lips offset what otherwise would have been an almost too handsome face.

Evan was unaware of Josh's scrutiny. Once dressed, he untied his sword from where it was lashed to the side of his saddle and strapped it to his side. Straightening to his impressive full height, he asked tersely, "Well? Will your damn Chickasaw be impressed enough with this?"

Josh's eyes took in the scarlet jacket with its gold braid and long, buttoned-back tails, the white and gold brocade waistcoat, the ruffled shirt, the skintight white breeches, and the gleaming black cavalry boots. With a snowy white muslin stock and black ribbon at his neck and another, wider black ribbon holding back his shoulder-length golden hair at the back of his neck, the officer did look striking. But it was much more than the colorful, well-tailored uniform that made the major look so impressive. The man himself, with his magnificent physique, his golden good looks, and his commanding, self-confident air put him a cut above other men.

Still, Josh didn't want the Englishman to know how

impressive he looked. Despite the surprisingly admirable qualities that Josh had discovered in the officer over the past few weeks, Evan had an arrogance about him that grated on the guide's nerves. It wasn't simply that Evan had noble blood in his veins. The entire British Army had an infuriatingly superior air, from the highest generals to the lowest privates. They all seemed to look down on the colonists, and Josh, like so many of his peers, highly resented it. For that reason he answered noncommittally, "Ye'll do," then added, "as soon as ye put on yer hat."

"Forget the hat," Evan answered in obvious disgust. "It's probably smashed beyond recognition. It wasn't meant to be folded away in a pair of saddlebags."

"Aye, I know, but put it on anyway," Josh persisted. "It's a symbol of yer position. The Indians won't mind a few wrinkles."

With something that sounded much like a snort, Evan turned to his horse, reached deep into one pocket of his saddlebags, and pulled out his tricornered hat. He mumbled beneath his breath as he tried to reshape it into a semblance of what it had once been. Then, seeing his efforts were fruitless, he slammed the battered headcovering onto his head, shoved the garments he had shed, along with his tomahawk and knife, into his saddlebags, picked up his long rifle, and remounted. Sitting on his horse, he asked Josh, "What are you staring at? And don't tell me the hat looks ridiculous. I warned you that it would be smashed beyond recognition."

But Josh wasn't thinking that Evan looked ridiculous at all. Mounted, he looked even more impressive, for he sat and rode his horse with such ease and grace that the guide had often thought the major and the powerful, sleek-muscled animal looked like extensions of each other. Was it because Evan's black stallion was a Thoroughbred, Josh wondered, well trained and a fine specimen of English horseflesh? There weren't many such animals in the colonies. Only the wealthy plantation owners could afford to have them shipped from abroad. Therefore, other than the better-heeled officers who brought their mounts with them, the British Army obtained most of its horses from the native-bred animals.

No, Josh had to admit that it was the man, not his trappings. With his noble bearing, his dynamic vitality that emanated in powerful waves, and his air of total self-confidence, Evan Trevor would have looked splendid sitting on the most miserable nag in the colonies. Then he became aware of Evan's steady blue gaze on him. "Nay, the hat doesn't look all that bad," Josh answered belatedly.

"Then if I've passed inspection, let's get going," Evan answered, picking up his reins. "I want to get this meeting over with."

Without another word, Josh mounted his horse and directed it toward the dark woods across the clearing. Evan followed. Leaving the warmth of the bright sunlight behind, they again rode through the dark, dense forest, the rancid smell of rotting leaves heavy in their nostrils. Twenty minutes later, they came to another, much larger clearing, where a big palisade had been built beneath scattered, towering trees.

Evan reined in. "This is it?" he asked.

"Aye. This is Promingo's home."

"I didn't know the Indians had forts," Evan remarked, looking up the long line of upright logs whose ends had been sharpened to a point.

"Aye, they do. These are permanent settlements, ye know. The Chickasaw had Indian enemies long before the white man appeared. If the truth be known, this is where we colonists got our ideas for buildin' our forts. I doubt if there are any like 'em in England."

As far as Evan knew, there weren't. Every fortress he had seen there was made of stone, whose bastions couldn't be burned and whose walls could be breached only by powerful cannons. No, there were none of these primitive log forts in Europe. Had there been, the armies there would have reduced them to ashes within minutes. Yet here, deep in the interior of this wild country, the French had held the British at bay for years from behind just such flimsy structures simply because the British could not haul their big guns across the rugged terrain. It had been a frustrating war for the British Army.

When they reached the huge gate of the palisade, it was open, but not a single soul in sight. Evan's eyes widened in surprise as he saw the large, circular town. "Now I know why you call it a town and not a village," he remarked to Josh. "It's much larger than I expected."

"This is one of the largest Chickasaw settlements," Josh answered, slowing his horse so Evan's could move up beside him. "It's been here for years and years. But then, so have most of their settlements."

"Then the Indians don't move about from place to place?"

"Nay, the Chickasaw have permanent homes. All the southern tribes do. They do a little huntin' and a little gatherin', but mostly they're farmers."

As they passed one of the homes, Evan looked at the small plot of cultivated ground next to it. The maize, planted in neat rows on the top of large dirt mounds, was barely a few inches tall, but already the leaves had taken on their characteristic long, narrow shapes.

"Their fields are awfully small for farmers, aren't they?" Evan commented.

"Those plots aren't their fields. They're just individual gardens. The tribal fields are on the other side of the town, beside the river."

Evan nodded, then squinted to study something he had spied between the scattered trees in the distance. "Do I see a flagpole?"

"Nay, it's a goal post for the ball games the Chickasaw dearly love."

"What kind of ball games?" Evan asked curiously, for he couldn't imagine savages playing games of any kind.

"There are several sorts. In one, the ball is moved with sturdy sticks, and the Indians aren't careful about who gets hit in the process. In another, the brave swallows a ball a little smaller than a chicken egg, then tries to run to the goal before he's caught by his opponents. If that happens, they jump on his stomach and beat on him until he vomits it up. In another game, the ball is kicked to the goal. It doesn't matter which form of the game is played—they're all vicious and bloody. Take my advice and avoid 'em, just in case ye're asked to join in. I'd as soon run the gauntlet."

As they rode farther into the settlement, passing sev-

eral large tribal granaries, Evan studied the individual
homes. They were much different from the long log
lodges that the Mingoes and Mohawks used, shared between several families. The Chickasaw homes were
made of wattle and daub over a log framework, and
they had thatched roofs. They didn't look much like the
log cabins the frontiersmen built, and they appeared to
be much sturdier. If anything, they resembled the cot-
tages on Evan's father's estates back in England, except
the Chickasaw buildings were larger and were whitewashed so that they gleamed in the bright sunlight.
That was impressive enough, but each home also had its
own corn and yam cribs and pens for pigs, chickens, and
cattle, as well as a well-tended garden.

Taking note of two detached buildings beside the
homes, Evan asked Josh, "What are those smaller buildings? Smokehouses?"

"Nay, they're hothouses, but different kinds. One is
the kitchen, where the fire is kept goin' at all times. It's
separated from the main buildin' to keep the homes
from gettin' so hot in the summer. It's a lot warmer
here than in England, ye know."

Evan nodded. He had yet to spend a summer in the
southern region of this country, but he had briefly visited a plantation in Virginia that had a separate kitchen
for the same reason—another idea the colonists had apparently picked up from the natives. "And the other
hothouse? What's it used for?"

"It's a sweathouse."

Evan's brow furrowed in confusion.

"A hothouse made just for sweatin'," Josh explained.
"If ye look closer, ye'll see there are no windows, like

the kitchen has. Inside, rocks are heated on a big fire in
the center of the buildin'. Then when they're red hot,
water is sprinkled on 'em to make steam. I tried it once.
It's hotter than Hades in there. Makes ye sweat somethin' fierce, even though ye haven't got a stitch of
clothin' on. The Indians claim it cleanses 'em, spiritually
as well as physically. Goin' to the sweathouse to be
cleansed is part of almost every one of their religious
rituals. A lot of Chickasaw claim it's invigoratin', too,
particularly if it's followed by a cold bath. They do it all
year 'round."

"The Indians bathe?" Evan asked in surprise.

"Aye, almost daily." Josh wrinkled his nose in distaste.
"Disgustin', isn't it?"

Evan wasn't surprised at Josh's reaction. The upper
classes of England bathed much more regularly than
commoners. But daily? That was carrying things a little
too far.

By this time, they had traveled deep into the settlement, but Evan had yet to see a solitary soul. For all
practical purposes, the entire settlement seemed deserted. Then, as they rounded the corner of a house and
came into the main square, Evan's breath caught. The
clearing was packed with Indians—men, women, and
children. He had never seen so many Indians in one
place—he judged there were at least a thousand.

Josh carefully guided his horse into the crowd, and as
they cleared a pathway for him, Evan followed, acutely
conscious of every dark eye on him. Had just one
Chickasaw smiled, he might have felt a little easier, but
every face was as impassive as if it were made of stone.
Not having the slightest idea what they were thinking or

planning was unnerving. But as they rode through the crowd and nothing happened, Evan felt a little less threatened and began to take a closer look at this far western tribe that so few white men had even seen.

He discovered that the Chickasaw were much better looking than any of the northern or eastern tribes he had seen. Most of the men were tall, surpassing even the usual European height, and well proportioned, with handsome features. They didn't shave their heads, leaving nothing but a line of long black bristles down the center, as the Mingoes and Mohawks did, a hairstyle that Evan thought made them look even more savage. Rather, the Chickasaw warriors' hair hung in long braids at one side of their heads, decorated with feathers or pieces of animal skin or strings of trading beads. Most of the men were wearing their traditional dress: a buckskin shirt, moccasins, fringed leather leggins, and a breechcloth made of stroud cloth—the scarlet red trading cloth of which they were very fond. But, much to Evan's surprise, quite a few of the younger men were dressed in togas made of the same cloth, as were many of the women—a costume that seemed more appropriate for an ancient Roman setting than the American wilds.

Then Evan turned his attention to the women of the tribe, and again he had a pleasant surprise. They, too, were taller than the average European woman, slim, with firm, well-proportioned breasts and legs. Their faces, with finely chiseled features and dark lustrous eyes, far surpassed those of any other Indian women he had seen in beauty. In fact, as a whole, the Chickasaw were much more handsome than any natives he had seen. Even their skin coloring seemed lighter, more of a golden brown than a deep copper tone, and Evan wondered if they weren't a race unto themselves.

As these thoughts were going through Evan's mind, he and Josh passed between two long, open-sided sheds that helped to form a square in which even more Indians were seated. Then Evan saw a large, circular open-sided building. He assumed it was the tribal meeting house, since it was elevated on a huge mound of dirt.

When they reached the mound, Josh came to a halt and dismounted, handing the reins of his horse and his long rifle to an Indian brave standing there. Evan followed suit, feeling a twinge of reluctance at giving up his gun. It was his only means of protection in an alien world. He followed Josh up the stone steps and down an aisle carpeted with red cloth that passed through a crowd of seated Indians. The aisle ended in a clearing covered with bear and panther skins, and in the center of this area flickered a low fire built on a solid rock dais.

Josh came to a stop. "That's their sacred fire," he said to Evan. "Only their *archi-magus*, their holy men, can touch it. Just thought I'd warn ye."

"Sacred? Then this is their temple?"

"Partly. They also use it for tribal business. With the Chickasaw, their religion is woven so tightly into their everyday lives that the two can't be separated."

"I see," Evan answered. "Where is Promingo? I expected him to meet me."

"And miss the opportunity for a grand entrance?" Josh chuckled and shook his head. "Not Promingo. Remember me tellin' ye the Chickasaw love pomp and pageantry? Well, he's Chickasaw to the bone."

Josh had hardly gotten the words out of his mouth when a loud cheer rang out, and all the Chickasaw came to their feet and waved the small tree branches they were holding in their hands. Evan whirled around at the sudden noise and saw a procession of Indians coming down the aisle that he and Josh had just traversed. The man at the head of the procession had to be Promingo, with his regal bearing and impressive dress. A feathered mantle embroidered with shells and copper beads hung from his broad shoulders, with iridescent green, purple, and rose feathers shining in the sunlight and the spread wing of a red hawk sitting like a fan at the back of his dark head. Copper bracelets circled his powerful biceps; a breastplate of some shiny golden metal covered his massive chest, and a panther skin hung around his waist and was wrapped around his loins. Ermine tails hung from the fringes of his knee-high moccasins. With his tall, muscular body, hawkish features, and black piercing eyes, he looked every inch the powerful, fierce chief Evan had heard he was.

Evan made these observations in just a few fleeting seconds, for he had hardly spied the chief when a young woman walking a few paces behind him caught his eye. Her graceful walk first drew his attention. It was so effortless that she seemed to be floating down the aisle. Then he noticed the gentle, tantalizing sway of her hips, the long, well-shaped legs that strained at the skirt of red toga she wore with each smooth stride, the proud thrust of her breasts, the seductive curve of the bared shoulder. A thick braid of lustrous black hair was coiled on top of her head and laced with pearls. Several other strands of various lengths hung from her slender neck and dangled from her ears.

Almost mesmerized, Evan focused on the young woman's face. Other than her high cheekbones, her features were finer than those of the other Chickasaws, and her smooth, flawless skin was a few shades lighter, making the natural blush of her cheeks and the rosy hue of her well-shaped mouth stand out even more. Then Evan noticed something that took his breath away: Her almond-shaped eyes were green! They were not a dusky green, but a pure crystalline green, and their luminous sheen seemed to give them a life of their own. Enraptured, Evan stared at the young woman. She wasn't just pretty, or simply lovely. She possessed a rare, exotic, stunning beauty that made his heart race and his breath quicken. That in itself was disturbing, for no woman had ever affected him so strongly. But even more he sensed a deep sensuality in her that seemed to cry out to the most primitive part of him.

Then and there, Evan made a startling and powerful discovery: Regardless of who she might be, or who he was—he wanted her!

2

Evan's attention was rudely but effectively drawn from the sensuous young woman back to his purpose in the Indian settlement when Josh painfully jabbed him in the ribs with his bony elbow. Even then, it took considerable concentration on Evan's part to focus on the powerful chief who was at that moment approaching him. His eyes kept wanting to stray to the fascinating creature who was now seating herself on a small bench set off to the side.

As Promingo stepped up to him, Evan wondered about the proper etiquette. He had been present at other meetings between military men and chiefs, but they had all known one another previously. Should he offer to shake hands or, if not, to smile? A smile was supposed to be a universal greeting understood by all, and he was well aware that he possessed a particularly dazzling one that could totally disarm his enemies and that never failed to make the ladies' hearts race. But seeing the stern expression on the chief's hawkish face,

Evan decided to do neither but, instead, to follow Promingo's strictly business lead.

"*Yo ish la chu anggona?*" Promingo asked Evan gravely.

"What did he say?" Evan asked Josh from the corner of his mouth.

"He asked if ye're a friend."

"Doesn't he know who I am?" Evan asked with a mixture of exasperation and alarm. "I thought you said all the arrangements had been made, that he was in perfect agreement with our plans."

"Of course he knows who ye are, and he *is* in agreement. It's just custom for them to ask that the first time they meet a stranger. Don't worry. I'll answer all his questions."

Josh turned to the chief. "*Yah-arahre-O, anggona,*" he said.

Promingo nodded solemnly and grasped Evan's right wrist with both his hands, then his elbow, then his upper arm by his shoulder. Accepting an eagle's tail from one of his medicine men, the chief waved it over Evan's head.

Again not knowing what to do, Evan asked Josh, "Am I supposed to reciprocate?"

"Nay, he's just pledgin' his good faith. It's assumed yers is good, or ye wouldn't be here."

Promingo and his entourage of advisers and medicine men sat down in a big circle on the bearskins that were scattered before the altar where the sacred fire burned. The chief motioned for Josh and Evan to join them. Once everyone was seated with their legs crossed Indian fashion before them, one of the holy men walked

to the fire. He lit the calumet and handed it to Promingo. As the long-stemmed clay pipe, decorated with
eagle feathers, was passed around by the medicine man,
Evan studied him curiously. Dressed in a toga made of
panther skins and wearing an impressive array of bone
and claw necklaces and armlets, the priest's face and
exposed skin were elaborately tattooed. The bone that
pierced his upper lip and his fierce black eyes made him
look imposing and very primitive, and once again, Evan
had a feeling that he had stepped into an alien world
whose civilization lingered on the fringes of the prime-
val.

When the holy man stopped before Evan and handed
him the pipe, the officer took it and inhaled deeply. To
his surprise, the tobacco was much milder than other
Indian tobaccos he had sampled. There was absolutely
no bitter aftertaste. In fact, it tasted even better than
the hybrid Virginia tobacco that had become such a
rage on the continent and that had made that colony so
successful. Briefly, Evan wondered if the Chickasaw
had access to the same West Indies tobacco that the
colonists had imported to improve the native plant, or if
their tobacco was, like they themselves, a breed unto
itself.

The pipe was solemnly passed around, signifying that
everyone who smoked vowed to speak the truth. Then
Promingo launched into a lengthy discourse. Evan
peered at him through the thick cloud of smoke that
hovered over the group and tried to pretend interest.
When the long-winded chief finally finished, Evan whispered to Josh, "What in the devil was that all about?"

"He was welcomin' ye."

"It took all that time to say welcome?"

"Promingo, like most of these southern chiefs, prides himself on bein' a grand orator. Besides welcomin' ye, he praised himself, his tribe, his council, his subchiefs, his priests, his British allies, and his Indian allies. Then he condemned his enemies, the Choctaw, and most vehemently the French. He positively loathes 'em, ye know."

Evan nodded, knowing it was that very hatred that made the Chickasaw Great Britain's best Indian ally and that was the reason he was here. "Tell him that I thank him for his gracious welcome, but that I'd like to get down to business. First, I'd like to clarify that he knows exactly why I'm here: to act as a military adviser on our combined war against the French in this area and the lower Ohio Territory. I'm here to help him formulate his battle plans and to coordinate his strikes against the enemy with ours, when applicable, but not to lead his warriors."

"He knows that," Josh replied. "Besides, his warriors wouldn't follow ye. Mohawks or Mingoes might follow a white man, but not Chickasaw. They're real particular about their war chiefs."

Evan didn't particularly like being told he wasn't good enough to lead a bunch of savages—it was insulting, considering he was a professional soldier and an accomplished officer. But Evan knew the rugged frontiersman had his own low opinion of him, and that made Josh's comment rankle all the more. He fought down the urge to make a caustic remark and instead said tersely, "Tell Promingo the first thing I want to do is to see this new fort he claims the French are building on the Ohio."

"I wouldn't say it that way if I were ye," Josh answered. "Makes it sound like ye don't believe him. He'll be insulted."

"Insulted, be damned!" Evan threw back, taking offense at the commoner correcting him. "To be perfectly honest, I don't completely believe his tale. Do you have any idea how far the French would have to travel to man and supply such an isolated fort? From New Orleans, no less? My God, that's well over a thousand miles away! And to do it by way of some backwoods river? That's an outlandish claim!"

"It's not just some backwoods river," Josh countered. "It's the Misho Sipokni! At least, that's what the Chickasaw call it. The Chippewa call it Mu-zu-see-bee. And take my word for it—ye've never laid eyes on such a river. Why, in some places ye can't hardly see across it."

"That's what the Indians and you crazy Goose Creek traders claim. That's there's a huge river out here somewhere, a river that makes the Thames look like a stream. But other than you traders, no white man has seen it, much less drawn a map of it—except for De Soto and his men, that is, and no one believes their wild tales. Christ! Those idiots were looking for the Seven Cities of Gold! I've never heard of anything so ridiculous!"

"Ye're wrong. Other white men have seen the river besides the Spanish. The French have seen it and even mapped it, the Indians claim, only they've been keepin' it a secret. Accordin' to the natives, the French buried those lead plates they use to claim land in the name of France down the entire length of the river."

Evan frowned. As much as he would have liked to, he couldn't argue with Josh. The French did keep what they found in this new country a closely guarded secret, and it was they and the Spanish who had explored the interior, while Great Britain had limited her explorations to the eastern coast. Why shouldn't they keep the river's existence a secret? Why give the enemy valuable information about the country that all three were vying for possession over, particularly if that information could be used by the enemy in an attack? Besides, maybe there was a huge river that flowed all the way to the Gulf of Mexico. Hadn't he just passed through forests he'd never dreamed could exist?

"This is not the time to be arguin' about whether or not the river exists," Josh continued, looking about uneasily. "We're makin' the Chickasaw suspicious with all this talk they can't understand. Besides, ye can see it tomorrow for yerself. It's just a stone's throw from here."

Josh turned to Promingo and said something to the chief. After the chief responded, Josh translated. "I told him ye'd like to see the new fort before ye make any suggestions on how to go about attackin' it. He said he could understand yer wantin' to scout it out for yerself, but to warn ye that it's a considerable distance. It'll take a good ten days to reach it. If ye want to see it in advance, he said he was sorry, but he had business to attend to here and couldn't accompany ye. However, he'll give ye a guide and a dozen warriors to protect ye, since ye'll be goin' into Illini territory."

"Illini? They're French allies, right?"

"Aye. And ye'll be passing through a bit of Shawnee territory too. Never know when ye might run into a huntin' party."

Evan would have preferred to travel with just a guide, but he knew he would be a fool to turn down Promingo's offer. The Shawnee were staunch French allies and, from what he had heard, were particularly brutal with their captives. "Tell Promingo I'll accept his offer and that I'd like to leave in the morning."

When Josh interpreted Evan's message, Promingo nodded and said something further to the Scot before he rose. As the chief came to his feet, the other Indians rose also, followed by Josh and Evan. Promingo turned and walked away, the others fell in behind him, and Evan knew the meeting was over.

When Promingo reached the young woman sitting on the bench, he stopped and said something to her. Evan's eyes were already on her, for they had sought her out of their own accord as soon as the meeting had finished. He saw a slight stiffening of her body before she rose and took her place behind the chief. As she followed Promingo from the meeting house, her head held as proudly as any queen's, Evan watched the sway of her hips—an incredibly seductive motion that seemed at odds with her regal bearing. His heat rose, and he asked in a voice hoarse with desire, "Who is she? Promingo's wife?"

There was no doubt in Josh's mind to whom Evan was referring. The Englishman was devouring the young Indian woman with his eyes. "Nay, she's more important than his wife—or his daughters, for that matter. She's his niece."

"His niece? How does that make her more important?"

"The Chickasaw trace their descent through the female, not the male. That's how titles and property are passed down. It's the women who are the heads of the clans, or sics, as we traders call 'em. They pass on the chieftaincy, but they can't be chief, although I've heard tales of that happenin' long ago. All of the southern tribes tell of a great woman chief who led the most powerful Indian tribe in the south. Story has it De Soto and his men ran into her tribe during his explorations and there was big clash. The Spanish tried to kidnap her and her ladies-in-waitin'. I don't know whether the Spaniards wanted the women or the lavish strings of pearls they wore, but the Indians were furious and chased the white men completely out of the area."

Evan was more interested in learning about the young woman than in hearing Josh's story. "Then the young woman is a princess?"

"Not exactly. The Chickasaw don't have royalty, but they do have a hierarchy—so much so that it determines where a person sits at tribal ceremonies and who they can socialize with. She belongs to a very important and powerful sic. Her brother will be the next chief, and then her son. Unless, of course, she abdicates that privilege to her younger sister."

"Why would she do that?"

"She might fall in love with a man from a sic below hers. It doesn't happen often, though—a woman of her station marryin' beneath her. In that way, the Chickasaw higher sics are like royalty. Marriages are taken very seriously and are often contracts of a political nature."

Evan understood. In Europe, women of nobility were often used as political pawns. Love seldom had anything to do with marriage.

"However," Josh continued, "the Chickasaw are different from us in a lot of ways too. Here the woman owns the property, and she can sue for divorce anytime she likes. If she doesn't like the way her husband is treatin' her or how things are goin', all she has to do is tell the man to leave."

Evan, a typical Englishman, firmly believed that it was the male's God-given right to be lord and master and that women were little more than possessions. For a woman any less than a queen to wield such power didn't sit at all well with him, and his feelings were clearly displayed by the disapproval on his face. Seeing it, Josh commented, "Aye, I know what ye're thinkin'. It's unnatural for a woman to be so independent. But despite the fact that Chickasaw women have the power to rule their own fate, they have by far much sweeter and even-tempered natures than our women."

Evan scoffed, and Josh was quick to say, "Nay, it's true. That's why I married a Chickasaw woman myself."

"You're married to one?" Evan asked in surprise.

"Aye, and she's a real pleasure. Of course, her bein' so experienced was an added boon."

Evan wondered if the Scot could possibly mean what he thought he meant, then decided not to make any assumptions. "Experienced in what way?"

"Why, in the art of pleasin' a man," the Scot answered without the slightest hesitation. "Now, in my estimation, that's one advantage the Chickasaw have over us. Their youths are perfectly free to experiment with one another, and by the time they marry, they're remarkable lovers."

"Then your wife wasn't a maiden?"

"Nay, and to be perfectly honest, I couldn't have cared less. She had her dalliances more out of curiosity or to satisfy her passions than out of any deep feelin's for the men. And like I said, I'm the one who bene-fited." Josh chuckled. "There's no cold fish in my bed."

"But aren't you afraid, with a past like that, she'll be unfaithful?"

"Nay. The Chickasaw take marriage very seriously, and adultery is strictly forbidden. Women are expected to get all that out of their system before they marry, and that's why the Chickasaw marry a little later in life than the northern Indians. They aren't bein' pressured by their passions, and by the time they marry, they're ma-ture and ready to fully accept their marital responsibili-ties. Besides, with divorce so easy, unfaithfulness isn't necessary. The woman doesn't have to sneak around and do it. She can simply cast her husband out. And she doesn't have to worry about her and her children bein' taken care of. She owns the property."

Josh turned and started walking away, and Evan fell in beside him. Apart from a few Chickasaw who had lingered to curiously stare at the Englishman in his bright red jacket, the temple and square around it had emptied.

As they walked, Evan thought over everything Josh had told him. He was both amazed and shocked. In his culture, a man would never openly admit that his wife had been hardly more than a whore, much less be pleased with it. Purity on the part of the woman was a prime attribute, so important that her failure to be a virgin on her wedding night could be grounds for annulment. Yet the Chickasaw men were not only unconcerned that their brides were not maidens, they actually took pride in their sexual experience. It was a concept that was totally at odds with Evan's upbringing. Then something else occurred to him. His people demanded total purity of their brides not just because of their moral beliefs. It was a means of assuring that the woman would foster no other man's child on her husband. Curious to know how the Chickasaw handled that problem, he asked, "How do bastards fit into the Indians' way of life? With all of the sexual freedom they're allowed, I'd imagine there are quite a few of them."

"Not as many as ye might think. That's one of the major reasons they marry—to legitimize their children. Unless the marriage price has been paid, they can't inherit titles or, in the case of females, property. But they don't make outcasts out of their bastards, like we do. They're accepted by the entire tribe without the slightest reservations and raised by the mother's family."

By that time, they had left the town square and were strolling down one of the wide avenues between the rows of houses. Evan glanced about, hoping to catch a glimpse of the beautiful young woman he had seen at the temple and wondering how he could seek her out. Learning of Chickasaw women's unusual independence hadn't cooled his desire for her in the least. The fact that there were no strict taboos about sex between single men and women and that it wasn't binding in any way just made her all the more intriguing. How the Chickasaws handled their independent, powerful wives was their problem, not his. He had no intention of courting the young woman, just bedding her. Apparently, all he had to do was catch her attention and make himself appealing.

Evan had no doubts about his capabilities in attracting the opposite sex. With his golden good looks, splendid physique, and strong masculine magnetism, he had more often been the pursued than the pursuer. All he had had to do was sit back and allow himself to be caught. Of course, he was always careful about who caught him. He wanted no liaisons with women who might have marriage or commitment of any sort in mind. That, of course, was totally out of the question. He had no intention of tying himself down to any woman. If nothing else, he had his freedom, he thought with a tinge of bitterness—and by God, he'd savor it. It was the only advantage he'd attained over his brother when his father had died.

Seeing Evan glancing around, Josh asked, "Are ye lookin' for Ash-heettla?"

Evan frowned, thinking the Chickasaw word sounded harsh. "Is that the young woman's name?"

"Aye."

"What does it mean in English?"

"Fire Dancer."

"Fire Dancer? That's not a particularly pretty name for a woman. Why did they name her that?"

"Remember me tellin' ye she's from a powerful and important sic? Well, nothin' is more important to the Chickasaw than their communal fire. They believe it represents the sun on earth and that from it comes all life. They never extinguish it, except durin' the Green Corn Festivities, their most important religious ceremony. Then, only the holiest women in the tribe are allowed to be in the temple, and they dance around the new fire. Fire Dancer will someday have that honor, but not until she is much older. Until then, it is a reminder of her station and the honorable role she's destined for."

"Her eyes are green," Evan remarked. "I didn't know there were green-eyed Indians."

"There're a few Chickasaw with hazel eyes, but none but her with green. Not even her brother and sister have green eyes. Ye see, she's not pure Chickasaw. She's a mestizo. Her mother was an indentured slave that the Creek took captive on one of their raids into the Carolinas."

The young woman was half white? Evan was surprised. But then, he supposed he should have guessed —her features were much finer than the others' and her coloring lighter. "The Creek?" he asked. "Then how did the Chickasaw come to have her mother?"

"The Indians have tradin' fairs, and one of the things they trade is their captives. It's always been that way. In that particular instance, Promingo traded off to the Creek some Choctaw braves he'd captured for the young woman's mother. She'd caught his fancy, and he planned on usin' her as a concubine. Except when he got back, his own mother saw her and decided to adopt her, since she didn't have any daughters to inherit the sic's property and to pass on the chieftaincy. I don't imagine Promingo was any too pleased with his mother's interference. I've heard that Fire Dancer's mother was quite a looker, and of course, beddin' her was out of the question for Promingo, since she had become his sister. Incest in any shape or form is strictly forbidden. They don't even allow unions with members of their own sics from other villages. They're afraid of feeble-mindedness."

Which shows better sense than some of our nobility back in Europe, Evan thought. There, marriages between cousins were rather commonplace and sometimes had disastrous results.

"The Chickasaw accept adoption for something as important as the chieftaincy?" Evan asked, finding it hard to believe. "I should think it would have to be pure bloodlines, particularly in view of their practice of hierarchy."

"Aye, it seems peculiar to us, but adoption is as legal and bindin' to the Chickasaw as bearin' the child from their own flesh and blood."

Josh pulled a plug of chewing tobacco from his shirt pocket. As he bit off a big chunk, Evan grimaced. He thought chewing tobacco a repulsive habit, yet everyone here in the colonies seemed to do it, even the more affluent. If they didn't chew it, they sniffed it, as did the higher class in England, carrying it in small, jewel-studded snuff boxes that they tucked away in their waistcoat pockets. Evan neither chewed nor sniffed, but he had become addicted to smoking, and at that minute, he would have loved a quiet pipeful. But he didn't know where his pipe was now. He looked around, wondering where the Indians had taken his horse.

"What are ye looking for?" Josh asked.

"Our horses. We need our things to make camp."

"We don't have to make camp. We're guests. They'll provide us with food and lodgin'. I guess I forgot to tell ye—we got so busy talkin' about other things—but that's where we're headin' right now. Promingo invited us to dine at his lodgin's."

Evan wondered if Fire Dancer would be there. His heartbeat quickened. "And where might that be?"

"Right over there," Josh answered, motioning to a home that was considerably larger than the others.

A few minutes later, Josh and Evan entered the chief's lodging. Evan looked about quickly and discovered that Fire Dancer was nowhere to be seen. He felt a keen disappointment as he slowly scanned the interior of the Chickasaw home. There was only one big room, and the floor was made of puddled clay that was swept so clean, it almost looked as if it had been polished. Against the walls were low, built-in beds that were padded with animal skins, wooden chests, and wicker hampers, which Evan assumed held the Indians' clothing and personal belongings. Bear and panther-skin rugs were scattered about, and in the center of the room was a low couch on which Promingo was perched.

Promingo motioned to Josh and Evan to have a seat on the bearskin rug before him. When the two men had done so, three women began to serve the men. They carried in colorfully woven trays on which sat wooden spoons and pottery bowls filled with a steaming stew, and placed the trays before the men. As the women performed their duties as hostesses, Evan studied them and discovered that they were all tall and slim and had a certain gracefulness that seemed to be an inherent

Chickasaw trait. But beyond that and the fact that they all wore red togas, any similarity to Fire Dancer ended. None of them could begin to compare with Fire Dancer's beauty, to say nothing of that seductive quality that had drawn him to her like a bee to honey. Then Evan noticed that the women's cheeks and chins were lightly tattooed. He wondered if Fire Dancer's were tattooed also—he had been too far away to notice. He hoped that wasn't the case. He didn't like the idea of anything marring the perfection of her face.

On several occasions, Promingo tried to carry on a conversation with Evan, as was his duty as host, but it was awkward and tedious with Josh having to interpret everything. Eventually, only the chief and Josh conversed, and although Evan was supposed to be the honored guest, he was left to listen to the language, which seemed to have too many harsh sounds and grated on his nerves. It was no small relief to the Englishman when the meal was finished and the two men could depart.

Just before he and Josh stepped from the chief's lodging, Promingo said something to Josh that made the Scot shoot a quick, surprised glance at Evan. Evan wondered what the chief had said, and when a big grin spread on the guide's rugged face, Evan became even more curious. As soon as the two men stepped from the cabin, he asked, "What did Promingo just say? I know it had something to do with me."

In the dim light of dusk, Evan saw yet another grin spread across the Scot's face. "Aye," he answered, "that it did. He said somethin' that I think will please ye."

Evan waited for more, but the Scot just grinned from

ear to ear. "Well?" he asked impatiently. "What's going to please me?"

"He said ye can have the guest cabin for your lodge for as long as ye're here. That's it back there." Josh motioned to a smaller cabin about a hundred yards from Promingo's. "Ye'll find yer things already there."

"That was very kind of him," Evan answered, strangely disappointed. "Is that where you'll be staying too?"

"Nay. My wife has members of her sic here. I'll stay with 'em. It's custom and expected of me."

Evan nodded. "Well, good night then."

As he walked away, Josh called out, "Wait! There's more to what Promingo said."

Evan whirled around with an impatient look on his face. He was weary of the Scot's company and was anxious to be alone. "Well?"

"He said he had instructed his niece to attend to yer every need and comfort. She's waitin' in the cabin for ye."

Evan sucked in his breath sharply. "My every need and comfort? Does that mean—"

Before Evan could finish the question, Josh finished it for him: "She'll share yer bed and ease yer loins? Aye. That was his instructions."

Evan's heart raced in anticipation. "Is this customary?"

"For honored guests, aye. Usually it's the chief's daughters or wives he loans out, but he must have noticed how taken ye were with Fire Dancer and wants to please ye."

Evan didn't find the custom particularly surprising or

offensive. European royalty often provided women for their honored guests' "entertainment." Nor did he stop to wonder if Fire Dancer was in accord with her uncle's plan. He assumed that since she was a part of Promingo's family, she fully accepted her duty and would perform readily, particularly since the Chickasaw took sexual liaisons so lightly.

Seeing an excited gleam come into the Englishman's eyes, Josh said, "Aye, ye're a fortunate man to have Fire Dancer in yer bed for yer stay here. There's not a more fetchin' woman in the entire Chickasaw nation. I'll wager ye're takin' a different view of yer mission now."

Evan was. During the entire trip across the wilderness, he had cursed his luck to draw this mission. But at that moment, there was no place on earth he wanted to be more than here. He turned and muttered to Josh, "I'll see you in the morning," then walked rapidly toward the cabin, his heart beating wildly against his chest.

3

As Evan told Josh about the arrangements Promingo had made for him during his stay with the Chickasaw, Fire Dancer was pacing within the cabin.

How dare he! she thought, furious with her uncle. How dared Promingo order her to play the role of concubine to the Englishman! Oh, it was customary among the Chickasaw to provide a female for their honored tribal guests, and as a member of the ruling sic that duty fell to the females of her family. But why hadn't Promingo chosen one of his wives, as he usually did, or better yet, one of his daughters, since her cousins so thoroughly enjoyed sex? Between the two of them, they had sampled practically every unmarried male in the settlement! Why, they were almost as whorish as those disgusting Indian women in the Carolinas that her mother had told her about.

Abruptly, Fire Dancer paused in her mental tirade. Tears came to her eyes, as they always did at the memory of her mother. It had been two years since she had died, and Fire Dancer still missed her very much. They had been unusually close, and her mother had instilled many of her Anglo convictions into her eldest daughter. One of those was the belief that a woman's virtue was one of her most prized possessions, that it was not given lightly, that only cheap women indulged in sexual liaisons with men for whom they felt nothing, that sex was meant to be a meaningful expression of one's deeper emotions and not simply a means of satisfying one's passion or curiosity. For those reasons, Fire Dancer was still a virgin. She had not yet found a man she cared enough about to give of herself, nor had she found one who could arouse her passion, although many had pursued her and tried.

So far, Fire Dancer had managed to keep the state of her virtue a secret. The braves who had unsuccessfully attempted to bed her had taken her rebuff very personally and had not revealed it to anyone. In a society where premarital sex was not only accepted but expected, the young men had feared they would be made a laughingstock if their failure were known. As a result, all the eligible braves in the tribe wondered if the others had been successful, but none had the courage to ask.

Nor did the women in the tribe know. The other girls in the settlement gossiped about their sexual experiences, but Fire Dancer refused to speak of her relations with men. Even her grandmother, Eastern Star, was in the dark, and Fire Dancer hoped she never became suspicious enough to ask. She'd never lie to her grandmother—she had too much respect for her. But she feared the old woman would be disappointed in her if

she knew her granddaughter was not following the
Chickasaw way but was adhering to the Anglo convictions of her mother. Eastern Star had always contended
that Fire Dancer's white blood showed more than her
brother's and sister's. Fire Dancer had never really
known if her grandmother disapproved of this—Eastern
Star had always been difficult to read, and Fire Dancer
never knew what she was thinking or feeling. But Fire
Dancer did know that she didn't want Eastern Star to
be displeased with her, and Fire Dancer was truly
proud of her Indian blood. She'd do everything in her
power to be worthy of the role she was destined to
inherit—everything except this. She could not give herself to a man for whom she cared nothing, particularly
one she had never laid eyes on until today, not even in
the name of duty. Her self-respect was too important to
her.

Was that why her uncle had done it? Fire Dancer
wondered suddenly. Had he guessed how she felt about
the custom, and did he mean to humiliate her by putting her in the position of being forced to bed a man
against her will? Did he somehow know she was still a
virgin? But why would he do something so spiteful?
Perhaps Promingo was still angry with her mother for
spurning his attentions and then being placed in a position where he couldn't touch her. Yes, that had to be it.
Her mother had told her how angry Promingo had been
when she refused to submit willingly to him, and how
that anger had been compounded when his mother had
placed her out of his reach. He had never forgiven either one, and he was now taking his spite out on her
daughter by forcing Fire Dancer to submit to a total

stranger. Well, she wouldn't do it, Fire Dancer thought, her fury once more coming to the fore. She wouldn't!

Her fuming was brought to a sudden end by a knock on the door. It had to be the Englishman. Suddenly her heart raced. It was all well and good to plan to refuse her uncle's orders, but would she have the courage to follow through with it? What if the white man told her uncle of her disappointing behavior, and Promingo passed that information on to Eastern Star? Oh, Promingo would just love to make her look bad in her grandmother's eyes! That would bring him almost as much pleasure as seeing her humiliated by having to submit. Or worse yet—what if the Englishman refused to take no for an answer and forced himself on her? That would be terrible. Besides the pain and degradation she would have to endure, she couldn't even accuse him of rape, not when she had been ordered by the head of the tribe to lie with him. Not only would she have no means of punishing him, the entire tribe would know of her humiliation.

While Fire Dancer was wildly thinking these disturbing thoughts, the door opened and Evan boldly stepped into the cabin. She was so stunned at his rudeness in not waiting for her to open the door that all she could do was stare at him.

Evan hadn't considered waiting for Fire Dancer to open the door because it wasn't a courtesy he would have given a whore, and he was already thinking of the beautiful Indian girl in those terms. She was there for one purpose—to satisfy his lust and nothing else—and they both knew it. As she came fully into view, he came to a halt and sharply sucked in his breath, thinking her even more beautiful and desirable close up. Hungrily, his eyes slid down her length, then moved back up to lock onto the proud thrust of her breasts. God, he thought, his passion rapidly coming to the fore, he could hardly wait to take those lush mounds into his hands, to taste her there.

Fire Dancer had at first been shocked by Evan's entering the cabin without awaiting her permission. Now, as his hot gaze slid over her body and locked onto her breasts, she was angered. How dared he look at her so lustfully! Why, she already felt defiled!

But when Fire Dancer stiffened in anger, it made her breasts jut out even more. They strained against the material of her toga so much that her nipples were clearly outlined. Thinking her an accomplished whore, Evan assumed that she was deliberately preening to show off her lovely, very female attributes. He stared, drinking his fill for a good minute, watching as her breaths became more rapid. Then he tore his gaze from her chest and looked at her face. Seeing her green eyes blazing, he totally misinterpreted it as desire on her part, just as he had thought her agitated breathing had meant excitement. A slow, smug smile spread across his face.

"Good evening," he said, nudging the door shut with the heel of his boot, then removing his hat and tossing it onto a low chest nearby. When Fire Dancer failed to respond and just stared at him, he said, "Oh, I forgot— you must not speak English." Once more his hot gaze slowly roved over her body. "But then you don't need to. You're not here for conversation, are you?"

Without taking his eyes from her, Evan removed his

coat, then the stock and black ribbon from around his neck. As he unbuttoned his shirt, he frowned and asked, "What are you waiting for? Take off your clothes! I want to see if your body is as enticing beneath that toga as it looks in it."

Fire Dancer was furious. She had never been treated in such an insulting manner. The warriors who had pursued her had at least had the decency to try to seduce her. But not this arrogant white man—no, he stripped right before her eyes without making the slightest romantic overtures, treating her as if she were simply something to be used! Why, he wasn't even treating her like a human being, much less the woman who would be the mother of this tribe's next chief. How dared he! Impotent with rage, she glared at him.

What was wrong with her? Evan wondered, finally getting an inkling that something wasn't quite right. Was she angry with him? But why? Certainly she didn't expect to be wooed. That would be preposterous—she was a whore. But then, she wasn't a whore, he reminded himself, not in the usual sense. True, she was here to perform a service, but she wasn't being paid money for it. Maybe she expected a few amorous overtures, a few compliments, like the women he usually bedded. Like her, they weren't professionals. Their reward was physical, not monetary, and ordinarily he didn't mind. The preliminaries to lovemaking were very enjoyable, particularly with beautiful women. Kissing, touching, tasting this one's flesh would undoubtedly be very exciting and arousing. Except that he didn't need any further stimulation. His swollen manhood felt as if it were about to burst in the tight confines of his breeches. Still, if that was what she wanted, a kiss or two couldn't hurt.

Evan tossed his shirt aside and walked to Fire Dancer, his warm smile turning to one of a more seductive nature. The promising smile on his sensuous lips would have been enough to unnerve any woman, but combined with the sight of his magnificent bare chest, Fire Dancer could only stand rooted to the spot and stare. She had been raised in a civilization in which seminudity of males was an everyday occurrence, but none of the warriors' chests seemed to have been as broad and manly as this Englishman's, nor were the muscles in their shoulders or biceps as large. Walking toward her with an easy swagger that bespoke utter confidence, the major exuded power and strength. Then Fire Dancer noticed the thick mat of golden hair that lay in a triangle across his broad chest and tapered to a fine line between the hard ridges of his abdomen before it disappeared beneath his breeches. His forearms were liberally sprinkled with the same. Fire Dancer had never seen so much hair on a man and she would have thought it would repulse her, but strangely it didn't. It seemed only to enhance his manliness, something that the arrogant Englishman didn't need. He fairly reeked of masculinity.

Evan came to a halt before Fire Dancer, his eyes avidly scanning her face as he said softly, "It's a shame you can't understand me. You're incredibly beautiful, you know. So beautiful, it takes a man's breath away."

Fire Dancer had been about to step away, but Evan's compliment brought warmth to her stomach. Then as he raised his hand and trailed his fingers lightly down the side of her face, his touch felt like fire. She flinched.

A sudden occurrence came to Evan. Maybe she'd been acting so reluctant because she feared him. "Don't be afraid," he reassured her, his voice still soft but husky with desire. "I won't hurt you. It won't be any different with me than with your men. We're built the same. Here," he said, taking her hand and placing it over his bulging manhood, "see for yourself."

Fire Dancer had been rooted to the spot by the strange magnetism that the Englishman seemed to possess. Standing as close as he was, his presence was so powerful that it seemed to surround her and left her feeling helpless and weak. But when he placed her hand over his hot erection, she was too shocked to move. She had felt in the past the proof of arousal of the warriors who had tried to seduce her, but the white man's felt enormous. A tingle of fear ran through her. No, he wasn't built the same. He was covered with hair and built like a stallion. Why, he'd rip her in two! She trembled at the thought.

Evan felt Fire Dancer's hand shake and again mistook her reaction for excitement. Thinking he had set aside all reluctance on her part, he removed his hand from where he had held hers over him, bent his head, and kissed the side of her throat, drinking in her scent. Never had he smelled anything as sweet. But Fire Dancer's sweetness didn't come from a heavy perfume, as with the other women Evan had known. Hers was a clean sweetness that was her very own womanly essence, and it was quite intoxicating. His head spun, and an incredible excitement seized him. His lips slid down the length of her throat as one hand fumbled with the knotted toga on the shoulder just below his mouth.

When Evan kissed her and ran his lips down the side of her throat, Fire Dancer's fear had disappeared like a puff of smoke in a strong wind. Her mother had kissed her, a quick peck on the cheek or forehead, but she had never been kissed by a man. Indians touched each other's bodies as a prelude to sex, but not with their lips. The Englishman's lingering lips felt so soft, so warm, so compelling—she was enthralled with the sensation of his kissing her, so much so that when her toga fell away from her to hang at her waist by the string of pearls she had tied there and his arms slipped around her back, she was still too mesmerized by the feel of his mouth trailing fire over her shoulder and across the soft rise of her breasts to move. It wasn't until his tongue darted out and she felt it like a hot, wet lash over her nipple that she finally regained her senses. Horrified at her breasts being bared and at what she had allowed him to do, she pushed away from him and yanked her toga back up.

Bewildered, Evan looked at Fire Dancer clutching her toga to her chest. "What in the hell is wrong with you?" he asked, stepping toward her. "I thought you wanted a little dallying before we got down to it."

As he stretched out his hands, Fire Dancer stepped quickly away. "No! Don't touch me!" she said.

For a moment, Evan was stunned. "You speak English?" he said in amazement.

"Of course I speak your language!" Fire Dancer answered hotly, her fury at his audacity once more aroused. "My mother was English."

"Yes, I know. But why didn't you speak earlier?"

"Because I was too furious with you to speak. How dare you come in here, strip halfway naked, then do such indecent things to me!"

Her outraged words brought a deep scowl to Evan's handsome face. Then he came to his own defense, objecting, "Wait a minute! I was told that Promingo sent you here to attend to my needs and that included my sexual needs. Am I mistaken?"

"No, you are not mistaken."

"Then why are you angry?"

"Because I have no intention of obeying my uncle."

"Why not? I've been told the women of your tribe are quite free with their favors, that experimenting with various partners is encouraged, that there are no taboos regarding sex between single men and women. Were these lies?"

"No, they were not lies."

"Then why do you object to me? I'd be just another partner."

Fire Dancer didn't want to tell the Englishman that he would be the first partner, not just another one. She fully intended to keep her virginity a secret. Not only did she not trust him with knowing it, it was none of his business. It was no one's business but her own. "I choose my own lovers, not my uncle."

"Did it ever occur to you that you might be making a mistake?" A slow grin spread across Evan's handsome face. "Perhaps I could teach you a few things about lovemaking, things my people do."

Like kissing, Fire Dancer thought, the memory sending a warm thrill racing through her. Then, furious with herself, she pushed the memory aside and said, "I do not wish to learn new things."

Evan was totally frustrated. She had aroused him to an almost painful pitch, and now she refused him release. Damn, he *had* to have her! He decided to take another approach. "Have you forgotten your uncle ordered you to do this? As I understand it, it's more or less your duty. Will you risk his wrath?"

"I am not afraid of my uncle," Fire Dancer answered bravely. "I told you, I and I alone choose my lovers."

Evan's eyes narrowed. "And what if I don't take no for an answer?"

Fire Dancer felt a tingle of fear. She knew he could easily overpower her. "You'd force me?"

Evan had never forced a woman in his life, nor had he ever pleaded with one, as he was doing now. God, the little savage had brought him low! he thought in exasperation. "No, I won't force you," he threw back angrily. "But I want to know what it is about me that you object to so strenuously. It's not as if it's a matter of your virtue. Christ, you've probably bedded every brave in this village. So tell me—why not me?"

His accusing her of being loose infuriated Fire Dancer all the more, and his thinking so little of her hurt, which bewildered her. She found she wanted to hurt him back and answered spitefully, "Because I find you personally repulsive."

The insult had the effect on Evan's heated senses of a dash of ice-cold water. His sexual frustration was quickly replaced with cold anger. He stiffened, a small muscle on the side of his chin twitching. "In what way?"

Fire Dancer was hard put for an answer. Actually, the

Englishman was by far the most appealing man she had ever met, with his golden mane of hair, his blue, blue eyes, his sensuous lips, and his tall, muscular body. And then there was that other, unexplainable attraction. Yes, he was by far the most exciting man she had ever come across, and he seemed to draw her toward him against her will. Her eyes fell on the mat of golden hair on his chest. She yearned to run her fingers through it, to see if it was as soft as it looked, but instead she said, "You have hair on your body. Chickasaw men don't. I find it repulsive."

Evan knew that Indian men didn't have beards, but he'd never paid any attention to whether they had hair on their bodies. Now that it had been brought to his attention, he realized they didn't. That Fire Dancer had chosen something over which he had absolutely no control infuriated him all the more.

Furious, he whirled away and walked to one of the built-in beds at one side of the room, saying over his shoulder, "I happen to have my preferences too. I like my women warm and willing. So get out! I need some sleep."

Fire Dancer sensed that the Englishman would not tell her uncle she had refused him. She knew he was a proud man because of how angry he had gotten when she had told him she thought he was repulsive. No, she'd stake her life on his holding his silence, but if she left now, she'd give herself away. "No, I will not leave," she announced.

Evan turned. "And why not?"

"Because I was sent to attend to your needs."

Evan had now been pushed beyond his limit. "You

know what my needs are!" he thundered. "You just refused me!"

Fire Dancer drew herself proudly up to her full height. "Do not yell at me," she said. "Do not ever use that tone of voice to me. I will attend to your other needs. I will cook for you, wash your clothes, keep this house, assist you in your bath. But I am not a servant, and I will not be treated like one. I am—"

"I know who you are!" Evan interrupted. "Some kind of a princess. But I don't need you. I'm perfectly capable of taking care of myself."

Fire Dancer knew that if Evan threw her out, Promingo would ask questions. "Your capabilities have nothing to do with it. This is a courtesy my uncle has extended to you as his honored guest. Will you insult him by refusing?"

It was a point well taken. Evan didn't dare insult Promingo. He needed his help—or rather, the British Army did. But God, he hated to back down—again! It seemed that since he had walked through the door, he and Fire Dancer had had a clash of wills, and she had won the contest.

To her credit, Fire Dancer sensed Evan's dilemma and didn't push the issue. Assuming a businesslike manner, she walked past him to the bed, pulled back the buffalo skin that served as a blanket, then walked around the cabin, drawing the shutters on the windows closed and blowing out the candles.

By the time she walked back across the room, Evan was sitting on the side of the bed and struggling to remove his knee-high boots. As Fire Dancer headed for another bed built into the other end of the wall from his, Evan said arrogantly, "Well, if you're determined to stay, you can help me get off these damn boots."

As Fire Dancer walked to him, Evan extended his foot. But when she took the boot in her hands, he said, "No, not that way. You'll never get enough leverage. Turn your back to me, straddle my leg, and pull."

Fire Dancer did as the Englishman directed, and as she tugged on his boot, Evan realized he had made a serious mistake. With the toga pulled up between her legs, the material was stretched taut across her buttocks, leaving little to his imagination. Evan tried to avert his eyes, but for the life of him, he found he couldn't. His hands itched to cup the soft mounds, and to his dismay, he found himself aroused all over again. By the time they got to the second boot, a fine sheen of perspiration had broken out over his lip. Wanting to get the agony over, he gently placed his foot on her buttocks. Immediately, Fire Dancer stiffened and glanced in alarm over her shoulder.

"I'm just going to give a little push to help you out," Evan explained, and before she could object, he pushed with his foot. The boot and Fire Dancer went flying across the room, and she barely managed to maintain her balance. Seeing the accusing look on her face when she turned, Evan said, "I'm sorry. I guess I should have warned you that might happen."

"Who usually helps you take off your boots?" Fire Dancer asked.

"When he's around, my batman."

"Who?"

"My batman. He's a combination of soldier and servant. All officers have them. Otherwise, I use my boot jack, but I don't know where it and my saddlebags are."

"Your bags are over there," Fire Dancer answered, pointing to a darkened corner across the room. "Would you like me to bring them to you?"

He could have saved himself the agony over the boots, Evan thought, then answered somewhat irritably, "No, don't bother. I don't need the damn things now."

Evan reclined on the bed. A moment later, the cabin was plunged into darkness as Fire Dancer blew out the candle by her bed. Then Evan heard a rustling that had to be made by Fire Dancer removing her toga.

Silence followed. Evan lay on his back, his arms folded behind his head, and stared out at the darkness, acutely conscious that Fire Dancer lay naked just a few feet away. His desire rose again, hot and urgent, and with it his manhood. But he was left to toss and turn, muttering darkly beneath his breath for the better part of the night.

4

When Evan awakened the next morning, the shutters were open and the sunlight was pouring into the cabin. But Fire Dancer was not there, and for that, he was glad. After his poor night's rest, he was in a foul mood, and he'd decided the sooner he got out of the settlement and away from her the better. He didn't want to be reminded of her humiliating rejection. Christ! He'd never thought he would live to see the day when he would be scorned by any woman, much less a savage.

The smell of food drifted across the room to him. He rose and walked to a bearskin in the middle of the cabin. There he saw a bowl of gruel and cup of milk sitting on a tray, and he knew Fire Dancer had left it for him, since she had said she would cook for him. He sank to the skin, crossing his long legs before him, and picked up the wooden bowl, noting that it was still warm. It occurred to him that Fire Dancer might be avoiding him, just as he was hoping to avoid her. For a moment the idea rankled, until he firmly told himself that was just fine with him if she was. Determined to put her out of his mind, he picked up the wooden spoon and dipped it into the bowl, taking a tentative taste. To his surprise, the corn mush was sweetened with honey, and although he would have preferred something more substantial, he ate it quickly. But ignored the cup of milk. He could never abide warm milk, no matter how hungry he was.

Evan rose and walked to one of the windows. As he passed by the bed where Fire Dancer had slept, he came to a halt. While his bed was covered with the skins of panthers and bears, hers was padded with fawn and buffalo calf skins. It looked so soft that he couldn't resist bending and running his fingers over them. It was a mistake, for the moment he did so, he became acutely aware of her lingering scent, and once again his desire for her made itself felt, much to his utter disgust. Muttering a curse, he rose and strode rapidly to the window, staring out and deliberately drinking in deep breaths of air to cleanse his nostrils of her tantalizing sweetness.

What in the devil was he doing here in an Indian settlement deep in the wilderness of this barbaric country, lusting after a savage? he asked himself. He didn't belong here, sleeping on a bed padded with animal skins, sitting on the floor to eat—mush! of all the disgusting things—planning to make an another arduous trip to scout out an enemy fort that might or might not exist. He belonged on his father's country estate back in England, sleeping on a feather mattress, eating a huge, satisfying breakfast served at a table by liveried servants, sipping hot tea while he conferred with his overseer on what needed to be done on the estate that day, or—if

Parliament was in session—in his town house in London, dressing in preparation for assuming his duties in the House of Lords as the ninth Earl of Linchester.

Yes, if it hadn't been for a trick of fate, that was where he would be—he, and not his blasted brother. How had he managed it? Evan asked himself for the hundredth time. How had his weak, cowardly brother managed to edge him out and be firstborn, cheating Evan of his rightful place? And yet his twin had done just that, had pushed him aside and laid claim to everything by the right of primogeniture. Edward had inherited the title, the lands, the property, everything. As second born, Evan had received nothing but the excellent education and gentleman's grooming his father had given him and a taste for expensive living that he couldn't afford.

So Evan had been forced to go out and make his own way in the world, and in that day and time, only two ways were considered suitable for a nobleman who couldn't inherit to accomplish this. He could become an officer in His Majesty's service or a minister in His Majesty's church. For Evan there had really been no choice. He was not minister material, not by any stretch of the imagination. Not only did he enjoy too many worldly things, he had a restless nature and, if truth be known, a taste for adventure. So Evan had let his younger brother become the minister for the family, and he himself had become the soldier.

But his bitterness in losing the title and all it entailed still remained. Had he missed out by a matter of years, as his younger brother had, it might have been different. But to be edged out by just seconds was hard to bear. Evan had always felt that he had lost the most important race of his life before he was even born.

Well, there was no use in brooding over it now, Evan thought. According to the last communiqué he had received from his younger brother, Edward had married and produced a son. Evan hoped the child would prove a worthier heir than his father. Not only was Edward a physical weakling and afraid of his own shadow, he had no appreciation of what he had inherited. He cared nothing for the estates, and through his mismanagement, they had all gone down badly. That hurt Evan even more deeply than losing out on the inheritance. He loved those estates, as had his father and his grandfather. He knew every nook and cranny of them, as well as the first name of almost every serf who worked them. That was how he knew in his heart that he should have been the ninth earl and not his brother. Such a deep caring for the lands entrusted to them had been ingrained in every earl since they had been bestowed by the king centuries before.

He was still mulling it over, Evan thought with self-disgust. And that he had come to be in His Majesty's army still didn't explain what he was doing out here in the wilderness among a group of savages thousands of miles away from his troops—why he, of all the officers in the British Army, had been chosen for this crazy mission. Evan scoffed, thinking the explanation was much like that for why he had lost out to his brother. It had been another case of bad timing. Maybe if he hadn't been present at the reception given for General Jeffrey Amherst or walked up to him at the precise moment Lieutenant Colonel John Bradstreet was praising

Evan for how well he had done in his service, the general would have completely forgotten that Evan had been on Bradstreet's lightning raid that destroyed an important French fort deep in enemy territory and would have picked another officer for this mission. But such hadn't been the case. The raid had been one of the British Army's few successes in this war, which was now dragging into its eighth year. Amherst was convinced the raid succeeded because Bradstreet had utilized both the Indian allies and the American rangers' methods of guerrilla fighting to the fullest. The general had been equally convinced that the experience Evan had gained on that raid qualified him for this mission. But Amherst was wrong, Evan thought. Evan didn't speak these savages' language, and he didn't understand their ways, as Bradstreet had; nor did he want to learn. He didn't belong here, and he didn't want to be here. Again, fate had dealt him a dirty blow.

"Good mornin'."

Abruptly torn from his musing, Evan jumped. Then, seeing Josh outside the window, he mumbled, "Good morning."

"What are ye doin' standin' there starin' out the window? I've been here a good five minutes, and ye didn't even see me."

"I had things on my mind."

"Aye, I figured that. What things?"

Evan was tempted to tell the scout it was none of his business, but instead he quickly fabricated. "The mission. Are Promingo's men ready to leave?"

"Nay. They won't be ready until noon."

Evan frowned. "I told him I wanted to leave this morning."

"Aye, but the warriors need to prepare 'emselves. They never go off on what could be a dangerous mission without cleansin' their souls and askin' Loak-Ishtohoollo-Aba's protection."

"Is that what they call God?"

"Aye, the great, supreme holy spirit of fire who resides above the clouds."

"Damn!" Evan responded in disgust. "I wanted to get an early start. What am I supposed to do until noon—twiddle my thumbs?"

"I was goin' to take ye over to see the great river this morning. Remember? The one ye don't think exists."

"All right, so it exists. But it would be pointless to make a special trip just to see it. I'll see it when we leave."

"Are ye thinkin' ye'll be travelin' to the Ohio by river?"

"Of course. That's the most logical means. You said the Ohio flows into this"—Evan paused, and a sneer came over his face—"great river."

"Ordinarily it would be. On any river but the Misho Sipokni, that is. It has such a powerful current that travelin' upriver is near impossible, particularly at this time of the year, when it's still runnin' high from the spring thaws."

"If that's true, how did the French get their men and supplies up to that fort they're supposedly building?"

"They only got a few keelboats through, and it wasn't easy. They had some hard pullin' and polin' to do, but they preferred that to runnin' the risk of gettin' caught by a war party of Chickasaw if they went overland."

"So that's how we'll be going? Overland?"

"Aye, and come back by river." Josh paused, then asked, "So do ye want to see the Misho Sipokni today or not?"

"I'll have a look. Come on in while I get some clothes on."

When Josh entered the cabin, Evan was standing in a corner and skimming off his uniform breeches. Josh glanced quickly around. Seeing no sign of Fire Dancer, he took quick note of the fact that both beds had been slept in. He thought it a little odd.

"Looking for something?" Evan asked sharply, very much aware that Josh was giving the beds a close scrutiny. Aye, something went amiss last night, Josh thought. Evan's warning tone of voice only confirmed his suspicions. He'd give his eyeteeth to know what went wrong, but he wasn't foolish enough to ask. He'd been around the major long enough to know he didn't take kindly to someone sticking his nose into his business, and when Evan was unhappy with someone, he could be very menacing. It had been a surprise to Josh to discover that Evan had this hard, dangerous side to him. He'd always thought of nobility as fearful weaklings with equally feeble characters, but the major was a man he most definitely didn't want to rile.

"Nay," Josh replied, pasting an innocent look on his face. "I was just curious. All these cabins are a little different inside, ye know."

Josh's answer didn't put Evan's suspicions at rest, and the guide knew it by the look on the nobleman's face.

Hoping to further distract him, he said, "Ye know, I've been wonderin' about somethin'. Ye said ye were with Bradstreet on his raid on Fort Frontenac. How did that happen? I thought he led a bunch of rangers and Onondagas under Chief Red Hand."

"He did. It just so happened that some of the rangers served under me. We were what was left of Lord Howe's command that hadn't been reassigned yet."

"Colonel George Howe? Commander of the crack Fifty-fifth Highlanders?"

"Yes, except it's not a crack outfit anymore," Evan answered, "and Lord Howe is dead."

The answer was given sharply, but Josh heard the sadness in it. "Aye, I know. He was killed at Fort Carillon, wasn't he?"

"No, actually it happened the day before. We were traveling in the direction of Ticonderoga on Lake Champlain and got lost. We ran into a party of French who were also lost. Shots were exchanged, and the French broke and ran. But Howe was at the first of the line, as usual, and he was killed."

"I heard he was an extraordinary officer."

"He was. He was also a good friend."

Josh wasn't surprised. Both men were noblemen, even though one had been a general and the other a mere major. Besides, Josh had heard that Howe was an unpretentious man who even liked provincials, so much so that he mingled with them and fashioned his method of fighting after the rugged rangers. "I've heard a lot about Howe. Is it true he issued rifles to his soldiers and made 'em cut off the tails of their uniforms?"

"Yes. His motto was, 'When in America, fight as the

Americans do.' Besides getting rid of the army muskets and coattails, he made his men wrap their legs in canvas, much as the Indians wrap theirs in buckskin, and carry all of their own provisions. He even deprived his officers. Like him, we had to cast aside our uniforms and wear hunting clothes, like these I have on, and give up our batmen, washerwomen, and champagne when we went into the field. For weeks, we survived on nothing but cornmeal and slept in the wide open. And all for nothing. The French cut us to pieces the next day. Major General Abercromby was in command. With Howe gone, he made the Fifty-fifth throw away their rifles and make a frontal attack with bayonets, along with his Forty-second Highlanders. It was a disaster. The French and the Canadians with their long rifles mowed them down."

Evan fell into a silence as he remembered that day. Up until then, he had never questioned the British Army's methods of fighting. Other than their cannons and artillery, they didn't fight with guns. The foot-soldier's Brown Bess was never meant to kill mass numbers by being fired. It threw a ball only a hundred yards and with little degree of accuracy. It was more or less an accident if a ball happened to find its mark and kill the enemy. No, what killed was a fierce, mass assault with bayonets. Nor did the officers fight with guns. They did battle with sabers.

But on that fateful day, everything Evan had learned about fighting seemed to be turned around, and although he had not been in agreement with Lord Howe before that, he soon saw the wisdom of the late viscount's beliefs. As usual, the British had no artillery of any importance with them. There were no roads in this country over which their heavy cannons could be transported, and the light artillery had too short a range to be of much good. Then the French refused to leave the protection of their fort to meet the bayonet attack. Their sharpshooter Canadians' long rifles could throw a ball several hundred yards with deadly accuracy, which turned the battle into a massacre. The British were forced to retreat in total panic, and Abercromby had to leave every bit of the useless artillery, ammunition, and supplies he had brought with him behind for the enemy to confiscate. Yes, it had been a horror, and Evan still had nightmares about it. He probably always would.

"Well," Josh drawled, breaking into Evan's thoughts, "I guess that's why ye carry that long rifle and know how to use it. Figured it strange. Ye're the first British officer I've seen tote one, much less know how to shoot one worth a damn."

"Yes, that's why," Evan admitted as he carried his boots to the bed to put on. "I decided that day that I wasn't going to be caught at that disadvantage again."

And that explained a lot of other things too, Josh thought as Evan donned his boots. He'd wondered why the Englishman had taken the long, difficult trip here so well. Evan hadn't seem to tire in the least, nor had he complained about the lack of comforts. Apparently his service under both Bradstreet and Howe had stood him in good stead. As for the bravery he'd shown when that mountain lion jumped him, Josh figured that was part of the man himself. Aye, that had been something to see, Josh thought in remembrance—the nobleman rolling around on the ground with that big cat, then coming to his feet as calm and cool as if killing a hundred pounds of animal fury with his bare knife were an everyday occurrence. Aye, there was a lot more than met the eye to this Englishman, and it was a shame. He would have made a damn good colonial.

Unaware of Josh's thoughts, Evan stood and said, "All right. Let's have a look at this mighty river."

Josh knew by the unnecessary emphasis that Evan put on the word *mighty* that he still didn't believe, but the Scot held his tongue as he led the major through the village and once more into the forest, deciding to let the river speak for itself.

Twenty minutes later, they stepped from the thick woods and came to a stop at the top of a high limestone bluff. "There she is," Josh said, bending slightly and sweeping his hand in a wide arch.

Evan stepped closer to the edge of the cliff and looked down. A stunned expression came over his face. The Mississippi River lay shimmering in the bright sunlight below him, its width stretched well over a mile from bank to bank. Amazed, he turned his head from side to side. From that high viewpoint he could see the mighty river curving through the forest for miles and miles both ways. Finally he asked, "Does it get smaller farther downstream?"

"Nay." Josh gazed down and said, "That river has got a hell of a lot of water in it. Why, it must drain half this country. The Ohio empties into it, and that's no small stream itself. And accordin' to the Chickasaw, there's another big river farther up past the Ohio junction that comes in from the west as straight as an arrow. They say that's where this river gets its yellow color, from that western river."

Evan looked across the river at the opposite bank. Unlike the side he stood on, it was almost level with the river, and it was covered as far as he could see with a thick forest. "What do you suppose is out there? The Pacific?"

"Well, maybe somewhere, but not anywhere near close."

"How do you know that western river isn't the passage to the Pacific that everyone has been looking for?"

"Well, it may be, for all I know. But the Pacific still isn't anywhere near close. The Chickasaw claim that out past that forest there's a huge stretch of land barren of everythin' but grass that grows up to a man's shoulders, and that past that there's a range of mountains that makes the Alleghenies look like anthills."

"How would the Chickasaw know what's out there?"

"Because that's where they claim they came from, long, long ago. From the west." Josh turned his back to the bank across from him and said, "We call these bluffs we're standin' on Chickasaw Bluffs. Almost the entire eastern side of this river has chalky cliffs, but this is one of the highest points, and ye can see for miles and miles from here. It's from these bluffs that the Chickasaw watch for French pirogues carryin' furs downriver to New Orleans. The Frenchmen try to slip past by hidin' under the trees on the opposite bank, but the Chickasaw can usually spy 'em anyway. Then they send their canoes out after 'em, and there's not many of those boats that get through, despite the swivel guns those Frenchmen carry. Besides these bluffs, the Chickasaw have several other bluffs they operate from farther upriver. I guess if the French could put the blame on anyone for not being as successful in this part of the country as they were in Canada, it would be the Chickasaw. They control almost the entire length of the river from the Ohio on down, except that part right around New Orleans. The French never could colonize out here because of 'em. They tried a few settlements, and the Chickasaw chased 'em off. And the French trappers play hell tryin' to get their furs down to New Orleans. Most of the time, they take their furs overland to the Great Lakes rather than have to tangle with these Indians."

Evan had never realized until that minute how valuable the Chickasaw's friendship really was. By controlling this vital river, they protected the British colonies' back door. Had they been French allies and allowed them to come and go all those years, the French would have had a much stronger hold on this area. Why, there might well be forts and settlements all up and down this river, as well as over the entire Ohio Territory, and if that had been the case, it would have been very difficult for the British to lay claim to it. Possession was nine-tenths of ownership.

Evan glanced down and saw huge fields being cultivated by the Indians between the bottom of the bluffs and the river's edge. The men were fashioning huge rows of mounded dirt while the women poked holes in them and dropped in seeds. "They farm down there?" he asked in surprise.

"Aye."

"But it's bottom land. Doesn't it flood?"

"Aye, but only in the spring, and that's what makes it such rich soil—all that silt it drops. It's also close enough to the river that the Indians can tote water to the fields in dry weather. The Chickasaw have been usin' those same fields for well over a hundred years."

Evan was impressed. He knew enough about farming from his father's estates to know that land eventually grew barren and crops didn't do as well. That was one reason the colonists were always moving westward in their quest for new, fresh land. He wondered briefly if the Chickasaw's long success at farming stemmed from the fact that the land was bottom land or if they knew some secrets that the white man didn't. Then, glancing toward the river shoreline and seeing a long line of canoes resting there, Evan put his thoughts about the Chickasaw farmers aside and asked, "Are you sure we can't go upriver to scout this fort?"

"Aye. Believe me, even as strong at paddlin' as the Chickasaw are, it'll be faster overland."

Evan glanced up at the sun. "What time do you judge it to be?" he asked.

Josh held up a finger and looked at its shadow on the ground. "About noon."

"Then we'd better get back. You said we'd leave at noon."

Josh scratched his nose with his long, bony finger. "Ye countin' me in on that *we*?"

"Of course I'm counting you. You're coming along with us as my interpreter."

"Nay, I'm afraid not. As soon as I pick up my things back at the settlement, I'm headin' home."

"But you agreed to be my guide and interpreter," Evan objected.

"I agreed to be yer guide to the Chickasaw village and to interpret for ye yesterday. That's all."

Evan was so shocked at the sudden turn of events that for a moment he didn't know what to say. "Did General Amherst know this when he made these arrangements with you?"

"Well, he didn't come right out and ask how long I'd hang around," Josh admitted, "but that doesn't make any difference. I agreed to bring ye here and take ye back. Nothing more."

"How can you take me back when you won't even be here?" Evan asked, his frustration rising.

"The Chickasaw know what village I live in. Send a runner to me when ye're ready to go back. A Chickasaw can run faster than any Indian on this continent. He could be there in less than a day."

"What if I personally asked you to stay?" Evan asked, taking another approach.

"Then I'd have to say nay." Seeing the major glaring at him, Josh hurried to say, "Look, I'm not just an ordinary trader. I'm an agent for the Goose Creek traders back in that Chickasaw village I come from. I've got a business to attend to. I need to get back to it."

"Did it ever occur to you that if we lose this war, you won't have a business?"

It was a point well taken. If England lost the war and France took over her colonies, Josh would no longer be able to get the cheap but superior British goods that gave him an edge over the French traders. "I'll fight when it comes time. When ye get ready to attack the fort, just let me know."

"I can't make any plans for an attack if I can't even speak Promingo's language. I can't do anything here, including going off with that scouting party. We need to have some way to communicate. I'm helpless without an interpreter. For Christ's sake! Can't you see that?"

"I didn't say ye wouldn't have an interpreter. I just said it wouldn't be me. Promingo has already made arrangements for an interpreter for ye."

"Who?" Evan asked in surprise. Then a sudden thought came to him; "The English factor in this town?"

"Nay, there's no English factor here. He died a few months back and hasn't been replaced."

"Then who is going to be my interpreter?"

"Well, I would have thought ye'd have guessed by now." A broad grin spread across the Scot's ruddy face. "Fire Dancer. Promingo has ordered her to go with ye."

5

Evan was so stunned by Josh's announcement that he was speechless for a moment. Then he recovered. "No! That's impossible!" he exclaimed.

"Why?" Josh asked in surprise.

"Because she's a woman."

"Aye, but what's that got to do with it?"

Evan couldn't tell Josh that she was a woman who had humiliated him and that for that reason he was anxious to put time and distance between them. He frantically searched his mind for a plausible reason, then came up with one that should have been obvious from the very beginning: "It will be too dangerous for her."

"Promingo must not think it too dangerous, and he's a better judge than ye. This is his country."

Evan quickly delved for another reason. "But still, it's inappropriate—a lone woman among all those men. Besides, we'll be discussing military objectives, strategies, things like that. She'll be bored to tears."

"I don't think Promingo is sendin' her along for her enjoyment. She's to perform a service. And she might not be so bored. Governor Oglethorpe in Georgia has been usin' a female mestizo servant of his as interpreter and Indian adviser for years. She goes everywhere with him, even into battle. That may be where Promingo got the idea for Fire Dancer."

Evan still wasn't willing to let go. "What about her younger brother? Why can't he perform this service? I should think it would be good experience for him."

"Neither he nor Fire Dancer's sister speaks English worth a damn. Besides, he's only nine years old." Seeing Evan about to open his mouth again, Josh cut in, "Nay, save yer breath. I don't know why ye're so dead set against Fire Dancer. But Promingo made this decision, and he won't tolerate anyone questioning his decisions, particularly if they have anything of a military nature about 'em. He's the chief here. His word is law. So if don't want to rile him, ye keep yer mouth shut and let him run the show."

Evan was enough of a military man to realize it was time to back down. A major didn't buck a general. Like it or not, he was stuck with Fire Dancer on a day-to-day basis. He had to admit that if he had been in the Promingo's place, he would have done the same thing—used the most capable person he had at his disposal. Promingo had settled his problem. Now Evan had to figure out a way to solve his own. Having to face Fire Dancer after last night would be bad enough, but he was honest enough to admit to himself that that was only the tip of the iceberg of what was bothering him. The real problem was that he still wanted her. Damn! If she was the only person in the tribe who could speak English well enough to act as his interpreter, why couldn't she have been old and toothless, or as ugly as sin?

As he and Josh walked back to the settlement, Evan mulled over his predicament. Josh was aware of his silence and the dark scowl on his face. The Scot no longer suspected that something had gone wrong between the major and Fire Dancer. He *knew* it. But for the life of him, he couldn't imagine what. Honest lust was such a simple emotion. How had they managed to complicate it?

When they reached the settlement, Evan asked, "Where do I meet my scouting party?"

"In the town square."

"And how do I go about finding my horse?"

"They'll have him waitin' there for ye, all saddled and ready to go."

"Then all I have to do is stop by the cabin and pick up my saddlebags, bedroll, and rifle."

"Nay, they'll probably be waitin' for ye also. Fire Dancer will see to that. Her other assignment still holds, ye know. She's yer woman, too, to care for yer every need as long as ye're with the tribe."

Josh shot Evan a quick glance to see his reaction but saw only the twitch of a muscle on the major's jaw.

As they entered the town square a few moments later, Evan saw the scouting party. A few of the Chickasaw were already mounted and apparently anxious to leave. "They'll be traveling by horse too?" he asked in surprise.

"Aye. Why do ye ask?"

"The Indians I dealt with up north always traveled by foot or canoe. I got the impression they didn't ride."

"Well, Chickasaw do, and they're damn good horsemen."

Evan spied his horse at the front of the line that was forming and Fire Dancer standing by its side and holding his rifle. Quickly, he glanced over her, noting that she was wearing a calf-length buckskin skirt, knee-high moccasins, and something that looked like a leather vest except that it had no buttons, tabs, or laces, and no sides. The two pieces of buckskin that crossed her breasts were held in place by a beaded belt, and the back was loose like a short cape. Her hair was styled the same, the large single braid piled on the top of her head, except that she had replaced the pearls with copper beads and a string of matching beads now dangled from each of her delicate ears. Becoming aware of her gaze on him, Evan looked directly at her face and saw, for one brief second before she hid it, a look of absolute fury in her green eyes. He knew then that she was as displeased with their arrangement as he. Well, he thought wryly, at least they had one thing in common.

Evan walked to where Fire Dancer was standing, and she handed him his rifle. Before he could even consider thanking her, Promingo stepped up to him and said something.

"My uncle wishes you a safe and speedy journey," Fire Dancer said, interpreting Promingo's words. "He looks forward to your return and making plans to attack the accursed Frenchmen."

"Tell him thank you, and I look forward to it also."

After Fire Dancer relayed Evan's words, another

Chickasaw stepped up to him. The man was about the same height and age as he, and he looked as thoroughly savage as Promingo. "This is Red Thunder," Fire Dancer informed Evan. "He is one of my uncle's sub-chiefs and will be in charge of this expedition. If you have any questions, or if you wish to confer with him on any matter, please make your desires known to me."

Evan nodded in acknowledgment, and the warrior nodded curtly back, then spun on his heels, walked to his horse, and mounted, surprising Evan by doing so on the off side. Evan swung into his saddle, as did the others. He glanced to his side and saw a horse being led to Fire Dancer. As she walked to meet it, Evan muttered to Josh standing by his side, "Christ, you'd think they could find a better animal than that for her. None of their horses look very good, but I've never seen a more miserable-looking nag. Why, it probably won't even make it through the day."

Josh laughed. "Nay, ye're as wrong as wrong can be. That's a Chickasaw horse. All of 'em are, and they're the most coveted horseflesh in the colonies. They bring higher prices than any other breed, even yer fancy British Thoroughbreds. Why, a man would kill for a Chickasaw horse."

"You've got to be joking," Evan responded with a totally disbelieving look on his face.

"Nay. They may not look like much, but there's no horse that can beat 'em for intelligence, for endurance, for speed, and for jumpin'. They've got pure Arabian blood in 'em."

"Arabian? How in the devil did that happen?"

"What ye're lookin' at is a direct descendant of the

Spanish horses De Soto brought with him. He and his men spent a winter right here in this settlement, ye know. When he left, he demanded carriers and women. The Chickasaw were so outraged that they attacked him. Needless to say, he left in a hurry, and in doin' so he left quite a few of his horses behind. That's why the Chickasaw have horses and the northern tribes don't. They had horses long before we came with ours."

Evan took a second look at the horse Fire Dancer was preparing to mount, and for the first time he noticed the small head, the characteristic set of the ears, the narrow chest, and the slim body of an Arabian. It was the animal's apparent listlessness and the dull, shaggy coat that had thrown him, the latter probably because the Indians knew nothing of currying. Then as Fire Dancer swung into her saddle, he stared, again caught by surprise to see a woman sitting astride.

Josh laughed at the expression on Evan's face. "Aye, that shocked me, too, the first time I saw a Chickasaw woman mount. But leave it to the Indian to be practical." He extended his hand. "Well, Major, I'll say good-bye for now. Like I said, let me know when ye plan to attack that fort. I'd like to be in on it."

Evan took the hand and shook it. "You can be sure I will."

As Red Thunder led the party from the town square, Evan fell in line behind the subchief, thinking he'd be damn sure Josh would keep his word. He was getting tired of fighting the colonists' battles for them. After all, they were the ones who'd lose the most if Britain lost this war, yet they seemed to be quite content to sit back and let the British Army fight it, each colony insisting it didn't have the money to wage a war and hoping its neighbor would bear the expense. Even at those times when the militia was called out, the colonists were so undisciplined and unreliable that they were useless. Like Josh, if they had business at home or crops to tend to, they simply packed up and left. If you accused them of desertion, they just laughed at you. And they were impossible to march. Instead of walking in file, they staggered out in every which direction as if they were taking a leisurely stroll, and they lagged behind, stopping to build fires and eat whenever the notion struck them. Dealing with them had been incredibly frustrating. Maybe he *was* better off fighting with the Indians. At least they knew how to follow orders and had a sense of duty.

As they entered the forest, Fire Dancer brought her horse up beside Evan's and took her proper place as his interpreter, although having to do so galled her. If this had been the only demand her uncle had made of her, she probably wouldn't have resented it nearly as much. She could understand her value as the only person in her tribe that spoke the Englishman's language well enough to act as a liaison between him and her people, and she wanted their joint military venture to be a success. But she had a feeling that her uncle had used her skills as an excuse to keep her by the Englishman's side, where she would have no respite from performing her more distasteful duties for him. Damn Promingo! Fire Dancer thought, using her mother's favorite curse. Had she not taken her Chickasaw duty so seriously, it would have been too much to ask. Now she would have to endure the arrogant Englishman's company from morning to night as well as play the role of his servant.

Evan had been aware when Fire Dancer moved her mount up beside his. He had detected her tantalizing scent before he even saw her. Now he pretended he wasn't aware she was there, but secretly he studied her from his peripheral vision. Although she was sitting in a most unladylike manner on her disreputable-looking horse, she looked queenly. Not even her knees, bare where her skirt had ridden up, or her half-naked breasts could detract from her regal bearing. Evan found that he couldn't draw his attention away from those bare areas of her body. The tawny skin on her arms, the side of the breast closest to him, even her knees looked so soft, so enticing. Noting the slender column of her neck, he remembered how sweet she had tasted, and he yearned to press his lips there once again.

Realizing he was allowing himself to become enflamed all over, Evan nudged his horse and trotted a few steps ahead of Fire Dancer so that she would be out of his side vision. Fire Dancer, aware that he had moved away, mistakenly thought he had done so because he considered himself too good to ride beside her. Her mother had told her that the whites looked down on Indians, and she had seen herself how the Anglo factor in their town had treated Indian women. He had used them in his bed but had always thought himself too much above them to marry one or even sit beside one in public. Of course, there were exceptions, like Josh, but apparently this Englishman wasn't of the same mold. It infuriated Fire Dancer that he would use her, yet scorn her for the Indian blood that ran in her veins. She spent the rest of the day staring at his broad back and seething.

That evening, when they stopped beside a small stream to make camp, Fire Dancer dismounted and reached for Evan's reins as he swung down from his horse's back. Evan caught his reins and jerked them back, asking, "What do you think you're doing?"

"I will care for your horse."

"The devil you will! I'll care for him myself. Otherwise he'll be looking like that miserable mount you've been riding."

Fire Dancer bristled. "You can care for your own horse if you like, but I will not tolerate you insulting my horse. She is not miserable! She is the best mare in my herd."

"Your herd?" Evan asked with a scoff. "Don't you mean your grandmother's?"

"No, I mean *my* herd! These are horses that she has already given to me, horses that have nothing to do with my future inheritance. And this mare is the best. She can outrun your horse anytime."

Even though Evan knew the Chickasaw horses had Arabian blood in them, he still thought they were the poorest horseflesh he had ever seen. He couldn't imagine any one of them beating his Thoroughbred in a race, particularly since his mount had won a fair share of money for him racing both in England and in the colonies. He looked Fire Dancer's mount over one more time and shook his head in disgust, for the animal didn't have enough spirit even to raise its head. "I'd put a wager on that if there were any way we could race."

"There is a place we can race."

"You mean back at the settlement?"

"Yes, at the ball ground. Then you will see."

Fire Dancer turned and walked proudly away, leading her horse to the stream. Evan led his own horse to the water, and while it drank, he watched Fire Dancer unsaddle her mare, swinging the small Indian saddle down as if it weighed nothing. Then she fed it a dozen or so ears of dry corn from a leather bag that had hung from her saddle. Then, just as Evan had suspected, she walked away without bothering even to rub the horse down, much less to curry it.

Evan unsaddled his horse, walked to the packhorse carrying his supplies, and removed a feedbag and sack of grain—something that he had paid dearly for in this country where mostly corn was raised. While his horse ate, he brushed it, aware that the Chickasaws were casting curious glances in his direction as they removed firewood and supplies from another packhorse and built a fire.

To Evan's surprise, Fire Dancer built them a separate fire, some distance from the larger one. As she spitted two dressed rabbits one of the braves had brought her and placed them over the fire, Evan never thought to object. He was accustomed to servants, both at home and from his batman, and Josh had done the cooking on their trip. So he sat back and waited, accepting this part of Fire Dancer's services as his due.

As soon as the rabbits were cooking, Fire Dancer slipped some yams into the ashes to bake, then mixed some cornmeal with some water, threw in a pinch of herbs from a small leather sack, fashioned the wet meal into cakes that she wrapped in dry leaves, and slipped them into the ashes at the edge of the fire. Evan watched this procedure with interest, for Josh's cooking had been limited to roasting meat and preparing a very basic stew. When Fire Dancer served him the meal, he had to admit that her cooking was far superior to the Scot's. He had never eaten the golden-colored yams before. They, like the little white native potatoes, were Indian foods that the whites had yet to adopt. He found their rather sweet taste strange yet pleasing to the palate, while the ash cakes were absolutely delicious. For a moment, Evan considered complimenting Fire Dancer, but glancing to where she sat resting on her heels as she ate from her wooden plate, he decided against it. Even before their little clash over the horses, something in her demeanor had told him she was angry with him, and he assumed it was about the night before.

After they had eaten, two of the braves erected a small lean-to of skins close to his and Fire Dancer's fire, the open side facing the fire and the back facing the warriors' camp. Then Fire Dancer spread skins on the ground under the lean-to. But it wasn't until she announced to Evan, "Your bed is ready" that it dawned on him that the structure had been built for him. He had thought it was for Fire Dancer, to allow her some privacy in this all-male expedition. He glanced to where the braves were bedding down around their fire, and he suddenly realized exactly why his and Fire Dancer's camp had been set at a discreet distance and a lean-to provided. They had done so not to give Fire Dancer privacy, but to give *him* and Fire Dancer privacy.

Evan wondered if he should refuse to sleep in the lean-to, for there was no doubt in his mind that Fire

Dancer had not changed her mind. She would cook for him, prepare his bed, even care of his horse—if he had allowed her—but she would not service him in that manner, and he well remembered what a miserable night he had spent the night before in her proximity. He could let her sleep in the lean-to and he outside, but he quickly rejected that idea, for fear the warriors would see and wonder. Evan couldn't stand for them to know of his failure, particularly in view of the fact that every one of them had probably shared Fire Dancer's bed at some time or other. No sooner had the thought crossed his mind than Evan was seized with a new emotion, one that he had never felt before. A jealous anger seized him.

Fire Dancer was still on her knees in the lean-to when she saw Evan rise and walk toward her. The hard look on her face and the dangerous glitter in his eyes alarmed her, for she had no idea they had been caused by jealousy. Despite his assurances that he liked his women warm and willing, did he mean to force her? she thought wildly. She quickly glanced at the warriors reclining near their fire, then saw Red Thunder standing across the fire and watching Evan intently. Would the Chickasaw come to her aid? Fire Dancer wondered. She had spurned his advances too—in fact, of all the braves who had pursued her, Red Thunder was the only one who been angered at her rejection. Fire Dancer suspected that he envisioned himself as her husband someday. No, she decided, she wouldn't ask Red Thunder for help. It might give him false encouragement. As difficult as it was to admit it, she would rather submit to the Englishman than him. At least the white man didn't have ideas of a permanent nature in mind.

As Evan dropped to his knees inside the lean-to, Fire Dancer quickly lay down with her back to him and pulled her blanket tightly around her. Her heart thudded in her chest as she waited for him to pounce on her. A moment passed, then another, and another. Finally, she risked a look over her shoulder. Evan had removed his shirt and was lying on his back, staring up at the skins that formed the ceiling. The flames in the fire behind him set his handsome features in profile and seemed to accentuate his powerful shoulder muscles, and they picked up the shining golden highlights in his thick hair. Even the hair on his chest and forearms glistened. Once again, she felt a strange urge to run her fingers through that V-shaped mat. A peculiar warmth formed in the pit of her stomach.

Fire Dancer jerked her eyes away and stared at the side of the lean-to, but it gave her no relief from the strange yearnings that were attacking her senses. She told herself to think of something else, anything but the man lying just a few feet from her, but her mind refused to obey. She remembered his kiss the night before and how wonderful and exciting his lips had felt on her breasts. Suddenly, with something almost akin to desperation, Fire Dancer wanted him to kiss her, to touch her. She waited breathlessly for well over an hour for him to make a move toward her, but she was doomed to disappointment: his deep, rhythmic breathing told her he had fallen asleep. Frustrated and bewildered, it was some time before she, too, slept.

6

When Evan met Red Thunder the next morning, he was stunned by the look of absolute loathing in the warrior's dark eyes. Evan was no fool. He quickly figured out that the subchief was angry at him because he thought the Englishman had bedded Fire Dancer. Evan was confident that he could have put the warrior's fury to rest, could have conveyed to the subchief his error in some way or another. It would have been the prudent thing to do, in view of the fact that the two were military allies and would in the future have to trust each other to guard their backs. But Evan was not in the least inclined to do so. He was thinking not as an officer but as a man. Even as he wondered why he was so possessive over a woman he had never possessed, and in all likelihood never would, he glared back at Red Thunder.

That day and the one following were much the same as the first. Fire Dancer rode slightly to the rear of Evan, but he was always acutely aware of her presence. During that time, he came to admire her endurance, for she never seemed tired at the day's end, and he knew she must be terribly sore from riding from dawn to dusk, day in and day out, then sleeping on the hard ground. She was certainly different from any woman he had ever known. Not only was she stronger physically, the lack of conversation didn't seem to bother her in the least. She didn't need anyone to entertain her. She seemed perfectly content with her own thoughts and her own company. Evan began to wonder what those thoughts were, which surprised him. He had never given a damn what a woman might be thinking, perhaps because most of the women he had known had seemed to be such mindless creatures. As time wore on, delving into the secrets of her mind became as tantalizing a prospect as coming to know the secrets of her body.

Although Fire Dancer was very successful at keeping Evan from even remotely guessing her thoughts, she was as overly conscious of him as he was of her. Her awareness of his presence was so strong that she couldn't keep her eyes, much less her mind, from him. Over and over, both kept straying to the handsome Englishman, lingering on his thick head of hair that seemed to glow even in the darkness of the woods, gazing at his broad shoulders and back, mesmerized by the subtle play of his powerful muscles beneath his shirt, or admiring the ease and confident manner in which he sat his horse.

That she had trouble concentrating on anything but him was disconcerting in itself, but combined with the strange feelings that just being around him evoked, Fire Dancer had to admit to a startling truth. He attracted her as no man ever had, and she wanted him to pay attention to her—yes, to be brutally honest, to make amorous advances. Not make love to her, though. The thought of the sex act disgusted her. But to touch her, kiss her, let her experience those exciting sensations again . . . But as time passed and Evan made no move toward her, this yearning over which she seemed to have no control became a source of acute frustration—and finally anger.

On the fourth day, Evan noted a change in their surroundings. The trees in the woods seemed to be thinning out, making the forest look more like those he had seen in England and Europe. That afternoon they rode into a lightly timbered, gently rolling land that was covered with lush buffalo grass sprinkled with wild flowers. He reined in and looked about in admiration, thinking he had never seen such excellent pasturage.

Fire Dancer, too, looked about herself, but in wonder. She had never traveled far from her home. Oh, she had heard there were areas like this, but she had never seen so much open land. Then she looked up, and her breath caught when she saw the wide expanse of sky. In her forest-world home of greens and browns, all she had seen was patches of blue over the clearings the Chickasaw had made and the ribbon of blue over the Misho Sipokni. Because it was so rare, blue had always been her favorite color, and now, seeing so much of it in one place, she felt overwhelmed.

"Well, we won't have to wait until we get back to your home to settle that issue of whose horse is the faster," Evan commented, drawing her attention away from the sky. "This looks like an excellent place to race. That is, if you still want to pit that nag of yours against my mount."

To Fire Dancer, Evan's words as well as his tone smacked of arrogance, and she took offense not on her mare's behalf, but on her own. She had not forgotten the way he had shunned her by pulling ahead of her the first day, or her anger at him for ignoring her. She wanted to punish him, to humiliate him, and she welcomed the opportunity to do so. "Yes, it does look like a good spot," she readily agreed.

Since Red Thunder was away scouting at the moment, Fire Dancer turned in her saddle and spoke to several braves riding behind her. Their ordinarily stony expressions quickly changed as wide grins split their faces. Then one of the warriors, Black Hawk, pointed to the horizon and said something to Fire Dancer.

Fire Dancer turned back to Evan and said, "I told them that you think our horses inferior to yours and have challenged me to a race. Black Hawk says there is a river up ahead that we can use as our finish line."

Evan was very aware of the braves' grins. Knowing they thought he didn't have a ghost of a chance made him all the more determined to win. He handed his rifle to Black Hawk. "That's fine with me. What will we wager?" he said.

Fire Dancer was at a loss. The Englishman had nothing she wanted. Except . . . But she didn't dare ask that. She was barely able to admit her desires to herself, much less to him. "My victory will be sufficient payment."

"Well, it won't be for me. If I win, I have a very different reward in mind."

"What, then? Furs?"

Evan's voice dropped an octave. "A kiss."

Fire Dancer sucked in her breath sharply, leaving Evan to assume her reaction was negative. Quickly he said, "No, you can't refuse my wager, not if you agree to race. And that's what I want if I win. I want you to kiss me of your own free will."

When Evan said a kiss, Fire Dancer had thought he meant he would kiss her, the very thing she had been wanting, and her heart had raced in anticipation. But when he told her he wanted her to kiss him, she felt insulted. Again he was treating her like a whore, she thought, wanting *her* to make advances to him. Her eyes flashed angrily, looking as if they were spitting green fire, as she stiffened in outrage. "It doesn't matter what you want. You won't win!"

Evan had been almost as surprised by his request as Fire Dancer. He had meant to say he would kiss her, but the other had just slipped out. Not until that minute had he realized he had been secretly fantasizing just that. But Evan wasn't a military officer for nothing. He always had a contingent battle plan, in case the first one failed. He responded to Fire Dancer's angry retort by saying, "Then as a consolation prize, I'll . . ."

Evan's words trailed off as Fire Dancer nudged her horse and cried out, "Hi-yi!" In a flash, the mare sped away, stunning Evan at the sudden, unexpected start of the race as well as its surprising speed. He would never have dreamed the slow-plodding, seemingly listless mare could fly like that. It was Evan's horse, and not he, who reacted. Accustomed to being raced, the stallion sensed what was expected of him and bolted forward like a shot out of a cannon, almost unseating Evan.

It didn't take long for the English Thoroughbred to catch up with the Indian mare. He was a strong runner. For well over a mile, the two horses ran neck and neck, manes and tails flying as they flew over one rolling hill, then another, and another, both animals thoroughly enjoying the total freedom of movement that had been given to them by their masters.

Fire Dancer, too, thoroughly relished the race. For the first time in her life she was racing in the wide open and not on the ball ground back at the village. There, she could only race back and forth, but here there was no confinement whatsoever. The countryside was a green blur, the scattered trees flashed emerald, and she loved the feel of the wind flying past her, tearing at her hair and clothes as her mare's slender legs gobbled up the ground and, as the animal took to the air, sailing over low berry bushes and small streams. She didn't even care that her braid came down and flapped wildly around her. The ride was the most invigorating, most exciting she had ever had. She had never felt so free, so alive, and she laughed with sheer joy.

Racing beside Fire Dancer, Evan completely forgot the contest between them. He couldn't take his eyes from her. As the wind whipped her long black braid about her and tore at the skin-covering over her breasts, giving him tantalizing, split-second glimpses of those tawny mounds, she looked wild and incredibly beautiful. When she laughed—an uninhibited delightful sound above the pounding of their horses' hoofs—he felt a sudden tightening in his loins. He wanted her, right then, right there. He leaned across the distance between them and reached for her reins.

It was at that moment that Evan's stallion fell back, making Evan's grasp fall short of its mark. The Thoroughbred had tried valiantly to keep up with the Chickasaw, but he didn't have the mare's endurance for long-distance racing. Over the next mile, he fell farther and farther behind, despite Evan's urgings. Finally, aware of how labored the stallion's breathing was becoming, Evan slowed him to trot.

Several minutes later, Evan entered the woods beside the river and spied Fire Dancer and her horse. The mare was prancing excitedly as Fire Dancer circled her, not quite ready to give up her run. With her tail held proudly high and her beautiful gait, the slender little horse looked every inch the Arabian she was. It wasn't until Evan's stallion trotted up to her that she stilled, giving a little victorious whinny.

Fire Dancer, her face flushed from the excitement of the race and her green eyes dancing with exhilartion, looked even more beautiful. "I won!" she cried out softly. "I told you my mare was faster."

Evan didn't reply. He dismounted, ducked beneath his mount's neck, and walked up to Fire Dancer. Without a word, he lifted her from the saddle. As he set her on her feet just inches from him, he said, "Yes, you won. I concede your victory. And now I'm going to collect my consolation prize."

"What consolation prize?"

"A kiss."

"But that's what you wanted for your reward if you

won—for me to kiss you," Fire Dancer objected. "You didn't win. I did!"

"Yes, I know. And for that reason, I kiss you. That was my consolation prize."

Fire Dancer's heart raced at the prospect, but perversely she said, "No! I won't allow it."

Evan's blue eyes darkened to indigo as he said in a husky voice, "I'm afraid you have no choice in the matter. I have it coming to me, and I'm a man who always claims his prize."

As Evan lowered his head, he slipped his hands from Fire Dancer's waist beneath the short skin cape on her back. Feeling his warm palms on the bare skin there, Fire Dancer gasped, then struggled to free herself. It was a useless effort, for Evan simply replaced his hands with one steely arm, then caught her chin in his free hand. She was totally unprepared for what happened next and jumped in surprise when his lips met hers. She stiffened, not knowing what would happen next.

As Evan continued to kiss her, as his mobile lips softly played on hers, wooing, then gently nibbling on the corners of her mouth, Fire Dancer's apprehension was replaced with another emotion. She was enthralled with the new sensations he was bringing her. She had never dreamed that anything could feel so utterly wonderful, and unknowingly, she relaxed. Her hands left his chest where she had been trying to push him away to slide around his neck.

Evan sucked in his breath sharply at the feel of Fire Dancer's breasts pressing against his chest. It was all he could do to keep from deepening the kiss, but he sensed that if he did so, it would frighten her away. He continued to sup gently at her lips, then ran the tip of his tongue back and forth over them, back and forth, enticing, silently pleading for her to open to him. When she finally did part her lips, he again forced himself to hold back, sliding his tongue ever so slowly down the length of hers, then back.

The parting of her lips had come instinctively to Fire Dancer, and she was floating dreamily when Evan's tongue slipped into her mouth. For a split second, she was shocked. His invasion of her body seemed terribly intimate, almost as intimate as if he had entered her with his manhood. But her outrage was short-lived. As his tongue sensuously stroked hers, as his hand slipped from her chin to caress the length of her throat, a sudden warmth invaded her, followed by an insidious weakness of her will as well as her body. All thought of objecting fled. She leaned into him, wanting his kiss to last forever, feeling a strange ache building between her legs.

As Fire Dancer pressed even closer, her full breasts flattened against his chest and seemingly branded him through their clothing. Evan felt a thrill of exhilaration run through him. He knew now that she wasn't averse to his touch, despite what she had said about his hairy body repelling her. She was as susceptible to seduction as the next woman. All he had to do was approach her more slowly, more gently, stoke her fires of passion until she no longer knew or cared who he was. Seducing her wasn't going to be easy. That would take time and concentrated effort. But Evan wanted her with an urgency he had never felt with any other woman. Drinking of the sweetness of her mouth was like taking a powerful aphrodisiac, making his senses reel and his aroused manhood strain painfully against his pants. All he wanted to do was tear off their clothes, throw her to the ground, and bury himself in her.

It was then that Evan heard the pounding of hooves. His soldier's instincts took command, and he jerked his mouth from Fire Dancer's just as the braves' horses cleared the trees. He automatically reached for the saber that usually hung at his waist, but his hand closed over the handle of his knife instead. Seeing who it was, however, he felt foolish. He had become so befuddled by his desire that he had completely forgotten about his Chickasaw escort. Quickly, he stepped behind Fire Dancer, using her as a shield to cover his blatant arousal from the others—something he considered much too personal for them to be laughing or joking about.

When Evan released her so suddenly, Fire Dancer had staggered and glanced about her dazedly before she finally came to her senses. Had the braves seen Evan kissing her? she wondered. A flush of mortification rose in her, for although Chickasaw youths practiced an unusual degree of sexual freedom, none would never dream of doing anything even vaguely sexual in the wide open in broad daylight. As Red Thunder rode up to her, swung from his horse, and began to angrily chastise her, Fire Dancer's embarrassment turned to fury, and she was just about to respond with equal anger when Evan asked, "What's going on?"

"He is angry because we left the group without his permission," Fire Dancer answered over her shoulder. "He says it could have been dangerous to us."

Like hell that was why, Evan thought. He knew the

subchief was angry because he'd seen him kissing Fire Dancer. "Tell him I'm perfectly capable of taking care of us, and that I have no intention of asking his permission if I decide I want to ride out for any reason. He's my guide, nothing more."

When Fire Dancer interpreted Evan's words, it was quite obvious that Red Thunder was even more infuriated. He spat a retort.

"Red Thunder said to remind you that Promingo put him in charge of this party," Fire Dancer said to Evan.

"He's in charge of the braves, not me. Promingo has no authority to give me orders, much less pass down that authority to Red Thunder. If Promingo thinks he has, he is in grave error. I'm here to act as a military adviser to Promingo, to collaborate, to fight beside him when the time comes, but not to follow his lead. I have my own chief that I answer to."

Evan didn't even wait for Fire Dancer to relay his words to Red Thunder. He turned his back on the subchief and walked way, leading his stallion down to the river for a drink. The Chickasaw leader listened to Fire Dancer's interpretation with absolute loathing in his dark eyes. He didn't dare refute what the Englishman had said—it was true, he had no any authority over him. But what angered Red Thunder even more was a moment of fear that he had felt when he saw the dangerous gleam in the major's eyes. He had known then that the white man could be a formidable foe, one he would be wise not to provoke. Still, it galled the subchief to have to back down, particularly in front of his men. Until now, he had hated the Englishman because of Fire Dancer. Now he hated him for himself. Vowing someday to get revenge, Red Thunder spun on his heels and walked away from Fire Dancer, calling out a command to his men to make camp.

That night, after Evan had finished his evening meal, he commented to Fire Dancer, "Before I came to this country, I'd never tasted maize in my life. We don't grow it back in England, you know. Over the past few years, I've eaten it as a vegetable both on and off the cob and as a meal in every conceivable form. I've had johnnycake, corn bread, corn muffins, and corn pancakes. But none have tasted as delicious as those ash cakes you make."

Evan paused to see Fire Dancer's reaction to his compliment to her cooking. She glared at him across the fire, just as she had been doing ever since they'd made camp. He knew she was angry because he had kissed her. He also knew she had thoroughly enjoyed the kiss, which only went to show just how perverse a woman could be. But Evan didn't want to seduce Fire Dancer, not at that moment. What he wanted was to bury the hatchet. "Look," he said, "I know you're angry about this afternoon, but you really can't blame me."

"Can't I?" Fire Dancer spat. "I told you not to touch me."

"Still, you can't blame me," Evan repeated, appearing totally unperturbed by her outrage. "You're a very beautiful woman, and a very desirable one. A man would have to be dead not to respond, and I'm a very healthy, normal male. So you see, what you're asking of me is nearly impossible."

Put in that context, Fire Dancer found it difficult to

hold her anger. Before she could think of a response, Evan added, "We got off to a bad start with that misunderstanding between us the first night. I got the wrong impression, and I guess I did appear rude. But I'd like to put that behind us if we can."

"Why?" Fire Dancer asked, bewildered by his amicable behavior.

"Because I'm curious about you. I'd like to get to know you a little better."

"Why?"

Dammit! Evan thought. Why did she keep asking him questions he didn't know the answers to himself? She was an uneducated, uncivilized savage passing through his life. Granted, she was beautiful and desirable, but the world was full of beautiful, desirable women, women who wouldn't spurn his advances, and after this mission was over he'd never lay eyes on her again. So why was he even bothering? Still . . .

Evan shrugged his broad shoulders and answered vaguely, "I just would, that's all."

It sounded like a strange request to Fire Dancer. Friends got to know each other, perhaps husbands and wives. "What is it you want to know?"

Evan was very curious to know how Fire Dancer felt about her mixed blood, but he sensed that would not be a good question to begin with. "Well, for one thing, I'm curious about your mother. I understand she was an indentured servant."

"She spoke of herself not as a servant, but as a slave."

"Perhaps that's how she felt about her servitude, but there is a subtle difference. An indentured servant sells himself into bondage for a set number of years, usually to pay for passage to this country. But a slave is sold into bondage by another, and the bondage lasts for life."

"My mother's bondage would have lasted for life, too, had she not been captured by the Creek. And she worked as hard as any of the slaves on that plantation— or harder."

Evan frowned. "Why did your mother indenture herself for life?"

"She didn't. It was to have lasted just seven years. But she fell in love with another servant, and he got her with child. Then shortly thereafter, he ran away. The man she was in bondage to was so angry that he took her to court, where the magistrate fined her heavily for bearing a bastard. Of course, my mother couldn't pay the fine, so her servitude was extended ten additional years. Her master claimed it would take that long for her to pay back the time she had lost during her pregnancy and raising the child, as well as what it would cost him to feed and clothe the bastard until it was old enough to earn its own keep. My mother said she would never survive that long, slaving from well before dawn until well after dusk. So she considered herself a slave for life."

Evan was prone to agree with Fire Dancer's mother. In all likelihood she probably would not have survived a life of hard labor that long, particularly in the Carolinas, where there were so many fevers. Nor was Evan particularly shocked by the story Fire Dancer told him. Until he came to the colonies and saw for himself, he had thought indentured servants fared much better than they actually did—that once they had served their time, they were free to make a better life for themselves here in the colonies. But unfortunately, a fairly high percent of them never saw the end of their bondage. Fines were placed on them for the slightest infractions, in many cases by magistrates who had been bribed by the bondsmen, and additional punishment was often meted out in the form of vicious public whippings that left a poor servant laid up for months or partially crippled, for which they were again fined. No wonder so many of them ran away. It was their only means of escape, next to death.

"What happened to your mother's child? Was it captured by the Creek too?"

"No, it died when it was three, from the pox. My mother was captured the next year."

"She didn't have very good fortune, did she," Evan observed, "going from one form of slavery to another?"

"She said it was easier being an Indian slave. The Creek did not work her as hard. They were not greedy like the whites. They did not try to amass a fortune. Nor did they want luxuries. They only wanted a home that would shelter them and to have enough food to live." Fire Dancer paused. "The Creek did not use her as vilely as her white master, either. She was not passed among the master, his sons, and their friends. She shared only her captor's bed, and he did not beat her or mistreat her."

Evan thought he had inadvertently found the answer to his question about how Fire Dancer felt about her mixed blood. Apparently, because of the way her mother had been treated, she didn't have a very high regard for whites. That didn't sit too easy with him. "But her captor turned around and sold her to Promingo," Evan pointed out. "That wasn't very kind of him."

"He had to sell her. His family had arranged a marriage for him, and his future wife would not allow my mother to stay. Besides, Promingo made him an offer he could not turn down."

"What offer?"

"A string of Chickasaw horses."

Evan remembered Josh saying that men killed for Chickasaw horses. But were the animals so coveted that a man would give up the woman he loved for one? But perhaps the Creek had not felt that strongly about Fire Dancer's mother.

"My mother said that was the best thing that ever happened to her," Fire Dancer continued when Evan failed to respond. "It led to her freedom."

"Yes, I know. Your grandmother adopted her. But was she really free? Could she have left at any time?"

"Why would she want to leave? What would there be for her to go back to? Her life was much easier here."

Evan was forced to admit that Fire Dancer was probably correct. Her mother had fared better with the Indians than with her own people. He'd been vaguely aware of the plight of the lower class back in England and of the indentured servants who were trying to escape bondage here in the colonies, but he had never stopped to give much serious thought to them. Fire Dancer's story of her mother brought him his first real insight into the social injustices practiced by his people, and he felt sincere compassion for the woman and a twinge of shame on behalf of his race. But Evan couldn't express these feelings to Fire Dancer. They were too new to him. Still, he did manage to say, "I'd like to meet your mother when we get back to the settlement."

"You can't. She died two years ago."

Evan heard the pain in Fire Dancer's voice, and his heart went out to her. He longed to take her in his arms and comfort her, a longing that was as bewildering as wanting to get to know her had been. For as an experienced, hardened soldier, he had thought himself inured to death and grief. "I'm sorry," he muttered lamely.

Fire Dancer knew Evan was sincere, and more than anything he had said or done, that softened her heart toward him. "Thank you."

"You know, she taught you English remarkably well."

Fire Dancer smiled. "She said that was the only thing she missed, speaking in her language. She thought Chickasaw sounded so harsh. She always spoke English to me."

A sudden thought occurred to Evan. Fire Dancer's English was good—too good for an ordinary commoner. "Who was your mother before she came to this country?"

Fire Dancer was a little taken aback by the intense look on Evan's face and his urgent tone of voice. "What do you mean?"

"Did she ever say anything to you about her life before she came to this country?"

Fire Dancer thought for long moment. "Yes, she did, once. Something about falling on hard times when she was a child. But she never explained what that meant."

As Evan opened his mouth to speak, Fire Dancer cut across his words, saying, "No, no more questions! It grows late, and I wish to wash before I retire."

As she rose, Evan said, "Wait! Bear with me just one more moment, please. Why did your grandmother adopt your mother? I know she didn't have any daughters—but why did she pick a white woman?"

"Because of the color of her hair. It was very pale."

"Like mine?"

Fire Dancer glanced up at Evan's golden hair and felt a strange little tingle. "No, it was much paler. Almost white."

"But what did that have to do with it?"

"There is a story among the Chickasaw of a queen with pale hair many, many years ago. She was very powerful and very wise. Some think she will return someday."

"Then your grandmother thought your mother was a reincarnation of this queen?"

"I do not know what that word means, nor do I know what my grandmother thought. She never gave any other explanation, except to say she thought my mother was a fitting heir."

Fire Dancer turned and walked away, her carriage as regal as always. Evan stared at her, wondering if her mother could have been royalty. She said her family had fallen on hard times—but then, she could just as well have been a wealthy merchant's daughter. They didn't talk like commoners either. Or maybe, he thought, fantasizing just a little further, maybe she *was* the incarnation of that Chickasaw queen from long ago.

Evan would have given his eyeteeth to know who Fire Dancer's mother had been, but it was a mystery that would never be solved. The only woman who knew the answer was dead.

7

After Fire Dancer left the camp, Evan sat for a few moments musing over everything she had told him. Then he rose and strolled into the woods, in the opposite direction in order to provide them both a measure of privacy. As he walked, he glanced at the larger camp in the distance, set beside the river; their own camp was set in the woods. He could barely see the warriors' fire. When he returned to the lean-to, Fire Dancer was rolled up in her blanket at the far end, as usual with her back toward him. Evan stripped off his shirt and moccasins and tossed them on the ground, then removed his knife and placed it beside them. He crawled in and lay down.

But he couldn't sleep. All he could think of was the intoxicating sweetness of her mouth that afternoon and the feel of her soft body pressed against his. His passion rose and, with it, a fierce determination to possess her. It was no longer just a matter of satisfying a physical craving. It had become a matter of survival, the only way he could get her out of his system once and for all. Otherwise he would never know another moment's peace.

Fire Dancer wasn't asleep. She had heard Evan enter the lean-to and had been just as tormented as he was by memories of his kissing her that afternoon. But now she was even more determined to keep him at bay than she had been before. His unexpected show of compassion that evening had stirred new feelings for him, feelings that confused her and seemed even more threatening than his physical advances. When he moved toward her and she felt his heat right behind her, she threw her blanket aside, rolled over, and came to her knees in a lightning-fast movement that stunned Evan. "Don't touch me!" she cried out. The long blade of the skinning knife that she held in one hand glittered in the firelight.

Evan looked at the knife pointed at his chest in utter surprise, then muttered, "What in the hell do you think you're doing?"

"Protecting myself. I don't want you to touch me again."

"Dammit, Fire Dancer!" Evan answered in exasperation, sitting up to face her. "It's unnatural for a man to sleep next to a woman he desires as much as I do you and keep his hands to himself." His voice lowered. "Besides, you don't mean that. You enjoyed my kiss this afternoon."

"No!"

"You pressed yourself against me, begging for more," Evan reminded her.

Fire Dancer remembered how wantonly she had behaved, and a flush of mortification rose on her face. But she wasn't about to admit it. "No, I didn't!" she denied emphatically, too emphatically.

Evan moved toward her. "Dammit, stop lying! Stop lying to me and yourself!"

"No! Don't come any closer!" Fire Dancer cried out, advancing the knife closer.

Evan came to a dead halt and glanced down at the knife that was less than an inch from his chest. Then he looked Fire Dancer directly in the eye. "Go ahead and do it. Kill me! Sink the knife into my heart."

Fire Dancer had never had any real intention of killing Evan. She had just hoped to frighten him away. Seeing her hesitation, Evan softly taunted, "Go ahead. Do it! Because that's the only way you're going to stop me."

With the swiftness of a striking snake, Evan wrenched the knife from her grasp, tossed it aside, and pushed Fire Dancer back to the ground, coming down over her.

Fire Dancer raised her hands to push Evan away. Then, feeling the mat of springy hair on his bare chest beneath her palms, she froze as a peculiar tingling ran up her arms and spine.

Evan, too, was acutely aware of where Fire Dancer's hands were. She had said that his hairy body repelled her, and he knew he could never force a woman. He wanted Fire Dancer to be as willing and eager as she had been that afternoon. But that afternoon he'd been fully dressed. Dammit, he thought, why hadn't he kept his shirt on?

For a long moment, the two were totally motionless.

Then, almost as if they had a will of their own, Fire Dancer's fingers moved—at first tentatively, then more boldly. As they felt the crisp hair over the hard muscles and warm skin, the tingles turned to electric shocks. Suddenly, her arms felt weak, too weak to push him away. The heat from his body seemed to engulf her, and his scent, of wood smoke, leather, and some faint musky smell, excited her and sent her pulses pounding. Fire Dancer knew she had lost her battle. The Englishman's strong sexuality was too powerful, and his masculinity, imprinted on every inch of his long frame, on every nuance, every fiber of his being, made her painfully aware that he was male and she was female. He appealed to something primitive within her, some deep, consuming need over which she had no control. From the moment they met, this moment had been inevitable. Just as ripened fruit must yield to the pull of the earth and fall to the ground, so she had been destined to surrender to Evan's attraction. She had never really had a choice. It had only been a matter of time. She squeezed her eyes shut as a little sob escaped her throat.

Evan recognized Fire Dancer's surrender for what it was. He knew she had done it with great reluctance. He bent lower over her, his lips so close to hers that she could feel his hot breath fanning her face. "No, don't feel that way. I promise you won't regret this. I'll make it good for you." He dropped a small kiss on the corner of her mouth, then the tip of her nose. "It will be the best you've ever had."

Evan's lips brushed across hers ever so lightly, and the tip of his tongue slid back and forth across her bottom lip, promising heaven and making her tingle all over. For what seemed an eternity, he teased and taunted, and Fire Dancer thought she would go insane if he didn't stop playing with her and really kiss her. Then as he finally gave her what she wanted, his tongue darting into her mouth and plundering her sweetness, she wondered through her spinning senses where he had learned to use his lips and tongue the wonderful way he did. She had always thought they were meant for speaking, but he made them instruments of exquisite pleasure as he kissed her again, and again, and again, his tongue sliding in and out, in and out, an exciting and breathtaking forerunner that mimicked the more intimate act of possession that would come later.

Evan's mouth left Fire Dancer's to blaze a trail of hot kisses across her face. He supped at the tender skin below her ear, making fresh tingles of delight run over her, while he untied the leather thongs on her belt. Then he pushed aside the buckskin that covered her breasts. Cupping one soft mound in his hand, he flicked his fingers across the nipple. When he heard Fire Dancer's gasp of pleasure as the bud rose and hardened, begging in its own way for more, and Evan was more than happy to oblige. He ached to taste her sweetness there.

Feeling the wet lash of Evan's tongue before he took the aching nipple into his mouth, Fire Dancer again drew in her breath sharply. Then as he began to suckle her while his fingers stroked her other breast, she felt as if a bolt of fire had shot to her loins, leaving her womanhood throbbing and burning. She caught the back of his head, tangling her fingers in the long, golden strands, lost in a sea of pure sensation. As his lips left that breast, she moaned in protest, then sighed blissfully as he took its jealous mate in his mouth. She arched her back, giving him even better access, thinking she'd die of this exquisite torture if he didn't stop, yet perversely, she did not want him to ever stop. The burning between her legs grew hotter and hotter; her breath came in ragged gasps. Each tug of his lips was both heaven and hell: heaven because nothing had ever felt so utterly wonderful, hell because she felt her excitement climbing higher and higher until that burning ache was almost unbearable. Not even realizing what she was doing, she twisted her lower body and pressed herself against Evan's hip, sobbing incoherently. "Please, please," she whimpered over and over.

Through his own reeling senses, Evan heard her plea and knew she was begging for release. Without leaving his feasting at her breasts, he deftly untied the thongs on her skirt and slid it down. As he stroked her bare thigh, Fire Dancer was vaguely aware he had stripped her, but she was too enthralled with the wondrous feeling of his mouth at her breasts to pay much attention— until she felt his hand slip between her thighs and cup the most intimate part of her. A brief tingle of alarm ran through her before the burning there took precedence over everything. Again she acted instinctively, pressing herself against his hand, then gasped in pleasure as his slender fingers slid through her dewiness, parting the aching folds before he found the burning bud of her desire.

Fire Dancer had thought nothing could possibly be more pleasurable and exciting than what Evan was doing at her breasts, but she quickly found out how very wrong she was. A whole new barrage of sensations attacked her senses, searing her to the soles of her feet and making her toes curl as he worked his magic there, teasing and tantalizing. Then, as the sweet yet frightening ripples became powerful undulations that rocked her body, she thrashed her head from side to side, her breath rapid and her heart pounding so hard, she feared it would jump from her chest.

Evan nuzzled the fragrant valley between her breasts, then raised his head and looked into her dazed eyes. His lips hovered over hers as he whispered thickly, "Didn't I tell you I'd please you?"

Fire Dancer couldn't answer. His voice seemed to come from far, far away. But then, Evan didn't expect an answer. He dropped a quick kiss on her lips and said, "But that was just a taste of what's to come."

Evan rolled away, stripped off his pants, and kicked them aside. As he took her back into his arms, her breath caught at the feel of his hot, bare skin against hers, then the crisp hair on his chest rubbing against her tender, swollen nipples, an incredibly exciting sensation. Feeling the blatant rigid proof of his arousal trapped between their lower abdomens, seemingly scorching her skin, a brief tingle of fear ran through her, for it felt very large and very menacing. But Evan gave her no time for her fear to grow. His mouth came down on hers in a demanding, torrid kiss that robbed her of all thought and made her passion ignite like a firestorm. She wrapped her arms around him, drawing him even closer, thrilling at the feel of his hard male body pressing against hers, kissing him back wildly as her hands greedily stroked the powerful muscles on his back.

Fire Dancer's intoxicating scent and the taste of her honeyed skin and mouth had excited Evan, but when she kissed him back so freely and caressed him, his passion soared to a feverish pitch of intense need. He could no longer hold back. Every fiber in his body was crying for release. He nudged her thighs apart with his knee and rose over her, placing fiery kisses over her face and throat and breasts as his hands slipped beneath her shapely buttocks to lift her. He plunged in, then stiffened as he heard her soft cry and felt her unbelievable tightness surrounding him.

Alarms went off in the back of Evan's mind, but he could no more stop himself than he could stop the sun from rising. Even after he buried his full length in her hot depths, he had no control over himself. His overwhelming need took immediate command of his body. Once more he covered her mouth with his, kissing her deeply as he began his movements, riding her hard and fierce:

Fire Dancer had cried out at the sharp pain caused by Evan's penetration. For just a brief moment reality had returned, and she had struggled. But as the pain became a dull ache, her full attention was centered on the feel of his hard, hot length moving inside her, his powerful strokes deep, bold, masterful. An intense, blinding pleasure overcame her, a madness that sent her heart pounding, her senses expanding, her breath rasping. She writhed beneath him, her fingernails digging into the skin on his shoulders as he filled her with the sweet fury of his fire. She forgot who he was, who she was. All that mattered were the glorious sensations he was making her feel. She wrapped her legs around his slim hips, bringing him deeper, glorying in his rasps of pleasure as she met him fierce thrust for fierce thrust. Higher and higher she climbed, feeling as if she were drowning in waves of shimmering ecstasy as an unbearable tension began to build within her. Then the ground fell away; time stood still. She heard a roaring, and lightning flashed in her brain as she shattered into a million flaming pieces and was thrown into a spinning black void.

Evan was the first to drift back down to reality. He lay where he had collapsed weakly over Fire Dancer, his face buried in the soft crook of her neck. Still dazed, his mind struggled to remember something. Then as it came to him, he raised his head and looked down at Fire Dancer, saying in a thick voice, "You were a virgin."

Fire Dancer heard the accusation in Evan's voice, but she felt too deliciously languid to respond. "Mmmm," she replied drowsily, wanting only to drift off into sleep.

Evan lightly shook one of her shoulders. "Dammit, you can sleep later. We need to talk."

"About what?" Fire Dancer asked irritably.

"This was your first time. You lied to me."

Being called a liar brought Fire Dancer to her senses, as if a bucket of cold water had been thrown on her. "I did no such thing!" she retorted. "I never said I had been with a man before. You just assumed it."

"Still, you misled me. You said you choose your own lovers."

"That didn't mean there had been lovers—only that I, and I alone, would decide who they would be."

Evan recalled the night Fire Dancer had spurned him, and he was forced to admit that he *had* made assumptions because of what Josh had told him. He felt a twinge of shame for the way he had behaved. But he could feel no shame or regret of any kind for what had just happened. It had been the best, the most exciting sexual experience he had ever had.

At the present time, Fire Dancer was feeling very vulnerable. She had forsaken her beloved mother's Anglo beliefs in a moment of passion, and now she felt ashamed of herself. What had gotten into her? she wondered. Had she let her hot Chickasaw blood get the better of her, or had this accursed Englishman cast some strange spell over her? Whichever, she couldn't let him know how strongly he affected her, for fear he would take advantage of the knowledge. She'd die before she became any man's love slave. No, her best recourse would be to treat the incident lightly, as if it had had very little meaning to her. So she said, "Besides, I don't see where it makes any difference if I've had other lovers or not. Someone had to be the first. It just happened to be you."

Evan frowned at Fire Dancer's answer. It mattered to *him* that he had been the first. The knowledge gave him a strange exhilaration. And he didn't like the way she casually brushed off their lovemaking, as if it had been nothing. His feelings puzzled him, for he himself had done the same thing in the past. He had never taken any of the affairs he'd had seriously, not since his very first in his youth. The women had been here today and gone tomorrow, his relationships with them fleeting and meaningless. Then why did Fire Dancer's nonchalant manner disturb him? he wondered. He should think he would have wanted it that way. Passion for the sake of passion—nothing more.

Evan was so preoccupied with his thoughts that he didn't notice Fire Dancer sit up and pull her blanket up around her shoulders to cover her nakedness. But when she said in a determined voice, "It won't happen again," he did take notice. His head flew up like a shot from a cannon.

Although Evan was very confused about his feelings, he was certain about one thing. His desire for Fire Dancer had not cooled in the least. Tasting of her passion had just whetted his appetite for more, and he was not accustomed to his desires being denied, particularly by some woman's whim. His eyes glittered angrily as he asked in a carefully controlled voice, "Oh? And may I ask why not?"

Fire Dancer was hard put to keep her eyes from Evan's naked body. With the firelight playing over his powerful muscles and his still damp skin glistening, he looked magnificent. A little thrill ran through her before she managed to jerk her eyes away and shrug her shoulders. "Because my curiosity about you has been satisfied, and I no longer find you appealing," she lied.

There was a pregnant pause before Evan replied, "Well, I'm afraid I disagree. It won't be the last time. Not by a long shot."

With that, Fire Dancer found herself flat on her back with Evan hovering over her. As he jerked the blanket away, she cried out, "No!"

Slowly, deliberately, Evan lowered his body over Fire Dancer's, pinning her down as he said in a voice husky with desire, "You can save your breath. I mean to have you anytime I want. You see, *my* curiosity hasn't been satisfied."

Fire Dancer gasped as Evan's heated skin came into contact with hers. Her nipples hardened and rose against the steely muscles on his chest. Then as one hand swept over her hungrily, she trembled with need. Furious at both him and her own body for betraying her, she cried, "I hate you, Englishman!"

Evan raised his head, and Fire Dancer saw that his eyes were blazing with desire. "My name is Evan," he muttered against her lips.

"I don't care what your name is! I hate you!"

At that moment, Fire Dancer felt a wetness slipping from her and bathing Evan's hard knee where he had insinuated it between her thighs. Feeling it, Evan scoffed, then growled softly, "Then you have a damn peculiar way of showing it."

Fire Dancer sobbed in frustration just before Evan's mouth came swooping down on hers in a fiercely possessive kiss. It was the last show of resistance she made before he once again took her to heaven.

The next day, as they followed the river northward, Evan looked around at the rolling, grassy hills around him. Once again, he thought that this country would make excellent pasturage. He had never seen such lush grass or tasted any so sweet—that morning, when his stallion had seemed to be enjoying it so vastly, he had pulled up a stem and tried it for himself. The grass seemed far superior to anything he had seen in England or on the continent. Beyond that, the area was laced with crystal-clear streams fed by springs and therefore would continue to flow even in the hottest, driest summers. Curious, he dropped back to where Fire Dancer was riding and asked, "Who does this land belong to? The Chickasaw, or some other tribe?"

Fire Dancer turned her head and glared at him with a look that brought a smile to Evan's lips. She had been casting him furious glances all morning, and Evan knew it was because he had forced her to surrender to him, not once but twice more during the night. He wondered why she had bothered to resist. Her resistance had been brief both times, and it had been quite obvious that she thoroughly enjoyed his lovemaking. He'd never known any woman as passionate or responsive. Maybe that was why he hadn't gotten his fill of her. My God, he had never made love to any woman that many times in one night. Not only had once always been enough, he had never dreamed he had such endurance. Even more perplexing, he still wanted her now, more than ever.

As Evan's eyes met hers levelly and patiently waited for an answer, Fire Dancer realized she was wasting her energy. The arrogant Englishman would never apologize for what he had done, nor would he care that he had made her angry. He was nothing but an insensitive brute. She jerked her eyes away and answered in an icy voice, "I do not know who this land belongs to. I have never been here before."

Evan peered in the distance where Red Thunder was riding far ahead of the group. Ever since their confrontation the day before, the subchief had deliberately made himself scarce. Evan didn't know if Red Thunder was doing it to avoid further disagreements between them or to frustrate him by not being available to answer questions. To hell with him! Evan thought, then glanced over his shoulder at the braves riding behind them. "Can't you ask one of them?" he questioned Fire Dancer, nodding his head in the warriors' direction.

Fire Dancer didn't want to do anything that might seem in the least bit cooperative. But Black Hawk was riding close enough to overhear, and she knew he understood just enough English to wonder why she would refuse the Englishman's request. She turned halfway in her saddle, motioned for him to bring his mount up beside hers and Evan's, and asked him.

"Loak-Ishtohoollo-Aba," Black Hawk answered.

"Who did he say?" Evan asked.

"God," Fire Dancer answered. "This is God's country."

Black Hawk said something else, and Fire Dancer interpreted. "My brother said our tribe sometimes bring their horses here to graze for a few weeks at a time to fatten them up. The closest village is at the head of this river, three days away, and they do not claim this land either."

"Your brother?" Evan asked in surprise. "I thought your brother was just a boy."

"I was using the Chickasaw term. You see, we have no word for cousin."

"This man is your cousin?"

"Yes, on my father's side."

Evan looked a little closer at the brave. He wasn't as

powerfully built as Red Thunder, but he was equally tall and much more agreeable-looking than the subchief, who seemed to wear a habitual scowl. "What's his name?"

Before Fire Dancer could answer, the warrior spoke up. "My name Black Hawk."

Evan shot Fire Dancer a sharp look. "He speaks English?"

"A little. I taught him when we were children, but I think he's forgotten most of it. He always seemed to understand more than he could speak."

Evan felt disappointed. He had hoped the warrior spoke enough English to be an interpreter when it came time to do surveillance on the French fort. He didn't like the idea of Fire Dancer accompanying him. It could be dangerous.

Evan glanced at the river, about a quarter of a mile away. From that distance it looked like a shimmering gray ribbon in the bright sunshine. "What's the name of that river?"

Again Black Hawk answered, rattling off something in Chickasaw that Fire Dancer interpreted. "Black Hawk said we have no name for it, but our Cherokee brothers call it Tannassie, after one of their chief villages that lay beside it."

"I didn't realize Cherokee country was so near," Evan remarked.

Again, Black Hawk answered.

"It isn't," Fire Dancer interpreted. "The river makes a big turn far to the south and curves back up into their hunting ground, near the big mountains that look like they are covered with smoke."

Evan gave Black Hawk a penetrating regard. Apparently the warrior understood quite a bit of English. It was a shame he couldn't speak more of it, Evan thought. Black Hawk seemed very knowledgeable about the country they were passing through and would be very helpful in creating the map he'd been ordered to make.

The latter proved to be very true as the three continued to ride side by side that day. Evan asked questions, and either Fire Dancer or Black Hawk replied, in which case Fire Dancer relayed the warrior's answer. After a while, their three-way communication didn't seem in the least awkward, and Evan found he was actually enjoying the two Indians' companionship.

It was toward sundown when Evan saw the herd in the distance. At first, he paid little attention to it, thinking it was yet another group of grazing deer or antelope. But when he got close enough to see the individual animals, he reined in sharply and stared in disbelief for a moment. "What in the devil are those odd-looking creatures?"

"*Yanasa,*" Black Hawk replied, grinning at Evan's incredulous expression.

"I believe your people call them bison," Fire Dancer informed him.

"I've never seen such a top-heavy, cumbersome-looking animal in my life. Are there many of them out here?"

Again Black Hawk answered and Fire Dancer interpreted. "There are small herds here and there in these open spaces. Sometimes you will find a stray in the forests, and the old bulls who have been run off by the younger males occasionally follow our herd of horses home. They are lonely and want companionship. Their meat is tasty, and their hides much larger than those of the deer. For that reason, we mount hunting parties for them. But there are not as many of them here as there are to the west, across the big river, where they come from. According to the old ones, they are so numerous there that the herds stretch from horizon to horizon."

Evan found this last hard to believe. It would mean tens of thousands of animals. "Are they dangerous?"

"Not unless you get in front of them when they are stampeding," Fire Dancer answered. "Then they will run you down. I have heard they are almost blind and will not swerve for anything, not even high cliffs. That is how many Indians hunt them, driving them from cliffs."

"But they couldn't possibly run very fast, not as monstrous as they are," Evan observed. "Why, some of them must weigh at least two thousand pounds."

A big grin split Black Hawk's face. "No run fast?" He laughed. "You see."

Black Hawk nudged his horse, and the pony leaped forward and raced across the open ground to where the herd of buffalo was grazing. Several other braves took off after him, apparently lured by the prospect of an invigorating run. Evan was amazed that the buffalo didn't seem to hear them coming. "They must be deaf as well as blind."

"You are correct," Fire Dancer replied. "Their hearing is not all that good."

"Then it must not be much sport to hunt them. They just stand there and let you shoot them, like a bunch of cows."

"They would not be there at all if we were upwind of them. They would have caught a whiff of our scent and stampeded long ago. They are almost blind and deaf, but they have an extraordinary sense of smell."

Not until the warriors were almost on top of them did the herd finally realize the danger. Then they bolted and flew away, running with their heavy, shaggy heads held down and making the ground shake. Evan was amazed at their speed. He never would have dreamed that anything that big could run that fast. Even the swift Chickasaw ponies were hard put to keep up with them.

After the buffalo had disappeared over the rise of a hill, Evan, Fire Dancer, and the others rode over the path they had taken during their flight. Evan was surprised that the ground wasn't torn up from the tremendous beating it had taken. The grass was flattened, but most of the stems were still intact, a silent testimony to the grass's remarkable resilience. Again Evan was impressed.

That evening they camped beside one of the streams that emptied into the river. Several braves scattered a coarse powder of some kind in the water, and Evan's curiosity was aroused. He walked to the river and, by the time he arrived on the scene, saw fish that had turned belly up and were floating on their sides in the water. He watched the braves wade in and pick up the larger fish. Then as Fire Dancer walked up beside him and Black Hawk stepped from the water and tossed three magnificent speckled trout at her feet, Evan asked, "What was that powder they sprinkled in the water?"

"The ground roots of *tephrosia*. My mother said they

call it the devil's shoestring back in the Carolinas. Pounded walnut bark can also be used."

"You're going to eat poisoned fish?" Evan asked, thinking he wasn't about to touch it.

"They are not poisoned. It just stuns them temporarily."

Almost on cue, it seemed, the fish lying on the grass began to thrash about wildly. "Is that the way you always fish?" Evan asked.

"Only if we are in a hurry. Most of the time the braves use bows and arrows or spears, and the women prefer to use basket traps."

When the fish on the ground had stopped flopping about, Fire Dancer picked them up and carried them to where the braves were setting up her and Evan's camp. Evan leaned against the trunk of a tree and watched as she cleaned and scaled the fish, then set them to grill over the coals. He was still leery about eating them, but the tantalizing aroma got the better of him and he relented. He was forced to admit that he had never tasted such delicious fish, and he wondered why his own people never cooked fish that way, over an open fire. They either baked it until it was as tough as a shoe or boiled it to pieces.

That night, when Evan made amorous overtures, Fire Dancer again resisted. But as it had been the night before, her resistance was short-lived. Evan wasn't an expert military officer for nothing. He stormed her defenses, giving her no time to rally between one dizzying, torrid kiss or bone-melting caress and the next, taking quick advantage of every weakness he had discovered during their previous lovemaking, doing things that made her twist and moan. Over and over, he drove her to the brink of ecstasy, only to withdraw, then once again assault her senses, prolonging the exquisite torment of her passion and making her beg for mercy.

When it was over, Fire Dancer was beyond knowing or caring that she had once again surrendered to the aggressive Englishman's powerful sexuality or that he still held her possessively in his arms. Feeling deliciously satiated, she dreamily snuggled closer to the man she had sworn to oppose, for the time being his willing captive.

8

The next morning when Evan awakened, Fire Dancer was nowhere in their camp. That wasn't unusual—he knew she bathed every morning. What was peculiar, however, was that she hadn't lit a fire before she left.

Evan walked downstream and bathed himself. When he returned to their camp, Fire Dancer was still absent. Peering at the warriors' camp in the distance, he noted that they seemed to be making no preparations for leaving but were lounging about their fire as if they had nothing to do that day. Puzzled, he walked to their camp and asked Red Thunder, "Have you seen Fire Dancer?"

When the subchief just glared at him, Evan asked in exasperation, "What in the hell is going on? Where has Fire Dancer disappeared to, and why aren't you making any preparations to leave?"

Feeling a hand on his sleeve, Evan turned and saw Black Hawk. "No leave today," the warrior informed him.

"Why not?" Evan asked.

A perplexed expression came over the brave's face, and Evan knew the Chickasaw didn't know enough English to answer. "Where is Fire Dancer?" Evan asked, thinking she would explain.

Black Hawk pointed to the woods off to the side of the camp. As Evan turned and started to walk in that direction, Black Hawk caught his arm and said sharply, "No! You not go there."

"Why not?" Evan asked, becoming more and more irritated.

"Bad medicine," Black Hawk answered gravely. "You not go. No man go."

"Look, I don't know what in the hell is going on, but I'm going to find Fire Dancer whether you like it or not."

Evan jerked his sleeve loose and strode rapidly away, acutely aware of the shocked expressions on the Chickasaw's faces. As he walked into the woods, he spied Fire Dancer sitting beneath a tree in the distance. As soon as she saw him, she quickly pulled a blanket over her head, which surprised and totally baffled him.

Before he reached her, Fire Dancer called, "Go away! You must not come here!"

Evan ignored her and continued until he stood over her. "What in devil is going on?" he asked. "Why are they acting so peculiar back there, and why are you hiding beneath that blanket?"

Fire Dancer had no qualms about answering—Chickasaw took the functions of their bodies very matter-of-factly. "My women's time has come. It is taboo for a man to lay eyes on me at this time."

Evan was a little shocked at Fire Dancer's direct answer. The women of his own culture tiptoed around that subject. Then the full implications of what she had said dawned on him, and he asked in disbelief, "Are you telling me that we're not going to travel because you're on your monthly?"

"Yes. I told you—it is taboo for them to lay eyes on me."

Evan didn't like holding up the expedition for any reason, much less for one that seemed so ridiculous. "That's no reason to delay us. You can ride with the damn blanket over you!"

"How will I see to guide my horse?"

"I'll guide it."

"No, you still don't understand. I must keep my distance too. If I were back at the village, I would go to the women's hut, where I would not be anywhere near a male. So you see, I cannot accompany you under any circumstances. Now leave, before the others get angry."

Evan glanced over his shoulder and saw the braves in the distance scowling at him. Realizing that they feared he would bring a curse down on them, he spat out, "This is absurd!"

"I do not care what you think of it!" Fire Dancer retorted. "It is the Chickasaw way." She paused. "Would you prefer they just left me here?"

"Out here in the wilderness? All alone? Of course not!"

Fire Dancer could have pointed out that she had been left all alone in the wilderness when she much younger, as part of the Chickasaw endurance rite for children, but she didn't. She held her tongue, letting Evan stew.

And stew he did. He was both angry and frustrated. Nothing had ever stopped him, either previously or on this present mission. He'd trudged over the most rugged of terrains, through terrible weather conditions, gone without food and water for days, fought the enemy against overwhelming odds, and yet he was being brought to a total stop by one lone woman. For Christ's sake, this was war, not some goddamn picnic! he thought. He paced back and forth before Fire Dancer, then asked in a brittle voice, "And may I ask how long this foolishness is going to last?"

"A few days."

Evan made a noise that sounded like a snort, whirled around, and stomped away. Beneath her blanket, Fire Dancer smiled. She was glad she had found a way to frustrate the arrogant Englishman, since she didn't seem to have the strength to spurn his lovemaking. He didn't dare try to force her to his will this time, not unless he was willing to risk the braves' wrath.

Personally, Fire Dancer had always thought that the Chickasaw custom of isolating women during their menses was silly. How could her blood possibly be perilous to males when it didn't harm her or the women in her company in any manner? What made it even more absurd was that Chickasaw warriors were fearless about everything else, so fearless that when they were captured by an enemy, they taunted their captors into inflicting even more and more torture upon them. Fire Dancer strongly suspected that many of the Chickasaw women felt the way she did, but she noted wryly that they didn't do anything to discourage the men's fear. They looked upon it as a time to relax and rest, a time when they could absent themselves from the fields and the drudgery of cooking and housekeeping without feeling any guilt. When Fire Dancer knew Evan was out of sight, she pushed the blanket aside and once more picked up the moccasins she had been beading. Yes, she thought, this was one month's confinement she was certainly going to enjoy. At least for a few days the *hottuck ookproose*—the accursed white man—couldn't practice his black magic on her.

For the next three days, the Chickasaw braves spent their time fishing, hunting, racing their horses, gambling with wooden dice, and playing chunky—a game in which they threw spears at rolling stones to see who could come the closest to where the stone stopped. The delay Fire Dancer had caused didn't seem to bother them in the least, except for Red Thunder, who stayed to himself and glowered even more than usual. But it irritated Evan no end. He was anxious to get the surveillance behind him and the mission done, and even though Black Hawk and the others welcomed him in their idle pursuits and shared their fire and food with him, he grew increasingly foul tempered.

Evan didn't think his exasperation at all unwarranted. It seemed ludicrous for the expedition to be brought to a complete standstill because of something as natural as a woman's monthly. What did puzzle him, however, was that he couldn't sleep at night. In part, it was because he was tormented by memories of making love to Fire Dancer, vivid recollections that always left his loins aching. That alone was unnerving. He'd never wanted a woman so badly that he'd lost sleep over it. But an even greater cause of his insomnia was his concern for her safety. Night after night, he lay in the lean-to straining his ears to hear any noises that might mean danger was approaching her; he peered through the darkness at the meager fire she kept going for any sign of a wild animal that might be sneaking up on her. He told himself that he was being foolish, that Fire Dancer was an Indian woman who could take care of herself, that if there were any real danger to her, surely the others would show more concern. But none of the arguments worked. Each night he kept his self-imposed vigil, until finally, around dawn, he dozed.

On the fourth morning, when Evan awakened after a poor night's rest and found Fire Dancer tending his fire and cooking his breakfast, he was greatly relieved. But he was determined he wouldn't show it. To openly admit that he had been so concerned about her safety would leave him strangely vulnerable, and Evan could accept no weakness of any kind in himself. When she handed him his breakfast, he growled, "Well, it's about time you put an end to this foolishness."

Fire Dancer hadn't expected Evan to be happy with her—she had known she was making him angry and had even enjoyed it—but his harsh words now seemed insensitive, and they hurt. "I have no control over what happened!" she retorted.

"Maybe not, but you didn't have to tell everyone. There was no reason for them to even know," he answered, motioning toward the warriors' camp.

Fire Dancer noted that, even so, Evan would have

known. He would have discovered it that night and would probably have been angry because he couldn't slake his lust on her, she thought bitterly. And to think that she had missed his company! It wasn't him she had missed. Why, he was nothing but a hateful, selfish brute. What she'd really missed was talking in her mother's tongue. Her eyes shot green sparks as she answered, "That would have been talking with *saente soolish,* a snake's tongue. The Chickasaw do not practice deceit. That's a white man's trait."

God, she was beautiful when she was angry, Evan thought as her green eyes flashed and her coloring heightened. But the way she had said *white man* made him feel that he was the lowest thing on earth. "You're half white," he reminded her.

"Only my blood. Other than that, I make no claim on the white race, nor do I want anything to do with them. My heart and my soul are pure Chickasaw."

With that, Fire Dancer turned and walked away, as aloof and regal as a queen.

That day, they traveled beside the river, and for all practical purposes, Fire Dancer might as well have been left behind. She was so furious with Evan that she wouldn't answer a single question, and she only stared straight ahead, as if he didn't even exist. Her anger baffled Evan. To his way of thinking *he* was the one who should be angry. It was he, not she, who had been unnecessarily delayed.

Because Fire Dancer was giving him the cold shoulder, Evan tried to converse with Black Hawk, but the Chickasaw's English was so limited that it soon became tiresome. He spent the rest of the day riding in silence and simply observing the territory through which they were passing, trying to memorize every bend of the river and every stretch of rapids so that he could transfer the information to his map later on.

That evening, as he was currying his horse, he saw the Chickasaw braves walking to the river and carrying long sticks in their hands. He thought that unusual, for he had never seen the men fish with fishing poles. When he was finished brushing his mount and feeding it, he walked down to the river and saw that the Chickasaw were using the sticks to dig in the mud and unearth shellfish. Evan had seen huge mounds of shells on the banks of the river, but not until he saw one of the braves taking a perfect pearl from the oyster he had just opened did he realize that the pearls Fire Dancer had been wearing the night he first saw her were freshwater. Why, there must be a fortune in pearls along this river! he thought, then gasped as the brave threw the pearl aside, apparently having deemed it not worth keeping, picked up the oyster, and tossed it into his mouth.

The incident caused Evan to do some serious reflecting. The general consensus in Great Britain was that this new country was a dangerous, unhealthy land ridden with terrible fevers, covered with a thick, ugly tangle of vegetation, and inhabited by bloodthirsty savages and wild beasts. From the very beginning it had been a disappointment: the first English explorers had found none of the riches the Spanish had found farther to the south, in Mexico and South America. Not until well over a century later had the British finally realized the country did have some value—its seemingly endless supply of land—and for the better part, that was the reason an Englishman braved this country. The land was cheap and plentiful, and if he had had the determination and industry to clear it and farm it, he could have made a comfortable living for himself here.

But Evan had seen enough of the new country now to realize that cultivating the land was only the tip of the iceberg. There were other riches here: the huge forests, as yet virtually untouched; the lush grasslands such as he was passing through; the mighty rivers whose power might someday be harnessed and that might yield unsuspected gems; and the mountains whose hillsides in all probability hid vast stores of precious minerals. America wasn't simply a country of unlimited farmland —or a source of endless furs, as the French tended to think of it—but a land of such vast natural resources, it was mind-boggling. It was no wonder Great Britain was fighting a war for this wilderness, yet he strongly suspected his country didn't even begin to realize its true worth. He himself hadn't, until he had gotten a closer look at it.

That night, after they retired to their lean-to, Evan fought a long battle with himself. That Fire Dancer had scorned him and treated him so coldly that day had irritated him no end, and he was determined not to succumb to her desirability. If she wanted nothing to do with a white man, then hell would freeze over before he'd touch her again, he told himself as he lay at his end of the structure. But this vow had no effect on his body. Her scent drifted across to him, sweet and tantalizing, and almost as if his body had a will of its own, he felt his passion rising and heat flooding his pelvic region.

Fire Dancer had lain stiffly with her back to Evan, waiting apprehensively for his touch. But when he made no move toward her, she was filled with a keen disappointment. This baffled her—surely, she didn't want him to make love to her! she thought, not that arrogant, selfish brute. No, she just wanted an opportunity to refuse him, to further frustrate him, to anger him. And this time she'd be successful in spurning him, she vowed fiercely. She waited and waited, each minute an eternity, until her nerves were crawling. Then, when his muttered curse broke the pristine silence, she jumped.

Evan roughly rolled Fire Dancer onto her back and bent over her, muttering against her lips, "Damn you for being so desirable, and damn me for wanting you!"

A little thrill of sheer joy ran through Fire Dancer, but then she remembered her vow and came alive with fury. She clawed and kicked and twisted wildly beneath him, as Evan struggled to subdue her. Finally, he managed to pin her arms to her sides and still her flying legs with his hard-muscled thigh. His mouth came down on hers hard, but when she bit his lower lip, he jerked his head away, released one of her arms, wiped the blood from his mouth, and glared down at her and spat out, "You damn savage! What in the hell is wrong with you?"

Fire Dancer's green eyes glittered. "I have told you over and over, Englishman. I do not want you for a lover."

Evan scoffed. "You're still lying. Your lips tell me one thing, but your body says another."

"No!"

Fire Dancer's hand flew out, her nails bared. Evan caught one wrist and twisted her arm behind her back, then caught the other wrist. Holding both arms pinned behind her body, he quickly stripped her with his other hand, then leaned so close his warm breath seared her face. "I'm going to prove to you once and for all that you're lying. Before I'm through with you tonight, you're going to beg me for it!"

"No!"

"Oh, yes, my little savage princess," Evan replied in a silky growl. "I promise you. You're going to beg."

It was a promise Evan kept. As she arched her back to give him better access, he feasted at her breasts, kissing, nipping, laving the mounds with his warm, wet tongue, sucking until Fire Dancer's senses were reeling and she felt weak with desire. He left a trail of hot kisses and little love bites as his head slowly descended across her rib cage and her stomach, slipping lower and lower, while his free hand stroked the sides of her thigh.

He dallied at her navel, exploring it sensuously with his tongue, then supped at it, making tingles of exquisite excitement race through Fire Dancer and her breath come in ragged gasps. Knowing she was beyond the point of resistance, Evan released her wrists and stroked her hips and thighs with both hands, his lips slowly and resolutely moving lower. Then he was dropping soft, butterfly kisses on the insides of her thighs, and Fire Dancer felt as if her entire body had been set to the torch, her secret woman's place throbbing painfully with need.

When she felt Evan's hands sliding under her hips

and lifting her, she arched her back in anticipation of
his lunge, thankful that she would find release and that
he would torment her no further. Then a shocking realization came to her. It was his tongue, not his manhood,
that was parting her, that was pressing against her there.

"No!" she cried out, catching his head in her hands
and jerking it up.

Evan's blue eyes, ablaze with the heat of his desire,
met hers. "Did you think I meant to let you off that
lightly? No, sweet savage, not by a long shot. I told you
you'd beg for it."

As he lowered his head, she closed her thighs tightly.
Without the slightest hesitation, Evan wrenched them
apart with his hands, and although she pulled painfully
on his long hair, his tongue laved her moist lips, and the
taste of her nectar excited him wildly and made him all
the more determined to keep his vow.

Fire Dancer's eyes widened in wonder as she felt
Evan's devilish tongue circling, stroking sensuously,
flicking like a flaming dart, then dipping lower. Ruth-
lessly, he teased and taunted, brought her over and over
to the very brink, then retreated until she was thrashing
and sobbing in frustration.

"Say it. Say you want me," he muttered from between her legs.

It took superhuman effort, but she managed to
whimper, "No!"

"No?" Evan's eyes glittered. "Very well, my sweet
savage. We'll see."

Evan dropped his head and proceeded once more to
drive her wild with his skillful lips and tongue. Fire
Dancer wished desperately she had the strength to re-

sist him, but her bones seemed to have melted. Every
nerve in her body had come alive and was strung tight.
Her heart was pounding so fast and hard, she thought it
would burst. She was being consumed in fire and
couldn't breathe. She had to have release. She had to!
She'd die if she didn't! "Please," she moaned.

Evan lifted his head, slid up her body, and looked
down at her. "What did you say?"

Fire Dancer was horrified by what had slipped out.
She bit her lips to keep from repeating it. Then she
gasped as she felt the moist, hot tip of Evan's manhood
where his lips had just been, circling, teasing, taunting
the same way his tongue had. She sobbed.

"Say it," Evan softly taunted. "Tell me you want my
fire."

It was an agony that he was so close to where she
needed him so desperately. Feeling him slip lower, hovering at the portal of her womanhood, she lunged, but
Evan pulled away, muttering hoarsely, "No, that won't
do. You've got to say it. Say 'please.' "

"Please!"

With a victorious cry, he drove into her with one
powerful, deep thrust that sent tremendous shock
waves racing up her spine and exploding in her brain as
her entire body convulsed. Dazed, Fire Dancer opened
her eyes and saw Evan smiling down at her. Then,
aware he was still inside her, rigid and throbbing, she
wondered vaguely what had happened.

But Evan didn't give her much time to wonder. His
mouth closed over hers in a deep, sealing kiss, and she
tasted herself on his tongue. Then he was moving, first
with slow, sensuous strokes that rekindled her fire, then

fast and furious, then slow again. Each thrust was an ecstasy, each withdrawal an agony as he once again brought her over and over to the shuddering brink, only to retreat, until she was writhing beneath him, her nails raking his back, sobbing, once more pleading for release. Finally, he gave her she wanted, what she'd been begging for. A star exploded within her, consuming her in a blinding flash of light that seared her brain, tore her asunder, and sent a million pieces spiraling into a dark void, where she was reborn in a bright shimmering light.

Later, after Evan had fallen asleep, Fire Dancer's practical Chickasaw blood came to the fore and she came to a conclusion. She decided that it was pointless, even silly, to fight off Evan's advances or to deny any longer that she enjoyed being his lover. Her greedy body betrayed her at every turn. All she was doing was wasting her energy and making herself foolish in his eyes. And there was really no reason for her to feel bad about it, despite what her mother had said. She was Chickasaw as much as she was white—no, more so, she amended, remembering what she had told Evan. What had happened to her now would have happened to any other Chickasaw maiden years ago. She had taken a lover, had given her body; it was as simple as that. But her heart and soul still belonged very much to herself.

And that was the way it would stay, Fire Dancer vowed fiercely. She would give her virile, exciting English lover her body, but never, never her heart.

Not her Chickasaw heart, and most certainly not her Chickasaw soul.

9

The next day, Evan and his Chickasaw escort entered another deep forest, and Red Thunder gave Evan the choice of staying overnight at the Chickasaw village at the head of the river along which they were traveling, or going on. Since they had lost so much time being delayed by Fire Dancer, Evan elected to pass through the village and go on.

Several hours later they entered the clearing where the village sat. As they passed through it, Evan noted that it was smaller than Fire Dancer's village but every bit as clean and neat. He was forced to admit that the Chickasaw towns put English villages and hamlets to shame. Not only were their homes well maintained and freshly painted, but they penned their animals, except for their dogs, and even they were better mannered than their English counterparts. Nor did the women toss their garbage and slop jars into the gutter, as they were wont to do even in London, creating a terrible stench, to say nothing of encouraging flies and rats.

What refuse and wastes couldn't be fed to the hogs, the Indians buried in the woods. The result was a much prettier and much better-smelling settlement.

Hearing the sharp squeals of pigs, Evan glanced to one of the pens where the animals were being fed. He remarked to Fire Dancer, "I've been surprised to find cattle and pigs this far west. They're not native animals."

"That's true," she said. "We did not have them until the white man came. The Spanish brought the *shook-qua*—the pigs—with them, like their horses. Many of them escaped in the woods, and we later captured them. Others we did not catch, and they became wild and dangerous, their meat so stringy and tough that we do not even bother to hunt them. They roam all over this area, from the river you call the Ohio to the big water far to the south."

"The Gulf of Mexico?"

Fire Dancer shrugged her shoulders. "We do not have a name for it, and I do not know yours."

"And the cattle? Did De Soto bring them too?"

"No. We traded for them with tribes far to the east, who stole them from the white man."

"I wouldn't think, with all the game you have, that you'd bother with them."

"We do not raise them only for their meat, as we do the pigs. The *pishi*—the milk—is just as valuable to us. Before the white man brought the *wahka*—the cattle—we did not have milk to drink."

Evan was surprised that the Indians prized milk as a drink. The British, neither back in England nor here in the colonies, didn't. As a general rule, milk was for making butter and cheese and for baking, but not for drinking, and the little that was drunk was consumed as buttermilk. No, the common British drinks were ale and, here in the colonies, rum, except for the frontiersmen, who of late had concocted a potent whiskey from corn mash.

They passed through the Chickasaw village and, on the other side, came to the junction of the river they had been following and the Ohio. The name came from an Iroquois word, *ohiyo*, which meant "great," and Evan could see why the waterway had been so named. While it wasn't as wide as the Misho Sipokni, its deep, fast-flowing, grayish-green waters stretched a good half mile from bank to bank.

Red Thunder said something to Fire Dancer, which she in turn translated to Evan. "Red Thunder said we will leave our horses here and go by canoe from here on. The French fort is downstream, midway between here and where this river empties into the Misho Sipokni."

"Perhaps we should continue with our horses," Evan replied. "Burning dugouts takes time."

Fire Dancer passed Evan's objection on to Red Thunder. After the subchief gave a curt reply, she turned to Evan. "We will not have to burn dugouts. Our Chickasaw brothers will loan us one of their canoes. Besides, we cannot go by horse. The forest is too thick, and there are no riverbanks."

Evan hated to leave his prize stallion behind in the care of the Chickasaw, but it seemed he had no choice. He dismounted and removed his saddlebags, then watched uneasily as the animal was led away with the others. He turned and walked to where the Indians were loading their supplies into the long canoe. Looking down at the boat, he asked Fire Dancer, "Are you sure this thing won't sink? I've never seen wood like that before. It looks like it's full of little holes, as if it were worm-eaten."

"No, it is just very porous, and therefore very light," Fire Dancer answered. "This canoe is made of cypress, a tree that grows in the swamps. It is swift and could even float on a heavy mist. It is virtually unsinkable. Nor will it rot, like an ordinary dugout."

Evan stepped into the canoe and sat in the middle, where the Chickasaw had thoughtfully made a comfortable pallet of skins for him and Fire Dancer. But he still wasn't convinced it was safe, despite her reassurances. The canoe was much larger than any he had ever been in, so large that three could sit side by side in it, but it rested far too low in the water to suit Evan. Not only was he leery of the type of wood it was made of, it seemed to be too damn big and heavy to float.

But when the Chickasaws pushed away from the bank, Evan found that everything Fire Dancer had said was true. The canoe skimmed across the water, seemingly as light as a feather. The braves, kneeling on both sides, dipped their paddles into the water every now and then to guide it rather than to propel it.

As they moved down the river and away from the Chickasaw village, Evan could see why Red Thunder had said travel by horse along the river was impossible. The deep water butted up against high, rocky cliffs that were covered with tangled honeysuckle, grape, and wild cucumber vines, the latter covered with starlike leaves and prickly little fruits. Scattered all along the cliffs were caves, some apparently very large, and above the cliffs the forest was a solid line of towering trees, like a green wall of a massive fortress. Gliding down the river with the warm sun beaming down on them, Evan had to admit that this was a far more comfortable and carefree way to travel than horseback. It seemed that all he had to do was sit back and enjoy the passing scenery.

He was leaning back on his elbows and watching the flight of a black turkey buzzard as it soared in the upper air currents above the river when Black Hawk, who was kneeling beside him and paddling, put his paddle down, stripped off his buckskin shirt, and tossed it down. Seeing Evan watching him, he explained, "Too hot."

Evan nodded in understanding. According to Josh, that was why the frontiersmen hadn't adopted the Indians' kind of shirt along with their high moccasins and leggins. They claimed the skin shirts were too hot in the summer and too cold and clammy in the winter. Evan was feeling quite comfortable in his linsey shirt. He wondered why the Indians didn't make their shirts out of fabric, as they did their breechcloths.

As the day wore on and the sun got hotter, more and more of the braves stripped off their shirts, their damp brown skins glistening in the bright sunlight as they paddled. Then, to Evan's utter surprise and horror, Fire Dancer, sitting across from him on the pallet, removed the buckskin vest that covered her breasts.

Evan glanced quickly about him to see if the others had noticed, then leaned forward and whispered, "For God's sake, cover yourself!"

Fire Dancer looked down at her buckskin skirt and answered, "I am covered."

"I'm talking about your breasts!"

"Why should I cover them? I'm hot!"

"It's indecent to bare yourself in public that way."

"Why?"

"Because there are men here! The sight might inflame them."

Fire Dancer frowned. "Inflame? Do you mean excite them?"

"Goddammit, yes!" Evan answered, feeling his own heat rise.

"The Chickasaw do not consider it indecent for a woman to bare her breasts. This is how we work in the fields when it is hot. The men are so used to seeing our breasts exposed that they pay no attention, any more than they would to our bare arms, or our necks, or our faces."

Evan looked around again. Not one of the Chickasaw was paying the least attention to Fire Dancer, and he was left to assume that they didn't look upon that part of a woman's body as sexual. That realization should have made Evan feel more easy, but it didn't. He simply didn't like it that the men could see Fire Dancer's beautiful breasts. Nor could Evan ignore the proud mounds with their impudent dark nipples that seemed to beg to be touched, to be kissed, to be tasted. No matter how hard he tried to divert his attention, he could always see them from the corner of his eyes. Finally, in desperation, he stripped off his shirt and tossed it over Fire Dancer's shoulders. "Here, wear my shirt. It's much cooler." As she started to remove it, he stayed her hand

and said, "No, please keep it on. If not for your comfort, then mine."

Fire Dancer glanced down, saw the telltale bulge in Evan's pants, and relented. She didn't want him to embarrass her. This was hardly the time or place for that sort of thing. She wondered why her mother had never mentioned the English custom, but now that she thought about it, she realized had never seen her mother bare-breasted. Fire Dancer had always assumed it was because she didn't want her sensitive skin to be sunburned.

The incident also explained why the Englishman paid so much attention to her breasts when he was making love to her. Chickasaw men didn't do that, she knew, nor did they do those other shocking, indecent things Evan had done the night before. They didn't use their mouths to make love. She had heard too many of the other women talking about their experiences to know that, and Chickasaw women were very candid about sex. She glanced across at Evan, her eyes zeroing in on his sensuous mouth. Then, remembering all the wonderful feelings those lips could bring her, a shiver of excitement ran over her, and to her horror, she felt her nipples hardening. If he wouldn't embarrass her, she would embarrass herself. What a shameful, wanton woman he had made of her. She jerked her eyes away and gathered his shirt around her, grateful for its covering, even though the rough material felt itchy.

That night, they beached their canoe on a narrow stretch of rocky land and made camp in a cave above it. The cave wasn't large enough for all of them to sleep in, so some of the braves made pallets in the boat. But the cave did conceal their fire from any French allies who might have been scouting.

As they continued downstream the next day, about midmorning, Red Thunder ordered the canoe again beached. He explained to Evan, through Fire Dancer, that the fort was around the next bend and that they would continue from here on foot. The canoe grounded with a solid thump, and after everyone climbed out, Red Thunder designated men to stay behind to guard the boat, then signaled for everyone else to follow him.

"Wait a minute!" Evan called, and Fire Dancer relayed it to the subchief. Red Thunder turned, scowling deeply. "Tell him I don't want you going with us," Evan continued.

"But I'm your interpreter," Fire Dancer objected. "You may have questions to ask."

"Black Hawk is going along. What he can't interpret for me, and what we can't communicate by sign language, I can ask later."

When Fire Dancer seemed to hesitate, Evan said, "Look, if we're discovered spying on them, this could be dangerous. Shots might be exchanged. I don't want you getting hurt."

Suddenly Fire Dancer didn't want to be separated from Evan, but she didn't have time to delve into that strange feeling. She said, "No, I will go. My uncle said—"

"I don't give a damn what your uncle said!" Evan interjected. "You're not going!"

Fire Dancer's feelings did a complete turn-around. There he was again, she thought, being domineering and arrogant. "You can't issue me orders!" she responded hotly. "I am not a white woman. I am Chickasaw!"

"This is no time to start that foolishness. You can assert your female independence some other time. You're not going!"

"You think not?" Fire Dancer retorted. "Well, you just watch me!"

As she started to step around Evan, Black Hawk blocked her path and said in a firm voice, "You no go."

"You too? Well, you can't tell me what to do either!" Fire Dancer answered in Chickasaw.

With that, she pushed her cousin aside and, motioning to Red Thunder to proceed, followed him.

"Can't you stop her?" Evan asked Black Hawk.

He shrugged. "No."

"I could tie her to the boat," Evan suggested.

Black Hawk scowled. "No. Make mad. Make plenty mad."

Evan thought the male Chickasaw should have exerted their authority years ago, even if it meant resorting to drastic measures that made the women hopping mad. Then maybe their women wouldn't have been so out of control now.

As the party made their way to the fort, the underbrush so thick they had to hack their way through it, Evan fumed. It wasn't until the fort came in view that he let go of his anger and his officer's instincts came to the fore. At a crouch, he crept to the edge of the clearing that the fort occupied, then eased himself to the ground on his stomach and peered through the lower branches of the bush behind which he was hidden. Curious himself, Black Hawk joined him.

The fort sat on a high cliff that overlooked a bend in the river. Only three walls had been finished, those that faced the river. The place was a beehive of activity, as the Frenchmen and their Indian allies worked to erect the two blockhouses facing the river, and from the woods all around them came the sounds of axes and saws being used. Evan did a quick head count and figured there were at least thirty men working in the clearing. But he had no idea how many were felling trees in the forest. He wished he and his party had come closer to dusk, when the entire company might have been in camp.

Turning his attention to the big pile of supplies sitting between the three walls, he noted that many of the boxes were long and narrow and could only contain guns. Barrels of gunpowder were also evident. He knew they didn't need that much ammunition just to protect this fort. Apparently, the French were planning to use this as a supply base for the line of French forts farther north and east.

Black Hawk touched his shoulder and whispered, "We go now."

"No, I want to see more."

"No!" the warrior whispered urgently. "We go. Listen!"

Evan strained his ears and heard the sounds of someone approaching in the distance. That was enough to galvanize him. He shimmied away from the bush, and he saw that the others, including Fire Dancer, were already hurrying away, veering more to the left than they had come to avoid the approaching footsteps. With his long legs, it didn't take Evan long to catch up with them, but their flight was impeded by the tangled underbrush. While the braves ahead of them hacked away at some particularly thick berry bushes, Evan spied an area to the side of them that didn't look nearly as overgrown. Why, it wouldn't even require his knife to clear the way, he thought. He slipped his knife into its scabbard, walked to it, and started to grab some of the vines hanging from the tree to pull them out of his way. Just then, Fire Dancer quickly stepped up to him, caught his arm, and said, "No!"

Thinking she was telling him not to go off on his own, Evan felt a keen edge of resentment. He realized he might not be as good a woodsman as the Indians, but he had learned something about getting around in a forest from his previous experiences, enough to guide his men to escape after their disastrous defeat at Fort Carillon. It wasn't enough that Fire Dancer had refused to obey him. Now she had the audacity to issue *him* orders!

"It will be shorter this way," he answered curtly.

"No, you must not—"

"Look," Evan said angrily, "I'm not one of your Chickasaw braves. You can't tell me what to do, either!"

"All right then!" Fire Dancer answered in exasperation. "Go ahead and touch the vines. You will be the one to suffer, not I."

"That's what you're talking about?" Evan asked in surprise. "The vines?"

"Yes!"

Evan looked at the curtain of vines he had been reaching for. "They're just ivy."

"No, they are not just ivy. They are poisonous. That's why the braves did not go this way."

Evan had never seen poison ivy, but he had heard the rangers talking about it. According to them, it could cause terrible blisters on the skin, and one man who had gotten it in his eyes had been blinded. He found it hard to believe—the vine looked so harmless.

Then Evan felt foolish. He didn't like being made to feel that way by anyone, particularly by Fire Dancer. He wanted her respect, even more than that of others. That discovery in itself was upsetting, and he found he couldn't bring himself to thank her. He couldn't get the words out. It seemed that that would have been an admission of his foolishness, and he couldn't force the words past his pride.

To his relief, Fire Dancer didn't wait for a thank-you or even seem to expect one. She was already hurrying after the braves who had cleared the path.

When they reached the cliff where they had left their canoe, they scrambled down and climbed into it. Evan had barely settled down when the braves pushed the long canoe into the water. Then, seeing they were going downstream, and not up, Evan objected, "We're going the wrong way! The Chickasaw village is in the opposite direction!"

"But we're not going back to the Chickasaw village," Fire Dancer answered. "I thought you realized that."

"No, I didn't," Evan answered, irritated that no one had bothered to tell him. "May I ask why not?"

"Getting back to Chickasaw Bluffs will be much quicker by river. We can be there in just a few days."

"All right, that makes sense. But what about our horses? You may not mind kissing those miserable nags of yours good-bye, but that stallion of mine is valuable."

Fire Dancer's eyes flashed. "Our horses are not miserable nags! They are just as valuable to us as yours is to you. They are all already on their way back to our village. Did you not notice that two of our braves stayed behind with them?"

Evan glanced around and did a quick count. There were only eleven braves now, where there had been thirteen before. "No, I didn't," he answered, again feeling foolish. For Christ's sake, he was an officer, trained to keep an eagle eye out for desertions and yet, he hadn't even missed the two men. Was it because he wasn't in charge that he hadn't noticed? Or had his preoccupation with Fire Dancer addled him?

As they came around a bend in the river, however, Evan's blood ran cold. Before them on the bend was the fort, and he realized the French had seen them. He could see them and their Indian allies in the blockhouses and on the walkways inside the high walls; the men were gesturing excitedly toward them and pointing their long rifles down at them. A split second later, he realized there was no turning back. Even if they had wanted to, they wouldn't have been able to. The French had picked the location for their supply base very well. As the river made its sharp curve around the bend where the fort sat, it narrowed and formed a shoot in which the water ran very fast. The rapid current caught the canoe, and it sped forward like a shot out of a cannon. Evan yelled, "Get down!" to Fire Dancer. Before she could bat an eye, he had shoved her down on the bottom of the canoe and covered her body with his.

The braves abandoned their paddling, and they too threw themselves to the bottom of the boat, relying on the current to carry them around the bend. Dusky arms and legs seemed to be flying everywhere around Evan as the warriors dove for cover. And not any too soon. Evan heard the roar of guns, and then balls were whizzing all around them and spattering into the water. Several hit the sides of the canoe, making dull thuds, but Evan had no time to wonder if any of them had penetrated the wood enough to sink the canoe. In a flash they were around the bend and flying down the river, the swift, hard turn spraying water all over them. Evan raised his head and got a bare glimpse of the pier the French had built on that side of the bend and the pirogues, each painted a different bright color, that were tied to it; then the canoe took another bend in the river, and his view was obscured.

The braves sat up, grinning broadly, their dark eyes glittering with excitement and their hair dripping from where they had been drenched. Then, feeling Fire Dancer struggling beneath him and muttering, "Get off of me!" Evan sat up, pulling her with him.

"That much fun," Black Hawk said to Fire Dancer as she emerged from underneath Evan.

"Yes, I suppose it was exciting," she answered, shooting Evan a resentful look. "I just wish I could have seen it as well as heard it."

Ordinarily, Evan would have enjoyed the thrill of danger as much as the others, but now he had been too filled with terror for Fire Dancer. It was another of those new emotions she'd brought out in him that left him feeling shaken. He scowled and said ominously, "We may not be out of danger yet. Just as we passed that last bend, I saw them running for their boats. I'm sure they're pursuing us."

"They no catch," Black Hawk answered confidently and slapped the side of the canoe. "Canoe too fast."

Evan, however, wasn't reassured. The rest of the day, he kept glancing back, but he saw nothing of the French. It irritated him that no one else showed any concern, that they were utterly confident of their escape. But what irritated him more was the enjoyment Fire Dancer had apparently gotten from their close brush with death, while he had been so afraid. He didn't like the havoc she was wreaking with his emotions, and he wondered why she, of all women, unearthed so much feeling in him.

That night, they once again camped beside the river and slept in a cave, but there were enough small caverns on the high cliff so that Evan and Fire Dancer had one to themselves. Despite his irritation at her that day, Evan couldn't resist taking advantage of their privacy to make love to her. Her desirability and his hunger for her were just too strong. He was surprised that she offered him no resistance, and sometime later, when she was sleeping in his arms, he smiled smugly, thinking he had mastered her in at least one way—in bed. And that was all that really mattered, wasn't it? he asked himself. That was all he had wanted of her: her passion, given freely, with no reservations.

Then the smug smile faded from Evan's lips. Deep down, he knew he wanted more. The problem was—he didn't know what that more was.

10

The next day the party came to where the Ohio River joined the Misho Sipokni, the merging of the two creating a river of massive proportions. Evan gazed at the river that flowed in from the northeast in awe. He didn't know where the Misho Sipokni began, but it had to be one of the longest watercourses on earth, and knowing that few white men had seen it, much less traveled it, filled him with excitement. Now he thought he knew what motivated explorers to brave the unknown: Discovery had its own rewards.

For a few miles the two waters didn't mix. They flowed beside one another, the bluish-green of the Ohio hugging the steep limestone cliffs on the east bank and the reddish-yellow of the Misho Sipokni flowing beside the thick cane brakes on the western side. When they finally did merge, the result was an ugly brownish liquid that smelled and tasted of mud and silt. But the water wasn't the only thing that combined. The two rivers' strong currents also merged and formed a current so powerful that their canoe shot down the river as if they had been riding on the crest of rapids and not just floating, although just to look at it, the river appeared smooth, almost somnolent. Now Evan could understand why the Chickasaw had not attempted to travel upriver, and he was amazed that the French had managed to get any boats up it at all. Transporting goods by keelboat was time-consuming and tedious even against normal river currents and over short distances. But pulling a boat by ropes from the bank while poling it from behind against the flow of a river as powerful as this one, for hundreds of miles through a wilderness filled with hostiles, had taken extraordinary perseverance on the part of the French. Contemplating this surprising accomplishment, Evan thought that the river's powerful current was perhaps one of his country's biggest allies in this war, although its aid was certainly unrecognized by those who were running the war back east, men who had only heard rumors of the mighty waterway's existence. Without its awesome current, the French would have been able to ship men, arms, and supplies at will all the way up to the Great Lakes and Canada, provided, of course, that they got past the Chickasaw. Because of the difficulty of getting French military supplies upstream, Great Britain might even win this war. Yes, the river played as important a role in shaping history as the Indians.

The shame of it was the river itself would never have much value as a means of trade, unless someone could figure out a practical means of traveling upstream. A truly successful trade would depend upon the flow of goods *both* ways. But if that ever happened, the possibilities of what this wilderness could become were mind-boggling. The Misho Sipokni could become to America what the Thames was to England and the Nile to Africa.

The sound of wings flapping, then a distinctive sound that could only be described as a *quoak,* tore Evan from his musing. He looked up to see a great blue heron flying overhead, its massive, dark gray wings spread a good seven feet from tip to tip. Unlike the thick forests, there were birds of every kind here along the river, both waterfowl and songbirds. Evan had never seen so many birds in his life. That morning, at dawn, they had made the most ungodly racket he had ever heard: cheeping, singing, quacking, quoaking, honking, warbling, trilling, shrieking. He had never known that birds could make so many different sounds.

He watched as a snowy male egret swept down on its nest at the top of a willow, landed, bowed to the female in the nest, and presented the stick he had brought her for the nest she was making. The female shrieked angrily, jerked the stick away from the other egret, and threw it to the ground. Dejected, the male flew away to search for another that might be more acceptable to his waspish mate. Observing the two, Evan thought that even the female birds out here were difficult creatures. For despite her warm giving of herself the night before, Fire Dancer had maintained an aloof demeanor all morning. It was hard to believe that the woman he had held in his arms the night before and the woman now sitting beside him were the same. This one spoke only if asked a direct question.

Hoping to draw her out, Evan decided that this was

as good a time as any to find out more about the French fort.

"Would you ask Red Thunder if he has a more accurate count on the garrison at that fort the French are building?" he said to Fire Dancer. "I counted about ten Frenchmen and twenty Indians before we were interrupted, but I know there were more in the woods."

Fire Dancer directed the question to Red Thunder, who stood at the front of the canoe with his arms crossed over his chest, a position he had maintained since they had successfully cleared the narrow river shoot that the fort overlooked. Red Thunder shot Evan a look that could kill, then answered. Fire Dancer said, "Red Thunder said there are supposed to be thirty soldiers at Fort Massiac and that the *tekape humma*—the red people—vary from time to time. There have been as few as twenty, but at other times well over a hundred."

"Fort Massiac?" Evan asked in surprise. "How does he know its name?"

Fire Dancer didn't have to ask Red Thunder. She knew the answer, as everyone in her settlement did. They all had heard the Frenchmen's agonized screams. "One of the boats the French sent upriver was captured with the enemy alive. They gave the fort's name and other information before they died."

Evan didn't have to ask how the Frenchmen had died. A shiver ran over him. "What other information?"

"The strength of the garrison, for one thing, and the location of forts farther up the Misho Sipokni."

Evan frowned. "We heard rumors of western forts, but we were told they were abandoned years ago."

"Some were. But there is at least one French settlement a few days upriver from where the Ohio and Misho Sipokni join. The French said the settlement is called Saint Genevieve. And there is another trading post, which also acts as a fort, farther north."

"How do you know this?"

"I heard my uncle talking about it."

"How much farther north is the fort?"

"A day or two."

"Do you know the fort's name?"

"The Frenchmen said it was called Saint Louis."

Evan fell silent for a moment, wondering if the fort posed any military threat to the British or if it was too far removed from the scene. It might need some investigating also. At any rate, he would have to report it to his superiors. Drawing his attention back to his present mission, he said, "Ask Red Thunder if he knows what tribes of Indians are at Fort Massiac."

Fire Dancer relayed Evan's question to the subchief, then answered, "He says they are mostly Shawnee, with a few Hurons and Delaware."

Evan frowned. The Shawnee were noted for being particularly vicious fighters. "What about Choctaw?"

"I don't have to ask Red Thunder that. I know there are none there. Their territory is to the south of us."

Evan had seen every warrior in the boat stiffen when he had said *Choctaw*. Curious, he asked, "What did the Choctaw do to make you hate them so much?"

"Do?" Fire Dancer asked in surprise. "They have always made war against us. They are our ancient enemies."

"But what started it between the two tribes?"

"I don't know, but they are treacherous and deceitful."

Evan wasn't particularly surprised by her answer. England had traditional enemies, too, particularly the French, and he couldn't remember what incident had precipitated the hostilities in the beginning. That had been centuries ago. But the French had not been in this country long enough to be ancient enemies of the Chickasaw. "And the French? Why do your people hate them?"

"In the beginning, we didn't. The first Frenchman to explore this river lived with us for almost a year, and unlike the Spaniards, he did not try to enslave us. For many years we traded with the French. The English came with their cheaper trading goods, particularly their rum, but still we felt no animosity toward the French. It was what they did to our friends the Natchez, and what followed, that turned us against them."

Evan frowned. "I don't think I've heard of the Natchez."

"I'm not surprised. As a nation they no longer exist. Except for a few scattered among the Chickasaw and Creek, they have been wiped from the face of the earth. They were a powerful, proud nation that lived far to south, near where this river empties into the big water you called the"—Fire Dancer paused, her brow furrowing as she tried to remember—"the Gulf of Mexico. When the French built a settlement at the mouth of this river, the Natchez befriended them, but the French proved to be as treacherous as the Choctaw, whom they took under their protection and armed. The French built a fort high on the bluffs overlooking this river on Natchez land. Fort Rosalie, they named it. The Natchez asked them to move it to another location, for it sat on their holy ground where their ancestors were buried. The French governor adamantly refused. The Natchez could not tolerate the desecration of their holy ground and had no recourse but to destroy the fort and those in it. Their ancestors demanded it of them. The French governor retaliated with a vengeance. With the help of the Choctaw, he attacked every Natchez town and village. The few who managed to escape fled to the Chickasaw and the Creek.

"The French governor demanded that the survivors be turned over to him. The Chickasaw refused. The governor swore to wipe us from the earth just as he had the Natchez and declared war on the Chickasaw. With the help of the Choctaw, he destroyed three of our villages before we threw them back. It was this unprovoked attack that turned us totally against the French. All we had done was give shelter to our friends. The Natchez were too few to be a threat to them any longer.

"We allied ourselves with the English and aided them in their attack on the French fort at Mobile. This angered the French governor even more, and he sent another large force against us, but again it was unsuccessful. Then, a few years ago, the French sent yet another expedition, aided by the Choctaw, against us from the south, and a second, aided by northern Indians, from the north, hoping to crush us between the two. Fortunately, the two forces did not arrive simultaneously, and we were able to defeat them both."

Evan remembered Josh mentioning that the Chickasaw had fought the French on three occasions, but Evan hadn't known what precipitated the hostilities, nor had he any realization that the French were so determined to see the Chickasaw annihilated that it almost bordered on a vendetta. It seemed strange, for it really wasn't like the French at all. On the whole, they got along much better with the natives of this land than with the British. From the very beginning, the French had been fascinated by the Indians. Their coureurs de bois made friends with the Indians, learned their language, respected their customs, adopted their habits, even married their women—something that the ordinary Englishman would never dream of doing. The British settlers had nothing but contempt for the Indians, and even when they aligned themselves with one tribe for protection against another, they looked down on the natives, considering them little more than animals, with no soul. Even among the traders who dealt with the Indians and lived with them, few accepted them as equals. Yet because of a French governor's arrogance and his total disregard for the Indians' beliefs and feelings—behaving more like a bullheaded Englishman than a Frenchman—the Chickasaw had turned to their more natural enemy and were now British allies.

This last thought brought Evan up short. What had he just called Englishmen? Arrogant and bullheaded? He wanted to retract the thought, but found in all honesty that he couldn't. He had seen that characteristic in some Englishmen with stunning clarity. His people did have a tendency to be haughty and proud and to put themselves above others—himself included. It was an admission that didn't sit well with him. He had never previously acknowledged any flaws in his character.

Feeling introspective, Evan fell silent as the canoe swept downriver, passing sandbars that varied in length from a few feet to several miles, covered with graceful willow trees whose long, slender branches waved gently in the breeze. Under the bright sun, the river sparkled as they skimmed past swirls and strange boiling spots where the water passed over obstructions on the bottom of the river. Both sides of the waterway were lined with thick canebrakes in which lurked panthers, black bears, razorbacks, rattlesnakes, and alligators, as well as muskrat and otter. Then the sound of a rumbling brought Evan from his musing. Looking to the eastern bank, he saw tons of earth and rocks that had sheared from the towering bank come crashing down on the cane, splintering the bamboo stalks into millions of pieces and sending water flying into the air.

Evan turned to Fire Dancer. "How often does that happen?"

"All the time. The banks are constantly being eroded and the river widened. That is why we stay in the middle of the river, to keep from being buried beneath one of those sudden landslides."

Evan turned his attention to an island they were passing, and his gaze briefly came to rest on a yellow warbler's basketlike nest that hung from one of the willow trees there. "I'm surprised at the number of islands."

"They are really sandbars, and they, too, are constantly changing. They form around a chunk of driftwood that gets snagged on something and grow from that. They may last a day, a month, a year, a hundred years. Sometimes they are there one day, and gone the next. The river never stays the same, nor does it always follow the same course. There are oxbow lakes all up and down it made from the river's old beds. Because the river never stays the same, not even from week to week, there are landmarks that we use to travel it, certain trees in the forest that tell us where we are."

Evan looked up at the dense forest on the high cliffs. From that distance, the trees all looked the same to him. Fire Dancer guessed his thoughts. "Do you see that tall tree with the shiny yellow bark? It is a sycamore. They are very common all up and down the river and usually very tall. Their bark seems to reflect the light, even at night. For that reason, we use them to guide us, or we use a tree that is misshapen and therefore distinctive."

Black Hawk, kneeling beside them and paddling, said something to Fire Dancer. She turned to Evan. "Black Hawk says to prepare yourself. The river narrows drastically up ahead and runs very swift and rough. Once we have gone through that bad stretch, we have the river demon to get past."

"What river demon?" Evan asked.

"The one that devours men and boats."

Evan had heard stories of sea monsters that resembled huge serpents and swallowed entire ships along with their crews and passengers. He had heard similar stories about such creatures inhabiting some of the lakes in Scotland, with several heads and horns on them. Was this the kind of monster the Indians were talking about? he wondered. But before Evan could ask, the boat was caught in a swift current, and it took his full concentration to hold on as the canoe flew down the narrow stretch of river, dipping and bobbing wildly, careening off twisted logjams and spinning crazily about. He was still reeling dizzily when the water finally smoothed out and the boat righted itself. He had barely gotten his bearings when Black Hawk thrust a paddle in his hands and commanded, "Paddle! Paddle hard!"

The command surprised Evan, for the Indians had not asked for any help from him thus far. Then remembering the warning about the river demon, he looked about him. What he saw was not a monster, but it had the same terrifying effect that a monster would have had. It was a huge whirlpool, whose spinning water made a loud sucking noise that made his blood run cold. A large uprooted tree floated in the water and was caught, then disappeared in the dark vortex as though it were no more than a stick. That was all the impetus Evan needed. He knelt and paddled like mad, just as the others were doing, but even with everyone putting every bit of strength they had into it, the canoe seemed to hover on the very edge, drawn around and around and around for what seemed like an eternity. Then they finally broke free from the tremendous suction and floated away. Exhausted and covered with a fine sheen of perspiration, they put down their paddles and drew in deep breaths, the muscles in their arms and backs aching from the unaccustomed effort.

Having revived slightly, Evan turned and looked back. Behind him, Fire Dancer was sitting back on her heels, her head hanging in exhaustion as perspiration dripped from her brow. Only then did he realize she, too, had picked up a paddle and was putting her back to the awesome battle against the whirlpool. He felt a strange mixture of emotions: anger at her uncle for making her come on this dangerous trip, and also a curious pride. The first feeling was understandable, but the second puzzled Evan. He had never felt proud of any accomplishment of any woman he had known in the past—but then, none of them had been like Fire Dancer. The women he was accustomed to would have cringed in fear, if they hadn't out-and-out fainted, but Fire Dancer had risen to the occasion and assumed responsibility for her own fate rather than depend upon others to get her out of danger. It was an example of her assertive Chickasaw nature. Such exhibitions of independence usually irritated Evan, but in this instance he couldn't help but admire her.

That evening, because both riverbanks were covered with a particularly thick growth of knee-high rice cutgrass, they decided to make camp on one of the larger islands. Evan was glad for the decision. He had cut his leg on one of the razor-sharp blades days before, and it was still sore. As the canoe skimmed beneath a willow, he ducked to avoid the low-hanging branches before they grounded on the hard-packed sand with a jarring thump.

Evan stood, his attention focused on the white scum from the seeds of the willows that floated on the water. Without looking to the bank, he started to step from the canoe. Fire Dancer pulled him back and said, "Watch where you step!"

On the ground where he had almost put his foot, Evan saw a black snake coiled, its body the size of a man's arm and its huge white mouth wide open as it reared its ugly triangular head. A split second later, he heard the roar of a gun and the head was blown to bits. He shivered as he watched the scaly body writhe in the sand. Glancing back across his shoulder, he saw Black Hawk, his rifle raised and still smoking.

"Thank you," Evan said, feeling rather foolish. "It was poisonous?"

Before Black Hawk could respond, Red Thunder growled something to the warrior, then jumped from the canoe and strode rapidly away.

"What did he say?" Evan asked Fire Dancer.

"He said Black Hawk shouldn't have wasted his ammunition. If you were foolish enough not to watch where you stepped, you deserved to die."

Black Hawk glared at Red Thunder's back and mumbled, "Him *ookproo-shed.*"

"What?" Evan asked.

"Black Hawk said Red Thunder was very bad."

"Because of what Red Thunder said?" Evan shrugged his broad shoulders. "I'm really not surprised. I know he doesn't like me."

"No, it is more than that," Fire Dancer answered. "None of the braves likes Red Thunder. He keeps himself apart. They follow him, but they do not like him."

"Fighting men don't usually like their officers, which is what I suppose Red Thunder is, and officers are supposed to keep themselves apart," Evan pointed out. "It's easier to discipline men that way. It would be very difficult, for instance, to have a friend whipped."

"Whipped? Is that how you get your men to obey you?"

"Sometimes. Men obey officers they fear."

"Then you don't try to earn their respect?"

Evan frowned. That had been Lord Howe's method. He had been a strict yet fair disciplinarian, and he had rarely resorted to literally whipping men into shape—the usual means of bringing men in line in the British Army. He hadn't just led—he had fought beside his men, never asking them to do what he wouldn't do himself. As a result, his men had had a deep respect for him and had fought to the death for him. Evan, too, had admired him, and he supposed that, if he ever got another command, he'd adopt a few of the nobleman's methods. But looking back on it now, most British officers' tactics in dealing with their subordinates did seem a little harsh. Still, he wouldn't go to the opposite extreme and become like the ranger officers. They mixed freely with their men and had almost no discipline in the field. Their orders were obeyed on the basis of persuasion rather than command.

"I suppose there's nothing wrong with earning respect," Evan admitted. "Is that why the braves don't like Red Thunder? They don't respect him?"

"No, it's not that. He is a very skilled warrior, and no one questions his bravery. From that standpoint, they respect him. It's just that they don't trust him. He's too ambitious, too . . ." Fire Dancer's words trailed off. She hated to say "vindictive," but that was what the warriors sensed in Red Thunder that they didn't like, and she sensed it was true. Black Hawk had once told her that the warriors feared that Red Thunder was so ambitious, he would go to any extreme to get what he wanted. Fire Dancer was prone to agree. Of all the men she had spurned, only he had become really angry, and she sensed that his anger had stemmed less from disappointment at her refusal than from her frustrating the other, more devious plans he had in mind for her. For weeks she had felt uneasy, half expecting him to jump her from behind or do something spiteful to her. At any rate, she felt just as the warriors did. There was something bad about Red Thunder, very bad.

Evan had no idea what thoughts were going through Fire Dancer's mind. He waited patiently, then prompted, "Too what?"

Fire Dancer didn't feel comfortable enough with Evan to voice her suspicions. What if he laughed at her? she thought. Besides, he was an Englishman, just passing through her life, a casual lover temporarily sharing her bed. He wouldn't care that she thought Red Thunder was somehow threatening. "It doesn't matter," she answered with a shrug. "The braves just don't like him, that all."

Fire Dancer stepped from the canoe. As she walked away, Evan felt a keen disappointment. She had been on the verge of confiding in him, and he wanted her to trust him. Once more, he had the strangest feeling that what she had been about to tell him was of the utmost importance.

11

Leaving their canoe secured on the bank of the sandbar, the scouting party walked through a grove of willow trees, under which a thick carpet of yellow daisylike flowers grew, to the center of the island. There, beneath several towering cottonwoods covered with tangles of grapevines, they made their camp.

While several of the Chickasaw collected firewood, Evan watched two others pull a few vines from one of the trees, strip off the glossy leaves and fragrant, white flowers, then fashion a large, basketlike trap. Evan knew that when they headed back toward the river, they would catch fish in the trap. But when they returned later and emptied the basket's contents on the ground, he was stunned. There, along with half a dozen good-size trout, was the biggest and ugliest-looking fish he had ever seen. At least five feet long, the bluish-black fish had a rather flat head, big protruding eyes, and long barbs around its mouth that resembled a cat's whiskers. While the trout were dead, the monster fish still had quite a bit of fight left in it as it thrashed about wildly on the ground, and Evan noted that the Indians gave the fish a wide berth, jumping back if it got anywhere near them.

As Fire Dancer walked up to him, Evan asked, "Are those barbs beside its mouth poisonous?"

"No, those are just feelers that help it see. It lives on the bottom of the river, in the mud, where it is very dark. But the vicious spines on the fins can be dangerous. If you get one in you, it is very difficult to remove, and even then it remains sore for several days."

Soon the fish stopped its thrashing, and as one of the braves began to dress it, taking care not to touch its fins, Evan asked, "They're not going to eat that thing, are they?"

"Yes, they're going to eat it," Fire Dancer answered as if he had just asked the stupidest question in the world. "And I hope they offer us some of it. It's very tasty."

Evan found that hard to believe. To his way of thinking, anything that looked that ugly couldn't possibly taste good, and if it lived in the mud, more than likely it would taste of it. But later that evening, he found how wrong he was. The grilled catfish was delicious, as were the orange mushrooms that Fire Dancer had picked from the trunks of the willows—which Evan had originally eyed with just as much suspicion as he had the fish. Of course, he had no objection to the strawberries she had found growing in a sandy, sunny location on the island. He was familiar with them. But he had never seen any so large or tasted any so sweet, and once again, he found himself impressed with the Indians' cuisine.

After they finished their evening meal, Fire Dancer left the camp, taking their wooden bowls with her. Evan assumed she had gone to the river to wash them, as she usually did. But when the sun began to fall and the shadows grew longer and longer, he remembered the snake they had killed that afternoon and began to worry. He rose and walked into the willow thicket where she had disappeared.

He found her at the other end of the island, sitting on a piece of driftwood, running her fingers through her loose, damp hair to dry it. Evan came to a stop behind her, realizing what had taken her so long was a bath, then gazed in silent admiration at her hair. He had never seen it hanging around her shoulders, had not realized it was so long that its curly tips fell to her hips. Once or twice during their lovemaking the big braid had come down, but it had never unraveled completely. Now her hair hung like a black silk curtain around her, with curls that she must have inherited from her English mother.

Then Fire Dancer turned and saw him. An accusing gleam came to her eyes as she asked, "What are you doing here?"

Evan flinched. She made him feel as if he had been caught spying on her, when all he had wanted to do was assure himself of her safety and protect her if necessary. He shrugged and answered, "I was wondering what was taking you so long."

"I took a bath and washed my hair."

"Yes, I noticed," Evan answered, then thinking his words sounded lame, added, "I thought you bathed in the morning."

"I do. But sometimes, when it is hot like today, I bathe in the evenings too."

Evan had never known a woman to bathe so much. In England, one bath a week was considered more than adequate, and the lower classes didn't bathe even that often. Aware of her green eyes on him, Evan wondered if he should gracefully depart, but he didn't want to leave. "Do you mind if I join you?"

It seemed a strange question to Fire Dancer. Had he missed her company? she wondered. Was that why he had come looking for her? Or was he just impatiently anticipating their lovemaking? The latter possibility distressed Fire Dancer. She had been silent all day, had dallied at her bath, because she had been thinking about their relationship. As much as she enjoyed the Englishman's lovemaking, she found herself yearning for something more, something she couldn't put her finger on. Feeling disappointed now, she answered rather sharply, "If you like." Then she turned her back on him and began to run her fingers through her long hair again.

Evan flinched a second time. He had hoped that she would say she enjoyed his company, but he should have known better. That would have been an English-woman's response, and Fire Dancer was very much living up to her independent Chickasaw image. Outside of his satisfying her sexual needs, she didn't want his company any more than she needed his protection.

Evan stepped up behind Fire Dancer and gazed out silently at the river, pondering why he had such a strong urge to protect her. Sure, he was a soldier by trade, he made his livelihood by protecting people, but wanting to protect Fire Dancer was much more personal. It wasn't something he felt he had to do, a duty he had to perform; it was something he needed to do to satisfy a craving he didn't begin to understand. But his need to shield her, however strange, was clearly doomed to being thwarted. She had proven herself perfectly capable of taking care of herself, and even more frustrating, his attempts to protect her had only irritated her. No, if truth be told, she was doing more to protect him than the other way around. He remembered that she had pulled him back from the poison ivy and the snake. All he had accomplished in his useless efforts to protect her —like coming to look for her this evening—was to make an ass of himself.

As the sun slowly set, turning the sky a reddish orange, the river reflected its color. The spectacular sunset served to turn both Fire Dancer's and Evan's brooding to the panorama nature was offering them. They watched the shadows fall, turning the river mauve in color, then purple, and then the stars appeared one by one as the sky darkened.

Gazing across at the riverbank across from them, Evan asked, "What are those lights over there?"

"Eyes. The green lights that look like sparks are the eyes of bullfrogs, the red spots, the eyes of the whippoorwills, the bluish-green ones are the eyes of muskrat digging for clams in the mud. The ones that glow in the dark are the eyes of raccoons."

Evan was amazed that Fire Dancer could distinguish different animals by how their eyes looked at night. "And those blinking lights in the forest? Are those fireflies?"

"Yes."

"I've never seen so many of them or their lights so bright," he commented. Then sniffed the air and asked, "And that sweet smell? Where is it coming from? I didn't notice any honeysuckle on this island."

"That's the smell of willow leaves," she answered, taking in a deep breath and relishing the familiar fragrance that she so loved. "It's always strongest at dusk."

For a long while, the two gazed out at the river, lulled by the soothing night sounds: the murmuring of the river, the chirps of the crickets, the throaty croak of the bullfrogs, the hoot of a night owl. For Evan it was a welcome experience. Not since he was a boy living on his father's country estate had he taken time to just stand and enjoy nature. It was also a new experience, for he had never shared his appreciation of nature's offerings with anyone, much less a woman. A peacefulness filled him.

Then he watched in awe as a huge moon rose over the forest, lining the treetops in silver, then cast a soft white light over all and making the river winding through the forest look like a glittering ribbon that some angry goddess had tossed down. "The river is absolutely beautiful at night," he remarked softly.

"This river is always beautiful," Fire Dancer answered, "regardless of whether it's day or night, or whether the sun is shining or it is raining, regardless of the season. Even in the winter it is beautiful with the icicles glistening on the branches and the rosy glow of the bark of the river birches."

Fire Dancer's voice had dropped an octave and had a husky quality about it. During the moonrise, Evan had stepped around the log and sat down beside her. He turned and faced her, seeing the soft, warm expression on her face. "You talk about that river almost as if it's a person and not a thing."

"The Chickasaw believe that everything has a soul, even the river and the land, for from it comes life. That is why our hunters pray before they go out to hunt; why we apologize to animals, our brothers, if we must kill them for food; why we make offerings of tobacco to trees before we gird or fell them, so the other trees will not weep. We care deeply about the country the Great Spirit entrusted to us and allows us to use. We love the land, the rivers, the forests, the animals, the ponds, the swamps, the little stretches of prairie—everything that is a part of it, for it is in turn a part of us. That is why we fight so hard to keep it, and why we will never leave it."

"And you?" Evan found himself asking out of the clear blue. "Would you ever leave it? You're half white."

"No, I would never leave my home," Fire Dancer answered emphatically. "It does not matter that I am half white. I told you, my heart and soul are Chickasaw."

Evan wondered why he had even asked if she would leave her home. For what purpose would she? There would be no reason for her leave. She had been born in this country and raised by these people, was destined to hold a place of honor among them. Yet her answer disturbed him, and more and more he found that he didn't like her discrediting the half of her that was white.

As Fire Dancer gathered her long hair to braid it, Evan stopped her. "No, please, leave it down. It's so beautiful that way." He ran his hands down its length, marveling at its silky texture and gazing at her face. In the bright moonlight, her skin seemed to glow, and her features took on an almost ethereal appearance. "You're beautiful," he muttered, "so incredibly beautiful."

As Evan bent his head to kiss her, Fire Dancer found she couldn't resist, no matter how lacking she found their relationship. The beauty of the night, its soothing sounds, and the strong attraction she felt for the Englishman had primed her for a night of love, and just the thought of his lips on hers filled her with a wild excitement. She couldn't fight his desire when she was so utterly helpless against her own. Sliding her hands over his broad shoulders, she lifted her head, and as his warm mouth covered hers, his tongue playing teasingly at the corners before slipping inside to gently ravish her heady sweetness, sensation erupted in her. A moan of desire rose from deep inside her as she pressed her body against his, wanting the kiss to last forever. By the time he rose and brought her to her feet with him, she was trembling with need and could barely stand.

With soft, exploring kisses and tantalizing caresses, Evan undressed her, stopping to dally at her proud breasts with their dark impudent nipples, his tongue laving, his lips nibbling, then lingering again at her navel. By the time her buckskin skirt had fallen to the ground and she stood naked before him, Fire Dancer was quivering all over.

Evan stepped back, his eyes hungrily sweeping over her, and Fire Dancer saw the blatant admiration in them. Knowing that he genuinely thought her beautiful, that he had not been complimenting her just to seduce her, excited her even more. Then, seeing that he was trembling, too, she realized that while he might reduce her to a weak, mindless, spineless creature with his torrid lovemaking, she held a tremendous amount of power over him too. It was heady knowledge that gave her the courage to boldly step forward and begin to undress him.

As Fire Dancer unbuttoned his shirt and pushed it back off his shoulders and down his arms, Evan stood perfectly still, both excited and surprised. It was the first time she had taken any initiative in their lovemaking, and he was hesitant to even move for fear she would change her mind and step back into her passive role. He had always been the aggressor, the one doing the seducing, and while she no longer resisted his advances, this was the closest she had come to openly admitting that she desired him as much as he desired her. That knowledge excited him as much the featherlike feel of her fingers on his feverish skin.

Fire Dancer was getting just as much enjoyment from touching Evan as he was from touching her. The feel of the powerful muscles on his shoulders and arms thrilled her, and as she undid the lacings on his pants, she was acutely conscious of the huge bulge straining just below her fingertips; then her heart raced at the feel of his throbbing heat as her fingers brushed against his flesh.

As Fire Dancer's fingers lightly touched his aroused sex, Evan's mouth turned dry. Then, as her hands slid down his thighs to push the pants down, he sucked in his breath. He stood for what seemed an eternity as she unlaced his high moccasins, acutely conscious of his released manhood standing at attention, primed and ready for action. It took all his control to keep from pushing her hands aside and finishing the chore himself. As soon she slipped his pants and moccasins off, he reached down and swept her up in his arms, taking her so much by surprise that she cried out softly.

He carried her to a willow, shouldering aside the curtain of graceful, slender branches that hung almost to the ground, then placed her on a mossy, moon-dappled spot. Kneeling beside her, he once more took in her beauty, his eyes slowly drifting over each curve and hollow. Then he covered her body with his, his mouth coming to rest at the sensitive nook between her neck and shoulder.

Fire Dancer gasped as Evan's heated flesh touched hers, as always acutely conscious of the crisp golden hairs on his chest rubbing against her aching nipples, as if they were making love to that very sensitive part of her of their own accord. As he slipped his hair-roughened thigh between her soft ones, she felt his manhood, rigid and hot and throbbing, pressing against her loins. She folded her arms around him, her hands stroking the powerful muscles on his back; then, feeling those muscles quivering in response, her heart quickened, and she pressed even closer, wanting with something akin to desperation to crawl inside him, every nerve tingling as her skin hungrily absorbed the feeling of his.

Evan's mouth lowered over hers in a deep, penetrating kiss that robbed her of her breath and all thought, and Fire Dancer was lost in sheer sensation. She was on fire for him, her bones melting, incapable of thinking of anything but the hot liquid feeling he was evoking in her.

His hands caressed and stroked, teased and tantalized as he kissed her from head to toe, drinking in her clean, sweet essence and glorying in her throaty moans and wild thrashing. The knowledge that he was bringing her such intense pleasure gave him tremendous satisfaction and made him want to prolong his lovemaking and put his own pleasure on hold. Evan never stopped to wonder why he was being so unselfish, for he had no ulterior motives. Unlike the other times he had made love to her, this time he didn't have to storm her defenses or play on her passion. He only knew that tonight he wanted to give and not receive, and unknown to him, this giving was passed on to Fire Dancer in a gentleness and a tenderness he had never shown before.

It was inevitable, however, that Evan's desire would make itself known so powerfully that he could no longer deny himself. But even then, he entered Fire Dancer with care. Not even her muscles surrounding him greedily or her scorching heat could rob him of his control. He clenched his teeth, then slid deeper. He lay savoring the feel of his rigid length inside her tight, velvety sheath, amazed at how perfectly their bodies fit together, as if they were made for each other.

It was a provocative thought that Evan never had a chance to explore. Fire Dancer wrapped her slender shapely legs around his hips in a vise so tight, he thought she would squeeze the life from him. A red haze fell over his eyes as his passion came surging to the fore.

"No, don't move!" he ground out between clenched teeth, still wanting to prolong her pleasure.

But Fire Dancer was beyond reasoning. Evan had

aroused her to such a feverish pitch, she thought she would burst if she didn't find release. It was she, not he, who drove them up those thundering heights to a soul-shattering release that left them weak and rasping for breath.

Long after their muscles had stopped trembling and the evening breeze had cooled their heated skin, Evan held Fire Dancer close. Both of them were content to listen to the murmur of the river, the rustle of the gently swaying willow branches, the repeated call of a whippoorwill somewhere in the distance. Finally, with great reluctance, Evan brought Fire Dancer to her feet. "We'd better dress and get back to camp," he said. "Red Thunder will be sending out a sentry soon. We wouldn't want him stumbling across us."

Fire Dancer knew the others assumed she and Evan were lovers and wouldn't be surprised that they had had a tryst in the woods, but she didn't want anyone to stumble across them either. Their spontaneous love-making had seemed so very private, so beautiful, that she didn't want anyone to know about it.

After they had dressed and were walking through the willow thicket back to the camp, Fire Dancer wondered why their lovemaking had seemed so special. Then Evan startled her by taking her hand in his big warm one, his long, slender fingers twining around hers as he brought her close to his side in an action that was pure Anglo, for Chickasaw did not hold hands. After she recovered from her surprise, Fire Dancer felt a wonderful warmth stealing over her, a warmth that had nothing to do with passion. Holding her hand seemed so caring.

Then Fire Dancer realized what it was that she had

been yearning for. She wanted Evan to care, truly care about her, not just for the pleasure her body could bring him. For Fire Dancer, it was an earth-shattering discovery that shook her to her roots. Somehow or another, she had let the arrogant Englishman slip past her defenses, and if she didn't take care, she'd lose her heart to him also.

12

The next morning when Evan awoke, the island was covered with thick fog. Putting on his damp clothing, he shook his head in disgust and walked to the fire where Fire Dancer was slicing bacon from a rack of salted meat—a process the English factors had taught the Chickasaw. "Everything is miserably wet again today," he said, "just as it was yesterday morning. Do you always have fog at this time of the year?"

Fire Dancer cut off a small piece of the bacon and tossed it into the fire, her daily offering to the Great Spirit. "There is always a morning fog on this river, regardless of the season," she replied. "Sometimes it just hangs over the water, and sometimes it rises and covers the forests at the top of the cliffs. But we do not mind it. Like the night dew, it waters everything and makes it green, and it has its own beauty."

Later, as they were pushing off from the island, Evan looked at the willows, whose long slender leaves were dripping with water, then at the peculiar greenish-gray fog that enclosed the entire river basin and obliterated the sight of the forests on either side. When Fire Dancer said the fog had its own beauty, he had thought her grossly wrong. To him, it just looked dreary and depressing, perhaps a little spooky with the ghostlike smoky swaths drifting across the brown water and the yellow sandbars. Then as the fog lifted, a pearly luminescence came to the upper levels. Suddenly the bright sunlight burst through and the droplets of water on the spider webs on the willow trees twinkled as though they had been sprinkled with millions of diamonds. Gazing at it with awe, Evan had to change his mind. It was really quite beautiful, with the trees twinkling, the water sparkling, and tiny rainbows winking here and there amid the underbrush where the light caught the water drops at just the right angle. And apparently the birds thought so, too, as they joyously burst into song.

By midday, the sun was so hot that heat waves rose on the baking sandbars, somehow reminding Evan of yellow corn bread just being removed from the oven. Then he spied a long wharf made of logs jutting into the river. Tied to this pier were two dozen or more canoes just like the one he was riding in. Seeing him eyeing the pier, Fire Dancer explained, "That is our village up ahead."

"Already?" Evan asked in surprise.

"Yes. Didn't I tell you it would be much faster by river?"

She had, Evan admitted, but he hadn't expected it to be quite that fast.

After they docked their canoe, Evan walked with Fire Dancer and the others to the end of the pier, where everyone stopped and removed their moccasins. When Evan stepped down from the pier, he found out why. The riverbank was pure mud, a good six inches deep, and it smelled to high heaven.

As they followed a winding path that went up the limestone cliff, the wet mud finally gave way to dry earth that crunched under their bare feet. They passed between two fields, where the corn was growing at least three feet tall and was covered with green ears whose golden tassels waved in the breeze. "This can't possibly be the same corn that was being planted the day I came to see the river," Evan remarked to Fire Dancer. "That was only a little over a fortnight ago."

"No, this is our early corn. It was planted six weeks ago. The field you saw is farther back, near the cliffs where the grapevines grow. It is planted there so it will ripen at the same time as the grapes. Then the birds do not bother the corn, since they prefer the fruit."

And the birds also explained the scaffold in the middle of the field, Evan thought, as an old Indian woman standing on it waved a small tree branch to frighten away some of the pests in the field. The flock of blackbirds took flight, spreading their colorful red wings, then flapped them loudly in protest at having their meal interrupted. "Then you have two crops of corn?" Evan asked in amazement. In England they did well to get one crop of anything before winter set in.

"Actually, we have three crops of corn. Our early corn, which is small eared, is the best eating corn, for it is very tender and sweet. Our summer corn is yellow and fleshy, but the kernels are very hard, so hard we have to soak them in water mixed with ashes to soften them."

Evan nodded. He had heard of the hominy the settlers made from that corn. He'd been told that it was pretty much the frontiersmen's mainstay. Naturally, they had picked up the process of making it from the Indians, along with the corn itself.

"The corn that ripens in the fall along with the grapes has the largest ears and is very white, with a soft grain," Fire Dancer continued. "It can be eaten, too, but mainly it is our bread corn, and therefore our main corn crop."

Evan took a second look at the cornfield. "The crop looks very good, but shouldn't you pull up those vines growing all over the stalks before they choke out your corn?"

Fire Dancer laughed. "Those are not just vines. They are peas and beans, and we deliberately plant them that way so they can trail up the cornstalks. Even after the corn has died and stalks have yellowed, they make good stakes. And the vines in between the corn plants are squash, melons, and pumpkins."

"The colonists claim the pumpkins are not worth much," Evan commented. "They use them for cattle fodder."

"Then they are very wrong," Fire Dancer answered with a scornful look on her face. "They are delicious, and like the other squash, they can be dried for later use in the winter."

Evan didn't doubt her word. So far, every new food she'd served him had been delicious. He looked again at the field. One plant stood out against the yellow and white blossoms. "What are those plants with the showy pink flowers?"

"Marsh-mallows, but their fruit is not edible. We eat the roots."

"Well, you certainly shouldn't starve, not with all you grow," Evan said, thinking that the Chickasaw were much better farmers than the majority of the colonists, particularly the frontiersmen, whose only crop was corn and perhaps some flax from which to make their linsey. Quite a few of the ones he had seen on his way west were on the verge of starvation.

"No, the Chickasaw have never gone hungry, not with our crops and what we gather from the woods."

Evan remembered the mushrooms, the yams, the white potatoes, and the wild onions that Fire Dancer had served him. They had been delicious, but few of the colonists would touch them, just as they refused to grow vegetables. The English had never cared much for vegetables, although they sometimes ate parsnips, turnips, carrots, and onions, but when they did prepare them, they overcooked them, just as they did their fish. Until he ate Fire Dancer's cooking, Evan had never realized that vegetables could taste so good, and he thought it a shame that the colonists couldn't learn more from the Indians than just how to build log cabins and forts.

"But I have heard of other tribes that are starving," Fire Dancer continued, breaking into Evan's thoughts.

"What tribes?"

"Some of the eastern tribes who gave up their farming to become hunters for the white man. They are constantly searching for deer, which the white man values greatly for their skins. When all the deer are killed off in an area, the tribes are forced to move to another, and they cannot take their fields with them."

Evan knew that what Fire Dancer had said was true. Buckskin was the current rage in Europe, which created a huge demand for the skins. But that was no reason for the Indians to be starving, he thought. "They can gather from the woods, as you do."

"No, like the wild game, those things the Great Spirit gave us will not last forever. He did not mean for us to strip the land to fill our bellies. We should take only what we need. The rest we should put our own labor into and grow for ourselves. That is the Indian way."

Evan had never stopped to think about it, but he supposed there was a danger in stripping the land. He had seen that for himself in some of the older settlements on the frontier. The colonists had complained that the game was growing scarce and that they had to travel farther and farther to get it—and no wonder, when they used turkey breasts for bread and discarded the rest of the bird, and when they shot deer for their hides and let the carcasses rot. The white settlers were terribly wasteful, and they could take another lesson from the Indians and learn to conserve what they had. Still, he was puzzled about something. "If that's the Indian way, then why did those tribes desert their farming and turn to hunting?"

"For the rum the white man trades them for the hides, or the brandy for the furs, in the case of the Frenchmen. Both are a curse to the red man. They make the Indian weak and muddle their thinking."

Evan laughed. "No, Fire Dancer. That's the way li-

quor affects all men. It muddles their thinking temporarily."

"No, it is not the same with the Indians," Fire
Dancer answered emphatically. "It cripples them per-
manently."

"How can it be permanent?" Evan argued. "The effect wears off as soon as you stop drinking."

"Not for the Indian, it doesn't. It is a curse!"

"Have you ever drunk any yourself?"

"No, Promingo will not allow it in our village."

"Then you're talking about something you don't know
anything about," Evan replied.

Evan's know-it-all attitude irritated Fire Dancer.
"No, I *do* know what I am talking about!" she said heat-
edly. "It is the white man's curse on the Indian. It takes
away his pride, cripples him, makes him weak and helpless."

As Fire Dancer rushed off in a huff, Evan stared at
her back. Why did she have to be so stubborn? he
thought in exasperation. Surely he knew more about
rum than she did. It was an Englishman's drink, for
Christ's sake, and the colonists guzzled it like water or,
rather, instead of water. It didn't affect people perma-
nently. In fact, from what he had seen, it had very little
effect at all. Why, even the children drank it.

And why did she have to be so intense about everything? Why couldn't she talk about things that other
women talked about? Then Evan realized that as a
Chickasaw, Fire Dancer didn't attend balls or parties,
didn't know what fashion was, didn't know or care what
the latest scandal was. If the truth were known, most of
the women he had known bored him to tears with their

frivolous, silly talk. But still, he wished Fire Dancer were a little less serious. It seemed that no matter what they talked about, they ended up arguing; she took the Indian point of view and somehow always put him in the position of having to defend the white. It was almost as if she were doing it on purpose, scorning everything the white man did to make him look little, while—dammit—she was half white herself.

Evan was still stewing when they reached the top of the high limestone cliffs and found Promingo waiting for them. The chief conferred briefly with Red Thunder, then dismissed him and the other braves. Turning to Evan, he initiated a conversation with him through Fire Dancer.

Evan informed the chief that he thought they should attack the French fort as soon as possible. He asked how many men the chief could commit to the attack and if the Indians needed more guns and ammunition, in which case he could request that a shipment be sent from Fort Laudoun, the nearest frontier fort. Promingo replied that the Chickasaw had plenty of ammunition, that he could supply fifty warriors himself, and that other Chickasaw tribes wished to be included in the attack and could provide a combined force of roughly another hundred.

Evan didn't particularly like this last—he didn't feel they really needed that large a force. The bigger their war party, the higher the risk that their march through the woods would be discovered, and he was counting heavily on surprising the French. But he was wise enough not to refuse the other tribes' offer, for fear they might take insult and withdraw their support from the British. Besides, he supposed, they wanted to get their licks in against the enemy too. But there was one thing he wanted to clarify. He said to Fire Dancer, "Ask Promingo if the warriors from the other tribes will convene here and march with us, or if we will meet them someplace along the way."

Fire Dancer relayed Evan's question to the chief. After Promingo had answered, she said, "My uncle says he will have them meet his war party at the Chickasaw village we passed through on the Ohio the day before the attack on the French fort."

"Do the Chickasaw have a calendar?" Evan asked Fire Dancer.

Her brow furrowed. "I'm not familiar with that word."

"Do you have a means of measuring days, months, and years?"

"We measure months from one new moon to the next and years from winter to winter."

"But you have no means of measuring days?"

"No."

"Then how will the braves from the other tribes know what day is the day before the attack?"

"Once Promingo has decided the day for the attack, he will send them a rope in which knots have been tied. Each day, a knot will be loosened. The day of the attack is the last knot."

Satisfied that the warriors from the other tribes would show up at the correct time and not delay the attack, Evan said, "Ask Promingo how soon he thinks we can leave."

Fire Dancer passed on Evan's question. Promingo

replied, and she said to Evan, "He said the war party can leave at sunrise five days from now."

"Five days?" Evan was surprised. "Why that long?"

"It will take the runners until tomorrow to reach the other villages. Then the warriors will need three days to prepare themselves. You see, it is our custom for our braves to fast and purify themselves for three days and nights before going to war."

A deep scowl came over Evan's face. "Ask Promingo if we can't forgo that foolishness. I want to attack before the French finish that last wall. If they finish it, we'll never be able to breach the stockade, not without cannons, no matter how many men we have. I saw that happen at Fort Carillon. We'd have to lay siege and starve them out."

Fire Dancer bristled. "It is not foolishness, and I would not dare ask Promingo to forgo the purification rites. He would be furious!"

"It's just going to delay us," Evan argued.

"It is a delay that cannot be helped," Fire Dancer answered firmly. "You will just have to take the risk that the French will complete that wall." Seeing an angry expression come over Evan's face, she quickly added, "And do not blame us for the delay. If anybody is responsible, it is you. You are the one who demanded to see the fort first. If you had taken our word on it, you could be attacking it this very minute."

Evan didn't like Fire Dancer's reminder, even if it was true, and his scowl deepened. Ignoring it, she said, "Promingo says to tell you that you are welcome to join in the purification rites."

Evan wasn't thrilled at the prospect of fasting and

joining in on God only knew what else, but to out-and-out refuse would insult the chief. "Tell him I said thank you, and I'll join for a while, but not the entire three days. I wouldn't want his braves to feel I was intruding on something so personal," Evan answered, hoping his excuse didn't sound too lame.

When Promingo seemed agreeable and nodded, Evan said to Fire Dancer, "There's just one more thing. Ask him to send a runner to Josh with the news of our plans. He promised to join the attack."

Fire Dancer passed Evan's message on to the chief, and as the chief walked away, she relayed Promingo's answer. "He said he would send a runner immediately and that he was glad Josh had agreed to join in the war party. He had been wondering who he could use as an interpreter."

"Well, thank God he isn't planning on sending you again," Evan replied, thinking it had been too dangerous to send Fire Dancer even on the scouting expedition.

But Fire Dancer had no idea that Evan was concerned for her safety, and she misinterpreted his words, thinking he was anxious to be rid of her. Yes, she had been a fool to think he might be seeking her company the night before, she thought bitterly, a fool to begin to hope that he might care for her. It was just as she had suspected in the beginning. He cared only about the physical pleasure her body could give him. That was not enough for her. If only she had the strength to refuse him.

For the second time that day, she turned and walked angrily away, leaving Evan wondering what he had said to rile her this time. She was decidedly cool the rest of the day, but that night she responded to his amorous advances with her usual passion. Long after she had fallen asleep, Evan lay in the dark, staring up at the log rafters in their cabin, deep in thought. He was finally forced to admit that he hadn't mastered Fire Dancer. She was just as independent as she had always been, giving only what she wanted, when she wanted. That she ran hot one minute and cold the next both bewildered and frustrated him. She was like no woman he had ever known, and he feared he was going to rue the day he'd met her. Fire Dancer was one woman he wasn't going to walk away from and easily forget.

Early the next morning, Fire Dancer took Evan to where the purification rites were to be held. From a distance, she pointed out what she called the winter cabin. Above the cabin was a tall pole on which a red and black striped flag flew. Fluttering beneath it was a torn and tattered Union Jack.

Staring in surprise, Evan asked, "Where did you get the British flag?"

"Josh gave it to us. We have flown it ever since."

That explained why it was so weathered, Evan thought. "And the Chickasaw flag? Do you fly it all the time also?"

"No, that is our war flag. We fly it only when our braves are preparing to go to war or are away fighting."

After Fire Dancer had left, Evan closed the distance between himself and the long, narrow cabin. Entering the structure, he saw Promingo and his warriors sitting cross-legged on the ground along each side of the cabin.

The braves had forsaken their buckskin shirts and leggins decorated with turkey cock spurs or fawn trotters tied to their fringes. Today, they were dressed for war, wearing scarlet breechcloths, their bodies slashed with war paint. A few sported breastplates made of bones or pounded copper. On the ground before them, each man had laid his weapons: his long rifle, his bows and arrows, his tomahawk, his scalping knife, and his special weapon for which the Chickasaw were noted—feathered darts with long, needle-sharp points.

Promingo motioned for Evan to be seated, and the Englishman watched as the priests passed out large shells filled with a black drink, chanting *"Yah-O-he-wah"* over and over. Evan expected the bitter drink to have some intoxicating or narcotic effect, but as he and the others drank shellful after shellful, the only effect he could see was that it made his heart race and his body sweat profusely. Not particularly liking what the black drink was doing to him, Evan drank sparingly, but the others guzzled the bitter drink. The sweat poured from their pores as many of them chanted along with the priests, while others mumbled what he assumed to be prayers. By late afternoon, Evan couldn't take it anymore. Not only was he bored to tears, but the chanting was getting on his nerves and the potent caffeine drink made him feel as if he were about to jump out of his skin. He excused himself and left, taking a brisk walk around the town before he returned to the cabin that he shared with Fire Dancer.

Discovering that she was not in the cabin, Evan went looking for her, driven by that strange desire for her company. He found her in the cookhouse, pounding dried kernels of corn into a coarse meal. Since the kernels were white, he assumed it was corn from last fall's crop. When she made no recognition of his presence, he said, "Good afternoon."

Fire Dancer had been pleasantly surprised when Evan agreed to attend the purification rite, but seeing him return too soon was a big disappointment to her. She had hoped he would take the Chickasaw custom to heart and remain the entire time. She refused to delve into why she wanted Evan to be more accepting of the Indians' ways. If she had, she would have realized she wanted him to be more accepting of her. She didn't want him to think of her as a savage and scorn her, as her mother had warned her white men were prone to do.

She set aside the wooden mallet she had been using, scooped up several double handfuls of the meal, and dropped them into a heavy black kettle beside her before she answered, "You are back so soon?"

Evan scowled at the strong hint of disapproval in Fire Dancer's voice. Surely she didn't expect him to stay at that ridiculous ceremony until its end, he thought. Well, if she did, she had another think coming, and his male assertiveness came to the fore. "Yes, I'm back. I saw no point in staying. Nothing was going on but a bunch of senseless chanting and a lot of drinking and sweating. What in the devil is that black drink, anyway?"

"It is a tea made from boiling yaupon leaves, and it is supposed to make you sweat, or so I have heard. That is how it cleanses the body and purifies the soul. And it wasn't senseless chanting. The priests were invoking the Great Spirit's protection in the upcoming battle."

Evan knew by her outraged tone that she had taken offense at his words. For a moment, he had completely forgotten she was Indian. He should have known better than to criticize their customs, he thought, particularly when they entailed religion. He cursed himself for a fool. Then something Fire Dancer had said caught his attention. "Why do you say you have only heard it makes you sweat?"

"I mean that I don't know what goes on at the purification rite in preparation for war. No woman does. It is taboo for us to be anywhere around it or for the men to discuss it with us. We aren't even allowed to be anywhere around when the priests are brewing the tea, although we gather the yaupon leaves."

Evan was surprised that the men kept the women away, since the women held such a strong position in the tribe otherwise. Apparently, the men had retained an age-old belief that war is a strictly male concern, and Evan heartily agreed with this. There was no place in waging war for women and their tender emotions. But Evan was curious about something. "If it's taboo for the men to even talk about it, how do you know about the purpose of the sweating and the chanting?"

"Because inducing sweating and chanting are a part of other rites, too, and they include women, although we use the sweathouses."

"What rites?"

"The Green Corn ceremony in the spring, for one. That is when we celebrate and give thanks for our successful harvest."

Evan had heard of this thanksgiving that the Indians practiced. Some of the settlers in the New England colonies had started to adopt the custom too. But now his concentration shifted from what Fire Dancer said to the cold tone of her voice. God, he thought, she could freeze hell over if she put her mind to it, and he hadn't come looking for a fight. Hoping to soothe her anger, he changed the subject. "What are you cooking?"

"*Sofki*. It's a corn soup."

Fire Dancer poured about a bucketful of water onto the meal, and as she started to lift the kettle to put it on the fire, Evan stepped forward and said, "Let me do that for you."

"That's not necessary," Fire Dancer answered coldly. "Indian women are accustomed to lifting heavy objects."

Evan was well aware of that. He had seen Indian women lift and carry loads that would have made a white man stagger. He sighed, striving very hard for patience. "I know that, but I'd still like to do it."

"Why?"

Evan ground his teeth. Damn! he thought. Did she have to challenge him on everything? "Because in my country that is how a gentleman treats a lady."

A lady? Fire Dancer thought. Yes, her mother had told her about ladies. They were women who were very highly thought of. A little thrill ran through her. But her mother had also told her ladies were weak, selfish creatures who expected others to wait on them hand and foot, hardly someone she would want to be.

Fire Dancer shoved Evan's outstretched arm aside. "Well, I am not a lady," she said, "and I do not want your help." As she turned her back to him and lifted the kettle, Evan rolled his eyes in exasperation.

"And I do not want you in my kitchen either," she added over her shoulder. "You are only in the way."

Her rebuke felt like a slap in the face. Evan turned on his heel and left the cookhouse, feeling once again bewildered, frustrated, and a little angry himself.

13

The next morning, Fire Dancer announced to Evan that their horses had been returned from where they had left them beside the Ohio, and she told him where he could find his stallion. He was happy at the news and looked forward to his old friend's companionship, particularly after Fire Dancer's cold treatment.

Evan hurried across the settlement and found his mount hobbled in an open grassy clearing along with the motley Chickasaw herd. The Indians must have pushed the horses hard to get them back in that short a time, but he was still shocked by his stallion's appearance. It wasn't the animal's coat that dismayed him— other than being splattered with dried mud and covered with burrs, the hair hadn't lost that much luster. But the Thoroughbred was absolutely exhausted and looked as if it might keel over at any minute, while the tough little Chickasaw horses looked as if they had never left their lazy grazing.

Evan spent the morning grooming his horse, and in

the afternoon he broke apart his rifle and meticulously cleaned it and sharpened his saber. He was determined not to seek out Fire Dancer, who had once again made herself scarce. If she didn't want his company, then that was just fine with him, he thought. He'd never forced himself on anyone. To the contrary. Women had always pursued him so much that Evan went out of his way to avoid *them*.

But the next day Evan found himself with nothing to do but pace the cabin restlessly. When Fire Dancer walked in, picked up a basket, and started for the door, he asked, "Where are you going?"

"To a pond near here to gather *wapato*, duck potatoes."

Evan didn't bother to give a reply, since none was required. He simply nodded his head, determined not to ask if he could join her and risk being repulsed again.

But Fire Dancer had seen his electric-blue eyes light up when she walked into the room—a sight that would be enough to make any woman's heart skip a beat—and then the disappointment on his face when he saw her leaving. Maybe he did enjoy her company, she thought, or perhaps he was just lonely. Regardless, something about his look, a certain yearning, tore at her heart, and she asked, "Would you like to come along?"

It took all of Evan's willpower to rise gracefully from the low couch where he was sitting and not jump to his feet in joy. "Yes, thank you, I would."

They walked through the town, past the palisade, then through the dark woods where the smell of honeysuckle hung heavy in the air. Thick roots jutting from the ground made their path treacherous. As the trees thinned out, Evan saw the small, shallow lake that was their destination. The water in the center sparkled in the bright sunlight, and the tree-shaded ground around the edges was covered with spikes of beautiful little blue-violet flowers. Staring in admiration, he paid no attention to where he was stepping, until Fire Dancer caught his arm and pulled him back. "Be careful!"

Evan glanced around, then looked down. A fluffy, speckled duckling stood in his path. "Where did that come from?" he asked.

"From the hole up in that tree," Fire Dancer answered, pointing to a tall, nearby oak. "That's where their nest is."

"But it's a duck. Ducks don't built nests in trees."

"Wood ducks do."

"It fell out?" Evan assumed it had, since the duckling was obviously too young to fly.

"No, it deliberately jumped out. Its mother whistled for it to do so. There she is, over there," Fire Dancer said, nodding toward the woods to one side of them, "with the rest of her brood."

Evan saw the mother wood duck and her ducklings beneath an ostrich fern. She waited until the duckling in the path waddled over to her, then led her brood away to the lake, the baby ducks falling into line behind her and quacking noisily. The nest in the tree where the duckling had been was a good fifteen feet up. "It's a wonder it didn't break its neck," he remarked.

"Yes," Fire Dancer agreed, "but even more amazing is the way the baby ducks take to water. They go in without the slightest hesitation, and they swim as if they'd been doing so all their lives. The mother doesn't even have to teach them."

They walked to the edge of the pool, where Fire Dancer stripped off her moccasins and, carrying her basket, waded in. Evan frowned. "I thought you said you were going to dig for potatoes."

She stopped beside a three-petaled white lily growing in the marshy shallows. "That's what I'm doing. The duck potato is the root of this arrow lily, and I'm digging it up with my toes."

A second later, a piece of white, thick root floated to the surface of the lake. Fire Dancer picked it up and placed it in her basket. Then she moved to another lily and did the same.

Evan was amazed at this novel way of harvesting food. "What are you going to use those for?"

"To make a different kind of ash cake."

If they were anything as tasty as the corn ash cakes she made, it would be well worth the work, he thought. He sat on the ground at the edge of the pond, content to watch Fire Dancer dig up the potatoes. He watched with amusement as a lazy, heavy-lidded bullfrog sat on a lily pad, patiently waiting for a dragonfly to fly by, the duckweed draped over its shoulder looking like a green cloak. Then he observed the ducks, who were also harvesting the potato. Their heads darted beneath the surface of the water, then bobbed back up with a tasty piece of root in their yellow bills.

A sudden urge came over Evan. He slipped off his high moccasins, rolled up his pants, rose, and waded into the pond. He didn't particularly relish the feel of the mud squishing between his toes, but if Fire Dancer could contend with it, so could he. He made his way to where she stood, passing several golden lotus blossoms sitting several inches above the water on their strong stalks.

Fire Dancer hadn't noticed him stripping off his moccasins and wading in. She was occupied with watching the mother wood duck and her brood of ducklings swim across the pond. A male wood duck had joined them, and his iridescent green, bronze, blue, and purple feathers shimmered in the bright sunlight and made the brown-and-white-speckled mother duck look dowdy in comparison. When a sudden shadow fell over her, she turned to see Evan standing beside her. "What are you doing here?" she asked in surprise.

Evan shrugged his broad shoulders. "I thought I'd help you. Tell me what to do."

Fire Dancer had not expected Evan to make such an offer—it was something a Chickasaw male would never dream of doing. Chickasaw men prepared the fields for planting, and they might dig for clams or mussels if no women were around, but they didn't dig in the dirt, much less the mud, for roots. That was definitely women's work. Taken aback, she didn't know what to say.

Seeing her hesitation, Evan grinned. "I know I probably won't be much good, but I'd like to give it a try."

It was the grin that did it. It was so open and appealing, so totally irresistible, that Fire Dancer felt a warm glow come over her and a strange little twisting feeling in her chest. She couldn't refuse but smiled back and said, "Dig your toes into the mud until you feel the root. Then just keep working at it until you've broken off a piece."

Evan did as Fire Dancer had directed him. It was harder than it had appeared. He found the root readily enough, but breaking it took some real grinding and a lot of concentration. Then she laughed, and Evan froze. The only other time she had openly laughed around him had been during their race, and it was such a beautiful sound, such a clear joyous sound, that it made his blood sing and his spirits soar.

"I'm sorry I laughed at you," Fire Dancer said when Evan stood perfectly still and stared at her. "But you looked so silly standing there in the water, twisting your hips."

Evan imagined he did look silly. Fire Dancer twisted her hips, too, but she did so with female grace. Still, he didn't take offense. He felt too relaxed and carefree. He laughed himself, a spontaneous rumbling that began deep in his chest, then reached his lips. It did strange things to her. "I imagine I did look ridiculous," he admitted. The root he had been working to free suddenly gave way and broke the surface. He pointed to it. "But I got results," he added.

As Evan reached for the root, which was floating away, he slipped on the muddy bottom. He would have fallen flat on his face if Fire Dancer hadn't caught his arm and righted him. The incident made them both laugh again.

They spent the next thirty minutes laughing at each other, twisting their hips to loosen the roots. It became a game to see who could come up with the most ridiculous gyrations. Even when Fire Dancer's basket was full to the brim, they continued to dig. When a crafty duck sneaked up on them and swiped a potato from the basket, it sent them into fresh gales of laughter.

Evan picked a potato from the basket and tossed it to a nearby flock of ducks. A mad scramble followed, with a lot of wing flapping and loud honking and quacking. Fire Dancer did the same, with the same results. By the time the two had given away at least half of their potatoes, they were surrounded by noisy ducks, and Evan had to throw a piece far across the pond for the couple to be able to wade ashore.

As they walked back to the village, still feeling light-hearted and gay, Fire Dancer marveled at the way Evan had behaved. He hadn't been at all arrogant. Rather, he had shown her a new, totally unexpected side to his personality, one that she very much liked.

Without either of them realizing it, Evan had bonded Fire Dancer to him in a manner that far surpassed all of his torrid lovemaking. He had reached out and touched her heart.

The next morning, Evan was awakened by a knocking on the door. Muttering a curse, he rose from the bed where he and Fire Dancer were sleeping, groped across the dark cabin, and opened the door. There, standing in the predawn light, was Josh.

"Well, it's about time you got here!" Evan whispered irritably. "What took you so long? When you didn't show up last night, I began to worry."

"About me?" Josh asked in surprise.

"Hell, no! You can take care of yourself. I was worrying about who was going to be my interpreter."

"There wasn't any need to worry. I knew ye wouldn't be leavin' until this morning. Didn't see any need to get here any sooner."

Evan still wished the frontiersman had shown up sooner. Then maybe he'd have gotten a decent night's sleep, instead of worrying that Promingo might take Fire Dancer along to interpret. "Well, I'm not sure we're leaving this morning," he growled.

"What do ye mean by that?"

"Shh! Keep your voice down," Evan whispered, glancing over his shoulder to where Fire Dancer slept. When Josh craned his neck to look over his shoulder, Evan said in a hard voice, "I'll be with you as soon as I get some clothes on."

A second later, the door was rudely shut in Josh's face. He grinned. He knew Evan hadn't invited him in because there was a naked woman in his bed, and that woman had to be Fire Dancer. Apparently the two had settled their differences.

A moment later, Evan stepped from the cabin, and as they walked together he said, "We're supposed to leave today, but I seriously doubt that these warriors will be in any condition to travel. They've been fasting for three days and nights."

"Oh, they'll be able to travel, all right," Josh assured him. "They don't need food. They feed off of their excitement."

"Well, I hope their excitement gets them through the day. I'd hate like hell to have to stop in the middle of the day and make camp. At least they won't be dehydrated, not the way they've been guzzling that black drink. They were putting it away by the gallons."

Josh stopped in his tracks. "Ye were there?"

"Yes. Promingo asked me to join in. Why are you surprised?"

"Because it's a rite reserved for men who have proven their courage. Not just any brave can participate, and I've never heard of a white man being asked. But I reckon Promingo thought ye'd earned the privilege, since ye're an officer. He doesn't know that British officers buy their commissions. He thinks they're like subchiefs, that they have to prove their bravery under fire before they can hold a position of command."

Evan didn't bother to point out that he'd earned his present rank. True, he'd originally bought his commission, that of a lowly lieutenant. But he had earned his rank as major the hard way—on the battlefield. He didn't bother pointing this out to Josh because he knew the frontiersman scorned him. The only way to overcome that scorn would be to prove the hard-headed Scot wrong, just as he'd had to prove himself to the Scots in the Blackwatch Regiment he'd commanded.

But if Evan felt no need to defend himself, he did regret having learned belatedly that the invitation to attend the rites had been a privilege extended to few white men. And he had belittled it to Fire Dancer! No wonder she had been so angry with him.

"I didn't realize it was an honor," Evan admitted. "If I had, maybe I would have stayed longer than one day. But that bitter drink with no food was making me jumpy and nauseated."

"Yeah, well, I do reckon yer stomach was rubbin' against yer backbone, and I've heard if ye drink enough of that stuff, it can make ye see and hear things that aren't there. That's why they drink so much, ye know, hopin' for a vision. At least, that's what one of my wife's relatives confided to me."

Fire Dancer hadn't told Evan this—she'd only said the ritual was taboo to women. "If they have another ceremony like that when we get back, I'll try to last a little longer," he said, still feeling somewhat ashamed.

"Ye won't have to worry about that. If we're victorious, the Chickasaw will dance and feast, and burn and torture a captive or two, but there'll be no drinkin' of that black tea. And thank God the Chickasaw aren't cannibals, like some of those Canadian tribes the French have aligned 'emselves with. They expect the French officers who fight with 'em to eat the flesh of their captives right along with 'em, and the poor bastards do."

Evan was horrified. He could suffer through drinking more of the bitter yaupon tea, but he could never eat human flesh. That would be carrying duty entirely too far. Nor could he stand by and watch captives being tortured and burned to death.

"There won't be any captives," Evan answered in a steely voice.

"How do ye know that?"

"Because you and I are going to see to it. There won't be any survivors to bring back and torture. That's one thing I can't stomach."

"How are we goin' to keep 'em from takin' prisoners?"

"Anytime we see a warrior taking a man alive, that poor bastard is going to be accidentally shot by one of us."

"If the Chickasaw figure out what we're doin', they're goin' to be mad as hornets."

"That's a risk we'll have to take," Evan answered, then walked away.

Josh stared at Evan's departing broad back in dismay and shook his head in disgust. Of all of the officers for the British to send for this mission, he thought, why did they have to pick one with principles? Hell, if they did what Evan proposed, they might well be killed themselves by the Chickasaw. Wishing he had found an excuse not to join in this raid, Josh halfheartedly followed the major.

Shortly after sunrise, the warriors emerged from the winter cabin. Just as Josh had predicted, they showed no signs of weakness from their three-day fast. After a quick breakfast, they mounted their horses, and following Promingo at the head of the file, they left the village, whooping boisterously and firing their rifles into the air.

Evan and Josh brought up the rear. Just before they passed through the opening in the palisade, Evan reined in, turned in his saddle, and searched the crowd of well-wishers who had followed the war party to the forest. He spied Fire Dancer among them, but somehow he sensed that she would be angry if he showed her any public affection, and he fought back his urge to blow her a kiss good-bye. But knowing that she had cared enough to follow, a warmth suffused him, and as their eyes met and held, he smiled, then waved.

*   *   *

Fire Dancer's grandmother, Eastern Star, stood at
the back of the crowd, remaining aloof as she always
did, which was one reason Fire Dancer never confided
in the old woman and rarely visited her—she had never
felt comfortable around the tribe's stern matriarch.
Eastern Star had heard that Promingo had given Fire
Dancer to the Englishman for his mistress while he was
with them. That did not disturb her—it was Chickasaw
custom. But she was curious about the man her granddaughter was spending so much time with, and the
town gathering to see the war party off gave her a good
opportunity to scrutinize him. What she saw impressed
her. The Englishman was not only very masculine and
physically appealing, but he seemed to have a strength
of character, a wisdom, a courage about him that she
had seen only in the best of chiefs. When the English
officer had smiled and waved to Fire Dancer, the old
woman wondered just how deeply involved her granddaughter was with the white man. Eastern Star didn't
understand the meaning of the wave. That was an European custom. But she did understand the smile the Englishman bestowed on her granddaughter. There was
about it a warmness, a closeness that surpassed physical
intimacy.

Alarmed, she glanced at Fire Dancer to see her reaction. It would never do for her successor to give her
heart to a man she could never marry, no matter how
exceptional he might be. That would lead to a miserable
life for the young woman, and although Eastern Star
never showed it, she did care deeply for the girl. Seeing
the stony expression on her granddaughter's face, the
old woman sighed in relief, thanking the Great Spirit

that Fire Dancer had enough sense to not to succumb to the Englishman's considerable appeal. The old woman turned and walked back to her cabin.

Fire Dancer's grandmother never knew how difficult it had been for Fire Dancer to put that stony expression on her face and maintain it. It had taken all her fierce will to keep from smiling and waving back, but she had been well aware that everyone in the tribe was watching. She had also been aware of Evan's disappointment when she had not responded to his farewell. The look on his face had torn at her heart. Not until the war party had disappeared in the forest did she turn and walk to her cabin, feeling very lonely.

The next couple of weeks seemed like an eternity to Fire Dancer. Each moment was like an hour; each hour, a day; each day, a year. She had never realized how lonely she had been since her mother had died. Evan had filled that terrible void for her, and more. In his presence, life had taken on a new, deeper meaning, and everything had seemed bright and beautiful.

She discovered that she not only missed his company, she yearned for his lovemaking. Every night, she lay in their bed, tormented by his lingering scent in the furs, her body aching for his touch. He had awakened dormant physical needs in her for which there was now no relief. Each morning after a night of tossing and turning, she had awakened feeling twice as tired as she had the night before.

Then, when her loneliness entered its third week, and everyone in the village began to speculate on why the war party hadn't yet returned, a new emotion took precedence over loneliness and physical yearning: fear.

Fire Dancer had never worried about anyone before, not the way she now worried about her English lover. She fretted night and day, unable to keep her mind on anything but her fear for Evan. What was delaying the war party? she wondered. Had the French finished the wall, as Evan had feared they would, and had the Chickasaw party been forced to lay siege? Or had the battle been fought and lost? Was Evan dead? Or worse yet, had he been captured alive, and was he at that very moment being horribly tortured?

The last was an unbearable thought for Fire Dancer, one that she didn't dare contemplate. She forced herself to think that the war party had laid siege.

On the nineteenth day, during the noonday silence when the townspeople napped in the heat of the day, the sound of gunshots brought everyone to their feet, followed by the frantic barking of the town dogs. Hearing the victorious singing of *Yo-He-Wah* over the dogs' barks, the townspeople rushed from their houses to greet the returning warriors as they paraded through the streets, carrying their fresh scalps on small branches of evergreens. Curiously, there were no captives with blue lines marked on their chest and arms to show they had been picked for burning. There were no captives at all.

When Fire Dancer reached the town square, she stood on her tiptoes and craned her neck, trying to see Evan in the milling crowd of warriors and excited spectators. But he was nowhere to be seen. She turned and peered in the direction the warriors had come from but saw only the dust cloud they had raised when they marched through the dry streets. Fear like none she had ever had seized her. She couldn't breathe, and an icy hand seemed to have clutched her heart.

Then she heard someone say her Chickasaw name. She turned to see Black Hawk grinning broadly. "I assume you are looking for the Englishman," he said in Chickasaw.

Surely he couldn't be dead, Fire Dancer thought, if her cousin was looking so happy. But her fear was still so strong she could hardly get the word past her lips: "Yes."

"He is with the rear guard. They will arrive shortly."

An immense wave of relief swept over Fire Dancer, and her legs were suddenly so weak, they threatened to buckle beneath her. She swayed, and Black Hawk reached out and steadied her.

"What took you so long to return?" Fire Dancer asked when she had recovered.

"The French had moved in a cannon and placed it in the breach between the unfinished walls. It had a longer range than our guns, and they held us at bay for days."

"Then how did you defeat them?"

"Some of the warriors from the other villages grew restless and angry. They rushed the fort without Promingo giving the order. It was a very foolish thing to do. When they were about halfway between us and the cannon, the French fired it at them and killed all but one of them, and he was wounded. Then two Shawnee came from the fort to take the wounded man captive, and we knew they were going to torture him within sight of the rest of us to torment us. We were all furious, but no one was as furious as the Englishman. He jumped to his feet and charged."

Black Hawk paused, shook his head, then continued. "I have never seen anything like it, Fire Dancer. The Englishman was fierce, snarling like a wild animal, and his eyes shot sparks. He didn't even take his gun with him. He left it behind and was waving that long knife the British officers carry over his head. One of the Shawnee had a rifle with him. He crouched behind a tree stump and fired it. The Englishman was running like a mad dog, weaving back and forth, and the bullet missed. Seeing him still coming, the Shawnee turned and ran."

"And then?" Fire Dancer was wholly caught up with the story. "What happened then?"

"The French turned the cannon directly on the Englishman and fired it. He was at so close a range, we all thought it must have killed him. But then the Englishman came like a streak of lightning from the cloud of smoke and ran right past the wounded Chickasaw and up to the French gun crew. I have never seen anyone use a knife the way the Englishman used his long knife. He felled three men as if they were no more than saplings. The other two turned to run, and we saw that victory was ours. Promingo didn't have to order us to attack—we rushed in."

Again Black Hawk paused, his black eyes sparkling with excitement. "The Englishman is a very brave warrior, the bravest I have ever seen. He fought like a demon that day. He would make a great war chief—except for one thing. He didn't leave any of the enemy alive to take captive. But still, I would follow him into battle any day, and many of the others say the same."

The Englishman had covered himself in glory. Fire Dancer sidestepped her cousin and headed for the landing. Before she could reach the woods, she saw the Chickasaw rear guard and Evan coming from the forest, his golden hair gleaming in the bright sunlight.

Spying her, Evan stopped in his tracks, and she, too, came to a halt. Their eyes met across the distance that separated them, and Evan held her by sheer eye contact until the others had rushed past her. Then a slow smile spread across his handsome face, a face that was still smudged with gunpowder.

Fire Dancer's insides felt as if they were melting. As Evan walked toward her with that confident swagger that was so much a part of him, an incredible joy swept over her. It was then that Fire Dancer realized that she had fallen in love with him. Somehow or other, the irritating, arrogant Englishman had slipped past her defenses and captured her heart.

14

The next morning, Evan was sitting on one of the three-legged stools in the cabin. Hunched over a chest, he was struggling to write his report to his commanding officer.

"What are you doing?"

He was startled by the sound of Fire Dancer's voice. She had been sound asleep when he left the bed, even though it was midmorning and sunshine was streaming through the open windows. He turned to face her. Propped on one arm, with her long black hair hanging around her like a silken cloak, her seductive green eyes heavy lidded from sleep, and her luscious lips still swollen from his torrid kisses the night before, she looked very inviting. He was tempted to put down his pen and rejoin her.

"I'm writing a report to my commanding officer."

With great reluctance, he turned his attention back to the task at hand. When he heard the soft padding of Fire Dancer's feet on the floor, he looked up, and his breath caught in his throat at the sight of her walking toward him totally nude. Desire rose in him, hot and heavy, and he clenched his teeth in an effort to fight it down.

Fire Dancer stopped beside him and looked down at the parchment. "What is *writing*?"

Evan forced himself to focus his attention on her question and not the lustrous curls at the junction of her thighs, a tempting sight that was level with his eyes from his low position on the stool. God, how he longed to kiss her there, taste her intoxicating honey. With almost superhuman effort, he turned away and picked up his quill pen. "It's a means of communicating with others without being present ourselves and, for that reason, is particularly handy in communicating over long distances. We put letters together to form words by drawing the shape of the letters with a pen."

Evan remembered Fire Dancer's mother. "Didn't your mother ever mention writing? Did you never see her write?"

"No, but who would she write to, and for what purpose? I told you, she was content here with the Chickasaw."

It was a valid point, one that once again revealed Fire Dancer's powers of logic. Evan felt a little silly that he hadn't thought of it himself, but it put him no closer to solving the puzzle of who Fire Dancer's mother had been.

As Evan wrote, Fire Dancer watched him form the tiny letters. She figured out on her own that the empty spaces were breaks between words. She was amazed that someone a long distance away would be able to look at the parchment and know what it said, or rather what Evan was saying.

Evan saw the rapt expression on Fire Dancer's face and realized she was fascinated. It pleased him that something from the white world had impressed her for a change, and he wished that she could see more of its better qualities. Then maybe she would stop thinking of herself as pure Chickasaw and acknowledge her white blood with pride. Once that had happened, maybe she would see him in a different light.

"Why did you stop writing?"

"What?" Evan asked, startled from his thoughts. "I was just thinking."

"Thinking about what?"

"Thinking about what I'm going to write next," he answered evasively. Then he turned halfway to her in his seat and looked up.

Fire Dancer felt the effect of those electric-blue eyes clear to her toes. Suddenly she became aware of his bare chest with its golden mat of hair and the powerful muscles on his shoulders. Her mouth turned dry with desire and she asked in a husky voice, "Can't it wait?"

Evan's heart raced and beat like a wild tom-tom in his chest, and he answered her in a croak. "No, I'm afraid not." Then he turned away from the temptation, saying, "Josh is going back east on business, and he'll deliver this if I have it ready by the time he leaves this morning. It's very important that my commanding officer know the result of our attack as soon as possible."

Again, Evan bent over his letter, thinking that he had never known duty to be so hard. But to his utter frustration, he couldn't remember what he had intended to write next. Seeing Fire Dancer step away from his peripheral vision, he sighed in relief, thinking that if she put distance between them, he might be able to concentrate.

But Fire Dancer had not walked away. She had just stepped behind Evan. She bent over him, her long hair falling around them both like a shimmering black curtain. She ran her hands down the length of his arms, then knelt behind him and dropped her hands to his lap.

Evan froze as she boldly cupped his manhood in her hand; a fine sheen of perspiration broke out on his forehead. "Later, Fire Dancer," he muttered. "I have—"

"Shh," Fire Dancer answered, running her tongue along one muscular shoulder. "Your writing can wait. I want you, Englishman."

For once Evan didn't object to Fire Dancer calling him "Englishman," for her voice had dropped to a seductive timbre that made his blood turn to liquid fire in his veins. Nor could he object to her interrupting his letter. He was putty in her hands as she undid the laces on his pants, and her fingers teasingly brushed his heated skin as she moved lower and lower. Then as his manhood sprung free, long and full and proud, she took him in her hands.

Evan groaned, and the pen fell from his hand, leaving a fine spattering of ink over the parchment. It was agony for him to sit while Fire Dancer ran her hand up and down his length and dropped feathery kisses on his shoulders, the hard points of her breasts brushing back and forth across his back. When he felt as if he were about to burst, he pushed his pants down past his knees, then shoved her hand aside and rose.

When he turned, Fire Dancer looked up from where she was still kneeling on the floor. As the bright sunlight streamed in the windows, every tiny little hair on his powerful body glistened, making him look as if he had been sprinkled with gold dust. The thick hair on his head was so brilliant that it looked as if a halo surrounded it. His eyes were blazing with desire and so blue, they were indigo. Fire Dancer stared at him with awe, thinking he looked absolutely magnificent, more godlike than human. She remembered that the Natchez had worshipped the sun, had spoken of it as a powerful god clothed in a golden mantle. Surely this was the Natchez sun god standing before her, fierce, proud, powerful, golden, and utterly beautiful. And for the time being, he was hers. She opened her arms to him.

Evan was more than willing to accept Fire Dancer's silent invitation, but he was too aroused to carry her to the bed. Instead, he lowered her to the bearskin rug behind her and, without preamble, entered her warm depths with a powerful thrust. Fire Dancer was ready for him, for she needed no further priming. She locked her arms and legs around him and dug her nails into the hard muscles on his back, his man scent and wild urgency exciting her all the more. She gloried in her virile lover and let the sun god she held so tightly in her arms take her to his heaven, where he bathed her in golden light and showered her with glittering stardust from a million bursting stars.

◦ ◦ ◦

The days that followed, when Evan waited to hear his commanding officer's response to his report, were a special time that Fire Dancer would treasure for the rest of the life. Once she admitted to herself that she had fallen in love with Evan, she was forced to face a hard, cruel fact: He would leave her when his business was finished, and their paths would never cross again. But she was not a woman to mope over what appeared to be a bleak future. She was much too practical to waste the present fretting about what tomorrow might, or might not, bring. She decided that she would enjoy her limited time with Evan to the fullest and store every memory away as if she were collecting items for a treasure chest. For once he walked out of her life, she knew that was all she would have of him—her memories, and they would have to sustain her for a lifetime.

Evan enjoyed their idyllic time together, too, although he didn't delve as deeply as Fire Dancer did into the reasons for it. He only knew that she was the most exciting mistress he'd ever had, and it had been far too long since he had taken time out from his military duties to really enjoy life and all its pleasures. He did sense a change in her, though. It wasn't just that she was as likely as he to initiate their lovemaking. He attributed her aggressiveness in that manner to her passionate Chickasaw nature. And she was just as argumentative if she thought she was right about something. For that reason, Evan went out of his way to avoid subjects that might end in disagreements between them. He didn't want to risk shattering the fragile new relationship they seemed to be developing. No, the change he sensed was something subtler, something he couldn't put his finger on. She seemed more amicable to him, and softer.

For a month, the two were almost constant companions. Evan even tagged along with her when she went to the fields to do her share of the labor, even though his presence was rather conspicuous. Chickasaw men cleared the fields, broke the ground, built the tall mounds of dirt on which the crops were planted, and took part in the harvest, but it was the women, children, and older members of the tribe who planted, weeded, and watered the crops. But Evan actually helped carry buckets of water from the river to the thirsty plants, and he became so accustomed to helping that he came to love the fragrant smell of the corn as much as the Indians. He even became accustomed to Fire Dancer stripping off her buckskin mantle and working bare-breasted.

One day when they were walking from the fields, Evan asked, "Why isn't your face tattooed like the other women's?"

"My mother said it wasn't necessary, that the Great Spirit had tattooed me himself."

He frowned. "How is that?"

She stopped and faced him, then ran a finger over her upper cheeks and the bridge of her nose. "See."

Evan saw a faint sprinkling of freckles, brought out by the sun. For a moment he thought to tell her that those were not tattoo marks but freckles, common among the English, but he decided against it. Apparently, Fire Dancer's mother hadn't wanted her daughter's beauty to be marred by the ugly bluish tattoos and had claimed she had already been marked to spare her

that. Evan heartily agreed. Fire Dancer's freckles were
appealing, but there was nothing attractive about the
tattoos—at least, not in his estimation. No, he wouldn't
give away the English captive's little ploy. "Of course. I
forgot about them."

As they continued their walk, Evan bit back a laugh at
how gullible Fire Dancer and others had been. He had
discovered something about Fire Dancer's mother in
the exchange. The English captive had been clever and
apparently not in total agreement with everything the
Indians did, as Fire Dancer was prone to make him
believe. He hoped the English in Fire Dancer was
stronger than she thought.

On several occasions, Evan was asked to go hunting
with the other men. On the most exciting of these, they
killed a ferocious bear. The Chickasaw revered the bear
even above the eagle and used its oil liberally in their
religious ceremonies, as well as for cooking and, scented
with wild cinnamon and sassafras, as a hairdressing.

The evening after the bear hunt, Black Hawk came
calling. He had done so frequently in this time, and
Evan had encouraged the visits. Evan was almost certain that General Amherst was going to command him
to investigate the French settlements in the area, particularly the fort known at Saint Louis, and he was determined not to take Fire Dancer as an interpreter again.
Black Hawk's visits gave Evan an opportunity to teach
him more English, and he had been very pleased with
the brave's progress. If Josh bowed out, he might be
able to use Black Hawk to interpret.

But on this particular evening, Black Hawk came because Fire Dancer was roasting the haunch of a bear his bullet had killed that day. He and Evan sat on the bearskin rug in the middle of the cabin, while Fire Dancer brought in the food from the cookhouse. As she set a large wooden mug in front of Black Hawk, he sighed, saying, "Ah, my favorite. *Sofki!*"

Evan had become fond of the slightly sour corn soup himself. He was always amazed by its deep yellow color. The ground corn from which it was made was white, and the soup didn't turn golden until the lye water, made from leaching ashes with water, was added.

Fire Dancer set wooden bowls of roasted bear meat before both men and at her own place. A moment later, she brought a tray with bowls of steamed corn, baked squash, and steamed wild artichokes, and a basket of ash cakes.

As she placed them in the center of the bearskin, Black Hawk snatched an ash cake from the basket. "And this is my second favorite!"

Up until recently, the ash cakes had been Evan's favorite, too, but since he had returned from the attack on the French fort, Fire Dancer had been making another dish frequently that had taken his fancy. When he saw her coming into the cabin carrying a kettle, he felt a deep pleasure in knowing that she had cooked it that evening.

When Fire Dancer lifted the heavy cast-iron lid on the kettle, Evan reached for one of the steaming corn husk rolls and peeled the husk away to reveal the baked mash that had been made from pounded corn and chestnuts. He tossed it into his mouth, savoring the taste of the mash and the spicy bean mixture within.

Back in England, kidney pie had been his favorite, but it didn't compare with this. As he reached for another husk, he became aware of Black Hawk and Fire Dancer watching him. He grinned. "In case you haven't already guessed, this is my favorite. At least for the time being," he added. "I'll have to be honest with you both." His eyes met Fire Dancer's. "I've never eaten such delicious food as what Fire Dancer has fed me here. It's impossible to really pick a favorite."

Evan had been lavish in his compliments of Fire Dancer's beauty, but he had never before complimented her on her accomplishments, something that she felt she had more control over than how she looked. She was extremely pleased by his praise, so much so that she felt sudden, unexplainable tears. She dropped her eyes so that Evan couldn't see, an action Black Hawk wrongly attributed to modesty and that Evan thought strange. He sensed her vulnerability at the moment.

Black Hawk observed the couple as they all fell silent eating. There was a radiance about Fire Dancer that he had never seen before, and a look of contentment about the Englishman. Black Hawk was no fool. Despite his youth, he knew the two were falling in love. Nor did he mistake love for desire. He'd been present at times when their physical attraction had been so strong, he could almost feel the electric current passing between them, could almost smell their hot desire. Tonight it was different.

The three had just finished eating and had settled down on the low couches that sat about the cabin when a knock came on the door. Evan glanced at Fire Dancer with a puzzled look on his face, then rose and opened the door. Josh was standing there.

At the surprised expression on Evan's face, Josh laughed. "I see ye weren't expectin' me back so soon," he said.

"Well, no, I wasn't," Evan admitted. "It's been only a month since you left. It took the two of us almost that long just to get out here. How did you manage to travel both ways in such a short time?"

"Ye forgot I was ridin' a Chickasaw horse." Josh strode into the cabin and greeted both Black Hawk and Fire Dancer.

"I didn't know you had a Chickasaw horse," Evan commented. "What happened to your bay horse?"

"My everlaster? He was good, but he didn't have the speed or endurance of a Chickasaw. I finally talked one of my wife's kin here in this village into tradin' with me. Of course, it wasn't an even trade. I had to trade two rifles along with my bay. Pennsylvania rifles. He wouldn't settle for anything but the best."

"But still, you got back awfully quick," Evan remarked. "Didn't you wait for General Amherst's answer to my missive?"

"Nay, I have his answer. He was in Williamsburg."

"What in the devil was he doing in the capital of Virginia? The fighting is going on up north."

"Pitt has recalled Governor Dinwiddie, and I say good riddance. He was the biggest bumbler the colony ever had."

Evan was in agreement. In the brief discussion he'd had with the governor of Virginia, he'd quickly seen that although the man thought himself a military genius, what Dinwiddie knew about military tactics he could have put in the eye of a needle and still have had room for the thread. Yes, the British Army could well do without him and his interference. However . . . "That still doesn't explain what General Amherst is doing in Virginia."

"Well, it's like this. Pitt was so pleased with General Amherst turnin' the war around that he appointed him governor of Virginia. Amherst came down to have a look at the colony, but he made it very clear to me that he wasn't goin' to stay in the colonies after the war is over. He said he'd turn the governin' over to a lieutenant."

Evan wasn't surprised. He knew General Amherst could hardly wait to get back to his beloved estate in England. In that respect, he and the general had a lot in common. But there was something Evan didn't understand. "What happened that turned the war around?"

"Well, for one thing, Fort Duquesne has fallen. They're callin' it Fort Pitt now."

"That's not news. That happened last year!"

"Aye, but it took a while for the news to get to Pitt, ye know." Josh paused with a thoughtful expression on his face. "Do ye suppose that's why the prime minister named Amherst governor of Virginia? Because Amherst renamed Fort Duquesne after him?"

"Amherst didn't name Fort Pitt," Evan informed the Scot. "It was suggested by a Virginian named George Washington." Evan continued in a disgusted voice, "Christ, Josh! Why did you come in here getting me all excited about turning the war around? Like I said, that happened last year."

"Aye, but I haven't told ye what's happened this year

yet." Josh paused in order to make his announcement more dramatic. "We've taken Fort Carillon."

It was at Fort Carillon that the British Army had suffered a terrible defeat and where Evan had lost the better part of his command and his good friend, Lord Howe. A sudden, fierce light came to his eyes, and he whirled around. "I hope to hell we beat the blazes out of them!"

"Well, nay, it wasn't like that, I'm afraid. The French blew the fort up and retreated when they learned that Amherst and his army were nearby. But it's being rebuilt. They've renamed it Fort Ticonderoga. General Amherst said his army is marchin' on Fort Crown Point and Fort Niagara right now and that he fully intends to take 'em."

Josh paused for a moment to let Evan absorb everything he had said. Then he added expansively, "And that's not all the news. General Wolfe has sailed up the Saint Lawrence River and put Quebec under siege. Aye, we've got those Frenchies on the run now."

Evan was stunned to hear of all that had happened since he left the north in the early spring. Prime Minister Pitt's battle plan seemed to have been put into action, with Amherst invading Canada by way of Lake Champlain and Wolfe attacking Quebec. But instead of being excited by the news, he felt a sinking feeling. "Then Amherst doesn't feel it's necessary for me to investigate the French settlements or Fort Saint Louis? He's recalling me?"

"Nay, he's not recallin' ye. He feels the war has been turned around, but not won. Accordin' to him, Quebec is goin' to be a hard nut to crack. By the way, he told me

to tell ye that he thought ye and Promingo did a fine job
and that the fall of Fort Massiac had a lot to do with the
French abandonin' Fort Carillon. They knew about it,
ye know. Amherst said they caught a few French lag-
gards. It seems Fort Massiac bein' destroyed shook
them up even worse than that raid Bradstreet made on
Fort Frontenac last year. They never expected an English attack comin' at them from that direction, their
back door. Ah, wearin' that scarlet coat of yers in the
battle was pure genius, Major. Pure genius! The
Frenchmen swore at least twenty Englishman were takin' part in the battle. Amherst thought it just a gross
exaggeration until I explained how ye captured the cannon singlehandedly and then were everywhere, fightin'
like the devil himself. It's no wonder they thought there
were twenty of ye. Amherst was real impressed."

The war wasn't the only thing that had turned
around, Evan thought wryly. So had Josh's opinion of
him. But that the Scot was talking of him in such glowing terms embarrassed Evan. He hadn't set out to be a
hero. In fact, what he had done had been rather foolish,
rushing in the way he had. He hadn't been brave, just
frustrated beyond his tolerance and mad as hell. The
only difference between him and the dead Chickasaw
was that he had survived. Hoping to change the subject
and remove himself from the limelight, he asked,
"Where is the missive Amherst sent me?"

"He didn't send any."

Evan frowned. "No orders? No nothing?"

"I reckon he'll give 'em to ye when ye get to Williamsburg. That's what he wants ye to do, ye know. Join

him in Williamsburg, so ye can discuss yer strategy with him."

"What strategy?" Evan asked in total surprise. "All I was proposing to do was some more investigating."

Josh shrugged. "The general didn't go into detail. All I know is he wants ye meet him in Williamsburg. But ye're going to have to make a quick trip of it. He'll be leavin' at the end of the month."

"The end of the month? That's just three weeks away!"

"Aye."

"I'll never be able to make that trip in that short a time."

"I made it in two weeks," Josh pointed out.

"You're a frontiersman. You know how to find your way around in the woods. I'd get lost. I'd never find my way back, not in that short a time."

"Aye," the Scot readily agreed. "That's why I'm takin' ye back."

A skeptical look came over Evan's face. "You're going to take me to Williamsburg, then bring me back here?"

"Aye."

"What happened to all that important business you had?"

"Ah, Major, nothin' could be more important than the war," Josh answered with a hurt expression on his face.

Yes, now that the British were winning, Evan thought with a twinge of disgust for Josh's sudden loyalty.

"Besides, I can conduct business while I'm in Williamsburg," Josh continued, "and send everything back by packhorse. Some of those packhorsemen are just as reliable as I am."

Now, that sounded more like the Josh he knew, Evan thought. "I suppose you want to leave early in the morning?" he said.

"That depends upon Fire Dancer. The general wants ye to bring her with ye."

Evan wasn't the only one who was stunned by Josh's unexpected announcement. So were Fire Dancer and Black Hawk. But Evan was the first to recover. "Why?"

"Well, I told him about her goin' along with ye on the scoutin' expedition, and she caught his fancy. He said she reminded him of Pocahontas and that he'd like to meet her."

"Who is Pocahontas?" Fire Dancer asked.

Josh answered before Evan could even open his mouth. "She was an Indian girl who saved the life of one of the first settlers. Since then, she's always been much admired by the colonists."

Evan realized that he had felt a sinking feeling because it would have meant leaving Fire Dancer. But he wasn't ready to be separated from her, not yet. The idea of her going with him to Williamsburg appealed to him greatly. Perhaps if she saw how her mother's people lived, she'd be more accepting of her white blood. He turned to her. "Come with me, Fire Dancer," he said. "It would be a wonderful opportunity for you to see how your mother's people live."

Fire Dancer was so stunned by his request that she was speechless. She stared at him.

"Aren't you even curious?" Evan asked, taking another approach.

Fire Dancer admitted to a certain curiosity. Not everything her mother had said about her people had been bad. But that wasn't what would motivate her to make the trip. It would give her more time with Evan to store up her precious memories.

Before she could answer, Josh suggested, "Maybe she needs to get her grandmother's permission to leave."

Fire Dancer whirled around, her green eyes flashing, and spat, "I do not need to get anyone's permission. I am a Chickasaw woman! I go where I please."

Josh drew back in surprise at Fire Dancer's outburst, and Evan bit back a chuckle. He would never have suggested such a thing to Fire Dancer. It was like waving a flag before a mad bull, and he'd learned the hard way to pick his words very carefully. It surprised Evan that Josh didn't know better, since he was married to a Chickasaw woman. But then, maybe his woman wasn't as fiercely independent as Fire Dancer.

Despite what Fire Dancer had said, she knew that what she had said wasn't completely true. She couldn't go where she pleased, because she wasn't just any Chickasaw woman. She was destined to rule her clan, to become the mother of the next chief. She had an obligation to the tribe. But she was determined not to retract her words and lose face. Instead she said, "I will not ask my grandmother's permission, but I will seek her counsel."

"When?" Evan asked anxiously.

"Tomorrow morning."

15

Early the next morning, Fire Dancer went to her grand-mother's cabin and told the old woman that she had been invited to visit the great war chief of the whites, and that she would be accompanied by the Englishman and the trader called Josh.

"Do you want to go?" Eastern Star asked.

"Yes, I do."

"Why?"

"Because I am curious about my mother's people and how she lived before she was captured."

Eastern Star sensed that that was only part of the reason Fire Dancer wanted to go, the smaller part. Her granddaughter clearly didn't want to be parted from the Englishman. It seemed what the old woman had feared had come to past. Fire Dancer had fallen in love with him.

"I think you did not come here to seek my permission, but that you have already made up your mind."

"I have," Fire Dancer answered, meeting her grandmother's fierce gaze evenly. "I am going."

"Then why did you come?"

"For your blessing."

Eastern Star wondered if Fire Dancer would change her mind if she refused to give her blessing, but it was only a fleeting thought. She knew Fire Dancer was most emphatically her own woman, that she ruled her life by her own counsel. She also knew that the girl was going to have to face a painful parting in the end. Perhaps it would be just as well if she did get a taste of the white man's way to see that it was not for her. She was too much Chickasaw. It might help her to more easily accept that which could not be.

"You have my blessing," Eastern Star answered.

Eastern Star had spoken very softly, and it momentarily bewildered Fire Dancer. Belatedly, she answered, "Thank you."

As she turned to walk away, Eastern Star said, "Wait! I have not finished." Fire Dancer turned. "I wish to speak to the Englishman."

"Why?"

Eastern Star smiled ever so slightly. It was not a question. It was a demand, something that few in tribe were brave enough to attempt of Eastern Star. But Fire Dancer dared, and that pleased the old woman.

"What I have to say to him is private," Eastern Star replied in a firm voice.

"He does not speak our language."

"I know. But I have been told that Black Hawk has learned much of his. Send Black Hawk and the Englishman to me."

Thirty minutes later, Black Hawk and Evan stood before Eastern Star.

"Netak chookoma," Eastern Star said.

"Good day," Evan replied, then repeated it in Chickasaw, for he had picked up a little of the language.

Eastern Star was pleased, but she didn't show it. Her face looked as if it were carved from stone. "You are to tell the Englishman this," she said to Black Hawk. "I expect him to return my granddaughter safely to this village and that no harm will come to her."

Black Hawk relayed Eastern Star's message word for word. Evan answered in an equally firm voice, "Tell her I will guard Fire Dancer's life with my own."

After Black Hawk had passed Evan's answer on, Eastern Star's and Evan's eyes met. Neither wavered. Then Eastern Star nodded, and Evan knew he had been dismissed. He turned and walked away.

As he stepped from the cabin, Eastern Star confided to Black Hawk, "It is not Fire Dancer's life that I fear for. It is her heart. I'm afraid she had fallen in love with the Englishman."

"Yes," Black Hawk answered solemnly, "and I think he loves her too."

This last came as a shock to Eastern Star. She had not expected it. White men took Indian women for lovers, had affairs with them, but they didn't usually get emotionally involved with them. The liaisons were almost without exception purely physical.

Still, the news would change nothing. The Englishman would still leave Fire Dancer in the end, and she would still be hurt. After all, he was not like the traders and packhorsemen, who sometimes married their Indian lovers and raised Indian families. He was an Englishman to the bone, and his world and Fire Dancer's were an eternity apart.

Evan, Fire Dancer, and Josh left an hour later on Chickasaw horses. Evan felt disreputable on the horse Fire Dancer had loaned him from her herd. Not only was the animal terribly shaggy and ungroomed, he was riding very low to the ground, and with his height he thought he must look ridiculous. His knees were pulled up almost to the top of the pony's back. He would have never agreed to this had Josh not said he planned for them to cover at least sixty miles a day. Evan knew his English-bred mount simply wasn't up to that kind of punishment.

But as they followed the old Chickasaw trail that the Indians called the Path of Peace through the dense woods, Evan eventually changed his opinion of the horse he was riding. Not only could the Indian pony keep up a steady, quick pace, it was far more sure-footed than his horse, and it had a surprisingly smooth gait. Now he could understand why the colonists preferred the little horses. Who cared what the animal looked like? No one was going to see it in these dense forests. Why, a man could pass within ten feet of them without being seen.

Just when Evan was feeling more comfortable with the Indian pony, the horse came to a sudden stop on the trail and went berserk, whinnying shrilly and rearing over and over. Caught off guard, Evan was promptly dumped on the ground. He didn't have far to fall, so he didn't receive much of a jolt. But his pride was severely injured. He'd never been thrown in his entire adult life, and since he had taken the lead after their noon break, both Josh and Fire Dancer had witnessed his disgrace.

He scrambled to his feet and hurried to the front of the horse to grab its reins. "No, stay back!" Fire Dancer called.

"Like hell I will!" Evan threw angrily over his shoulder. "I'll teach this goddamn horse to throw me!"

But before Evan could catch the reins, the animal came to a stop as suddenly as it had gone berserk. The only sign of its frantic behavior was its rapid breathing. "What in the blazes got into him?" Evan asked as Fire Dancer trotted her horse up beside him.

"That," she answered, pointing to ground in front of the horse.

Evan peered at the ground. He could see pieces of something in the dark pathway. "What is it?"

"What's left of the rattlesnake your pony killed. They're very poisonous."

"I didn't hear anything. Don't they rattle before they strike?"

"Not always," Josh answered, squeezing his horse between Fire Dancer's and Evan's on the narrow trail. "And he probably didn't see it either. Probably smelled it."

"How do you know it was a rattler?" Evan asked. "Maybe it was some other kind of snake."

"Nay. A rattler is the only thing that can make a Chickasaw horse go crazy like that. They hate rattlers something awful," Josh informed him.

"Yes, I noticed," Evan answered wryly. "I just wish he'd given me a little warning."

◦ ◦ ◦

On the evening of the third day, Josh said to the two, "French Lick is about a mile up ahead. There's a tradin' post nearby. We can stay there the night and get a hot meal."

"A trading post?" Evan asked, surprised. "Way out here in the middle of nowhere?"

"Aye. It's been there since '14, when its owner, Charles Charleville, built it. Only English tradin' post this side of the Alleghenies, as far as I know."

"Why didn't we stay there when we passed through here on our way out?" Evan asked.

"I didn't think it was necessary. But since Fire Dancer is travelin' with us and it looks like it might rain, I reckon it might be a good idea."

Evan looked up at the solid canopy of limbs and leaves above him. Not a piece of sky could be seen. "What makes you think it's going to rain?"

"I can feel it in the air. We're goin' to have a downpour before daylight for sure."

About an hour later they reached a clearing in which a large log cabin sat. They hobbled their horses in the clearing where the animals could munch on the grass, then placed their saddles and their supply pack under a lean-to at the back of the cabin beside the bundles of firewood that the trader sold.

They stepped into the trading post, and Fire Dancer looked around curiously. She had heard that the Cherokee built their cabins of logs—the white man must have copied theirs. The cracks in the logs were stuffed with moss mixed with mud, and all around there were pegs on the walls from which things were hanging: harnesses, saddles, black kettles, powder horns, bullet molds, long-handled skillets, lengths of rope, hoes, shovels, axes, snowshoes, traps, smoked hams, and slabs of bacon. One corner of the room was piled high with buckskins and furs; in another there were casks of bear oil, molasses, and gunpowder and sacks of cornmeal, grain, and dried beans stacked almost to the ceiling.

Evan also looked around. He had been in more than a few of these trading posts, and he was glad this one had a wooden floor instead of dirt and was cleaner than most. He wanted Fire Dancer to be impressed by the way the white man lived.

Suddenly, a loud male voice boomed out, "Josh? Josh McDougal, is that you?"

"I reckon it is, Charlie," Josh answered with a chuckle.

Evan and Fire Dancer turned and saw a heavy-set, red-faced, gray-haired man standing behind a long counter that ran the length of the cabin. On the wall behind him was a display of long rifles and vicious-looking knives and tomahawks.

"What brings you here?" Charlie asked, coming around the end of the counter, then shaking Josh's hand so hard, it looked as if he nearly dislocated the shoulder joint. "I haven't seen the likes of you for nigh on five years."

"Me and my friends here are on our way to Williamsburg, and I thought I'd ask if we could spend the night, since it's goin' to storm," Josh explained.

Charlie gave both Evan and Fire Dancer a piercing glance, but he didn't ask for an introduction. Out here, too many men were running from the law, and it was safer not to be too curious. "Aye, won't be fit for man or beast out there tonight," he answered. "You're welcome to sleep by my fire, for a fee of course." He pointed to a table before the fireplace with benches on both sides of it. "Have a seat."

Both men placed their long rifles beside the door, and as they walked to the table, Evan was amazed by the two traders' conversation. There hadn't been a cloud in sight when they rode up, yet both had agreed it was about to storm.

Evan stepped aside and let Fire Dancer slide down the long bench before he joined her. Josh sat on the opposite side. Charlie walked up to the table, drying his hands on an apron that was none too clean.

"Charlie, I'd like ye to meet my friends," Josh said, "Fire Dancer and Major Evan Trevor."

Evan nodded, and Fire Dancer smiled. "Glad to meet you," Charlie answered, then said to Evan, "I reckon I know who you are. You're the officer that led the attack on Fort Massiac."

"I was there, yes, but I didn't lead the attack. Chief Promingo of the Chickasaw did." Evan frowned. "But how did you know who I am?"

"Easy. Every Indian, trader, fur trapper, and packhorseman is talking about you and the way you took that cannon singlehandedly. You're a hero."

Evan glared at Josh. Josh held up a hand and said, "It wasn't me, Major. The Indians have got a grapevine of their own, ye know."

Evan looked at Charlie. "I'm sure everything you've heard was much exaggerated. I'm not a hero."

"Maybe, maybe not. But I'd like to buy you a drink.

What will you have? Ale? Rum? I've got some good French brandy.

"Brandy, thank you."

"And you, Josh?"

"I'll have rum."

"And the lady?" Charlie asked Evan, for he had not missed the officer's possessiveness. There was no doubt in his mind which man the Indian girl was with.

Fire Dancer's eyes flashed. "I do not drink!"

Charlie turned to her with a surprised look. She was clearly a mestizo, with those European features. There were quite a few with mixed blood out here, sons and daughters of the traders and packhorsemen, but none had her beauty and striking green eyes, and certainly none spoke English as fluently. If the mestizos spoke their fathers' language at all, it was usually very broken and unsure. But not so with this feisty lass, he thought, biting back a smile. Not only did she know the language, she wasn't in the least afraid to speak out. "Is that so? Well, you're the first Indian I've seen turn it down. But I got other things you can drink. How about a cup of tea?"

"Sassafras?"

"Nay, this tea comes from China."

Fire Dancer had never heard of China. She hesitated, and Evan spoke up. "Do you have any apple cider?"

"I reckon I've got a keg somewhere," Charlie answered. "I have kegs of everything else."

Fire Dancer shot Evan a suspicious look, and he responded, "No, it's not alcoholic. It just tastes good. I'd like you to try it."

The look in Evan's blue eyes had just a hint of pleading in it, and Fire Dancer found she couldn't refuse. She nodded in agreement. Charlie hurried behind the counter, then pulled a bottle of brandy and a keg of rum from under it. "I have to hide the liquor under here. It's the only thing I've ever had stolen." He disappeared behind the counter for a while, and the three could hear him rummaging through kegs and bottles. Finally he reappeared, holding a keg of cider in his hand. "Thought I had one around here," he said.

While Charlie poured their drinks, Fire Dancer ran her fingers over the weathered tabletop, marveling at how smooth it was. Observing her, Evan said, "The table is nice, isn't it? The split logs that the table and benches are made of are called puncheons. The floor is made of them too."

"Yes, it's nice," Fire Dancer admitted. "I suppose it would be easier to write on."

"And eat on," Evan added with a chuckle, realizing that Fire Dancer hadn't guessed the table's real purpose. "But just wait until we get to Williamsburg and you can see some real English furniture. We have tables called desks just for writing."

Charlie walked up to the table, carrying a tray with four heavy pewter tankards. When he set Evan's drink before him, Evan looked at it in dismay. If he drank that much brandy, he'd be under the table.

Seeing the expression on his face, Charlie said, "Sorry I haven't got a proper glass to serve it in, Major, but I don't have many requests for brandy out here. Most of the men prefer rum."

"That's quite all right," Evan answered. He didn't imagine the trader did have many requests for the

French drink. Brandy was expensive and not nearly as intoxicating as rum.

Charlie sat down on the bench beside Josh. "What's the latest news on the war?" he asked.

The question had been directed to Evan, but it was Josh who answered. He told Charlie everything he had learned on his recent visit back east. When he finished, Charlie said, "So we're going to win this war, after all? Thank God! And I hope it's final this time. These blasted Indian wars have been going on since the turn of the century."

"Nay, Charlie, I think this one is it," Josh answered.

"Well, that's a relief. You don't know how I've sweat blood all these years, never knowing from day to day if I'm going to lose this trading post and my livelihood."

"I'm amazed that there's enough business out here to keep you going," Evan remarked.

"You'd be surprised at the traffic that comes through here, particularly since Dr. Walker discovered that old Indian trail through the Alleghenies ten years ago."

"You didn't come by way of the Cumberland Gap?" Evan asked in surprise.

"Hell, no. I didn't know about it way back then. None of us traders did."

"Then how did you get here?"

"Like the Goose Creek traders, around the end of the mountains, through the Carolinas. But I always figured there was a trail over those mountains someplace. Tried my damnedest to find out from the Indians that traded with me, but they wouldn't tell me. But now that we know where that trail is, the colonists are going to be swarming over those mountains, particularly if we win this war. Then I'll be sitting pretty."

"That might not be for a hundred years or more," Evan pointed out.

"Nay, it won't be that long," Charlie answered confidently. "They're already moving into the big valley between the Alleghenies and the Cumberland Mountains. And there've been two land companies selling land along the Ohio ever since Walker got back with his news. All they've been waiting on is for this mess about what country the land belongs to to get settled. Maybe I won't live to see it, but they're coming. They aren't going to let nothing stop them, not the mountains, not the Indians, not nothing. They'll keep moving westward. They won't stop until—"

"Until they reach the Pacific?" Evan prompted.

"Aye, wherever the hell that is."

Evan still seriously doubted that it would be less than a hundred years. Then turned to Fire Dancer and asked, "How do you like the cider?"

"It's very good," she replied. "How is it made?"

"From squeezing the juice out of apples."

Seeing the skeptical look coming over her face, Josh laughed. "I know what ye're thinkin'. But we don't use crabapples. Why, those runty little things aren't nothin' but a core covered with a skin as tough as leather. That cider comes from trees we brought from England that have apples on 'em as big as my fist."

Fire Dancer found it hard to believe that there were apples that big, and the expression on her face clearly showed it. "Honest to God," Josh added.

Fire Dancer turned to Evan for confirmation. He

smiled. "It's true," he said. "Cross my heart," then made the motion on his chest.

"What does that mean?" Fire Dancer asked.

"I swear it's true."

Fire Dancer's eyes filled with wonder. Then she held out her tankard. "May I have another?"

Evan smiled, pleased that for the second time he had found something to impress her.

Shortly thereafter, Charlie served them their evening meal. When he set a three-pronged object beside Fire Dancer's wooden spoon, she looked at it, then asked Evan, "What is that?"

Before Evan could open his mouth, Josh answered, "That's a fork. Don't see too many of 'em in the colonies, although I understand they've had 'em in England for a while. Right, Major?"

Evan was getting a little irritated that Josh butted in whenever someone addressed him. He shot the trader a resentful glance, then answered, "That's correct. It's used to eat with, particularly meat. That's the purpose of the prongs—to spear the meat."

Fire Dancer looked down in the stew in the wooden trencher sitting before her. "Where is the meat?"

It was a good question. Evan looked down at his trencher and saw that, as usual, the stew had been boiled so long, the vegetables and the meat were indistinguishable. "Just use your spoon," he muttered, feeling a keen embarrassment, not necessarily on Charlie's behalf, however. He was embarrassed that Fire Dancer was being given a classic example of just how poorly the English cooked their food.

They were just finishing their meal when they heard first distant rumble of thunder.

"There she comes," Josh remarked, cocking his head to one side. "I told ye it would rain before mornin'," he said to Evan.

Shortly thereafter, a pack train arrived. The eight men stacked their freight in the lean-to behind the cabin and staked their horses, then crowded into the trading post, asking for shelter for the night. Charlie readily agreed and offered them food. But the men were more interested in drinking than eating, and they lined up at the trader's counter as if it were a bar. There they stood and downed one tankard of rum after another.

From the table, Evan eyed them warily, for they were an unsavory-looking group with long stringy hair, unkept beards, and dirty clothing. As their voices got louder and louder, their language got more and more obscene. Evan was incensed that they should speak so disrespectfully in front of Fire Dancer. When one of them called another a "bugger," Evan cringed, for he found that obscenity, frequently used by the commoners, particularly offensive. He leaned across the table and whispered to Josh so Fire Dancer couldn't hear, "If they don't keep their voices down, I'm going to go over there and bash a few heads together. They have no right to talk that way in front of Fire Dancer, even if they do think she's nothing but an Indian."

"That's not why they're not watchin' their language. Hell, Fire Dancer is an Indian. They don't expect her to understand English. Besides, she probably doesn't know what those words mean, anyway. I can't see her mother teachin' her that."

It was a good point, and Fire Dancer didn't appear to be insulted, but as the group got rowdier and rowdier, Evan became more uneasy. He rose from the table, and Josh asked, "Where are ye goin'?"

"To get my rifle. I'd feel better with it at my side."

"Why?"

Evan nodded curtly to the men.

"Are ye afraid they'll try somethin' with Fire Dancer?"

"Yes."

"Well, ye can forget that. If one of 'em even so much as looks cross-eyed at her, Charlie will blow their brains out, and they know it. He's got a mighty respect for women."

Now that Josh mentioned it, Evan realized that the men hadn't even cast a glance in their direction, which was unusual. But he still didn't like the idea of Fire Dancer sleeping with those men all around her. He contemplated taking her outside to sleep, but a particularly loud crack of thunder and the sound of the wind preceding the storm rattling the heavy door changed his mind. He rose and walked across the cabin to the end of the counter where Charlie was bent over and writing something in a ledger.

With his back to the other men, Evan asked, "Is there someplace more private where Fire Dancer can sleep?"

Charlie looked up in surprise. "I don't have a separate bedroom, if that's what you mean. This isn't an ordinary."

At that moment, one of the men laughed particularly

loud, and both Charlie and Evan cast him a displeased look. Then Charlie said, "But I can see why you're concerned about her. We wouldn't want her getting kicked in the face, and they'll be thrashing around in their sleep something awful tonight. They always do. I won't let them have enough liquor to pass out. And I'd rather bed down with a bunch of mules." He turned sideways and pointed to a narrow bed built into the wall that was obscured by the counter. "She can have my bed for the night. I'll sleep on the floor. But I'm sleeping back here, too, so I can keep one eye on my liquor. That's why my bed is in here and not out there."

Evan didn't object, particularly since Josh had told him Charlie had a great deal of respect for women. "Thank you, and I'll be more than happy to pay you for it."

"That isn't necessary."

"No, I insist."

Charlie scratched his head. "Well, all right then. That will be a buck."

"A what?"

"A buck! A buckskin!"

"I'm afraid I don't have any buckskins."

"All right, then, I'll take a couple of ounces of black salt." Seeing the blank look on Evan's face, Charlie asked, "You don't have any of that, either, do you?"

"No, I don't. I don't even know what it is."

"That's the thick dark crust of potash you get when you boil ashes in water. We skim it off the top, cool it, and use it as salt. It's valuable out here."

Evan nodded. He knew salt was valuable in the wilderness. Not only was it needed to live, but so much of the meat was preserved by salting it. This was the first time he had heard of black salt. He felt rather foolish, until Charlie asked, "If you don't have any buckskins or any black salt, what were you going to pay me with?"

"Why, good English coin," Evan answered, as if it were the stupidest question he had ever heard.

As he reached into the pouch of his hunting shirt for his purse, Charlie waved his hand in the air and shook his head. "Don't bother," he said. "I have no use for coin out here. It's worthless."

Evan had never felt so frustrated. By British standards, he was well-off. He had saved almost all his wages, and combined with the money he had won on his horse and the small inheritance he had gotten from his mother, he had put a tidy sum aside. But out here, he was a pauper. "I'll ask Josh if he can loan me a"—he paused, his nose wrinkling in distaste, then finished—"a buck."

"No, Major, that's not necessary. The girl can have my bed."

"But—"

"No," Charlie interjected firmly. "I want to do it for the girl. She's a fine lass."

Later that night, as Evan lay with his feet to the fireplace along with Josh and the packhorsemen, he was gouged by their elbows and kicked as they restlessly tossed and turned in their sleep. He might have consoled himself that he had saved Fire Dancer from the misery he was going through, except he knew that in the tightly closed cabin, she could hear their loud snoring and smell the stench of rum, unwashed bodies, and stale tobacco smoke just as well as he. That in itself was bad enough, but when the rain came down in earnest, the roof leaked, and one leak was right above the bed where she was lying.

Evan felt disgust, and a keen disappointment. He had wanted Fire Dancer to be impressed by the white man's way of living. He could only hope that the rest of the trip would not be as miserable a failure as this night had been.

16

The next day, Evan, Josh, and Fire Dancer passed French Lick. It was usual to see animals, especially deer, at the salt springs, licking the crust on the ground where the water had evaporated. But today, Indian women were standing to one side of the spring and boiling water over a fire. Evan tensed, looking around for the braves.

"Relax, Major," Josh said. "They're Cherokee. They're a friendly tribe, remember?"

Evan had known the women weren't Chickasaw because they wore their long braids down, not piled on top of their heads. But other than that, he couldn't tell one Indian from another. "What are they doing on Chickasaw land?"

"This isn't Chickasaw land. It's Cherokee territory from here until we reach Virginia, except for a little spot of huntin' ground the Shawnee have claimed to the south of here."

"How far south?" Evan asked. The Shawnee were most definitely unfriendly.

"Far enough that they won't bother us," Josh answered.

The next day they reached the foothills of the Cumberland Mountains and left the deep forests behind them. Fire Dancer was filled with awe. She had never seen hills before, much less mountains. She kept her eyes glued to the towering, purplish peaks of the Appalachians in the distance, amazed that they actually reached as high as the clouds that capped them.

When they rode through the narrow pass that Dr. Walker had named after the Duke of Cumberland, Fire Dancer couldn't get enough of it. She turned from side to side in her saddle—the scenery was absolutely spectacular. Two major rivers had their beginnings here, the Tennessee and the Kentucky, and they cascaded over breathtaking falls shrouded with misty rainbows and tumbled over wild rapids through narrow, rocky gorges. When they reached the highest rim of the pass, Evan and Fire Dancer reined in beneath a pine tree and paused for a moment, admiring the beauty all around them.

"When we passed through here earlier this year, it was springtime," Evan informed Fire Dancer, "and everything was blooming. There were splashes of color everywhere you looked from the redbud and dogwood trees, the wild azaleas, rhododendron, and mountain laurel. I wish you could have seen it then. It was beautiful."

Fire Dancer couldn't imagine it any more beautiful than it was. From her lofty viewpoint she could see fifty miles in every direction, which made her feel as if she were standing on top of the world. This was what the eagle saw, she thought, when it soared high in the sky. The Chickasaw thought the bird blessed because it was a creature of the upper kingdom where the Great Spirit lived, but at that moment Fire Dancer thought the bird blessed just because it could enjoy such a commanding view whenever it wished. Seeing a shadow cross the ground, she looked up, expecting to see one of the majestic birds. Instead, she saw the wisp of a cloud floating overhead, so close that she reached up to touch it. But its nearness was only an illusion. Realizing Evan was watching her, she felt foolish, and a flush rose on her face.

"Don't be embarrassed," Evan said softly. "I did the same thing." Then hearing Josh calling to him, he said, "We'd better go."

As Evan turned his horse, Fire Dancer took one last look at the beautiful view. The trip was well worth the time and bother just to have seen this. Even after Evan had ridden a short distance away, she sat trying to commit each detail to memory. Then, satisfied that the breathtaking panorama was etched in her mind forever, where it, too, would become a part of her treasure chest, she turned her mare and followed.

As they were coming down the trail from the pass into the wide valley between the Cumberland and the Allegheny mountains that the colonists called "the trench," they entered another dense forest. Suddenly, Evan sat bolt upright in his saddle, every muscle primed for action. "What's that noise?" he asked Josh.

Josh cocked his head. "It sounds like a bell to me," he answered.

Having thought it was a bell himself, Evan relaxed. "Do you think there's a pack train coming? Their horses wear bells around their necks."

"Aye, but they usually tie the clappers when they're goin' through a forest for fear of alertin' any Indians that might in the vicinity."

"I thought you said we were in Cherokee country and safe."

"We are, but those packhorsemen don't know the Indians like I do." Josh listened again. "Ye know, I'd almost think it was a settler's cow. They let 'em run loose in the woods, ye know, and the bell is how they find 'em."

"There are no settlers way out here, not this far west."

"Aye, I know. That's why I said *almost*."

About five hundred yards down the trail, they came to a frontiersman who was leading his family through the forest. The trio moved aside for the settlers to pass on the narrow path, and the frontiersman gave them a curt nod of thanks. The man, dressed exactly like Josh and Evan except for the hat of braided cornhusks on his head, was carrying a long rifle and leading a horse on which his wife, holding their infant, sat sidesaddle. The woman was wedged between as many crates and barrels as the animal could carry. Following her horse, on a lead rein, was a second horse carrying an axe, a hoe, a few sacks of corn, a barrel of gunpowder, an iron pot and long-handled skillet, pottery jugs, pewter mugs and wooden noggins, and clothing rolled into big bundles.

Behind the second horse was the cow, also loaded down. The bell hanging from its neck rang loudly, and its tail swished at the cloud of flies following it. Bringing up the rear was the family dog, its long nose to the ground as it crisscrossed the trail. It raised its head just long enough to give a few sharp warning barks to the three people sitting on the side of the trail as it trotted past.

Evan and Josh stared at the settlers until they disappeared into the forest. Both men found it hard to believe that the couple was going that far away from civilization. Even though they were in territory claimed by Virginia, the frontier was on the other side of the Allegheny Mountains they had yet to cross.

Fire Dancer, however, had stared for an entirely different reason. Her full attention had been on the woman: her butternut linsey dress, the dingy neckcloth crossed over her bosom, her bare feet, and her limp brimmed sunbonnet. As Evan turned his horse, he saw the puzzled expression on her face. "What is it?" he asked.

"That is the first time I have seen a white woman's clothing. What is that strange thing she has on her head?"

"It's called a sunbonnet. It keeps the sun off of her face."

"Why does she want to do that?"

"So her skin won't burn and turn dark."

The "turn dark" caught Fire Dancer's attention. When her mother had covered herself, she had said it was to avoid the pain of sunburn.

"Aye," Josh chimed in, confirming what Evan had

said. "White women are very vain about their skin. They think the paler they are, the prettier. It's a bunch of hogwash as far as I'm concerned. I like to see a little color on a woman's face."

Fire Dancer wondered if that was what Evan thought —the paler, the prettier. For the first time, she was acutely conscious of the dusky color of her skin. "And the cloth around her neck? Does it have a purpose too?"

"Yes, it's worn for modesty's sake in public, so that the top of her breasts in the low-cut bodice can't be seen," Evan answered.

Fire Dancer remembered the day she had bared her breasts and Evan had become upset with her. Revealing her breasts wasn't wrong, but she hadn't realized how much stock the white man put in keeping them covered. She looked down at the mantle she wore on her chest. The two skin strips covered the tops of her breasts, but she could see the sides and the valley between the two mounds. She wondered if she should wear a piece of cloth around her neck too. She didn't want others thinking her immodest. Then she remembered that she was Chickasaw. The white man did not set her code of conduct, not even the golden-haired one riding beside her. She kneed her horse and rode off.

When they left the forest, they entered a hilly, rocky countryside, and that afternoon they had their second encounter with settlers that day. A frontiersman had built a flimsy structure in which upright logs were simply lain against a frame. One side was completely open and faced the fire. Beside the "half-faced camp" was a small cornfield overgrown with weeds.

After they passed it, Evan asked Josh, "Is that all they're going to build, that lean-to?"

"Aye. Ye see, there are three kinds of settlers out here on the frontier. The kind like those we just passed are mostly hunters. They don't stay put. They don't mean to build anything permanent. They have no farm animals or fences. The next kind is the poor farmers. They build a cabin, put in a crop of corn and maybe one of flax. They have a plow horse and a milk cow. They build fences, weak fences. They stay, but they never do well. They just barely make ends meet.

"The last kind is the real farmer. He has a little money to invest in his farm. He builds strong fences and a barn for his animals, buys good tools, and plants in earnest, enough to trade for the other things that make life good. You won't see too many of that kind here in the trench. The ground is too rocky for any decent farmin'. It's more suited to raisin' cattle."

From time to time throughout the day, they passed small farms, and just as Josh had predicted, none had a look of real permanence. The cabins were poorly built with a crude hominy block in the front yard and a still in the back. The crops were withered in the hot sun, and the fields overgrown with weeds; the fences were weak and down in many places. In some instances the cow was in the field eating the corn and trampling down the stalks. The only other sign of life was the occasional dog that barked ferociously from open cabin doors.

They crossed the mountains the next day, and Evan could see that the first farm they passed was different.

There was not only a cabin and a barn, but a smoke-house, a fowl house, and pigpen. The corn crop was lush and green, the tobacco almost ready for cutting, and the flax ripe and waving in the gentle breeze. Evan was so busy watching the farmer swing his sickle back and forth as he cut it that he didn't realize for a moment that Fire Dancer had stopped and was staring at the field. He turned and rode back to her. "What's wrong?" he asked.

"The seed on the grass that man is cutting is the same color as my mother's hair. I have never seen that color anywhere else."

Fire Dancer's mother had had flaxen hair and green eyes, Evan thought. It was fairly typical coloring for an Englishwoman and was generally considered quite at-tractive by his people. He glanced up at the dark hair piled on top of Fire Dancer's head, so black it had a bluish sheen to it, and he was glad she had inherited her Chickasaw father's hair. Along with the darker shade of her skin, it made her eyes stand out and look so striking. Yes, he very much liked her unusual coloring.

Josh rode up to them, saying, "If ye two can tear yer eyes away from that farmer for a minute, I'd like for ye to look at the top of the farmhouse. Ye'll see something ye won't see when we get closer to the coast."

On the roof of the cabin, a boy was carrying a chicken. Evan assumed he was bringing it down from where it had flown and been roosting. But then he ex-claimed in surprise, "Why, he threw the chicken down the chimney!"

"Aye," Josh answered with a laugh. "That's how they clean their chimneys out here. All that wild flappin' of its wings as the chicken falls brushes the soot away. They don't have chimney sweeps out here. As far apart as these farms are, I doubt if there ever will be enough demand for 'em."

A moment later, the chicken emerged from the cabin, squawking indignantly, its feathers as black as tar. The three laughed. "Maybe it's just as well the chimney sweeps stay away," Evan remarked. "This method is a lot cheaper."

A little farther on, they came to the farmer's orchard. Again, Fire Dancer stopped and stared, this time at one of the trees growing there. Its leaves were long and slender like the willow's, but larger. "What is that tree with the yellow fruit?"

"That's a peach tree," Evan answered.

"And the one with the small, odd-shaped green fruit?" she asked, motioning to a tree with an oval-shaped leaf.

"That's a pear tree, but the fruit isn't ripe yet," Josh answered. Looking over her head, he said to Evan, "Peaches and pears aren't native to this country either."

"Then you've never eaten a peach?" Evan asked Fire Dancer.

"No."

"Well, you've been missing a real treat," he answered, pleased that he could introduce her to a new food for a change. He rode his horse over to the heavily laden tree, plucked one of the plump golden peaches from it, and handed it to Fire Dancer. "I don't think the farmer will mind you having a taste," he said.

Fire Dancer bit into the peach, then wiped away

some of the sweet juice that had dribbled down her chin. "It's delicious!" she exclaimed.

"Peaches are my favorite fruit," Evan told her. "In fact, that looks so good, I think I'll have one."

"Why we don't we just pick us a dozen or so?" Josh suggested. "Don't look to me like that farmer is too interested in pickin' 'em. Half of 'em are layin' on the ground and just rottin'.'"

The two men plucked a few more luscious-looking peaches from the tree and slipped them into the pouch sewn into the front of their loose, wraparound shirts. As the three rode away munching peaches, Evan said to Fire Dancer, "There's a plum tree over there that's bearing too. Do you want a few of those?"

Fire Dancer looked at the tree. "No, just the peaches," she answered. "The plums look rather small."

"They're not nearly as small as the wild plums I've seen," he pointed out.

"But you've not seen a Chickasaw plum," Fire Dancer answered. "It is as big as my fist, or bigger."

When Evan looked skeptical, Fire Dancer said, "No, it's true. My people brought them from the west when they came to live beside the Misho Sipokni." Seeing he still looked doubtful, she laughed. "I cross my heart."

The next day they came upon a community of fifty or sixty log cabins that were strung along a creek for ten miles or so. There was even a little mill, the wheel making a creaking noise as it turned slowly in the water. At the end of the line of cabins, in a large clearing studded with half-rotten tree stumps, was one of the frontier

blockhouses that the Virginians built to protect themselves from Indians.

"They've got a tradin' post inside the fort," Josh informed them. "We'll stop here to pick up some more
supplies."

As they left the stream and rode to the top of the rise
where the fort was, they passed several people lugging
buckets of water up the hill. Evan asked Josh, "Why do
you colonists always built your forts away from the
streams? If the Indians lay siege, you're setting yourself
up for defeat without any water."

"Because the streams lie in the lowlands, and every
time a good rain comes, they flood. But you're right,
Major. It does make for a problem. I've been in more
than one siege where we had to find volunteers to go
down to the creek to get water." Josh grinned. "Of
course, that was necessary only after we ran out of rum
and corn whiskey."

As they approached the fort, Fire Dancer stared at it
curiously. The palisade of logs was like those the Chickasaw used, but the two-story blockhouses that jutted out
over the tall walls at each corner were something the
colonists had added. As they rode through the open
gate, she was surprised to see that the settlers had built
their cabins side by side along the palisade so that their
back wall was actually the wall of the fort, while their
fireplaces all faced the center of the stronghold. She
was impressed by this ingenuity. Not only had the white
men conserved wood, but during an attack the roofs of
the cabins could be used as parapets, on which the settlers could stand and fire down over the walls.

As they crossed the dusty interior of the fort to the

trading post at the rear, they heard the sharp ring of metal hitting metal as a blacksmith pounded on a red-hot horseshoe. They passed a pack train going out; the sturdy little horses were loaded down with barrels and bushels strapped to their sides, and the bells hanging around their throats clattered noisily. Two children ran across the open area in front of them. The little girl was wearing an apron and a miniature sunbonnet just like the ones the women passing the time of day standing in front of one of the cabins were wearing.

The trio stopped at a hitching post in front of the trading post. As Evan swung down from his horse, he bumped Fire Dancer, who was also dismounting, as usual on the off side. Evan swung back up on his horse to allow her room, and two Indians unloading their horses next to them caught his attention. As the trio walked into the post, Evan commented to Josh, "Those were wolf pelts those Indians were unloading. Is there that much demand for them? Why, they must have had at least fifty."

"As furs they have little value, but wolves pose a big threat to the settlers' livestock out here, so Virginia pays a bounty for the pelts. Bounty huntin' can bring in a tidy sum, and both Indians and white men do it. But the white men aren't as careful hunters as the Indians. They're bad about layin' their wolf traps on main trails. I fell into one of those pits one time. Broke my ankle and had a devil of a time gettin' out. They're eight foot deep, ye know."

"Why don't they use spring traps, like they do for other wild animals?" Evan asked.

"Because they aren't any good for holdin' a wolf. A wolf will chew its leg clean off to get loose."

They walked into the dim interior of the trading post and up to the counter, where the owner was occupied with a customer. On the wall behind the counter was a sign that advertised a pound of powder for a dollar and a half; another sign said both "bucks" and "roanoke" were accepted. Hanging a little below the sign were several sheaves of cured tobacco.

While Josh placed their order, Fire Dancer walked over to a table on which lengths of calico were displayed. She picked up a handful of material and examined it curiously, for she had never seen fabric with a print on it. "Would you like it?" Evan asked. "If so, I'll buy it for you." He thought he'd borrow on Josh's credit if he had to.

"What would I do with it?"

"You could make a dress from it."

Evan's answer was a simple statement of fact, but Fire Dancer misinterpreted it as criticism of her Indian clothing. "No, thank you," she replied curtly, and stalked away from the table to examine a stack of furs sitting in one corner.

Evan was bewildered. He had no idea what he had said that offended her.

As they left the trading post, a drunken Indian came into the building, reeking of rum, and bumped into them. Fire Dancer gave the man a long look as he staggered away. Then as they were riding from the fort, they saw two frontiersmen carry another intoxicated Indian past the gates and unceremoniously dump him beside still another brave sprawled there.

Fire Dancer gave Evan a sharp, accusing look, then kneed her mount and trotted ahead of him and Josh. This time Evan knew what had displeased her. He said to Josh, "Fire Dancer told me that the rum the whites sell them is a curse on the Indian."

"Aye, ye could say that," Josh admitted. "They seem to be more susceptible to it than us. Ye'll see a lot more drunkards among them than the white man—women and children included. Then they hang around the forts or trading posts beggin' for it.

"Besides that, many of 'em get crazy on it, and there's no tellin' what a berserk Indian might do. For that reason, drunkenness upsets the Indians' methods of dealin' with crime. They usually have clan vengeance—an eye for an eye and a tooth for a tooth. If the man who the crime was committed against can't seek his own vengeance, one in his clan will do it for him. But what the Indians can't figure out is, if the criminal didn't know what he was doin' while he was drunk, should he be punished?"

"If you colonists know what it's doing to them, why do you continue to sell it to them?" Evan asked angrily.

"Look, I'm a businessman," Josh answered in a hard voice. "If they want it, I'll sell it to 'em."

"And you don't think you have any moral obligation to them whatsoever?"

"Hell, no! I'm not their keeper."

"Goddammit, Josh! You're not like these other settlers, who think Indians have no soul. You've lived with them. You know better. You owe them something."

"That still don't make me their keeper. They can say

no. Besides, if that isn't the pot callin' the kettle black, I don't know what is!"

"What do you mean by that remark?" Evan demanded.

"I mean ye don't have any right to accuse me of bein' underhanded, not when ye're just as guilty. Or have ye forgotten how the British Army sends pox-infected blankets to the Indians?"

Evan had forgotten. "Those Indians are our enemies. That's a part of war."

"Is that so?" Josh asked with a sneer. "Well, I heard they weren't all enemy tribes, not that I can see where it makes any difference. Seems like an underhanded way of fightin' a war—killin' women and children."

Josh kneed his horse and trotted ahead, leaving Evan to do some serious thinking about what had been said. In the end, he was forced to admit that he had been just as guilty. He'd known what was going on but had turned a blind eye toward it. Like everyone else in the British Army, he'd thought the Indians little more than animals. It hadn't been until he'd lived with the Indians, until Fire Dancer had taught him that they were just as human as he, that he had come to appreciate them, and the one that he appreciated the most was at that moment very angry with him. Knowing that her anger was justified only added to Evan's remorse. Not only wasn't he making any headway with Fire Dancer that day, he seemed to have taken a very clear step backward.

17

Three days later, Evan, Fire Dancer, and Josh rode into Williamsburg. As they led their horses down the main thoroughfare, a wide sandy street named after the Duke of Gloucester, Evan was beaming. Now he'd finally be able to impress Fire Dancer and make her proud of her English blood. The frontier was behind them, and in most cases, the Anglo way of living there was even cruder and more backward than the Chickasaw's. Here was real civilization, a genteel manner of living that in this land would come the closest to what he'd been accustomed to in England.

Fire Dancer *was* impressed and excited by the new sights and sounds of the colonial capital, and she didn't try to hide it. Her eyes were wide, and she looked from side to side, eagerly scanning the neat brick buildings and taking in the busy activity of the business section through which they were riding. Tradesmen, with their long flowing sleeves rolled up and wearing leather aprons, brushed shoulders with Negro slaves dressed in tattered homespun and gentlemen elaborately clothed in tight, knee-high breeches, white hose, black shoes with shiny buckles, full, knee-high coats, long brocaded waistcoats, and stark-white ruffled shirts with frilly lace jabots at the neck. Most of the gentlemen carried walking sticks, a symbol of their higher social status, and wore tricornered hats, while the tradesmen and the blacks were bareheaded. The latter's dark brows were beaded with perspiration in the summer heat as they unloaded heavy hogsheads of rum from wagons or carried the chaise longues that the well-to-do city dwellers used for transportation around the town.

At first, Fire Dancer saw only two other women—a tavern maid standing at the door of one of the ordinaries and a Negro slave carrying a basket of vegetables from the open market farther down the street. Both were dressed like the women on the frontier, wearing long dresses with neck scarfs and barefoot, except the black woman had a turban around her head. Another woman stepped from one of the shops, and Fire Dancer took in her highly pompadoured hair, the ruff around her neck, her tightly laced bodice, and her elbow-length sleeves with their deep lace ruffles. After the woman was helped into a coach and it drove away, its wheels sending up a spray of sand from the street, Fire Dancer asked Evan, "What was wrong with her hips?"

Evan laughed. "Nothing," he said. "Below her skirt, sewed to an undergarment known as a petticoat, are metal hoops called paniers. They're what make her hips stick out that way."

"She deliberately distorted her body's shape?" Fire Dancer asked in disbelief.

"Yes."

"But why?"

"Women think it makes them more attractive. A female's hips are naturally curved. They're just exaggerating them." Evan suddenly thought the current fad was as absurd as Fire Dancer did.

Hearing the crack of a whip and the clatter of an approaching wagon behind them, the three moved their mounts to the side of the street to allow a dray piled high with kegs of molasses to go by. As it rolled past, Fire Dancer caught a glimpse of an Indian in a crowd of men walking down the opposite side of the street. The brave was wearing a bright red and blue broadcloth coat with brass buttons, breeches of some golden fabric, shiny black shoes with high red heels and glittering silver buckles, a filthy white ruffled shirt, and a turban with an ostrich feather on it. Fire Dancer realized that he was trying to mimic the gentlemen, but instead of looking impressive, he looked ridiculous. She knew the whites thought so, too, for she saw them smirking behind his back. She felt a keen embarrassment on his behalf.

"Where do you want to stay?" Josh asked Evan. "Since it isn't public times, we can take our pick of the ordinaries."

Evan was glad it wasn't "public times," that the House of Burgesses wasn't in session. It had been when he was in Williamsburg the past spring, and the town had been so crowded, he'd had to pay through the nose for a room. Even then, the politicians had carried their arguments into the common room in the tavern, yelling back and forth and pounding on the tables. Combined with the incessant gambling and business transactions that always took place in the colonial taverns, the noise had been so loud that a man could hardly think. "I stayed at the Raleigh Inn the last time I was here." The nearby inn had a bust of Sir Walter Raleigh over its entrance. "It has a billiard room as well as a public chamber for dining."

"Aye, it's a nice place," Josh agreed. "Some consider it the best ordinary in Williamsburg." He paused. "Are ye goin' to see General Amherst today?"

"No. It's been a long, hard trip, and I'm sure Fire Dancer would like to recuperate before she meets him. We'll go tomorrow."

"Aye, there's no rush," Josh agreed, "not if he's not leavin' until he told me he was. That won't be for two days yet." He looked around. "Since ye won't be needin' the animals anymore today, why don't I take the horses around to the stables at the back, and ye and Fire Dancer go on in and get yer room. I'll get back with ye in a day or two. I've some business to attend to."

What Josh had said was partly true. He did have business to attend to in Hampton. However, that could wait until tomorrow. What he had in mind for today was to find some of his drinking friends and do some carousing. He knew Evan and Fire Dancer wouldn't miss him —from the hot looks they had been shooting in each other's direction for the last hundred miles, he knew they were making their own plans for a celebration.

Evan and Fire Dancer meanwhile dismounted and removed the saddlebags containing their clothing. Then, handing the two animals' reins to Josh, they stood back while he led them and the packhorse away. Evan was glad to have the guide out of the way for a while. He had been wanting some private time with Fire Dancer, although not just intimate time, as the guide had assumed. He wanted to spend some time where the Scot wouldn't be butting in or interrupting. Evan took Fire Dancer's saddlebag from her, then tossed it and his own over his broad shoulder and led her into the building, carrying his long rifle in his other hand.

They walked down a dimly lit hallway and passed the billiard room, where several gentlemen were playing the game and two more at a table in the corner were involved in a game of checkers. They turned at a large opening and walked into the common room, where light spilled through the open shutters over the windows. Since it was midafternoon, the room was empty except for several well-heeled planters sitting at one of the heavy mahogany tables and sipping peach brandy—a southern drink of which the Virginia gentry was very fond, male and female alike. As Evan and Fire Dancer walked by them, the men gawked at her, and Evan knew they were staring at her half-covered breasts. It was all he could do to keep from turning and telling them to keep their eyes to themselves. But he knew he really couldn't blame the men. It was an accepted practice among his people that any woman who revealed herself so openly deserved to be ogled, was probably even seeking that attention—particularly if she was one of those promiscuous Indian women.

Evan forced his anger down, and when they stopped at the counter at the back of the room, he said to the tavern owner, "Good day. I'd like the best room you have available."

The man peered over the top of his half glasses. "Don't I know you?" he asked.

"Yes, I was here last spring. You put a chest of mine in storage for me."

"Aye, I remember now, Major. It's just that"—the tavern owner hesitated; he had started to say Evan looked harder and more dangerous—"I didn't recognize you in that clothing. You were wearing your uniform when you left here." He glanced to the side to be sure the tavern wench drying tankards at the end of the counter couldn't overhear, then leaned forward and said, "I've also got that other you gave me for safekeeping. It's locked in my safe."

It was his savings and the letter to his younger brother in case he didn't return. They had better be safe, he thought. "Thank you," he said. "I'll make it worth your while."

The man nodded, then asked, "Did you say you wanted my best room?"

"Yes, for the lady and myself."

The innkeeper had carefully schooled himself and showed neither shock nor disapproval at an officer having an Indian mistress. He certainly wasn't going to refuse to allow the savage to stay in his inn, which he ordinarily might have done. The major was one man that he didn't want to rile. On his last visit, a local bully had gotten out of hand and started a fight, downing three men before he turned on the major, who had been sitting in a corner of the room and quietly drinking. The bully soon regretted his rash action. The officer had made such quick work of the pest that everyone had been stunned. The innkeeper had never seen anyone's fists move that fast or strike that hard, and the major hadn't even looked particularly angry. He'd been unbelievably calm and cool and had treated the incident as if it were just an unsavory chore that had to be done. Aye, this was one man the innkeeper wouldn't want to see angry, and the planters at the table staring so rudely at the Indian girl were already making him very nervous. He hoped that the officer hadn't noticed their lecherous looks.

"If you'll just follow me, Major," the innkeeper said, coming around the counter. "I think I have a room that will please you."

Evan and Fire Dancer followed him from the common room and down the hall. At the end of the hallway, the innkeeper opened a door and showed them the room. "This is my best room," he said. "You won't be bothered by any noises, either from the common room or from the street back here."

Fire Dancer slowly looked around, while Evan's gaze quickly swept over the room. "This will be fine," he answered. He leaned his long gun against the wall by the door. "If you'll just send my chest and a bath."

"Aye, and would you like something to eat?"

"Not now. I'll order our dinner later."

The innkeeper left, closing the door softly behind him, and Fire Dancer continued to look about her in wonder. This one room was almost as big as the cabin she and Evan had shared. In one corner, sitting on a raised dais, was a huge four-poster bed covered with a canopy. The canopy was made of blue cotton print, the same as the drapes on the windows and the dust ruffle. Covering the bed was a light quilt made from scraps of the same material on a blue background. In the corner opposite the bed was a round mahogany table surrounded by four "spool" chairs for dining, and in the wall between the sleeping and dining areas was a brick fireplace. A large press, a lowboy, a writing desk with a chair, two small tables, and two heavy upholstered chairs made up the rest of the furnishings, and about the highly polished wooden floors, several hook rugs were scattered.

Thinking she had never seen so many pretty things, Fire Dancer walked to the small table beside the bed and fingered the glass hurricane shade over the candle. "What is this for?" she asked.

"It lessens the danger of fire, and disperses the light."

She stepped up to bed and placed her hands on it with her fingers spread, testing it. It felt incredibly soft. She turned and sat down on it, amazed at how deeply she sank into it.

Seeing the expression on her face, Evan said, "That's a feather mattress, and the pillows are made of down, the soft underfeathers of birds. It's quite an improvement over those corn-husk mattresses you find on the frontier."

"Yes, it is," Fire Dancer replied, remembering the lumpy mattress she had slept on in the trading post. "And much softer than my fur-padded bed."

Evan grinned with satisfaction, pleased that she was impressed.

Fire Dancer walked to the fireplace and observed the andirons in the fireplace, then the tongs, shovel, and bellows on the hearth. Picking up an object with a long wooden handle and a round brass object on the end, she asked, "Is this used for cooking?"

"No, that's a bed warmer." Evan walked to where she was standing, tossing their saddlebags onto one of the big chairs, and turned back the half lid on the pan. "Hot coals are placed in here," he said, "then the pan is placed under the covers and run between the sheets to warm the bed. Of course, we won't be using either it or the fireplace in this heat."

Fire Dancer wondered why they would ever need bed warmers. It seemed a lot of trouble to her, when body heat would accomplish the same thing in a short time. She placed the bed warmer back on the hearth, turned, and crossed to the writing table, looking at the pewter inkwell with its feather quill pen and the sanding box. Then she picked up a odd-shaped object. "And this? What is it used for?"

"That's a twenty-four-hour glass. It's used for measuring time." He took the glass from her, turned it over, and set it back down on the desk. "It takes exactly twenty-four hours for the sand in the top part of the glass to spill into the bottom, which marks the passage of one day."

Fire Dancer remembered that Evan had once asked her if the Chickasaw had a calendar. To her the white man seemed overly concerned with the passage of time. The Indians didn't need a glass with sand in it to tell them a day had passed. The rising and setting of the sun did that. She looked up at the wall behind the desk and saw a large piece of parchment on which there were many black markings. She knew it was a map, for it looked very similar to the one Evan had been working on. "What is that a map of?"

"The thirteen colonies." Evan pointed to a place that was almost in the middle of the map. "This is where we are. Williamsburg, Virginia. It's Virginia's second capital. The first was down here"—Evan slid his finger downward—"at Jamestown, but it was unhealthy spot, subject to flooding and ridden with fevers. After the fourth statehouse there burned down, the Virginians decided to move the capital here on higher ground, on what they call the Middle Plantation."

A knock at the door interrupted him. He opened the door, revealing two husky boys with a heavy chest between them. "Ah, thank you, lads," he said congenially. "You can put it over there at the end of the bed."

The two boys carried the chest to where Evan had directed and set it down. As they straightened, they started in surprise, for they had not noticed Fire Dancer when they walked in, and the last person they'd expected to find there was an Indian. Evan watched their expressions turn speculative, then snide as they realized why she must be sharing his lodgings. Their reaction infuriated Evan. He was tempted not to, but he reached into the pouch of his shirt, pulled out his purse, and fished out a coin for the two. Then he said in a hard voice as he handed them the money, "Mind your manners the next time, or there won't be any more."

The boys didn't need a verbal warning. The murderous expression on Evan's face would have been enough, and they were astute enough to guess why he was angry. They snatched the coins and rushed away. When they returned a few moments later lugging a big brass tub, they were very careful to keep their eyes from straying and maintain blank looks on their faces.

They rushed from the room the second time, leaving the door open, and Fire Dancer stared at the long, shiny tub they had placed in a corner of the room. The rim of one end was much higher than the other, and the tub sat on short pedestals that looked like an animal's paws. She had never seen such a peculiar-looking object in her life and couldn't imagine what it was used for.

Evan laughed at the expression on her face. "It's a tub for bathing, as well as for relaxation. It's made in that shape so you can lean your head back on the higher rim and just soak."

"You bathe indoors?" Fire Dancer asked in surprise.

"Yes."

At that moment, the boys, joined by two others, came into the room. Each toted two heavy wooden buckets of water, which they poured into the tub. It took three trips before the tub was half full, at which point Evan called a halt and gave each lad a coin for his efforts.

As soon as the boys left the room, Evan walked to the windows and closed the shutters. "You go ahead and bathe first, before the water gets cold," he said over his shoulder.

Fire Dancer needed no urging, for the tub of water looked very inviting. She stripped and stepped in; moving very cautiously so as not to upset the tub, she sat and stretched out, leaning her head on the back rim of the tub.

Evan turned and, seeing Fire Dancer already in the tub, grinned. It was obvious from the look on her face that she was enjoying her new adventure. He picked up a bar of soap that the boys had left them and carried it to her. "I think you might want this," he said.

Fire Dancer had never felt anything as relaxing as lying in the warm water. She could easily have fallen asleep. Hearing Evan's voice, she opened her eyes and accepted the soap. With reluctance, sat up and began washing.

Evan sat in one of the big upholstered chairs and removed his high moccasins, then leaned back in the chair and watched Fire Dancer bathe. For a while he was content to enjoy her obvious pleasure. Then he became more and more aware of her nakedness, and his desire for her, always just barely below the surface, came to the fore. When she raised one shapely leg, the tawny skin glistened in the filtered light from the window, and he stood and walked to her, a determined expression on his face.

Fire Dancer was so preoccupied with her bath that she didn't notice Evan undressing a few feet to one side of her. By the time she did, he was just tossing aside his last article of clothing. She glanced up and saw him coming toward her. Somewhat taken aback, she muttered, "I'm sorry. I didn't realize I was taking too long."

"That's all right. The tub is big enough for two."

"You're going to bathe with me?" Fire Dancer asked in disbelief.

"Later, maybe."

The husky tone of Evan's voice drew Fire Dancer's attention to his eyes, and she noticed that they were smoldering with desire. A quick glance downward confirmed what she had seen in his eyes: He was at full arousal and ready for her. As he stepped into the tub,

Fire Dancer still couldn't believe that he actually meant to make love to her there.

Evan entered the tub, and as he pushed her back so that her head again rested on the high rim of the tub, he carefully eased his body down over hers. "Do your people do this often?" she asked. "Make love while they're bathing?"

"I've never done it before," Evan admitted, his voice husky with desire. "The notion just struck me. I thought it might be novel."

Fire Dancer had no idea what *novel* meant, but at that moment she couldn't have cared less. She was acutely conscious of Evan's heated skin against her full length, pressing chest to chest, abdomen to abdomen, thigh to thigh. Trapped between their lower bellies, his magnificent erection pulsated with a life of its own, and she could feel every muscle in his body tense with anticipation. His barely leashed sexual energy was at that moment so powerful that the air seemed charged with electricity and the water surrounding them seemed to ripple. Fire Dancer's heart raced, and suddenly she wanted him with an intensity that was almost painful. She slipped her arms around his broad shoulders, glorying in the feel of his muscles trembling at her touch.

Evan ran his mouth the length of Fire Dancer's slender neck. He nibbled on her earlobe, then pulled it into his mouth and sucked on it, making wonderful shivers of delight course through her and the water ripple even more so. Slipping his hands around her back and under her buttocks, he massaged the twin mounds and then lifted them, then deftly entered her, his manhood as true as an arrow. To Fire Dancer it seemed as if every nerve ending in her body suddenly shifted to that part of her body, and her full concentration was on the feel of his rock-hard length inside her and his tremendous heat filling her, seeming to scorch her entire pelvic area. Her muscles contracted tightly around him of their own accord, and both gasped at the intense pleasure they felt.

Evan slipped his mouth from her ear to her temple and kissed her lightly there, then whispered in a ragged voice, "Put your legs around me."

Fire Dancer did as he requested, drawing him even deeper into her hot, tight depths and bringing another gasp of pleasure from both of them. He lifted his golden head and looked down at her face. Their eyes locked and held, his a vivid blue and hers a deep emerald green. Never had they been so profoundly aware of each other's powerful sexuality. A current seemed to pass back and forth between them everywhere their bodies touched, electrifying and exciting them to new heights. Evan did not have to even move a muscle for their passion to climb higher and higher, to spiral upward as their breathing came in ragged gasps and their hearts beat wildly in unison. Then as they hovered on the breathless brink, so close to reaching their fulfillment yet not able to do so, Evan came to his knees to make the thrust that would push them over.

Unfortunately, the tub had a weak foot, and when Evan moved, the foot gave way. The tub suddenly tumbled over, spilling Evan, Fire Dancer, and its water onto the floor. The impact wasn't hard enough to knock the two lovers apart, and they lay still entwined on the wet floor, staring at one another in utter surprise; then, seeing the look of disbelief on each other's face and realizing how silly they must look, they both laughed.

"I guess that wasn't such a good idea after all," he admitted.

Fire Dancer cast the tub a sideways glance. "Yes, but it's a shame," she replied. "It might have been interesting."

Evan disengaged himself, then rose, lifting her in his arms as he did so. Carrying her toward the bed, he said, "Well, we won't let a little accident stop us."

"What about the water?" Fire Dancer asked.

"What about it?"

"Shouldn't we try to soak it up with something before it ruins the mats?"

"To hell with the rugs! If the innkeeper doesn't want ruined rugs, he shouldn't send tubs with weak feet."

"It wasn't weak until you got in too," Fire Dancer pointed out.

"You're right," Evan answered, stepping up onto the dais where the bed was.

"But—"

"Shh," Evan interrupted. "If he complains, I'll pay for the blasted rugs."

As he lowered her to the bed, she asked, "Shouldn't we dry off first? We'll get the bed wet."

Evan lowered himself over her. "Stop worrying!" he said in exasperation. "I couldn't care less about the rugs or the bed. I wouldn't give a damn if the entire world were engulfed in water." His voice lowered several octaves. "I want you, more than I've ever wanted you before, so much that I think I'm going to burst if I don't have you soon. Right now, that's all that matters."

She glanced down at his erection and saw that what he had said was true. It looked immense as it jutted from the golden nest of hair at his groin. The skin was stretched so tight over the rigid, swollen organ that it looked as if it might burst. The intensity of his desire for her thrilled her and swept aside all concern for the damage they might be doing to the innkeeper's property. She opened her arms to welcome him.

But instead of embracing her, he bent his head to lick away a trickle of water on one breast, then another on her abdomen. Then he kissed away the glistening beads of water in the hair between her legs. For a moment, she thought he was going to make love to her there, and just the thought was enough to make her tremble all over, for she knew only too well what wonderful delights his skillful mouth and tongue could bring her. She opened her legs to him in breathless anticipation.

But Evan proved once again what an unpredictable lover he was. He plunged into her depths, his thrust so powerful and masterful that she climaxed almost as soon as he buried his steely length inside her. Before she had recovered, his hot mouth descended onto her lips in a ravishing, demanding kiss that gave as much as it took and sent her senses spinning all over. She kissed him back in wild abandon as he fiercely rode her to yet another tumultuous, escalating explosion, and another, and another, until she seriously feared she would die of ecstasy if he didn't give her some relief. When Evan finally allowed himself his own fiery burst of rapture, Fire Dancer was so utterly exhausted that she fell into a deep sleep almost as soon as she drifted down from the glorious heights.

As she slept, Evan looked down at her from where he still lay over her and felt a deep regret. He still wanted her, and it wasn't just because they had been forced to abstain from lovemaking during their long trip. If he had made love to her a score of times within the last twenty-fours, he'd still want her. It seemed he could never get enough of her—and that puzzled him. He had never been driven by passion, had always considered men who were to be weak and irresponsible, had never dreamed that he might become a slave to his own desire. In the past, women had simply been meaningless flirtations, to be used to satisfy his manly needs from time to time. Yet he couldn't help himself when it came to Fire Dancer. No matter how many times he possessed her, his hunger for her was never totally satisfied. If anything, making love to her just whetted his appetite for more. It appeared that the Indian maiden had brought him to his knees.

Evan smiled at the thought of Fire Dancer as a maiden. Thanks to him, she was a far cry from being one, and yet he still thought of her that way. In his mind, she was still innocent and pure, and he knew she would always be, no matter how many times he made love to her or how passionately she might respond. For a moment he pondered this oddity: How she could be so wildly unbridled in giving of herself, yet seem so virtuous? Then he realized it wasn't her body but her inner being that made her appear so pure and untouched. Hers was a special beauty that she held fiercely to herself, one that could never be corrupted or marred by the passage of time. Evan was glad for it, but it was also a part of her that she held away from him, and it was the reason he could never truly claim her as his.

At that moment Evan realized what the "more" he wanted from Fire Dancer was. He wanted all of her, that beautiful inner being as well as her passion and her body. Why he wanted this was a puzzle to him. He had no intention of getting emotionally involved with her, or so he thought. Yet knowing he could never have all of her filled him with an unexplainable sadness.

Tenderly, he brushed aside a wisp of damp hair lying across Fire Dancer's forehead and kissed her there. Then he rose from the bed, pulled the covers around her, placed a screen in front of the bed to shield her from prying eyes, and walked to the door to summon fresh bath water, his heart still heavy.

18

Fire Dancer slept through the rest of the afternoon, the evening, and the entire night through and awakened the next morning entirely disoriented. The first thing she became aware of was the incredibly soft feather mattress beneath her. She was sunk so deeply into it that it seemed to threaten to engulf and smother her. That was frightening enough, but the room was totally unfamiliar. She shook her head, trying to rid herself of the cobwebs in her sleep-befuddled mind and remember where she was.

"Good morning."

She started at the sound of Evan's deep voice, then rolled over and saw him bending over the bed and smiling down at her. For a moment she allowed herself to drowsily bask in the warmth of his shimmering blue, blue eyes. Then everything suddenly came flooding back, and she sat up, the covers dropping to her waist. "It's morning?" she asked in surprise.

"Yes."

"I slept all night?"

"And the afternoon and evening before," Evan answered.

Fire Dancer heard a hint of disappointment in his voice and misinterpreted it as censure. No wonder, she thought. He must think her terribly lazy. "I—I must have been tired," she answered, still finding it hard to believe that she had slept so long.

"Yes, the trip was long and exhausting."

It wasn't just the trip that had exhausted her, Fire Dancer thought, remembering Evan's long, fierce lovemaking the afternoon before. Where did he get his amazing endurance? she wondered. Could someone die from too much excitement? At times she had thought her heart was going to burst, it was beating so hard and so fast. Why, it was a miracle she survived it! But the memory made her blood warm and her loins tingle.

Seeing a flush come to her skin, Evan knew she was remembering their torrid lovemaking. He bent a little lower and dropped a kiss on the dark peak of one rosy breast, then watched the nipple harden in response. "I'd crawl back into that bed with you and stay there all day if I could," he said in a husky voice, "but that's impossible. We have an audience with General Amherst, remember? So stop looking so damn tempting and get up! Breakfast is on the table."

As he rose, turned, and walked away, Fire Dancer saw that he was dressed in his uniform, except for his coat and tricorner hat. His broad shoulders strained at the gleaming white material of his shirt, and his tight breeches molded his narrow hips and taut buttocks. As he stepped around the screen and out of her line of vision, she slowly climbed from the bed. Her muscles felt stiff, and her back ached. Pulling a sheet from the bed, she wrapped it around her and walked gingerly around the screen. Breakfast was on the table, just as Evan had said.

As he saw her approaching, Evan asked, "Why are you walking that way?"

"I'm stiff, and my back aches."

"Is it from the bed?" he asked.

"Is that what caused it?" Fire Dancer asked in surprise.

"I don't know. I'm stiff when I've slept on something harder than I'm accustomed to, but I've never heard of anyone getting a backache from a bed that was too soft."

"But that must have been it," Fire Dancer argued. "I've never had a backache in my life. I'll sleep on the floor from now on."

Sleep on the floor—when a feather bed was available? What a total waste of comfort! Evan thought in horror. And he had hoped to impress her with his way of living. He felt keen disappointment. "Why don't you try it another night or so, to allow your body to get used to it?" he suggested.

"Why? There's no point in getting used to it. When I go back to my Chickasaw bed, it will seem too hard," she answered with maddening logic.

As she stepped up to the table, he pulled one of the heavy spool chairs out for her. She gave him a quizzical look. "It's customary for a gentleman to pull a chair out for a lady," Evan explained.

Fire Dancer's eyes flashed. "I told you, I'm not a

lady! I'm not helpless! I don't need to be waited on hand and foot!"

Her and her damn independence, Evan thought. "I know that, and I didn't mean to imply that you are helpless," he answered in exasperation. "This is simply a courtesy that men give women. I was trying to be polite. It comes as automatically to me as saying good day."

In that case, Fire Dancer could not object to it. The Chickasaw also practiced courtesy and politeness, and she couldn't blame Evan for the fact that his customs were different from hers. "I'm sorry," she muttered. "I didn't understand. But I don't like being called a lady."

"I gathered that much," Evan answered wryly, "but I don't understand why."

"My mother said that ladies are very spoiled and self-ish."

Then her resistance wasn't just a matter of fierce independence, Evan thought in surprise. Yes, her mother would naturally have had a low regard for the women she worked for, since she had been an indentured servant. He shrugged. "I'll have to admit that your mother wasn't altogether wrong. Some of the women of the gentry are spoiled and selfish. But when I called you a lady, I didn't mean it that way."

"Yes, I realize that now," she answered, then sat on the chair he had pulled out. He pushed the chair in and walked around the table to his own chair, feeling that he had won a small but important point.

Meanwhile, Fire Dancer was admiring the delftware plates, saucers, and cups, whose rims were circled by blue flowers and leaves. She picked up the cup sitting before her and said in surprise, "It's so light."

"Yes, compared to pewterware or wood, it is. It's called delftware. You'll also find a lot of white salt glaze here in the better homes in the colonies. That's a milky white pottery with scalloped edges and embossed pictures. It's really quite pretty. We have sets of both in my home. We also have a set of china—it's made of porcelain and very delicate, so thin you can almost see through it."

Fire Dancer realized that, for all of the intimacy they had shared, she really knew very little about Evan personally. "Where is home?"

"Back in England," Evan answered with a shrug.

Fire Dancer sensed that he was being evasive, but her curiosity had been aroused, and she was determined to know more about him. "I know that, but where?"

"It doesn't matter. It's no longer my home. It was my father's. Then when he died, it became my brother's. That's the law in England—the eldest son inherits everything. It's just that I still think of it as home. I suppose I always will."

Fire Dancer heard the bitterness in his voice, but she sensed that it went much deeper, that he had been hurt, and that made her hurt for him. "It saddened you to lose it, didn't it?" she asked softly.

Evan stiffened, and a hard warning look came into his eyes. He had never discussed his feelings about losing his father's legacy with anyone, nor had anyone dared attempt to pry into those feelings—not even his closest friends. They had learned the hard way that Evan was a man who would reveal his thoughts, but never his feelings. Those he guarded closely.

Fire Dancer could tell by his reaction to her question that she was infringing on something that he considered very private, but her concern for him gave her the courage to pursue it. She reached across the table and covered one of his big hands with her small one. The act seemed so genuinely caring that it broke down all the barriers Evan had erected over the years. His disappointment, his hurt, and his resentment came spilling forth as if a dam had burst. When he was finished telling her his story, he was shocked by all that he had revealed. He rose from the table, walked to the window, stared out for a moment, then turned back around. "I'm sorry," he said. "I didn't mean to get so carried away."

Evan's revelations about himself had given Fire Dancer a better understanding of him and made her appreciate him all the more. Knowing he'd had dreams and had suffered disappointments made him seem much more human, and she was particularly impressed that it was the loss of the land he grieved, more than the wealth and prestige. His love of the land was something she could understand, for she felt the same way about her wilderness home. "No, don't be sorry," she answered. "I'm glad you did."

Evan was actually glad too. Voicing his feelings had been a tremendous relief, almost like lancing a deep, festering sore. He wished he had done it years ago, but he had never found anyone he felt he could confide in. He wondered why, of all people, he had bared his soul to Fire Dancer. Confidences were something you shared with friends, not lovers, and yet he felt comfortable about what he had done. She had been so understanding.

When she reached for the pot of tea sitting on the table, he said, "That's probably cold by now. In fact, our entire breakfast is. I'll order us some more."

Later, as they ate their breakfast, Fire Dancer mused over everything she had learned about Evan. She had known by his manner and speech that he was a cut above the usual Englishmen with whom the Chickasaw dealt, but she had never dreamed he had noble blood or that he came from such wealth and high position. She supposed she should have guessed as much when they reached Williamsburg. He seemed so at ease in these surroundings, with all the comforts that where so amazing and so foreign to her.

In that respect, his revelations about himself were a double-edged sword. She understood him better, but she also realized how drastically different they were. Just as she had always claimed, she was pure Chickasaw, and he was pure Anglo. Bloodlines had nothing to do with it. Who a man was and who a woman was, was determined not by their birth but by the culture in which they had been raised. Despite the fact that they were lovers, their cultures had absolutely nothing in common. It was a sobering realization, and it left her saddened.

Seeing the expression on her face, Evan said, "What's wrong? You look as if you've lost your best friend."

That was just the way she felt—as if she had lost someone very dear to her. She realized now that she had agreed to come with Evan on this trip not only to have more precious time with him but to give him time to fall in love with her. But now she knew how futile her hopes had been. Evan wasn't like the colonists—transported Englishmen who had come to this backward country to find a better life. He came from the wealthy and powerful upper crust. He already had the better life.

And noblemen didn't fall in love with women beneath them, certainly not with "savages." They were even more class conscious than the Chickasaw. Her mother had told her that. Oh, Evan might come to feel fondness for her, she admitted. But that would mean nothing. He was fond of his horse. No, what she wanted was love, the deep, abiding emotion she was beginning to feel for him, and that could never be. She had been chasing an impossible dream.

When Fire Dancer didn't answer, Evan prompted her. "Didn't you hear me?" he asked softly. "I asked what was wrong."

Realizing that her dreams could never come true brought a deep pain to Fire Dancer. Suddenly, she felt terribly alone and terribly homesick. "I miss my home. I want to go back."

Nothing she could have said would have disappointed Evan more. "We just arrived," he argued. "There are so many things I want to show you!"

"I don't want to see them," she answered adamantly. "I only want to go home."

How could he impress her if she refused to see the things he wanted to show her? he thought in frustration. And just a moment before, he had been thinking that he felt closer to her than ever, that they had reached a new, undefined plateau in their relationship. Then out of the clear blue, she announced that she wanted to go home. He'd never figure her out, not in a million years. Her moods were as unpredictable as quicksilver.

"All right, we'll go back," Evan answered in a terse voice. "But not until we've accomplished what we've come for. You agreed to an audience with General Amherst, and I won't let you back out of it."

"You can tell him I changed my mind and did not come with you."

"No, I can't. He knows you're here. I sent word to him early this morning, and we have an appointment with him shortly after noon." After she had absorbed this information, he asked, "Are you going to break your word?"

Fire Dancer's eyes flashed. "A Chickasaw never breaks her word!"

There she went again, Evan thought, his own temper rising. She totally ignored her Anglo blood. "Good! Because I don't break mine either!" He rose from the table and pushed back his chair. "Now that that's settled, you'd better get bathed and dressed. Then we'll go to a dress shop to pick up something for you to wear."

Fire Dancer's head shot up. "What do you mean, pick up something for me to wear?"

"I mean a dress. Certainly you're not planning to wear your buckskins to meet the governor of Virginia."

"And why not? It is what the Chickasaw wear, and I am Chickasaw."

"You're half white!"

"No!" Fire Dancer answered, coming to her feet. "I am all Chickasaw!"

Her claim infuriated Evan all the more. "I don't give

a damn who you say you are! I forbid you to wear that garment to meet the governor!"

There he went again, Fire Dancer thought. Being arrogant and demanding. And now she knew why he was that way: because he was a nobleman and accustomed to having people obey him. "You cannot forbid me to do anything! You are not my master!"

"Dammit, I know that! But I won't stand by and watch you being ogled."

Fire Dancer drew herself up proudly and said in a cutting voice, "If you are ashamed of me, you should not have asked me to come."

"Where in the hell did you get that idea?" Evan asked. "I didn't say I was ashamed of you! I'm talking about the garment, not you. It's too revealing. Half your breasts show." Evan ran his hand through his golden hair in frustration. "Dammit, Fire Dancer, I know you don't think that top is immodest, but my people do. So please, for my sake, don't wear it."

"I should forsake my native clothing so I won't embarrass you?"

"It's not a matter of embarrassing me. It's what I know those men will be thinking when they see your breasts revealed that way. It makes me madder than hell to know they're lusting after you."

"Why?"

Fire Dancer's candid question took Evan aback. Why would he get angry? he wondered. He'd never cared how much the other women he'd taken up with had revealed themselves to other men. But with Fire Dancer, it was different. He felt much more protective, much more possessive of her. "I don't want them thinking bad thoughts about you, that's all," he replied, his answer partly evasive and partly true. "You're not a loose woman."

Fire Dancer didn't want the men to think bad thoughts about her because of her Chickasaw clothing. She didn't wear it to seduce. It was simply her woods garment. "In that case, I will wear my town clothing."

"You mean that togalike garment you wrap around you?"

"Yes."

She would still stand out like a sore thumb in the crowd and people would stare, Evan thought. He wanted to save her from that indignity as well. "I still think a dress would be more appropriate. You'd blend in with the crowd better. You wouldn't have to wear the paniers, if that's what you're objecting to."

Fire Dancer remembered the Indian she had seen the day before and how ridiculous he had looked. She feared that if she dressed in the white woman's clothing, she would look just as ridiculous, and the colonists would laugh at her behind her back. After all, no dress could hide the color of her skin or her high cheekbones or her unusual female height—all strong Chickasaw characteristics. No, she decided firmly, she would not make a fool of herself that way. She didn't care if the colonists stared at her, but her fierce Chickasaw pride would never tolerate their ridiculing her. "I will dress in my own clothing."

Evan had no idea what was going on in Fire Dancer's mind. If he had, he would have admired her courage. As it was, he thought her insistence on wearing her own clothing was simply another show of stubborn independence. But he refrained from saying so, for fear she might wear the offensive buckskins just out of spite. He nodded curtly. "I'll order a bath for you, and while you're bathing and dressing, I'll see about getting us some transportation."

Evan left the room, and as he walked down the dimly lit hallway, he wondered where his plans had gone astray. Nothing was working out as he'd hoped.

19

Two hours later, Evan and Fire Dancer were seated in an open chaise longue and being carried to the governor's palace by four husky black slaves. As they traveled down the street, colonists in other chaises and on foot were staring at Fire Dancer, but much to Evan's relief, their looks were more awed than anything else. Evan thought he knew why. While her red toga was simplicity itself, the impressive strings of pearls around her neck, in her dark hair, and dangling from her earlobes were hardly commonplace. The gems would have made a queen envious, and the colonists were astute enough to realize their value. But what Evan didn't realize was that most of the people were admiring the woman as much as the pearls, for Fire Dancer looked not only beautiful with her exotic coloring but absolutely regal with her dark head proudly high.

As they approached their turn, Evan gazed down the street. In the distance, over the tops of the trees, he could faintly see the cupola of the capitol. "I wish you would reconsider," he said to Fire Dancer, "and let me show you more of Williamsburg. There's a theater just past the capitol where they present Shakespeare's plays almost nightly. I'd particularly like to take you there."

Fire Dancer's mother had told her of the theater and how men dressed in rich costumes acted out a story on a stage much like the dais in their Indian temple. The Chickasaws loved storytelling in any form, and ordinarily she would have been tickled to death to actually see a play. But not even the lure of seeing a play could draw Fire Dancer from the depths of her depression. Much to Evan's disappointment, she made no reply.

They turned from the Duke of Gloucester Street onto Palace Street. The thoroughfare ran through the palace green, a wide grassy stretch that was lined with catalpa trees, and ended at an elaborate ironwork gate. When they passed through the gate and Fire Dancer saw the governor's palace, her breath caught at the sight of the brick building with its dormers in the roof, its cupola, and its towering flagpole where the colorful Union Jack fluttered. Not only was it a very impressive-looking building, she had never seen a two-storied structure before and wondered what kept it from toppling over. She broke her long silence to ask in awe, "This is the capitol?"

"No, the capitol is at the end of the Duke of Glouces-ter Street, the same street our tavern is on. It's the building where the House of Burgesses meet, the rep-resentatives that make Virginia's laws." He paused, see-ing her frown. He was only confusing her. To help her understand the legislature's function, he said, "You might compare the representatives to your tribal council. They make laws, but only if the governor, like your chief, approves. This is the governor's palace, where he both works and lives. Of course, compared with palaces in my country, it's very small."

Fire Dancer could hardly believe that this massive building was someone's home, even if he was a chief. She wondered if Evan's home had been as large and impressive as this, and once again she felt a painful pang that their worlds were so far apart.

Evan didn't notice the pained look that came to Fire Dancer's eyes. Indicating a one-story building that jutted about seventy-five feet from the north face of the palace, he said, "I understand that addition was built only a few years ago. It contains a ballroom and supper rooms. Out back are the formal gardens and orchards."

They stopped in front of the palace, and the chaise was lowered to the ground. A footman dressed in colorful livery helped them from the chair, and after climbing a short flight of stairs, they were greeted at the heavy wooden door by another servant similarly clothed.

"Good day, sir," the servant said to Evan.

"Good day," Evan replied. "I'm Major Trevor. I believe General Amherst is expecting me."

"Yes, sir, he is. If you'll just follow me."

Evan and Fire Dancer followed the servant into the building and walked down a wide hallway whose floors were made of black and white marble. Seeing Fire Dancer looking curiously at the leather buckets hanging on the walnut-paneled walls, Evan said, "Those water buckets are kept there in case of fire, since this building almost burned to the ground. If you remember I told you, the capitol at Jamestown burned down four times. It seems the Virginians have a problem with fires."

Fire Dancer looked at the fireplace set in one wall of the hallway. If the whites didn't build their homes with so many fireplaces, they wouldn't have to worry, she thought. A fireplace in every room seemed to her a luxury that wasn't needed. She doubted that it got any colder here than it did in her part of the country.

The servant led them into a spacious drawing room and told Evan that the general would be with them shortly. After he left, Fire Dancer looked around and saw that the room was furnished even more luxuriously than their room at the tavern. Her gaze moved over the gleaming mahogany Chippendale furniture, the fine set of Queen Anne chairs with their needlework seats, the cherrywood fold-down card table, the heavy damask draperies at the windows. Then she crossed to a strange piece of furniture and ran her fingers lightly over the top of its wooden cabinet.

"That's a spinet," Evan informed her. "It makes music."

The Chickasaw used bamboo flutes, hide drums, and cymbals fashioned from shells for making music. Fire Dancer couldn't imagine how this odd-looking, boxlike object could make music or what kind of sounds could possibly come from it. Evan was about to show her, his fingers hovering over the keyboard, when General Amherst walked into the room and said in a cheerful voice, "Good day, Colonel. I'm glad to see you had a safe trip back."

Evan spun around and answered, "Good day, General Amherst." He wondered why the general had addressed him by the wrong title. Surely he hadn't forgotten he was a major.

As Fire Dancer turned from the spinet, General Amherst said, "And this must be the young lady Josh told me about. Fire Dancer, I believe he said?"

Evan cringed, half expecting her to take offense at being called a lady and to tell the general so in no uncertain terms. But to his relief she smiled politely and answered, "Yes, I am Fire Dancer."

As Evan's commanding officer walked across the room, she noted that he was slim and not much taller than she was herself. He was also older than she had expected—his brown hair was streaked with gray. All in all, she was rather disappointed with the white war chief. He wasn't nearly as impressive-looking as her uncle.

General Amherst came to a stop before Fire Dancer. "Josh told me that you bravely accompanied Colonel Trevor on that dangerous surveillance of the enemy through the wilderness," he said, "but he didn't tell me you were so beautiful."

Fire Dancer knew the general's compliment was sincere, for she could see the admiration in his eyes. A flush rose on her face. "Thank you for your kind compliment," she replied, "but what I did wasn't all that brave. My home is in the wilderness. I don't consider it so dangerous."

Evan couldn't believe his ears. How could she say such a thing? he wondered. Still, it had been he, and not Fire Dancer, who had worried about the dangers, he knew, and he hadn't been worried on his own behalf, but hers. Not once had she shown the slightest fear, which had been the source of a great deal of frustration to him at the time. But remembering it all now, he was proud of the way she had behaved. "I'm afraid Fire Dancer is being too modest, sir," Evan said, overriding her dismissal of her bravery. "At times we were in grave danger. Once we had to run from a barrage of bullets the enemy shot as we were departing, and another time we were almost sucked into a monstrous whirlpool in the river. At neither time did she show any fear."

General Amherst gave Fire Dancer a quick appraising look. "I agree with you, Colonel. These are hardly everyday occurrences, even in a wilderness."

Evan frowned. That was the third time the general had addressed him by the wrong rank. Seeing his scowl, General Amherst asked, "Is something wrong, Colonel?"

"Yes, sir, there is." Evan hesitated, then said, "Excuse me for correcting you, but I'm a major."

A grin spread across the general's lean face. "Not anymore you're not. You've been promoted to a colonel."

But Evan's scowl only deepened. "Sir, if taking that cannon at Fort Massiac had anything to do with it, I'm afraid the tale has been greatly exaggerated. It wasn't an act of bravery, despite what Josh might have told you. If anything, it was downright foolish."

"Let me be the judge of that." The general's firm voice brooked no argument. Then he smiled. "Besides, that wasn't the only thing I took into consideration," he said. "You should have been promoted after the Fort Carillon defeat, for the way you successfully led what was left of the command back to safety. If it hadn't been for your decisive leadership, we might have lost the entire force."

The mention of Fort Carillon directed Evan's attention from his unexpected promotion to the war. "How is the war going, sir? I understand Quebec is under siege."

"Yes, General Wolfe managed to get up the Saint Lawrence, even though the French sent fireboats against him twice and laid siege. But I am in no way confident that the city will fall. It sits at the top of a high bluff overlooking the river. We'll have to make an amphibious assault, and I'm not certain we'll be successful."

"So the war could still be a long way from won?"

"Indeed. For that reason, I want you to investigate that western fort and settlement that you've heard the French have made. We can't afford to leave any stone unturned."

"I agree."

"And while you're at it, make a map of the area, as you did before," General Amherst instructed. "I don't know if you realize it or not, but the information you recorded on the map you sent me is all we know of that area. It is invaluable to us."

He turned his attention back to Fire Dancer. "Excuse me. I didn't mean to appear rude, discussing business that way."

"I don't mind. I'm very interested in how the war is progressing. My people have a stake in this struggle against the French too."

It was a point of calm logic that the general would not have expected from a woman, least of all from one as young as Fire Dancer. How different she was from the young women he knew, he thought—women who seemed to think their sole purpose in life was to be entertained and admired. Not only was she beautiful and brave, she was much more poised than he had ever dreamed a mestizo could be, even if she was an Indian princess. And he suspected that she was usually intelligent for a female. The general gave her a long, thoughtful look.

When Josh had first told him about Fire Dancer, he had been personally curious. That was why he had asked to meet her, and he expected to meet a mestizo woman who had shown unusual bravery and let it go at that. But now that he had seen that there was so much more to her, he realized she could be a great asset to the war effort. "My dear," Amherst said, "I have a favor to ask you."

Both Fire Dancer and Evan had wondered at the general's close scrutiny of her. But they were stunned at this remark. "What favor?" she asked a little belatedly.

"I don't know if you are aware of it or not, but here in the colonies support for the war has not always been the best, particularly in these southern colonies. The war seems far removed and unreal to the colonists here, and they're for the better part unconcerned about what happens in the northern colonies and the northwest, where the actual fighting is taking place, and where the French are arousing the native tribes against the colonists. Here in Virginia proper, they're protected from those kinds of attacks by the mountains. As the commanding officer in charge of all the operations against the French here, I find this attitude frustrating."

The general seemed to be beating around the bush. "I'm afraid I don't understand," Fire Dancer said when he paused. "Just what is it you want of me?"

General Amherst smiled at her question. He liked her directness and assertiveness. He wished a few more of his officers had those qualities—the majority of them would let him ramble for hours before they dared interrupt him. That this young lady dared pleased him even more. "I'm sorry, my dear. I don't suppose you need all that background information. This is what I propose. One of the wealthy planters here is having a reception and ball in my honor at his plantation tonight. I'd like for you and Colonel Trevor to attend as my guests. I'm hoping that your presence and the story of the part you both played in this war will make the colonists more aware of its reality—and help them appreciate just how important our Indian allies are."

Evan shot Fire Dancer a quick glance, fully expecting her to refuse. When she hesitated, he said, "I'm sorry, sir, but we'd planned to leave as soon as this audience is over."

"But why? You just arrived this morning."

"Fire Dancer misses her home."

The general turned directly to Fire Dancer. "Won't you reconsider?" he said. "Surely one day wouldn't make that much difference to you, but it might make a big difference to our war effort. As you said, your own people have a stake in this war."

Fire Dancer was very eager to get back to her home, but she couldn't refuse the general. She no longer had just herself to consider. What had started out for her as a visit to satisfy her curiosity had acquired a political aspect. She had become an envoy of her people, and as one of the Chickasaw ruling clan, it was her duty to aid their allies in whatever way she could. She looked the general directly in the eye. "I will attend," she said.

"Thank you, my dear! Somehow I knew you wouldn't let me down."

Evan was surprised at her answer but was just as pleased as the general. "At what plantation are the reception and ball to be held, sir?"

"At Thomas Moore's plantation. Perhaps you know him?"

"No, I don't know many colonists personally—only those I've had occasion to work with, like Mr. McDougal. But if Thomas Moore is well known in Williamsburg, I'm sure the driver of the coach I hire will know how to get to his plantation."

"There's no need to hire a coach. You can travel with me. As I said, you're my guests. Be sure to bring bedclothing—we'll be staying overnight."

Evan wasn't surprised to be staying overnight. The same was true of balls in England—they usually lasted into the early morning hours, and many ended with an early breakfast. Only the guests who lived close by left when the ball ended, a ball at a country home. But this overnight might be a problem. "Don't you think it would be better if we left after the reception and dance? Mr. Moore may not have room for any more overnight guests."

"Of course he has room! Why, he must have thirty bedrooms in that huge place of his, and most of the guests will be local plantation owners and businessmen from town. They won't be staying overnight."

"But I'd hate to impose, particularly since he didn't invite us personally," Evan argued, hoping the general wouldn't take offense at his objections.

"I can see your point, Colonel. And ordinarily I might agree that it's improper, if not downright rude, for me to invite guests, when I'm a guest myself. But Moore is not a personal friend of mine. And there's no doubt in my mind that if I weren't the new governor, he wouldn't give me the time of day. You know how the colonists feel about the British Army, including its top officers. So, it's quite obvious to me that the reason he is giving this reception and ball in my honor is to impress me, in the hope that I will grant him favors in the future, and to impress the other plantation owners. He's using me, Colonel, and I don't particularly like being used. Besides, in all likelihood, he won't mind. All these plantation owners seem to have guests from England, and it isn't at all unusual for them to stay for months at a time."

Evan didn't mind imposing on one of the scornful colonists in the least. Besides, the general had made it quite clear that was how it would be.

"In that case, sir, I think Fire Dancer and I should get back to our ordinary to pack and return here before it's time to depart." Evan thought he would also have to find something appropriate for Fire Dancer to wear, then convince her to wear it. Yes, he was going to need every moment he could possibly get. He had a battle to fight between now and the time the coach arrived.

"There's no point in your coming back here," the general answered. "I'll have my coachman stop for you on our way out of the city. At what ordinary are you staying?"

Evan was relieved at the general's suggestion. That would give him even more time. "The Raleigh."

The general nodded and said, "Expect us around five, but don't eat beforehand. We're also going to be dinner guests. I hope you have a hearty appetite."

Evan knew the general would love to see him eat the plantation owner out of house and home if at all possible, simply out of spite. He gave his commanding officer a conspiratorial smile. "Well, you know how bad army food is, sir," he said. "I may not be able to contain myself."

Their eyes met in perfect understanding, and the general chuckled. Then Evan looked around for Fire Dancer, and spied her standing before the fireplace across the room.

"That marble plaque in the mantle seems to draw everyone's attention," General Amherst remarked. "It depicts a rural hunting scene. The deer are so lifelike, you expect them to move at any moment."

Evan wondered if that was why Fire Dancer was staring at the plaque so intently.

"Ah, Colonel," the general said in a low voice, "she is truly lovely. So beautiful, so graceful, so poised. Yes, Fire Dancer will make quite an impression on these colonial bumpkins. They'll see what a real Indian princess looks like. From what I have heard, for all of her bravery, Pocahontas wasn't all that pretty or impressive looking."

Fire Dancer wasn't a princess, not in the technical sense. But Evan didn't bother to correct his commanding officer, because she was the closest thing to one, with her high position in her tribe, her regal bearing, and her rare exotic beauty. Still, he had taken note of a very important point. If Fire Dancer was to be presented as an Indian princess, she would have to wear her native dress—otherwise she would lose her authenticity. But he was determined not to let her go to the reception and ball in that faded red toga. If she was to be presented as an Indian princess, she would dress the part. He'd see to it, by God!

Evan stepped forward. "Fire Dancer, if we're to be ready by five, we should leave."

"What's the hurry?" General Amherst asked. "Surely, there's time for me to show Fire Dancer the gardens. They're quite lovely, you know."

"As much as I regret it, I'm afraid not, sir." Evan searched for an excuse to leave now. He was almost certain that Fire Dancer would resist his plan, and he didn't want the general witnessing it. "My dress uniform has been packed away for some time and will need pressing, and my sword is undoubtedly rusted. Also, I've misplaced my dress gloves, and I'll have to shop for replacements. I wouldn't want to appear at such an important function looking anything less than immaculate —not if I'm to represent His Royal Highness's army."

"Indeed, not!" the general agreed. "In that case, you are dismissed."

Evan took Fire Dancer's arm firmly in hand. She started to object, for she had glimpsed the beautiful garden from the window and would have liked to see it. But Evan whispered, "I'm warning you, don't resist me! If you do, so help me God, I'll throttle you!"

Fire Dancer didn't resist as Evan led her from the room. Instead, she nodded good-bye to the general, who smiled and nodded back. But beneath the poised and graceful surface, she was once again fuming at Evan's arrogance and overbearing attitude.

20

Fire Dancer waited until she and Evan were seated in the chaise and moving before she exploded. "How dare you threaten to throttle me! Just try it—I'll cut your heart out!"

Evan had been expecting her anger and wasn't in the least perturbed about it. The black slaves carrying the chaise weren't as unaffected, however—they missed a step and almost stumbled. "Calm down," he said firmly. "What I said back there is true. We need to use this time to get ready for the ball. We've got to find you something appropriate to wear."

"I told you, I will not wear the white woman's clothing!"

"Of course not," Evan agreed, which took her completely aback. "That's not what I had in mind. Let's find you something better than that faded stroud cloth you're wearing. After all, this is an important occasion. Everyone will be dressed in their very best, and so should you. You don't want to look dowdy, do you?

Think of what a poor impression of the Chickasaw that would give these colonists."

In appealing to Fire Dancer's tribal pride, Evan had hit upon the perfect means of persuasion. She realized that as their representative, it was her duty to look her very best. No, she would not shame her people by appearing dowdy. "Is there a trading post here where I can find more stroud cloth?" she asked.

"Does it have to be stroud cloth? Can't you use some other material?"

If there were any taboos against using other fabrics, Fire Dancer didn't know about them. The traders had simply never given the Chickasaw any other. "I—I suppose any material could be used, as long as it's new and not faded."

Evan could hardly believe his success, but he was very careful not to show his exultation. If Fire Dancer knew he had looked upon the matter as a contest between them, she might do a complete turn-around. She could be unbelievably stubborn. "Then we'll go to a dressmaker's shop. They have every imaginable kind of cloth. Surely we'll find something there."

Evan gave the bearers instructions to take them to the best dressmaker's shop in Williamsburg. The slaves wove in and out of the streets until they came to a small frame house with a white picket fence around it and a small garden beside it. Evan might have thought the bearers had brought him to the wrong place, for the house was clearly in a residential area, but then he saw a small sign hanging from a post out front that read MRS. SMITH, DRESSMAKER OF THE HIGHEST QUALITY.

The bearers had set the chaise down beneath the cool

shade of one of the trees that lined the street, and Evan helped Fire Dancer from it and led her down the gravel walk. When he opened the door to the shop, a bell over it rang, startling Fire Dancer. She looked up to see what had made the tingling sound. When her eyes lowered once again, they widened in surprise. The entire front of the house was one big room with tables on which bolts of material of every possible hue on earth were displayed. Fire Dancer had never seen so much color in one place. For a moment, she was simply overwhelmed. Then she stepped up to a bolt of flaming red on a nearby table and began to finger the material.

Evan followed her. "Are you considering that piece?" he asked.

"Yes."

"Why don't you get something in another color?"

"Why? I like red. It is the Chickasaw's favorite color."

"I'm well aware of that. But there might be another color that is more suited to you personally."

Since she had never had a choice, this hadn't occurred to Fire Dancer. And red really wasn't *her* favorite color—she preferred blue. She turned and looked over the room. There were bolts of every imaginable blue in every imaginable type of material, from heavy brocades and velvets to the sheerest of silks. Then, seeing a brilliant royal-blue silk shot with golden threads, she made her way to it and lifted the free tail of the bolt in her hand, marveling at its lightness and the way the golden threads shone. The intense blue reminded her of Evan's eyes, and the gold resembled his hair. She had never seen anything so beautiful in her life. She turned to Evan. "This is the one I want," she said.

All along, Evan had had a different color in mind, and he, too, had spied his choice. He snatched the bolt from the table. "What about this one?" he asked, holding it out for her inspection. "Did you notice it?"

Fire Dancer looked at the bolt. Made of a shimmering silk, it seemed almost iridescent. Its color changed from a pure crystal green to a deep emerald and to every subtle hue in between as the light caught it from different angles. While the color didn't appeal to her much, she was fascinated with the fleeting transformations. She looked from the green to the blue in indecision.

Hoping to sway her, Evan said, "The green will accentuate your beautiful eyes."

"But the blue is so beautiful itself."

"Yes, it is," Evan answered, with no idea why Fire Dancer was so caught up in it. "But a dress color should be chosen according to which is the more flattering, especially for an occasion as important as tonight."

"May I speak to you in private, sir?" A cold, haughty voice came from behind Evan. Evan turned and saw a thin, hatchet-faced woman. "This way, please," she said, walking to the back of the room.

Evan frowned, handed the cloth to Fire Dancer, and followed the woman. When they were out of Fire Dancer's hearing, the woman said, "Sir, I must ask you to leave. I do not allow Indians in my establishment." The woman's long nose rose a few notches in the air. "I cater to only the best."

Evan glanced to the side and noticed other customers in the shop, three women standing in a corner, glaring at him in affront. Evan saw red. If they had not been pressed for time, he would gladly have given the hateful woman a scorching retort, then taken Fire Dancer and left. It took all his considerable will to force his fury down and say in a tight voice, "Then perhaps you had better reconsider, madam. The young woman to whom you are referring is a Chickasaw princess who happens to be the honored guest of Governor Amherst."

At the mention of the governor's name, the woman's eyes widened. She glanced at the other women and stared at them for a moment, as if weighing whose approval was more important to her, theirs or the governor's. Then she turned back to Evan. "I'm most sorry, sir. I didn't realize," she said.

"I'm sure you didn't," he answered caustically, feeling nothing but disgust for the woman. He nodded curtly, turned, and walked back to Fire Dancer.

"I still haven't decided," she said, gazing down at the bolts. So caught up had she been in trying to make a choice that she hadn't realized the conversation with the shop owner had been about her.

"Then take both of them, but wear the green tonight," Evan answered, picking up both bolts.

Having solved her dilemma, he returned to the proprietor, who was now whispering to the other women. Seeing him approach, the woman broke away, walked up to him, and took the bolts. "Would you like to see the trimmings that go with these and my fashion dolls?" she asked.

"That won't be necessary. We're not having a dress made. I just want the material."

"Sir, I'm sorry if I offended you earlier," the woman answered. "But I *am* the best dressmaker in town, if you're thinking of finding someone else. Also, I think you'll find that my prices are quite reasonable."

"It's not that," Evan replied curtly. "The princess doesn't wear dresses. She intends to wrap the material around her, like what she's wearing right now."

"Oh, I see." The dressmaker was flustered, then recovered her poise. "How many yards will you need?"

Evan had no earthly idea, and seeing the blank look on Fire Dancer's face, he realized she didn't know either. "Just pull it off of the bolt," he instructed the dressmaker. "She'll tell you when to cut."

The dressmaker placed the bolt of green material on her cutting board, then rolled it over and over and over until Fire Dancer told her to cut. She repeated the procedure with the blue bolt. All the while, the other women were craning their necks to get a glimpse of Fire Dancer. Apparently, they had been told of her importance and had withdrawn their objections to her shopping in the place. But that didn't change Evan's opinion of them in the slightest. He still thought them bigots. As soon as he paid for the purchase and the proprietor handed the wrapped packages to him, he took Fire Dancer's arm and led her from the shop—but not before he shot the women a look of pure loathing.

When they reached their room at the ordinary, Evan pulled his dress uniform and boots from the chest and dropped them off with the tavern owner to be pressed and shined. He quickly did his own last-minute shopping, purchasing a new shirt, a lace jabot, and a hat, as well as dress gloves. A small brocade valise caught his eye, and he bought that, too—for Fire Dancer.

When Evan returned to their room, she had dressed her hair and was struggling to wind the long length of green silk around her. Stepping into the room, Evan stopped in his tracks. He had known the green would bring out the striking color of her eyes, but that hadn't fully prepared him for the arresting sight before him.

Having no idea what he was staring at, Fire Dancer said in frustration, "I know it doesn't look right. I've had a terrible time with it. It's so soft and slippery that it won't stay in place." She held out the long tail of the silk. "And I don't know what to do with this extra material. I've wrapped it around me three times, and I still come out with this left over. I must have misjudged its length. Do you have something to cut it with?"

Because the silk was so much thinner than the cotton, it clung to Fire Dancer's curves more. Evan thought she looked absolutely beautiful. He closed the door, walked to the bed, and dumped the packages and hatbox on it. "It's just that the material drapes more softly. It looks right. It looks beautiful." He took the excess material from her and draped it over one shoulder. "Don't cut this off. Wear it this way," he said.

Fire Dancer looked over her shoulder at the length of shimmering material cascading down her back. It reminded her of the feather mantle her uncle wore, and for that reason she didn't object to it.

His neatly pressed uniform and polished boots had been delivered, so Evan hurried to dress. "There's a valise in that big package on the bed. You can carry your personal articles in that instead of your saddlebag. And why don't you pack that piece of blue material? You can

wear it tomorrow." Evan didn't bother to tell Fire
Dancer to pack bedclothing, since she didn't wear any.

"Where are you going to pack your things?"

"I have my own valise."

"Why can't I put my things in with yours?"

Evan turned from where he was stripping off his
shirt. "Because we won't be sharing the same room,
since we're not married," he said. "It simply isn't done,
not when you're invited to stay at someone else's
home."

"Lovers must refrain from making love at those
times?"

"Well, I suppose that's the idea, but it doesn't always
work out that way. There's usually a lot of slipping
around, and the lovers sneaking into each other's beds
in the dead of night."

"And everyone knows this?"

"Usually, unless they're terribly naive."

Fire Dancer didn't know what *naive* meant, but it
didn't matter. She thought the whites' method of dealing with lovers was terribly hypocritical. She packed
while Evan was dressing.

Turning from the small mirror on the wall where he
had been tying his jabot, Evan noticed Fire Dancer's
sandals. They weren't the braided straw ones she usually wore. "Where did you get those?" he asked.

Fire Dancer lifted one slender foot to better show off
the sandal, with its twin ropes of pearls that crossed her
instep. "I made it from an extra length of pearls I had
and the bottom of a pair of sandals. My others looked so
plain."

Her ordinary sandals certainly would have looked out

of place. He would have suggested buying her a pair of slippers, but he had known she would refuse. "That's very clever, and they look very pretty," he remarked. Then his eyes swept over her length. "No, I take that back. You look beautiful. Absolutely beautiful."

Fire Dancer knew by the smoky look in his eyes and the husky tone of his voice that he spoke the truth. She had been feeling just a little insecure in the unaccustomed material and new sandals, but his compliment gave her back her self-confidence. "Thank you," she muttered.

Evan had sensed her fleeting vulnerability, and it had touched a powerfully protective chord deep within him. Never had he wanted to shield her from the world, to keep her safe, to hold her to him, more than he did at that moment. Suddenly, the spell was broken by a knock on the door and the innkeeper's voice calling, "The governor's coach is here, sir!"

A few moments later, Evan and Fire Dancer were seated in the coach across from General Amherst. As the coach pulled away, the general said to her, "You look ravishing, my dear. I'm afraid you're going to put all of the English ladies to shame."

"Thank you," she muttered absently, staring at the general's head.

"Is something wrong?" Amherst asked her, aware of where her gaze was glued.

"Your hair has turned white in just a matter of hours."

Her candid observation amused the general, and he chuckled. "No, I'm afraid not, my dear. You see, this

isn't my hair. It's a periwig, and it's powdered to make i`
look white."

Seeing the puzzled expression on her face, Evan explained, "It's customary for ladies and gentlemen to
wear powdered wigs to evening socials."

"But why would anyone want white hair, to look
old?" Fire Dancer asked.

"That's a very good question, my dear," the general
answered. "Unfortunately, I have no answer for you. I
have no earthy idea what idiot came up with the practice, but it's considered fashionable and therefore is accepted. Thank God, wigs are used only for evening wear
now. I once had to wear the silly, hot things all the time.
I notice you aren't wearing one, Colonel."

"No, sir," Evan answered. "I lost mine on the trip
down here, and to be perfectly honest, I completely
forgot to buy another, what with my hasty preparations
and all."

"It's just as well. Quite a few of these colonists don't
wear them."

The three sat back and enjoyed the view as the coach
drove through Williamsburg, then out into the countryside. For miles and miles, they passed fields of tobacco,
where the broad leaves were being cut by the slaves and
thrown on the back of wagons. Later the leaves would
be driven to the tobacco shed where they would be
dried until the fall, then pressed into a hogshead and
shipped to England.

"The tobacco crop looks good," Evan remarked.

"Yes, I've heard the harvest is going quite well this
year. The plantations here are remarkably large. None
of the estates back in England have so much land, as

you well know, Colonel. I understand the average plantation here is twenty-three thousand acres, yet only a thousand might be under cultivation. The rest is just waiting to be cleared and used when the soil in the present fields is worn out."

"What do you mean, when the soil is worn out?" Fire Dancer asked.

"Tobacco depletes the soil quickly," Amherst answered. "After several crops the fields have to be abandoned and new ones cleared."

"Why do they abandon their fields? Why don't they plant peas and beans?" Fire Dancer asked.

"I'm afraid there is no demand for peas or beans, either here or in England," the general pointed out. "Tobacco is the money crop."

"I understand that. But even if they plowed the peas and beans under, it would be worth their while. They could plant tobacco again. That is what the Chickasaw do. We have been using the same fields for hundreds of years."

Seeing the doubtful look coming over the general's face, Evan said, "It's true, sir. I don't understand why, but rotating the crops seems to prevent this depletion of the land caused by planting tobacco year in and year out. And I can personally attest to the excellence of Chickasaw tobacco. It's a smaller-leafed variety, but it's just as smooth and sweet as the Roanoke."

"That's very interesting," General Amherst replied thoughtfully. "Perhaps I'll suggest it to one of the planters."

Evan seriously doubted that the planter would listen, particularly if he found out it was the Indian method of farming. The white men were too quick to discredit the Indian, so positive of their own superiority in everything, including the growing of native crops. No, the white men would have to see it for themselves before it would dawn on them that they were doing it all wrong, and that probably wouldn't happen until there was a shortage of land. Yes, he admitted regretfully, the white man was incredibly wasteful.

21

The sun was just setting and the slaves were plodding
wearily from the fields when Evan, Fire Dancer, and
General Amherst arrived at their destination. Fire
Dancer leaned forward and peered out the coach window, curious to know what a plantation looked like, for
her mother had lived on one. It looked more like a town
than someone's home, with slave quarters, a kiln for
making bricks, a smokehouse, a blacksmith's shop, a
kitchen house, a carriage house and stables, a barn, a
fowl house, and a dairy. And sitting right in the middle
of this, at the end of the deeply shaded circular drive-
way, was a two-story brick home that was every bit as
impressive as the governor's palace—if not more so, for
it had two cupolas and a deck on its hip roof and was
flanked by two advance buildings surrounded by formal
gardens.

The trio were led into the plantation house by a butler dressed in a brilliant red and white livery and wearing a periwig like the general's. He opened the heavy

wooden door, and the first thing that caught Fire Dancer's eye was the huge crystal chandelier hanging from the hallway ceiling. Catching the light from the setting sun, the glass dispersed the rays and sent a kaleidoscope of colors dancing over the walls. Then they followed the servant across the rose-colored marble floor and down the hallway, passing expensive oil landscapes that lined the whitewashed stucco walls.

Stepping into a wide doorway, the butler stood to one side so the three could pass, then announced to the plantation owner, "Governor Amherst and his guests have arrived, sir."

The crowd of men and women in the spacious parlor turned and stared at Fire Dancer in disbelief. An Indian woman wearing a green togalike garment was obviously the last thing they had expected to see. Then a red-faced, heavy-set, middle-age man dressed in a dark green evening suit and gold brocade vest recovered from his surprise and hurried from where he had been leaning on the fireplace mantle. "Forgive me, Governor," he said as he crossed the room, "I didn't hear your coach drive up."

"That's quite all right, Tom," General Amherst answered. "I didn't expect you to meet me at the door." He motioned to Evan and Fire Dancer. "And I hope you don't mind me bringing guests along. They just arrived this afternoon, and I could hardly desert them. May I present Fire Dancer, of the Chickasaw nation, and Colonel Evan Trevor, one of my most valuable officers? My friends, this is Thomas Moore, the owner of this beautiful plantation, and his wife, Abigale," the general added as the short, stocky mistress of the house walked forward.

"How do you do," the Moores muttered simultaneously. Both were still somewhat in a state of shock at Fire Dancer's appearance and at the fact that the governor had introduced her as his friend. Evan and Fire Dancer returned the greeting. Then, belatedly, Abigale said politely, "We're more than happy to have your guests stay with us, Governor Amherst. Any friend of yours is a friend of ours. Let me introduce them to my guests from England."

Abigale took Evan and Fire Dancer around the room and introduced them, while General Amherst followed and greeted them, for he had been introduced to the visitors from England at a previous dinner party. Evan noticed that almost all the visitors had a minor title and that their manner was decidedly cool. Undoubtedly, being forced to keep company with a half savage and a common soldier didn't sit easily with them.

After a while, however, everyone had settled down. The general and Evan sipped on glasses of peach brandy like the other guests in the room, while Fire Dancer nursed a glass of water that she had requested in lieu of wine. "Isn't one of your guests missing?" General Amherst asked Moore. "It seems to me that when I was here for dinner a few nights ago, there was a young countess."

"Vanessa? No, she's still here. She'll be with us as soon as she's dressed."

A few moments later, a hush fell over the room. Seeing everyone staring, Fire Dancer turned and saw a young woman poised in the doorway. She presented a lovely picture with her beauty, her expensive ball gown, and her glittering diamonds, but Fire Dancer was astonished at the powdered wig the woman wore on her head. Lavish strings of jewels were draped all over it, and a bird's nest with a pair of stuffed doves nestled in it. But what amazed her was the fact that the wig was a good three feet tall, and she couldn't imagine what kept it from toppling over.

Arriving late so she could make a grand entrance, Vanessa posed in the doorway on purpose. She knew she was beautiful, and she expected admiration as her due, just as she expected everyone to kowtow to her because she was a countess. As the men in the room rose to their feet, she caught sight of two brilliant red coats off to one side of the room. She gasped, and her gray eyes widened in disbelief. "My God, Evan!" she cried out. "Is that really you?"

Everyone watched in surprise as the countess ran to Evan, threw herself into his arms, and kissed his cheek. Evan was surprised and pleased to see Vanessa and hugged her back. He stepped back and replied with a chuckle, "Yes, it's really me."

"What are you doing here in Virginia?"

Before Evan could answer, Moore stepped forward. "Excuse me, Countess," he said. "Do you know the colonel?"

Vanessa gave a little laugh. "Of course, I know Evan Trevor! He, his twin brother Edward—the Earl of Linchester—and I all grew up together in Sussex."

Eyebrows were raised when Vanessa revealed Evan's noble blood, and he sensed the Englishmen's snobbish attitude toward him change. He had always expected and received such shows of respect back home, but now, knowing it was based on his noble birth alone, not merit, it filled him with disgust.

"Well, Evan?" Vanessa continued. "What are you doing in Virginia? I thought you were assigned somewhere in the northern colonies."

"Perhaps I can answer that question," General Amherst said, stepping forward. "Good day, Countess," he said, nodding to the young woman.

"Good day, General," Vanessa answered.

"I asked Colonel Trevor to meet me here in Williamsburg," he continued, "so that I could honor both him and Fire Dancer for the part they played in the fall of Fort Massiac, on the Ohio River. Unfortunately, I have to depart for the northern colonies tomorrow and cannot throw a ball in their honor, as I had intended. So I brought them with me this evening, to share in the honor the Moores are according me. God only knows, they are much more deserving than I."

Having revealed his purpose, General Amherst waited while his hosts absorbed this information. Even if Evan and Fire Dancer were the hero and heroine of the hour, it was clear that the two weren't too pleased by the startling announcement. One of the male houseguests, asked, "Did you say Fort Massiac, sir?"

"Yes, I did," the general answered.

"Everyone has been talking about the fort and the remarkable bravery of the English officer who led the attack. But I thought the officer was a major."

General Amherst smiled at Evan. "Colonel Trevor *was* a major, until I promoted him a few hours ago," he replied. Then the general stepped aside, revealing Fire

Dancer. "But we mustn't forget the princess's bravery or the critical part she played in that important victory."

General Amherst's announcement that Fire Dancer was a princess had the same effect as throwing a bomb would have, which was just what he had planned. Not only did he want to shock the group, he hoped to bring the snobbish houseguests down a peg or two—particularly the countess, for he disliked the spoiled and self-centered young woman. Pretending surprise at the stunned looks on everyone's face, he said, "Oh, I must have forgotten to tell you that Fire Dancer is nobility, although I can't imagine how I could possibly forget something as important as that."

Evan knew by the expression on Fire Dancer's face that she was about to object to being called a princess. That would have blown the story the general was telling to bits and made him look the fool. He quickly stepped forward. "Yes, someday Fire Dancer's son will be chief of the Chickasaw," he said.

Evan's intervention made Fire Dancer pause, and her moment to object was lost when one of the guests asked General Amherst, "But just what did the princess do that was so important?"

"Because she speaks fluent English—her mother was an English captive, you know—she accompanied Major Trevor as his interpreter on his dangerous reconnaissance of Fort Massiac, without once giving thought to her own safety. Without her aid, the battle plan could have never been laid, and without the help of our stalwart Chickasaw allies, the critical fort could have never been destroyed."

Evan had no objections to General Amherst praising

Fire Dancer—in his opinion, she had behaved bravely. But he thought the general was overdoing his praise of him. No matter what anyone said, Evan didn't believe the fort had been critical, and he thought he was a far cry from being a hero. But he understood that the general was telling the tale to these Englishmen to assure that all the rest of the guests would hear of it later. The houseguests were all clearly intrigued—all except Vanessa. She looked more suspicious than awed, Evan thought, and he wondered at it. Did she know the general was grossly exaggerating everything? But how would she? For all her beauty, she had never been particularly astute.

At that moment the butler entered the room and announced that dinner was served. Before Evan could turn to escort Fire Dancer, Vanessa took his arm in a firm grip and all but dragged him from the room. Fire Dancer saw the possessive action and the look of pure loathing the countess shot her over her shoulder before she and Evan stepped from the room. Fire Dancer knew that the two had once been lovers, from the countess's warm greeting and from Evan's obvious pleasure at seeing her again. That was a painful realization, but without Evan she felt lost in this alien world.

It was General Amherst who rescued her, saying as he extended his arm to her, "May I escort you, my dear?"

Seeing the other women laying their hands on top of the men's forearms to be escorted, Fire Dancer followed suit and allowed the older man to guide her from the drawing room.

When they stepped into the dining room, Fire

Dancer paused at the sight of huge twin chandeliers hanging from the ornately swirled ceiling. She had never dreamed there were that many candles in the entire world. There seemed to be thousands of them, their flames flickering and sending shadows dancing over the walls. Then Fire Dancer saw the long table, and her breath caught. Covered with an exquisite linen cloth and decorated with huge bouquets of flowers, it was set with gold-trimmed china in a delicate rose pattern, fine crystal goblets, and gold-plated serving ware. With the servants standing in vibrant, gold-trimmed uniforms behind each chair and with the jewels the women were wearing, Fire Dancer had never seen so much glitter and sparkle, so much richness.

Somehow sensing that she was feeling a little intimidated, General Amherst led her to the table and saw to it that she was seated beside him, even though he knew that that was not where the hostess had intended her to sit. Evan and Vanessa were sitting on the opposite side of the table several seats down.

As soon as they were seated, Evan remarked to Vanessa, "I certainly didn't expect to find you here in the colonies. Why didn't the count come with you?"

"Then you haven't heard the news?" Vanessa asked in surprise. "I thought Edward would have told you."

"No, I don't correspond with him," Evan answered stiffly. "What news?"

"My husband died two years ago."

The news was imparted with absolutely no regret, which didn't surprise him. The marriage had been arranged, and Vanessa had never loved her husband. In fact, she had never even been fond of him. "How did it happen?" he asked.

"A hunting accident."

Vanessa leaned forward and said in a low voice so no one could overhear, "I'm a very wealthy woman now, and free to marry whom I like."

Yes, she could remarry now, Evan thought, and still retain her title, which meant so much to her family and, if truth be known, to Vanessa. That was why she hadn't originally married Evan, although they had been lovers and she had vowed that she loved him. She had wanted a title and all the prestige it entailed, but Evan had not been able to give her that. She had walked out of his life —the only woman he had ever thought he loved—and Evan had carried his bitterness and anger for years. But strangely, he had never been angry with Vanessa. She had only done what everyone had expected of her, including himself. No, his anger had been directed at the irony of fate that had made him the second born and not the first and that had thereby cheated him of his first love.

When Evan failed to respond, Vanessa repeated, "Didn't you hear what I said? I'm free!"

Evan knew what Vanessa was suggesting: Now that she was a widow, she could marry him. But Evan found he had absolutely no desire to marry her. He no longer loved her. Somewhere over the years that emotion had died, and all that was left now was the feeling of friendship that remained from their childhood years together. Because of that friendship he found he couldn't hurt her either. Cautiously, he said, "I'm glad you're free, and I hope you find what you're looking for."

Vanessa sat back. What was wrong with him? Find whatever she was looking for? *He* was what she was looking for! *He* was what she wanted! She had never known a man as exciting as Evan, as manly, as masterful —and she had taken lovers freely. None had ever held a candle to him. Surely he couldn't have stopped loving her. Why, she was what every man desired—beautiful, titled, wealthy, and accomplished in all the social arts. No, he must not have understood what she was hinting at. Apparently, he wasn't as perceptive as he used to be. She vowed make sure he understood her before the evening was over.

The meal lasted a full two hours as course after course was served, each course accompanied by a different wine poured from the Moores' personally monogrammed bottles. To Fire Dancer, the dinner seemed to last a lifetime. Not only was it awkward to eat with the unaccustomed heavy gold-plated service, she had no one to talk to, although conversation was flowing as freely as the wines. General Amherst would have entertained her had it been up to him, but he was kept occupied with questions coming from all directions. The woman sitting on the other side of Fire Dancer felt she had nothing in common with the Indian, even if she was a princess, and gave her husband her full attention. Adding to Fire Dancer's misery was the fact that Evan seemed to have completely forgotten her, for Vanessa kept engaging him in reminiscences about their childhood and their homes.

As the dessert plates were being removed, Evan said to Abigale, "I would like to compliment you, madam. The meal was absolutely delicious, the best"—he hesi-

tated, about to say the best he had ever eaten at an
English table anywhere—"the best I've eaten in the colonies."

"Thank you, sir."

"Yes," General Amherst added, "the food was remarkably well prepared, and there were several dishes
that I've never eaten anywhere else. Have you imported
a cook from some exotic place?"

"No, sir," their host answered. "Our cook is an Indian"—Moore had been about to say *slave* but feared
Fire Dancer would take offense—"servant. More and
more of the planters are using them as cooks, along with
the Negro slaves from the West Indies. They use ingre-
dients and herbs that we've never heard of, but as you
can see the results are delicious."

He should have known the cook was Indian, Evan
thought, casting a warm, appreciative look in Fire
Dancer's direction. But she didn't notice. Her eyes
were downcast as she rearranged the napkin in her lap
for the tenth time in a futile effort to relieve her utter
boredom.

22

Fire Dancer thought tedium would be behind her once the dinner was finished, but she was mistaken. While the other female houseguests were freshening up and resting before the ball began, she was forced to stand between Evan and General Amherst in the receiving line and greet the local guests. After an hour of smiling and nodding at the steady stream of ladies and gentlemen parading before her, she had a pounding headache. She knew these colonists hadn't been a bit impressed with her, either as a princess or as a heroine. Unlike the English guests, the colonists had been here long enough to become prejudiced against all Indians, and her efforts to act as a diplomatic envoy of her people were doomed to failure. The colonists would never genuinely respect Indians—there was simply too much bad blood between them. She knew their smiles were false, given only for the governor's benefit, and although she couldn't see their scorn, she could feel it. For that reason she felt a great relief when the Moores broke up the receiving line and announced that the ball was about to begin.

As soon as his hosts were out of earshot, General Amherst turned to Evan and Fire Dancer. "Thank God, that's over!" he said. "I dearly hate standing in receiving lines. It's such a waste of time. How could anyone possibly remember that many people's names? That's just one more reason I'm going to turn the governing of this colony over to a lieutenant."

"I'm in perfect agreement, sir," Evan answered in all honesty.

"If you two will excuse me," the governor continued, "I'm going to step out into the garden and have a quiet smoke."

As the governor walked off, Evan led Fire Dancer into the ballroom. For a moment, they stood to one side and observed the milling crowd. Then, spying Vanessa across the room, Fire Dancer said, "I thought you said your women never exposed their breasts, that that was considered indecent and immodest, that that was why they wore the scarfs around their necks."

Evan saw that every woman in the room was wearing a low-cut gown, exposing a great deal of bosom. Not a fichu was in sight. He shrugged and answered lamely, "Evening wear is different."

It certainly was different, Fire Dancer thought. The countess's full breasts were about to pop out of her tight, low-cut ball gown. "Why is evening wear different? Because seduction is an accepted nighttime pursuit?"

Fire Dancer had hit the nail on the head, forcing Evan once again to see the hypocrisy the whites practiced. The Chickasaw bared their breasts with no shame because they did not feel it wrong, while the English-women hid their bosoms modestly in the daytime, then exposed them blatantly at night in hopes of drawing the men's attention to them and making the males desire them. Fire Dancer's candid observation disturbed him, but he was accustomed to her total honesty, her direct-ness. What caught his attention more was the scathing tone of her voice. It had seemed almost brutal, as if she had meant her words to be personally hurtful. He shot her a curious glance.

Fire Dancer wasn't usually spiteful, but for a moment her strong Chickasaw desire for vengeance had come to the fore. She had been hurt that the colonists had scorned her and that Evan had deserted her in favor of Vanessa. She wanted to lash out at both him and them.

Evan was just on the verge of asking her what was wrong, when Fire Dancer jumped at a sudden sound. "What is that?" she asked in alarm.

Evan chuckled. "It's the musicians."

"That is your music?" Fire Dancer asked in horror, for the screeching of the violins played on her nerves.

"No, they're just warming up." Then the ensemble began to play a minuet. "*That* is our music," he said.

The sounds were much different from the music the Chickasaw played, but Fire Dancer had to admit that it was soothing and rather pretty. Then the guests lined up, the gentlemen on one side of the room and the ladies on the other and began to perform the graceful, stately dance for which the music had been written. She watched in enthrallment as the women's wide silk and satin skirts swished and the pale colors of their ball gowns shimmered beneath the lights of the chandeliers. Their jewels twinkled, and the elaborate gold and silver decorations on the men's dark suits glittered. Even their powdered wigs seem to glow in the light of hundreds and hundreds of candles.

No sooner had the dance ended than Vanessa broke away from her partner and rushed to where Evan and Fire Dancer were standing. "I wondered where you had disappeared to after the receiving line broke up," she said to Evan. A little pout came to her lips. "I thought you would ask me for the first dance. It's been so long since we've seen one another."

"I was keeping Fire Dancer company," Evan pointed out.

"Well, just because she can't dance is no reason for you not to enjoy yourself." Vanessa looked Fire Dancer directly in the eye. "Don't you agree?" she asked. "Why, there's no telling when he might have another opportunity to attend a ball as lavish as this one."

Fire Dancer didn't dare object—that would look as if she were being selfish. "You don't have to keep me company, Evan. Go ahead and dance."

"Yes, go ahead and dance with your old friend, Colonel," General Amherst said, stepping up to them. "I'll keep Fire Dancer company."

Fire Dancer raised her head proudly. "That's not necessary, General. No one has to keep me com—"

"Shh, my dear," the general whispered, cutting across her objection. Looking about, he bent his head so that only she could hear and confided, "It will give me an excuse not to dance. Then no one will know how terribly clumsy I am."

Fire Dancer's and General Amherst's eyes locked. Something told her the governor wasn't just being polite, that he meant what he said. She smiled and nodded in agreement, and Vanessa rushed Evan away before he could make any further objection.

Vanessa and Evan danced one dance, then another and another, and another, all at her insistence. Evan found he much preferred Fire Dancer's company, but he couldn't find a graceful way to escape Vanessa's clutches without being out-and-out rude. He wondered what he had ever seen in her. The dewy beauty she had had in her youth had faded, and he could see she tried to cover it beneath a thick layer of leaded powder and far too much rouge. Her constant, senseless chatter wore on his nerves, while the smell of her strong perfume made him feel a little nauseated. Besides, it didn't cover her faint body odor from not bathing regularly. Having become accustomed to Fire Dancer's clean, sweet scent, he found Vanessa's offensive. He kept glancing longingly in Fire Dancer's direction.

Seeing his look, Vanessa sighed. "For God's sake, Evan!" she said irritably. "Will you stop worrying about that savage? She's not your responsibility."

Evan stiffened at the word *savage*, then said in a tightly controlled voice, "She's not a savage. The Chickasaw are just as civilized as we are. Besides, she's not pure Indian. Didn't you hear General Amherst say her mother was an English captive? And I am responsible for her—I accompanied her here."

Vanessa was unaware that Evan had taken personal insult; nor had it dawned on her that Evan might have a genuine concern for the Indian girl. "But you are not responsible for her by choice," she responded. "You only brought her because the general ordered you to. And now he's taken her under his wing and relieved you of that burden." Vanessa paused. "The old fool. He should have never brought her. Princess or not, she doesn't belong. Why, she's not even dressed appropriately. She sticks out like a sore thumb."

Evan highly resented Vanessa's criticism of Fire Dancer, but he couldn't argue her point. Fire Dancer was conspicuous in her simple green costume. To begin with, the material was too dark—the other women were wearing pale colors, as was customary for evening wear. Their elaborate dresses had tiers of rich lace on their underskirts, at their elbows, and in their low-cut bodices. Lavish bows and ribbons seemed to be everywhere, and the array of rubies, diamonds, and emeralds they wore only made them look more overdressed. Their wide-hipped gowns, which made a mockery of their natural feminine curves, and their wigs, which looked false instead of rich, made the women look cheap and vulgar, while Fire Dancer looked elegant with her natural coloring and her simple clothing. Even her pearls were more appropriate, glowing with warmth they took from her skin, not glittering like shattered pieces of ice.

No, Fire Dancer didn't belong here. But Evan felt no shame on her behalf, only pride. She didn't need trappings to make her look beautiful or regal or graceful. Those qualities were an integral part of her, just as her honesty, her courage, her keen intelligence, and her integrity were.

The last thought took Evan by surprise. He had never

thought of integrity as a female attribute, but Fire Dancer was sincere and fiercely loyal to her beliefs. It was one more of the many virtues he had come to appreciate in her.

Evan cast another look in Fire Dancer's direction. He wondered if she knew she was being ostracized, that the colonists snubbed her not only for her appearance but for her Indian blood. She didn't look uncomfortable. To the contrary—she appeared totally self-assured, as if she were in command of the entire ball. But Evan sensed that she was putting up a brave front. Fire Dancer was no fool. As proud as she was of her Indian blood, she was bound to know how the others felt about her, and he knew her well enough to know she wasn't unaffected by their scorn. Evan felt a pang of deep regret that he had put Fire Dancer in such a position. General Amherst could not have known better, but he should have. Evan had had more day-to-day contact with the colonists than his superior officer had, and he knew how prejudiced they were against Indians. Not even the Chickasaw being their allies changed that. It was a matter of using the native tribes' animosity against one another to attain the white man's purpose. And he should have known that the English guests wouldn't truly accept Fire Dancer either. He knew how terribly snobbish the nobility could be, particularly the lower nobility. No, if they had any interest in her at all, it was simply as an oddity, someone to gape at, just as they stared and marveled at a two-headed calf at a fair.

As Evan mused, Vanessa led him into yet another dance, and he performed the familiar reel automatically. Yes, he thought, he had made a grave error in bringing Fire Dancer to the ball. In fact, he should never have brought her back east with him. His hopes of making her proud of her white blood had been dashed to the ground. Nothing in the Anglo way of living or behavior had impressed her. If anything, he had given her cause to be ashamed of her English blood. The entire trip had been a failure.

Across the ballroom, Fire Dancer was struggling to endure the ordeal. She was very much aware of the glances sent in her direction. A few were curious, but the majority were openly hostile, and with her keen Chickasaw hearing, she had overheard more than one hateful remark. Adding to her misery, Evan continued to ignore her. She had hoped he would return to her side after a dance or two, but she could only conclude that he stayed with Vanessa by choice, that he preferred his old lover to her. It seemed as if the ball were lasting an eternity. When General Amherst asked her if she would like to take a walk in the garden, she accepted the invitation gratefully. At least she wouldn't have to watch Evan and Vanessa enjoying themselves.

For well over thirty minutes, the two strolled through the formal garden in silence, weaving through the maze of sculptured evergreens and passing the statues and iron-wrought benches along the gravel pathway. Fire Dancer relished the fresh air as much as the solitude, for the odor of the burning bayberry candles and the strong perfumes the guests wore had made her feel a little ill.

Finally, General Amherst said, "I must apologize to you, my dear. I should have never asked you to come here. I had no idea that the colonists harbored such strong feelings against your people. I suppose I'm very naive from that standpoint. Since I've come to this country, I've been too busy plotting military strategies to notice, and I've never been much for socializing, not even back home. When I'm not performing my duties as a soldier, I've always led a quiet country life."

Fire Dancer agreed that her coming to the ball had been pointless. Nothing had been accomplished that would improve relations between her people and their English allies. No, the only thing the ball had accomplished was to make her more determined to reject her white heritage. She had seen nothing in Anglo culture that made her proud of that half of her bloodline. They were everything her mother had said they were—vain, selfish, snobbish, bigoted, and bent on pursing physical pleasures—and the sooner she put distance between herself and them, the better. "You don't need to apologize, General," Fire Dancer said graciously. "But if you don't mind, I would like to retire. The evening has been tiring."

"Of course, my dear. I understand. I wish I could do the same. I'm feeling weary, myself." He took her arm. "Come," he said. "We'll go back to the house and find our hostess."

Back in the house, they found Mrs. Moore close to the hall doorway. Fire Dancer noticed that the woman didn't seem in the least disappointed that Fire Dancer wished to retire, but then, Fire Dancer hadn't expected her to. Her hostess seemed to be just as glad to be rid of her as she was to be going. Abigale called a servant and asked him to show Fire Dancer her room.

Before she followed the servant away, General Amherst said to her, "Good night, my dear. I hope you sleep well. We'll be leaving around midmorning."

"Midmorning?" Abigale asked in surprise, breaking into the conversation. "I thought you were staying for lunch."

"I'm afraid not, Abigale. My ship sails on the evening tide."

"But it's only a two-hour drive back to Williamsburg. You'll have plenty of time," Abigale argued.

"No, madam. I have quite a bit of packing left to do," General Amherst answered firmly, shooting Fire Dancer a look that told her he was only making excuses for an early departure.

"I'll be ready, General," Fire Dancer answered, strongly suspecting that the older man was as eager as she to be rid of the place. Saying good night to her reluctant hostess, she turned and followed the servant.

Abigale was still trying to convince General Amherst to stay longer when Evan walked up and said, "Excuse me for interrupting, sir, but have you seen Fire Dancer? I can't seem to find her."

"She and I went for a long walk in the garden, and now she has retired. A servant took her upstairs just a few moments ago." Seeing Evan's surprised expression, General Amherst explained, "She's not accustomed to our late hours, and I saw no purpose in her staying up."

So, Evan thought, the general had realized his error and released Fire Dancer from her commitment. "I couldn't agree more, sir. It seems our strategy wasn't well thought out, and there's no reason for her to suffer for it, particularly since she hasn't fully recuperated from our long trip." Evan spied Vanessa coming across the ballroom to them and had a distinct urge to run like hell. "If you don't mind, sir, I'd like to be excused also," he said quickly. "I'm afraid I haven't completely recuperated either."

Abigale had had no objection to Fire Dancer leaving the dance early—the "savage" was nothing but an embarrassment to her. But Evan was another matter entirely, particularly since the countess seemed so happy to be reunited with her old friend. "Oh, surely you're not going to retire so early, Colonel. Why, the ball has hardly begun!"

"I sincerely hope not, Abigale," General Amherst said before Evan could respond. "I was planning to retire in an hour or so myself." Seeing an aghast expression come over Abigale's face, he added, "I'm sorry to disappoint you, but we're soldiers, you know. We're not accustomed to staying up all hours of the night. But that doesn't mean you have to cut your ball short. We don't want to spoil your pleasure."

"Oh, no, sir," Abigale said quickly, knowing full well how inappropriate it would be to continue the ball after the guest of honor had departed, "I wasn't planning on the ball lasting much longer than that." She turned once again to Evan. "Are you sure you won't reconsider?"

"Reconsider what?" Vanessa asked, stepping up to them and slipping her arm possessively around Evan's.

"Colonel Trevor is going to retire," Abigale informed her.

Vanessa couldn't fathom why Evan would want to leave the ball early—unless it was because he was eager for the two of them to get together privately. And that

was exactly what Vanessa had been planning all evening
—for the two of them to renew their intimate relationship as lovers. Her heart raced with excitement. She
could hardly wait. But it wouldn't do for them to leave
the ball together. That would be too obvious. She'd
have to wait awhile, then claim a pounding headache.

"That's a shame, Evan," she said, surprising everyone. "You're not feeling ill, are you?"

"No, I'm tired," Evan answered, frankly suspicious of
Vanessa's concern. "I'm not accustomed to these late
hours anymore."

"I'll ask one of my servants to see you to your room,"
Abigale said, relieved that the countess was taking the
news so well.

Evan said good night to Vanessa and General Amherst and followed Abigale from the room. Yet he had
an unsettling feeling that he hadn't escaped Vanessa's
clutches.

After Fire Dancer had been brought to her room, she
stripped off her clothing and climbed into the bed. She
had never felt so tired in her life, and she knew it was
from emotional, not physical, exhaustion. But sleep
wouldn't come.

At first, she thought it was because the bed was too
soft. But even after she had left it and lain down on a
rug, she couldn't sleep. She was tormented by memories of Evan and Vanessa talking, laughing, and dancing
together. For an hour she tossed and turned. Then she
heard a soft knock. Remembering what Evan had told
her about lovers sneaking into one another's rooms at
night, her lagging spirits soared. He'd come! she

thought, throwing back the sheet she had dragged from the bed and jumping to her feet. Evan had come to her, not to Vanessa.

Before she could open the door, Fire Dancer heard a second knock. Suddenly she wasn't sure that the knock had been on her own door. Carefully, she cracked it and looked out. No one was there. Peering down the dim hallway, she saw someone standing before another door. It took a moment for her to realize the woman was Vanessa, since the countess had removed her wig and her long brown hair was down. When the door opened and light spilled out into the hallway, Fire Dancer realized that the countess was clothed in a sheer nightdress that hid nothing from view.

"What took you so long to answer the door, darling?" Fire Dancer heard Vanessa ask whoever was standing inside the open doorway.

Fire Dancer gasped as Evan stepped from the room. He looked quickly both ways down the hall, then took Vanessa's arm and yanked her into the room, closing the door quickly behind them.

Fire Dancer didn't have to see any more. What she had feared had come to pass: Evan had forsaken her for his old lover. Feeling crushed and terribly betrayed, she closed the door, hurried across the room, and threw herself onto the bed, burying her head beneath the pillow as tears and soul-wrenching sobs came loose.

Down the hall, Evan was not at all happy to see Vanessa. He had pulled her into the room only so no one could see her seminudity. "What the hell are you doing here?" he asked as soon as the door was shut.

His anger took Vanessa aback. "Why . . . I think that should be obvious," she answered.

As Evan's eyes quickly slid over her body, Vanessa's inherent conceit came to the fore. It had not dawned on her that Evan might find her unappealing, that he might refuse her. She stepped forward, slid her arms around his neck, and pressed herself against him, saying seductively, "It's been too long since we've made love, darling. Much too long. I've never forgotten how good it was between us. I can't begin to tell you how many nights I've lain awake thinking about it, thinking about you."

Evan's body turned rigid as he steeled himself against the feel of Vanessa's soft curves. What he felt at that moment was revulsion, not desire. He caught both her arms in his hands and pulled them from around his neck, then stepped back from her. "You're right, Vanessa," he said. "It has been much too long. Things have changed."

Vanessa couldn't have been more shocked if Evan had slapped her. It took a moment for her to recover. Then her eyes narrowed suspiciously. "Are you talking about that savage?" she asked.

An urge to protect Fire Dancer rose in Evan. "Fire Dancer has nothing to do with this."

"Oh, for God's sake, Evan!" Vanessa said angrily. "I'm not stupid. I know you've been lovers. I thought so the moment I laid eyes on her. And this may surprise you, but I understand. I've learned a lot about men's passion since you and I were together. I know men can't control their lust as well as women can. Stuck out in the wild the way you were, you turned to whatever was available, and I don't hold that against you, or any other affairs you may have had. I know those women meant nothing to you, that I'm the only woman that you ever loved."

"You're wrong, Vanessa. I do care about Fire Dancer."

Vanessa stared at Evan in disbelief. "You can't be serious," she said. "You can't possibly be in love with that —that slut!"

"Watch your tongue!" Evan said between clenched teeth. "I won't tolerate you insulting her!"

Vanessa's eyes widened. "Then you are in love with her?"

Evan wasn't prepared to delve deeply into his feelings for Fire Dancer. He only knew he cared. "What I feel for her is none of your concern," he answered scathingly. "The point is, I neither love nor desire you anymore."

Furious, Vanessa stepped farther back and said icily, "You're right, Evan. Things have changed. *You* have! The Evan Trevor I knew had some pride. He was a man of discerning tastes. He would have never aligned himself with a lowly—"

"Don't say it!" Evan interrupted, his blue eyes flashing. "I warn you. Whatever insulting name you were going to call her, don't! Because if you do, I won't be responsible for what I might do."

A shiver of fear ran through Vanessa. She had never seen Evan so enraged, so dangerous-looking. She didn't doubt for a minute that he might follow through on his threat. The color drained from her face, which made her thickly powdered face look even pastier. "You really are infatuated with her, aren't you?" she muttered.

"As I said, my feelings for Fire Dancer are none of your concern. But I will tell you this much, Vanessa. She's more woman than you could ever begin to be. There's more beauty, poise, courage, intelligence, and honesty in her little finger than there is in your entire body."

Evan turned, walked to the door, and opened it, then said in a hard voice, "Good night, Vanessa."

Stunned by the turn of events and Evan's rejection, Vanessa walked stiffly from the room. Not until she reached the hallway did she forget her fear and become outraged. How dared he! she thought. How dared he insult her and send her on her way. She was a countess!

Just as Evan was closing the door, she whirled around. "Then go to your savage whore and wallow in your lust and see if I care!" she said vindictively. "The filthy little bitch deserves you. But don't be surprised if she gives you a disease. That kind opens her legs to anyone and everyone!"

Putting distance between them had given Vanessa a false sense of courage. Now, seeing the absolutely murderous look coming over his face, she froze for a moment, then turned and ran down the hall.

It took a while for Evan's anger to cool. Then he remembered the hostility to which Fire Dancer had been submitted that evening, and he wondered how she was faring. Was she feeling alone? Was she frightened?

Evan smiled at this last thought. He couldn't imagine Fire Dancer frightened of anything. But he wanted to go to her, and he wasn't motivated by desire. He wanted to go to her because she might need him.

This time, Evan knew enough to scoff at this thought. His desire to protect her when she didn't need protecting seemed to be his major downfall. Besides, if anyone saw him, they would think he was slipping into her room for a tryst, and he wouldn't cheapen what they shared by sneaking around. Their relationship had always been in the wide open; they had never hidden anything, and he liked it that way. Of course, they hadn't flaunted it either. That would have been as tasteless as sneaking around like a thief in the night.

Having made his decision, Evan retired for the night. But sleep was elusive. He found he missed Fire Dancer's presence beside him. Even on the trail she had been close by. Knowing she was near, that they were sharing the darkest hours of the night when people are most vulnerable, had given him a strange sort of security. It seemed that she didn't necessarily need him, but he needed her. It was an admission that shook him to his very roots.

23

Fire Dancer was vastly relieved that General Amherst intended to keep his promise for an early departure later that morning. She had hardly slept a wink all night, and she couldn't wait to put the plantation and its painful experiences behind her. But despite her eagerness to get away from the scene of her humiliation as she prepared to make her exit, she dreaded coming face-to-face with Evan. To behave as if nothing had happened would be very difficult, if not impossible. Drawing on her years of training in self-discipline that had been given her in preparation for the day her son would rule her clan, she descended the stairs and walked from the house, looking absolutely regal despite her weariness and the emotional battering she had undergone. Not until she saw Evan standing beside the coach, his golden hair gleaming in the sunlight and his blue, blue eyes shimmering, did her rigid composure break. Feeling as if someone had reached into her chest and wrenched her heart out, she missed a step, then regained her footing.

Evan didn't notice her missed step, but he did notice her face as the footman helped her into the carriage. He had never seen her looking pale and drawn, and there were dark circles beneath her eyes. After she and the general exchanged pleasantries and Evan took his seat across from her, he leaned forward. "Are you ill?" he asked.

"I've never been ill in my life!" Fire Dancer answered sharply.

Evan attributed her sharpness to the same strange malady that must be causing her paleness. A sudden thought occurred to him, one that terrified him. Had she caught one of the fevers that plagued this wet, low country? "Are you sure? You don't look well."

"I'm tired!"

As Evan peered even closer, it seeming to Fire Dancer as if he were trying to look into her soul. "Please! Just leave me alone!" she snapped.

When she turned her head and stared pointedly out the window, it dawned on Evan that she was very angry. But why? he asked himself. Did she blame him for bringing her here, for putting her in the position where she could be scorned? But he sensed that that wasn't it. Her anger seemed much more personal.

Evan had no idea what had triggered Fire Dancer's behavior. But he did know that he couldn't pursue what was bothering her until they were alone. He sat back and studied her, a puzzled expression on his face.

From his corner of the coach, General Amherst had heard the exchange, although he had pretended to be absorbed with something they were passing. He had suspected from the moment he first saw how beautiful the Chickasaw girl was that the two might be lovers. Then, at the dance, when Fire Dancer let her guard slip for just a moment, he saw the hurt in her eyes when Evan and the countess were dancing. Then he had known the girl was in love with Evan. He had assumed the feelings were not mutual. English officers frequently took native mistresses when they were assigned in foreign lands, but few ever became emotionally involved with them. Thinking that was the case, he had taken pity on Fire Dancer. That was why he had invited her for the walk, to remove her from a painful situation, and why he had been so agreeable to her retiring early. Then, when Fire Dancer had climbed into the carriage this morning, the general had correctly assumed she was angry because she had discovered Evan didn't return her feelings. The fury of a scorned woman seemed the same the world over, regardless of race.

But Evan had thrown his commanding officer an unexpected curve when he had shown deep concern for the young woman's welfare. Perhaps Evan was more deeply involved that he had first thought. The general found that that didn't disturb him in the least, which surprised him. As a rule, commanding officers didn't approve of their men making permanent liaisons with native women. Once such couples went back to England, the wives usually couldn't cope with living in a strange country with strange people and strange customs, where they were generally unaccepted and forced by prejudice and misunderstanding to live on the fringes of society. The strain on the women was too much, and more often than not the unions ended in disaster. But Fire Dancer was different. Not only did she possess a keen intelligence, she had an unusual strength of character. The general suspected that once she set her mind on something, nothing and no one could stop her from accomplishing it, even adapting to another environment. He could understand how Evan could fall in love with her. Unfortunately, the young woman herself appeared to have no idea of Evan's truly affectionate feelings.

Still, General Amherst was much too wise to try to interfere. He knew that lovers had to work their problems out in their own way. He held his silence and stared out his window just as pointedly as Fire Dancer did hers.

Fire Dancer didn't see any of the scenery that flashed by—she was too furious to even notice. But only a part of her anger was directed at Evan. She was just as angry at herself for giving both her body and her heart to a man whose only interest in her had been gratification of his physical needs. She had behaved just as foolishly as her mother, even after she had vowed she would never make the same mistake. She wondered if her mother had felt as hurt, as devastated, when the man she loved had walked out on her. Fire Dancer had never dreamed such pain was possible. Last night, she had cried even more tears than she had when her mother had died, and she had felt just as empty inside. But she had only herself to blame. She had known all along there was no future with Evan, that she would lose him in the end. Even if he had loved her—which he obviously didn't— they had never walked in the same world.

After they reached Williamsburg and the coach rolled away, she and Evan returned to their room in the inn. No sooner had the door shut behind them than she turned on Evan. "I want to go home," she said firmly.

"I know. You told me that yesterday," Evan answered in exasperation. "And now I want to know why. Why did you make that decision out of the clear blue, and why are you so angry at me?"

Ordinarily, Fire Dancer would have been honest with Evan, but now she deviated from her usual behavior. She couldn't answer either of his questions without revealing the depth of her feelings for him, and she had vowed that she would never let him know how much his betrayal had hurt her. Her fierce pride was all she had left. "I do not wish to discuss my feelings. All I want to do is go home."

"No! I'm not going to let it go at that! Is it because of the way you were treated at the ball? If so, I apologize. If I had known how rudely they were going to behave, I would have never brought you."

"I said I do not wish to discuss it," Fire Dancer replied stiffly.

Evan no longer merely suspected that what had angered Fire Dancer was personal. He knew it. He quickly reviewed the events of the evening before. "Is it because I spent so much time with Vanessa?" he asked.

Evan watched as a mask seemed to drop down over Fire Dancer's face, and he knew he had hit the nail on the head. "She's an old childhood friend that I hadn't seen in a long time," Evan explained. "I thought you realized that. Then I couldn't get away."

Fire Dancer's anger overrode her caution. "You were more than friends. You were lovers!"

"Yes, at one time we were," Evan admitted frankly. "But that was a long time ago."

"No, it was not a long time ago! Vanessa went into your room last night."

Suddenly all the pieces of the puzzle fit together. "So that's it?" Evan asked, relieved that he had finally discovered the reason for her anger. He had no doubt that he could clear up the confusion. "You think I invited her?"

"No, I don't think it. I *know* it! She asked why you took so long to answer the door. Then I saw you pull her into the room as if you couldn't wait to make love to her."

"I didn't want anyone to see her half naked and make the wrong assumptions. And that's exactly what you're doing, Fire Dancer. Making wrong assumptions, just as she assumed I was expecting her and would welcome her to my bed. But nothing happened. I sent her away."

Deep down, Fire Dancer desperately wanted to believe Evan. But after being scorned by the colonists, her inbred Chickasaw suspiciousness of white men was too strong. She was determined not to give the Anglo an opportunity to humiliate her or play her for the fool. "Do you really think I'm so stupid as to believe that, that I'm nothing but a gullible, naive Indian? No! I don't believe it!"

By virtue of his noble birth, Evan had never been a man to give explanations to others, and if it had been anyone but Fire Dancer now, he would not have even bothered. Had she realized that, his attempt to explain to her now would have told her volumes about his feelings for her. But she wouldn't listen to his explanation, and her all but calling him a liar infuriated him, for he was a man of his word. "All right then! Believe what you want. Have your jealous temper—"

"I am not jealous!" Fire Dancer interjected hotly. "I do not care enough to be jealous. I am angry! You have insulted me by taking another lover before you dissolved our affair. Even the Chickasaw, whom your people scorn so much, have the decency to be constant to their lovers and honest with them. They do not sneak around on them. If they tire of them and wish to take on a new lover, or an old one"—she added meaningfully —"they have only to announce their intentions. If you do not have the courage to call our affair at an end, I do." Fire Dancer took a deep breath and forced the words from her lips. "It is over between us. You are never to touch me again."

Fire Dancer saying she didn't care enough to be jealous hurt Evan deeply. It appeared that all she was concerned about was her pride, and Evan was just as fiercely proud, if not more so. He stepped back a few steps, and the short distance might as well have been an ocean as he said in cold fury, "Since you have made your feelings quite clear, I am in perfect agreement. I'll get my things and move to another room. We'll leave tomorrow morning."

Not until Evan agreed to end their affair did Fire Dancer realize that she had secretly wished he would continue to try to convince her of his fidelity. Now, with all hope for a reconciliation removed, she felt as if the ground had suddenly disappeared beneath her. Sudden tears welled in her eyes and threatened to spill over. As he strode past her to gather his things, she looked about the room and remembered his torrid lovemaking. She couldn't stay in this room with all its memories, she thought as a totally alien, panicked feeling crept over her. "No! We'll leave now. This moment!"

Evan heard the urgency in her voice and wondered at it. "That's impossible! I don't even know where Josh is staying," he replied.

"We will go without Josh."

Evan might have been willing to try to find his way back to the Chickasaw stronghold if he had been alone, but despite the anger and hurt Fire Dancer had dealt him, he cared too deeply about her to risk endangering her. "No, we will *not* go without him," he answered in a firm tone of voice.

"Then find him so we can leave today. This town is not that big."

"By the time I find him, it could be almost dark. It would be pointless to leave that late," he argued.

"We can travel through the night," Fire Dancer persisted.

"No. I think we both need a good night's rest before we begin the long trip back."

Fire Dancer knew she wouldn't be able to sleep in this room with its memories. The night would be even more painful than the one she had just had. "Then I will go by myself."

Evan saw from the determined expression on her face that she wasn't making an idle threat. She had no fear of the wilderness. "Why are you being so damn

unreasonable?" he asked, running his hand in exasperation through his thick golden locks.

Fire Dancer refused to answer. She looked as if she
had turned to stone, and Evan knew that nothing he
could do would force her to speak. This wasn't just ordinary stubbornness. It was the same determined will that
Chickasaw warriors called upon when they were being
tortured by their enemies. Frustrated beyond his own
endurance, Evan thundered, "All right, then! I'll go
look for Josh! But you're just being spiteful!"

Evan stormed from the room and the inn. Much to
his surprise, he found the lean Scot sitting in the common room of an ordinary not too far down from the
Raleigh Inn with some of his friends. Motioning to him,
Evan waited impatiently as the guide rose and walked
toward him, carrying his tankard with a pottle—two
quarts—of rum with him. When Josh came to a stop
before him, Evan glanced at the tankard. "How many of
those have you had?" he asked.

"Why?"

"I'm wondering if you're fit for traveling," Evan answered brusquely. Then he explained that Fire Dancer
was homesick and that they were leaving for the wilderness immediately.

Ordinarily, Josh would have balked or at least asked
for more explanations, but now he refrained. He could
tell that Evan was in no mood for questions or resistance of any kind, and Josh had gained a healthy respect
for the Englishman's anger after Fort Massiac. He
downed his tankard of rum, said good-bye to his friends,
and told Evan he would meet him at the stables as soon
as he had collected his things.

They rode out of Williamsburg a half hour later. Josh knew that Fire Dancer's homesickness was not the reason for their sudden departure. It was quite obvious by both her and Evan's abrupt behavior that the two were at odds with each other. Josh wondered what had happened in his absence, but he did not have the courage to ask. As a matter of fact, conversation of any kind was nil for a good hundred miles. Then one night, after Fire Dancer had fallen asleep, Josh broke the long silence by asking Evan, "I assume General Amherst has sent ye back to investigate that settlement and the other fort?"

"Yes."

"Do ye mind if I go along?"

Evan was surprised at the request. "There may not be any fighting, if that's what you want to get in on," he said. "If they don't pose a threat to us, there's no purpose in starting anything, particularly when we're that deep in enemy territory."

"I agree. That's Sioux and Omaha country. Ye sure don't want to tangle with 'em if ye don't have to. Even the Chickasaw would agree not to antagonize 'em. They're both big nations, and fierce as hell."

"Then why do you want to go along?"

"I'm curious. There aren't any Englishmen that's seen that part of this country as far as I know. I'd like to know what's out there. Besides, if we win this war and that territory becomes ours and the French pull out, there will be a hell of a lot of Indians out there with no one to trade with. Havin' been to that country would give me a jump on the other Goose Creek traders. Why, this might be my golden opportunity."

"I figured your motives must be monetary," Evan remarked. "But haven't you forgotten something? That's not territory that Great Britain is fighting for. Even if we win this war, it will still belong to the French."

"So what? The French claimed all the land west of the Alleghenies, but that didn't stop the Goose Creek men from settin' up a trade with the Indians there. Only thing that's kept us out of the land farther north and west has been those French forts, and if the French lose this war, they'll pull their soldiers out and give up on any ideas of settlin' that land, since they'd no longer have access to it by way of the Great Lakes. The only thing left in that territory will be some French trappers, and they'll be just as happy as the Indians to have someone to trade with—and they won't give a damn that that someone is an Englishman. They're businessmen just like me."

Evan strongly suspected that Josh was right. Not many businessmen would let loyalty to their country get in the way of their profits. That's why there was such a healthy smuggling trade going on between Great Britain and France right now, war or no war. "You're welcome to come along, but I warn you, we're not going to dally. I don't want to risk getting caught in an early snowstorm."

"Aye, a few of the trees' leaves are already turnin' colors." Josh paused. "If we traveled a few hours longer every day, we could cut a week or so off this trip."

Evan found Josh's suggestion very appealing. For him, the trip was miserable, being so close to Fire Dancer every day, for despite everything, he still wanted her. Several times, he had thought of burying his pride and trying once more to reason with her, but nothing in her demeanor had hinted that she would listen. She behaved as if he didn't exist. Perhaps it was just as well, Evan consoled himself. They were going to have to part sooner or later. He'd known that all along. He only wished for them not to part with bad feelings between them. Maybe then he wouldn't feel so empty, so lost. "Let's do it. Travel an hour or so later every day." He glanced in Fire Dancer's direction. "It shouldn't add too much of a strain on"—Evan hesitated when he realized he was putting his concern for Fire Dancer before himself—"any of us."

Josh saw the same pained look in Evan's eyes that he had seen in Fire Dancer's when the young woman didn't think anyone was looking. He knew they both regretted whatever had happened between them, and he wished he knew how to help them resolve their differences, for his sake as well as theirs. Traveling with them was very uncomfortable.

Ten days later, when the three arrived at the Chickasaw stronghold, the forest was ablaze with color as the trees donned their fall dress of vibrant scarlets, oranges, and yellows. But that was the only change that had come about. Fire Dancer and Evan were no closer to resolving their differences than they had been when they left Williamsburg, and she had disappeared almost as soon as they passed through the palisade that surrounded the town.

With Josh as interpreter, Evan held a hasty conference with Promingo and told him of his orders to investigate the French forts and settlements farther up the Misho Sipokni and of his plans to destroy them if they seemed to pose any military threat. Promingo was in agreement and offered Evan a Chickasaw escort. For a moment, Evan paused, wondering if he should risk offending the chief if he set a condition. Then he instructed Josh, "Tell him I appreciate his offer, but I'd like to request that I be in charge of this expedition. If that's not possible, then I would to request that someone other than Red Thunder be in charge. The friction that was between us on the first surveillance has not been resolved."

Josh conveyed his message to Promingo, and the chief's answer clearly surprised the Scot. He said, "Promingo said he had heard about that problem and was sorry it had happened. He said that ordinarily his warriors would refuse to follow a white man, but that you had gained their respect at Fort Massiac. He's given his permission for you to be in charge, but he would like someone clearly marked as second in command, in case something happens to you. He wants to know if you have any suggestions."

Evan wanted Black Hawk. Not only had the brave become fairly adept at English, Evan had come to like and admire the Chickasaw warrior for himself. He wondered if what had happened between himself and Fire Dancer might change how the brave felt about him, if he might withdraw his friendship. But he realized that Fire Dancer would tell no one what had happened, not even her favorite cousin. Her pride would not allow it. "Tell him I'd like Black Hawk, if that could be arranged."

Promingo agreed to Evan's choice without hesitation, and plans were made for their departure the next morn-

ing. It was decided that the expedition would go by
boat, since it was unknown if the territory they were
entering could be crossed by foot or horseback. The
river had fallen by now, and the current was not as
strong as it had been in the spring and summer. Josh
noted that although traveling by river upstream might
take a little longer and more muscle power, it would be
much faster if they ran into a large enemy party and had
to make a rapid escape.

That night, Evan found that he couldn't stay in the
little cabin that he and Fire Dancer had shared. It held
too many memories, and he, too, was convinced that
there was no hope for a reconciliation. He wanted only
to finish his mission and go back to England, to put the
entire episode behind him and try to forget it. Under
cover of darkness, he slipped from the cabin and spent
the night in the woods, close to the river where the
expedition would depart in the morning. But even
there, he couldn't escape. The sweet scent of the willows on the riverbank below drifted up to him, vividly
recalling to him the night he had made love to Fire
Dancer on the sandbar. He couldn't sleep. But it wasn't
the ache in his groin that kept him awake—it was the
strange ache in his heart.

Back in the village, Fire Dancer was faring no better.
She faced the lonely night heartbroken and yearning for
what should never have been—but had. Despite everything, she still loved Evan. Not even his betrayal could
change that. She was terrified that something might
happen to him on the upcoming expedition, her fear
now even stronger than when he had gone off before. It
was then that Fire Dancer did something that she had

never done before. She prayed to Loak-Ishtohoollo-Aba, her God, and then, just to be safe, to his God. When she was finished, she was forced to admit to a bitter truth. It didn't matter if the two gods were one and the same. What mattered was that she had made the distinction and had still done it. She had given her all to the Englishman, despite her promise to herself. She had given her body, her heart, and now, her fierce Chickasaw soul.

24

Evan and his party left the Chickasaw Bluffs landing early the next morning, while the dew was still dripping from the willow trees. The twelve men traveled in a large cypress canoe and hugged the flat western side of the river where the current wasn't as strong, but it still took every man rowing and one poling from behind to make any headway.

Three days later, they came to the junction where the Ohio River joined the Misho Sipokni, then veered left and followed the Misho Sipokni northward. Here the river was much like the Ohio, lined with steep limestone cliffs that were topped with thick forests ablaze with color and dotted with sturdy little red cedar trees that clung tenaciously to the sides of the lofty banks. Here they found the going a little easier, for without the added flow of water from the Ohio, the current wasn't quite as strong. At night, they made their camp on the narrow gravel banks and climbed up to the top of the massive water-chiseled cliffs in search of game, blueberries, and a peculiar fruit with pinkish-orange flesh that Josh identified as a persimmon.

A week into their voyage up the uncharted river, they saw the first human beings they had encountered on this lonely stretch of water. Some French trappers suddenly appeared, coming around a bend in the river, and it was quite obvious from the expressions on their bearded faces as they floated by in their bright blue pirogue with the moose antlers on its bow that they were as surprised to see them as Evan and his party were. For a tense moment, Evan held his breath for fear the *voyageurs* would go for their guns, but fortunately they didn't. After they had passed, Evan remarked to Josh, "Thank God those trappers had enough sense not to try anything. But I'm frankly surprised our braves didn't attack them."

"Nay. They took yer lecture seriously about no shootin' unless ye gave the orders. They're well disciplined. Besides, they don't really dislike the French trappers. If anything, they think of 'em as kindred spirits, since they spend their lives in the woods close to nature. It's the French soldiers that they hate."

Three days later, after the steep banks had given way to undulating land, they came across what Evan assumed was the settlement of Saint Genevieve. But it was so small that they almost passed it without even realizing it was there, for it was just a few scattered cabins at the top of a high hill. Apparently the Frenchmen in the settlement didn't notice them at all, as there was no cry of alarm. Since it was of no military value, Evan didn't even bother to give it closer scrutiny and moved on. But from that point on, they traveled a little more cautiously. According to what the French captives had told the Chickasaw, the fort wasn't far from the settlement.

Late the next day, they found what they had come for. Sitting among the heavily wooded rolling hills on the western side of a crescent-shaped bend in the river was a French stockade that had to be Fort Saint Louis. Below it, on a long sandbar, were scores of pirogues and Indian canoes.

Fortunately, Evan spied the fort before he and his men were seen, and they quickly took cover in a thick woods on the same side of the river as the fort, since dangerous rapids curved under the steep bluff on the eastern bank of the river and made a landing on that side impossible. With only Josh and Black Hawk to accompany him, Evan slipped through the woods and for two days kept the fort under surveillance. During that time, Evan didn't see a single soldier. The only thing that seemed to be going on was a brisk trade. Deeming the fort no more of a military threat than the settlement, Evan called the expedition to an end.

The three men made their way back to camp, but when Evan announced that they would leave that night, he knew from the disappointment in the Chickasaw faces and from their grumbling that they were not pleased. Thinking he had guessed the reason for their unhappiness, he said to Black Hawk, "Tell them I'm sorry that there wasn't a fight, but I explained in the very beginning that we were just a scouting party. It would be foolish to attack without good cause this deep in enemy territory."

"They are not unhappy because there was no fight,"

Black Hawk answered. "They do not wish to antagonize the Sioux and Omaha. We do not need more enemies at the present time. No, the braves are disappointed that they will not get to see the Big Muddy that our ancestors traveled when they moved eastward."

Evan frowned. "The Big Muddy?"

"Aye," Josh said, breaking into the conversation, "the big river that comes from the west that I told ye about. Remember? Well, the Omaha named it the Big Muddy."

"Oh, yes. I remember now."

"Aren't ye curious to see it yerself?" Josh asked. "To find out if it really exists? I am!"

Evan was curious. Like so many others, he wondered if there was a northwest passage to the Pacific and China in this vast land that was waiting to be discovered. His own mission was twofold: not only to find out if the rumored French settlement and fort existed, and if they had any military value, but to make an accurate map of the river and its adjacent territory. He had done both, but his map would be much more valuable if he could verify the existence of this rumored western river and chart it. Excitement filled him, then a sobering thought. "We don't know how much farther this river may be—if it even exists—and winter is coming on."

"But we do not think the Big Muddy is much farther," Black Hawk argued. "The French captive who told us about the fort said it was less than a day's walk farther north."

"Why, that couldn't be more than ten or fifteen miles away!" Josh interjected. "And we wouldn't even have to go by river, if ye're worryin' about runnin' into someone and givin' our presence away. We could trek through the woods. They're thick enough to hide us, but not so thick that we'd get lost. And they ought to be fairly safe. Everyone else is usin' the river to travel."

Evan's excitement came surging back. He grinned. "Well, it looks like you two have taken care of any arguments I might have had. But I'll have to set some limits. We can't wander around out here too long."

"Aye, that's fair," Josh agreed.

"How long will we have?" Black Hawk asked, his dark eyes glittering with excitement.

"A week. We'll leave tomorrow morning."

Black Hawk announced Evan's decision to the others, and the braves went wild, whooping and hollering so loud that Evan feared they would be heard at the fort. They quieted when he cautioned them, but the pitch of their anticipation was so keen that night that it was almost palpable, and no one slept more than a few winks.

The next morning, they hurriedly cooked breakfast on a fire made from cottonwood, since the wood produced no smoke when it burned. They hid their big canoe deep in the woods, packed up what little supplies they had brought with them, and began to walk northward, staying far enough in the woods that they could not be seen, but close enough that the river was always within sight. Just as Josh had predicted, the woods were deserted, although there was considerable traffic on the river, leaving Evan to assume that the trappers and Indians were laying in their winter supplies. By midday, they suspected they were getting close to where the Big Muddy flowed into the Misho Sipokni, because the latter looked as if it were two rivers flowing side by side, just as it did where the Ohio entered it: the water on the western side was a dirty, rusty red, and that on the left was a pure bluish-green. For miles and miles, the river stayed that way; then that evening, the party ran right into the junction of the two large streams.

As they stood on the limestone bluff that overlooked the new river, no one doubted that they had found the Big Muddy. It was, as the Omaha claimed, big and incredibly dirty looking, for it carried with its swift current an unbelievable amount of silt and crushed iron ore from the distant Rockies. It came directly from the west, looking at sunset like a twisted scarlet ribbon that ended in a bloodred sun.

Evan had given the Chickasaw a week, and they held him to it. They wanted to see more of the land their ancestors had come from, and Evan was just as interested for his own reasons. They followed the turbulent river as it wound its way through towering cliffs the water had chiseled in the high, windswept land dotted with trees and huge sunflowers and covered with a thick, tall grass. The Chickasaw were enthralled with the country. Being woodland Indians, they had never seen so much wide open space or such huge herds of elk, antelope, and buffalo, or such a cloudless sky that was such a deep blue. They were fascinated with a plant that appeared more and more often as they moved farther west, its thick, pulpy, paddlelike leaves covered with wicket thorns. Neither Evan nor Josh could identify the cactus, for they had never seen one either. They examined the Sioux burial platform they came across at length, but the warriors were very careful not to disturb the body, for Chickasaw had a profound respect for the dead.

Evan had never seen a burial platform, but Josh identified what the scaffold and the buffalo-skin-wrapped object lying on it was. "Why don't they just bury their dead underground, like everyone else?" Evan asked.

"The Sioux do it to keep wild animals from diggin' the body up. The Choctaw use burial platforms, too, but they have an entirely different reason—so they won't have to dig the body up when it's decayed. They're ancestor worshippers, ye know. They keep their relatives' bones in big jars in bone houses. The Chickasaw used to do that, too, a long time ago, particularly their important chiefs. But now they just bury their dead sittin' up, facin' the sun, except for the women. They're buried in reed coffins."

Evan's attention was still on the odd manner of burying people. "They wait until all the flesh falls from the bones and then collect them?" he asked in a mixture of amazement and disgust.

"Aye, all of the southern tribes used to do that, except the Choctaw. They're too impatient to wait. When the body putrefies, they hire a bone picker with long fingernails to cleanse the bones of their flesh."

Evan's stomach rolled, and a horrified expression came over his face. "Aye, it's a revoltin' practice," Josh said. "That's one reason the Chickasaw scorn the Choctaw. That, and the fact that they practice infanticide."

The next day, there was a decidedly cool nip in the air, and Evan ordered the party to turn back. The Chickasaw didn't object. Their curiosity had been satisfied. Upon their return to their old camp, they retrieved their canoe and departed under the cover of darkness.

With the strong river current to aid them, the party made much better time on their trip back to the Chickasaw village, and they were spied by the sentry on the towering bluffs long before they arrived at their destination. They were met by what seemed to be the entire town almost as soon as they had docked. The Chickasaw asked endless questions, and the returning braves answered excitedly. Evan glanced around, secretly hoping he would see Fire Dancer in the crowd, but he was disappointed. He did, however, get a glimpse of her grandmother in the distance, looking very forbidding and stern-faced.

Shortly thereafter, Evan, Josh, and Black Hawk held a conference with Promingo and reported everything they had seen. The chief seemed disappointed that the fort appeared to be of no military value. Evan suspected that he would have liked to get one more lick in against the French before the war ended.

After they finished giving the chief their report, Evan told Josh to tell Promingo that he was leaving, since there was no point in his staying any longer, and that he thanked him for all of his help and hospitality. But before the Scot finished telling this to Promingo, the chief interrupted with some news of his own that apparently startled the trader.

"What did he say?" Evan asked.

"He said ye might as well forget about going back for a while. The Cherokee are on the warpath, and they aren't lettin' any white men pass through their territory —not even traders they know."

"When in the hell did that happen?"

"I guess while we were gone."

"But I thought the Cherokee were on friendly terms with the colonists."

"They were. Some of 'em were even fightin' on our side down in Georgia under Governor Oglethorpe, attackin' the Spanish forts in Florida." Josh paused thoughtfully for a moment. "And I'll wager that's what this is all about. I heard that a party of Cherokee returnin' from a raid on the enemy in Florida was attacked by some settlers and totally wiped out. The settlers didn't even ask if they were friendly Indians or not. All they cared about was that they were Indians. The massacre had the entire Cherokee nation in an uproar. I reckon things must have finally come to a head."

"I don't blame them for going on the warpath," Evan said angrily. "That's a hell of a way to treat your friends and allies. Those stupid, goddamned settlers! I wish I could get my hands on them."

Josh's fiery red eyebrows rose at Evan's outburst. This certainly wasn't the same man he had brought west a few months ago, he thought. That man hadn't had any respect for Indians either. But Evan's attitude had changed, and Josh only wished more white men could learn to appreciate the red man, or at least come to realize that, like the white man, there were good and bad among them.

Promingo said something, and Josh quickly interpreted it. "Promingo said ye're welcome to stay as his guest for as long as the Cherokee are on the warpath."

Evan wasn't particularly excited by the chief's invitation. He had been eager to get away from the village and the nearness of Fire Dancer. But he realized that Promingo might be risking his friendship with the Cherokee to harbor a white man, and he was grateful. "Tell him I accept and thank him for me."

When Josh finished passing that message on, Evan said, "Ask the chief if he thinks I can get a letter through to Fort Laudoun by way of a Chickasaw runner. I'd like to let General Amherst know what we found—or rather, didn't find—on our expedition."

Josh passed that message on, and to Evan's relief, Promingo was in agreement.

That night, Evan wrote his report to General Amherst and put it in a leather pouch. Before he handed it to Josh to deliver to the runner, he slipped the map he had made in with it. When the Scot accepted the pouch, Evan asked, "What will you do now? Go back to your own village?"

"Aye, in a few days or so. My wife's relatives have asked me to go on a hunt with 'em tomorrow mornin'. I didn't want to appear rude by rushin' off, so I agreed. I thought maybe ye'd like to go along, since ye don't have anything pressin'.'"

Evan was grateful for the distraction the hunt would lend him and the opportunity to get out of the Chickasaw village. "Thank you. I would."

The next day, Evan, Josh, and the hunters left the Chickasaw village and hunted for several days. They were on their way back to the stronghold on the fourth day when Black Hawk suddenly appeared, tearing through the woods as if all the demons in hell were after him. He sped past the hunters up to Evan, then said through ragged gasps, "You must come quick!"

"Why? What's wrong?" Evan asked in alarm.

"Fire Dancer . . ." Black Hawk paused, trying to catch his breath.

"What about Fire Dancer?" Evan asked anxiously, catching his shoulders and shaking him. "What's happened to her?"

"She has been captured by"—Black Hawk paused to draw in another deep breath, then spat as if there were something foul tasting in his mouth—"Choctaw!"

25

When Black Hawk uttered the name of the Chickasaw's most hated enemy, every brave in the hunting party gasped. Evan and Josh were so stunned, they were speechless. When he had recovered from the shocking news, Evan asked, "They attacked the town?"

"No. There was just one boat of them. They apparently captured Fire Dancer while she was in the woods gathering *pacans.* Another woman saw her in their boat and ran back to the village to give the alarm."

"But how did she know they were Choctaw?" Evan asked, his shock replaced with an icy fear for Fire Dancer's life. "Maybe they were Shawnee or Delaware."

"Nay, she'd never mistake another Indian for a Choctaw," Josh informed Evan. "The Choctaw foreheads are horribly disfigured by placin' sandbags against 'em while they're infants. That's why the colonists call 'em flatheads."

"And we found the imprint in the mud from where

they had grounded their canoe," Black Hawk said. "It was clearly a Choctaw canoe, for they carve their war canoes, even the bottoms. Promingo ordered a party of warriors to go after them, and I knew you were probably near and would want to come along."

"I do," Evan answered grimly.

"Me too!" Josh chimed in.

"Then we must hurry."

Black Hawk turned to the hunters and quickly explained what had happened. The braves didn't hesitate to unload the game from the horses that were carrying it and offer them to Black Hawk and the white men. The three quickly mounted and raced back to the village. Evan stopped by his cabin to pick up his saber and more powder and balls. Then they rushed to the pier below the bluffs, where a war canoe had been readied and loaded with supplies and a group of angry warriors who were anxiously pacing and awaiting their arrival.

Within minutes, the big boat was launched, and the Chickasaw were in hot pursuit of the abductors. But the Choctaw, in a swift, light canoe made from cypress, had a head start on them. All day they sped down the river, and the more time that passed without sighting the Choctaw, the more despondent Evan became. Finally, he said to Josh. "It's hopeless. We'll never catch up with them."

"We will eventually."

"Eventually? How? They might not even be on this river anymore. They could have turned off on any of the small streams that empty into it, and we'll never find them."

"Ye couldn't. I couldn't. But he can."

Josh nodded at the wizened old man standing in the bow of the boat, the skin on his thin arms and legs looking like old, wrinkled leather. "Who's he?" Evan asked.

"Our guide. He's supposed to be an expert on trackin' Choctaw."

"But that's my point. How can you track anyone on water? There are no tracks. They could have turned off anywhere."

"Aye, but he's got a pretty good idea where they will leave the river. The Choctaw are creatures of habit, just like anyone else. They have their favored streams."

About two hours before sundown, the ... man squinted at the eastern bank, then motioned for the boats to move in that direction. Evan saw nothing but a solid line of cattails, until they had almost reached them. Then he saw that there was a slight break in the wall, where the cattails leaned to both sides, and on the water below them was a scum of fallen brown pollen. Aiming their boat at the break, the Chickasaw passed through the cattails, making them rustle and sending several birds that nested among them flying into the air. Evan expected them to ground and he braced himself for it, but to his surprise, behind the cattails was the mouth of a narrow stream, which they followed as it twisted and turned beneath a thick canopy of overhung tree limbs, making it look like a long, dark tunnel.

That night, as they sat in the darkness eating jerky and the fruit from a nearby pawpaw tree, Black Hawk said, "Our guide says he does not think the Choctaw know they are being pursued. They have been too careless. Apparently they do not know one of our women saw them."

"How have they been careless?" Evan asked. "Are you talking about that break in the cattails back there?"

"Partly. But more important, our guide says they are burning a fire. They would not dare do that if they even suspected they were being followed."

Evan peered into the darkness. "I don't see anything."

"No. He does not see it either. He smells the smoke."

Evan couldn't smell smoke—only the musty odor of half-rotten leaves. But Black Hawk's words gave him hope. If the Choctaw didn't know they were being pursued, then they had a much better chance of taking them by surprise and recapturing Fire Dancer alive. The terror he had been living with since he discovered she had been abducted abated slightly.

The next day they followed the stream into a swamp, and Evan got his first look at cypress trees. They stood like towering giant sentinels, their reddish trunks gnarled and ancient-looking, their feathery leaves yellow now and dropping to the water below, where they would rot and turn the water the color of tea. As they wound around the knobby knees that protruded from the submerged roots and were surrounded by the duckweed that made the water look slimy, a shiver ran over Evan. The place looked dark and forbidding; the dead silence was eerie, the smell fetid. He sensed danger lurking everywhere, and on several occasions he actually saw it. A huge water moccasin suddenly dropped from a limb of a tree under which they were passing, frightening him before he had the presence of mind to knock the dangling snake away with his paddle. A little while later, several alligators sunning on one of the banks slithered into the water and followed them, their peculiar red eyes glowing in the dark shadows; one actually snapped at their paddles. Then Evan saw leaves moving on the bushes on one of the banks. A swamp deer, its hooves unusually large and spread to support its weight on the mud, stepped forward and dropped its head to drink. A split second later, Evan heard a hair-raising scream and saw a yellow flash come from a tree above the deer. As the cougar's long fangs sank into the deer's vulnerable throat and its claws dug into its back, Evan turned his head, not wanting to witness the violent death.

When they left the swamp, again following a narrow stream, Evan was vastly relieved. He turned to Josh and asked, "Where do you think they're taking Fire Dancer?"

"Judgin' from the direction we're headin', I'd guess Koosah. That's their main town. Or they might be takin' her to Mobile. It's about a hundred and eighty miles farther south."

"Mobile is a French fort. Why would they be taking her there?"

"They might figure they'd get a good price for her as a slave, since she's unusually beautiful."

Evan summoned the courage to ask what he had been putting off for fear of what the answer might be. "What will happen to her if we don't rescue her?"

"Well, like I said, either they'll sell her for a slave to the French—who may or may not ship her to the West

Indies—or whoever claims her as his captive will make her his concubine."

Evan swallowed hard. "Then she's already been raped?"

"Nay. They save that for when they get back to their settlement. Most of these Indians take a vow of celibacy when they're raidin' or makin' war. It's sort of a pact with the Great Spirit: If he'll protect 'em, they'll behave 'emselves. And something else the Indians don't do, in case that's worryin' ye—they don't gang rape. Only the man she belongs to can use her that way. That's why a lot of the women who were captured at those frontier forts by the French and their Indian allies at the beginnin' of the war decided to ally themselves with an Indian captor instead of one of the French soldiers. Otherwise they got raped by the entire garrison." Josh paused. "The biggest danger to her is goin' to be when we attack. Then they'll try to kill her. All tribes do that —kill the captive quick. It must be some kind of cardinal rule in Indian fightin'."

Evan already knew that. That was why he had been so relieved to hear that the Choctaw didn't know they were being pursued.

"There's always the possibility that we'll be taken captive ourselves," Josh continued. "Ye know what will happen then. They'll torture us. If that happens, take my advice and act real brave. It wouldn't hurt even to egg 'em on. Then they might let ye die with yer manhood still intact. That's the prize, ye know—yer manhood."

Evan hadn't known, and just the thought of it made him feel a little sick. But he was determined not to be captured alive, if that was what it came down to. He'd fight to the death.

A little while later, they entered a pleasant country interspersed with wooded .hills and abounding with creeks and springs. The smell of pine was pungent in the air, and the foliage on the occasional sweet gum trees was spectacular. Suddenly the land dipped, and they found themselves in another swamp. Here the cypress trees were draped in Spanish moss that fluttered in the breeze, looking like gray wraiths among the dark shadows. Several times that day, the stream dwindled down to nothing and they were forced to carry the canoe, sloshing through mud that came to their ankles and shouldering aside cane at least fifty feet high. These were the times that they all dreaded the most, for the canebrakes were full of poisonous snakes, alligators, vicious razorbacks, and black bears, and they kept a sharp eye out. Then the stream would suddenly appear again, and they would climb back into the canoe until the next time the water gave out. This peculiar country couldn't seem to decide if it wanted to be land or water or something in between.

The second night, they reached another hilly area. They camped in a deep woods, again with no fire. Their guide disappeared for a few hours, and when he returned, he announced that the Choctaw party was close enough to attack that night. A battle plan was quickly drawn up. It was decided that Evan would try to secure Fire Dancer's release before the others moved in, and if that was not possible, he would try to prevent the Choctaw from killing her until the others could engage the enemy.

Leaving two men behind to guard the boat, Evan, Josh, and the Chickasaw cautiously picked their way through the dark woods. Evan smelled the smoke from the enemy's fire long before he saw the dim red glow through the trees. An outlying sentry was discovered, and one of the Chickasaw quickly and silently disposed of the hapless man before he could sound the alarm. When they crept up to the perimeter of the clearing where the Choctaw had made their camp, they dropped to their stomachs and studied the scene.

Evan's primary concern was Fire Dancer. He quickly scanned the camp and spied her off to the left side, sitting on the ground and leaning against a pine. Her hands were tied behind the tree, and her ankles were tied together with a piece of rawhide. With her head resting on one shoulder, she looked to be asleep, and as far as Evan could tell from that distance, she didn't appear to be harmed in any way.

Having assured himself that she was alive and unharmed, he peered at the Choctaw lying closest to him and was filled with revulsion. The warrior's head appeared to be horribly misshapen—the unusually high forehead was flat up to the hairline, where it jutted forward, making his nose look out of place. That and the lurid tattoos all over him and the bones that pierced his nose and upper lip made him look hideous, and he smelled to high heaven from the alligator oil he used to repel mosquitoes. Tearing his eyes away, Evan counted nineteen braves sleeping around the fire, which meant the Choctaw had a six-man edge on them.

Evan motioned for the Chickasaw to circle the camp, then crept through the woods until he reached the side of the camp where Fire Dancer was tied. He fell to his stomach and shimmied across the clearing that separated them until his nose was practically in her hands. Carefully, he removed the knife from its scabbard at his side, placed the blade next to the rawhide string, and cut the bonds. Fire Dancer awakened with a start.

"No, don't move!" Evan whispered urgently, as the narrow tree to which she was tied offered him no concealment.

Fire Dancer could hardly believe her ears when she heard Evan's voice. She had thought there no hope for her rescue, that when she was discovered missing, everyone would assume she had been dragged off by a wild animal, since her abductor had been very careful to leave no trail between where she taken and where the boat waited on the river. An incredible surge of relief raced through her. Then, seeing one of the Choctaw roll over in his sleep, she closed her eyes and feigned sleep.

Evan waited until the man who had moved was still once more, then shimmied around the tree to cut the bonds holding her ankles together. Just as he placed the knife to the rawhide, one of the Choctaw awakened, spied him, and yelled.

All hell broke loose in the camp as the Choctaw scrambled to their feet. The Chickasaw rushed in simultaneously, screaming their bloodcurdling war cry. "Run!" Evan yelled to Fire Dancer as he jumped up. He dropped his knife and pulled out his saber to engage the four Choctaw running toward him with their knives bared and tomahawks raised. He ducked as one tomahawk flew over his head, then swung his saber back and forth with a vengeance, the blade flashing in the fire-light.

Behind him Fire Dancer was trying desperately to get to her feet, but the bonds that had held them had cut off her circulation, and her numbed feet would not support her. She kept falling to her knees. Balls from the Choctaw guns whizzed everywhere around her and Evan as the enemy tried desperately to kill her and the man protecting her.

Snarling, eyes blazing, his golden head gleaming in the firelight as he slashed and stabbed furiously with his long, lethal blade, cutting down the warriors rushing him as if they were no more than shoots of cane, the Englishman seemed to the Choctaw more like a demon from the underworld than a human being. For many of the Choctaw, it was their last thought. They were shot while trying to focus their gun sights on the wild man or were downed by the Chickasaw's well-aimed knives and tomahawks. The few that remained fought to the death in desperate hand-to-hand combat, much preferring that to what the Chickasaw would do to them if they captured them alive.

Within minutes, the fierce battle ended. Evan stood over the four men he had slain in a pool of blood and looked wildly around as the gunshots and war cries still echoed in the woods, not yet realizing it was over and expecting to see more of the hideous Indians rushing toward him. He was oblivious to the blood running down his temple from where one of the bullets had grazed him and to the fact that his sleeves had been cut to ribbons, as his heart raced from the adrenaline that had poured into his bloodstream. Smoke rolled over the camp, and bloody bodies were scattered everywhere. Then he saw one of the Chickasaw drop to his knees and scalp a Choctaw lying on the ground, and it dawned on him that the fight had ended and the abductors had been soundly defeated.

Remembering Fire Dancer, he whirled around, tossed his saber aside, and dropped to his knees beside her. Still on her knees, she stared at him, for she, too, had thought he looked absolutely terrifying. She had never seen anyone fight so furiously, and she had no idea that he had done so not out of anger, as he had at Fort Massiac, but out of fear for her life.

Seeing the blood on her face, Evan touched it and said in alarm, "You're hurt!"

"No, it's just blood that splattered on me," she answered numbly; then, as blood continued to run from the wound on his temple, she said, "But you have been wounded. You're bleeding."

Evan raised his hand and felt the wound. "It's nothing to be concerned about. It just grazed me," he said.

Suddenly, he pulled her into his arms, and embraced her so tightly, she found it difficult to breathe. "Thank God, you're safe!" he said in an anguished voice that seemed to be torn from the depths of his soul. "I don't know what I would have done if anything had happened to you. Oh, God, Fire Dancer, I love you! I never dreamed I could love someone so much. I love you so much, it hurts."

Again Fire Dancer had trouble believing what she had heard. Evan learning to love her had seemed even more hopeless than her being rescued. She pushed away from him, searched his face as if looking for confirmation there. *"Chiklooska ke-e-u chua?"* she asked.

Evan hadn't consciously meant to tell Fire Dancer that he loved her. It wasn't until she asked if he lied that he fully realized that his deep love for her was a profound truth, and he didn't regret admitting it. His Chickasaw beloved had not only lit an unquenchable fire in his blood, she had captured his heart. He looked her deep in the eyes and answered solemnly, *"Aklooska ke-e-u-que-Ho."*

Fire Dancer didn't even realize she had asked the question in her own tongue until Evan had answered, "I do not lie" in Chickasaw.

"I love you," Evan repeated.

Tears of happiness swam in Fire Dancer's eyes. "And I love you," she answered.

Evan hadn't realized that Fire Dancer's love was what he had been striving for, yearning for, wanting so desperately for so long. It surpassed even his need to protect her—something that he had finally managed to accomplish that night. He felt the sudden sting of tears in his own eyes, and a choking feeling came to his throat as a powerful surge of pure emotion swept over him. He didn't know whether to kiss her, shout for the whole world to hear, or jump up and down for joy. He settled for embracing her, and Fire Dancer hugged him back just as tightly.

To the others in the camp, the two seemed to cling to each other for an eternity, still on their knees, and despite the fact that the Chickasaw didn't approve of public shows of emotion, no one begrudged the couple their happiness. The warriors pretended not to notice, while Josh grinned from ear to ear.

Finally Evan broke the embrace and rose, bringing Fire Dancer to her feet with him. As he framed her face in his hands in preparation for kissing her to seal their vows, she cried out softly and pulled away. Then he noticed the dark bruise on her jaw just below her left ear. Gently, he placed one finger under her chin and turned it to get a better look. Fury filled him. "Which one of these bastards did that to you?"

"None of them." Fire Dancer's eyes flashed with remembered anger. "Red Thunder hit me with his fist when he was trying to subdue me."

"Subdue you?" Evan asked in surprise. "What are you talking about?"

Both Black Hawk and Josh had overheard what Fire Dancer said. They rushed forward in time to hear her answer: "He followed me into the woods and overpowered me, then carried me to where the Choctaw were waiting in their canoe and turned me over to them."

"He planned and executed your abduction?" Evan asked, unbelieving.

"Yes, he did. He told them to take me to the French at Mobile, that they would give them a good price for me since I was Promingo's niece. But I think they planned to keep me themselves. They hate my uncle even more than the French do."

"This is treachery!" Black Hawk said angrily. "Red Thunder will pay."

"Yes, he certainly will," Evan agreed in a hard voice, his eyes glittering with fierce determination. "But I still don't understand why he did it."

"Because he wants to be the father of the next chief, and as things are, I am the woman who is destined to bear that child. He wants the prestige and the power he thinks it will bring him. I always suspected he had some ulterior motive—he became very angry when I spurned his advances years ago. While you were gone to investigate Fort Saint Louis, he approached me again, and I turned him away. He knew I was in love with you. He waited, thinking if you were killed or didn't return, I would change my mind and eventually accept him. But just in case, he had already approached the Choctaw. Then you returned, and he followed through with his plan to do away with me."

"But why you?" Evan asked. "If he felt I was such a threat, why didn't he kill me, or try to?"

"Because he knew I'd suspect him if you met with an 'accidental' death. So he decided to get rid of me, then court my younger sister. She is young and naive and very impressionable. He had already made advances, and she didn't spurn him, as I had."

"Ookproo-shed!" Black Hawk spat. "I always knew he was very bad. I go now. You will be avenged."

Evan caught the warrior's arm. "No, I'll avenge her! She's the woman I love," he said angrily.

"Don't interfere in tribal justice, Evan," Josh warned. "Vengeance is for blood kin. It's Black Hawk's place to do it, not yers. Besides, Red Thunder has probably already hightailed it. He wasn't countin' on that woman seein' the Choctaw with Fire Dancer. It'll take some trackin' to find him. I'll admit ye've become a pretty good woodsman, but ye still can't hold a candle to Black Hawk."

"Then I'll go along with him," Evan answered.

"Nay, ye'll only slow him down, and the sooner Black Hawk can pick up Red Thunder's trail, the sooner he can bring the bastard to justice. Ye can't begin to run like Black Hawk can. No white man can."

"Run? You mean he's going overland from here?"

"Aye. The Natchez Trail is not far west from here. It's an old Chickasaw trail that they used to use to trade with their old friends, before the French wiped 'em out. Why, Black Hawk can probably be on Red Thunder's trail by the day after tomorrow."

As much as Evan wanted to take part in avenging Fire Dancer, he knew he had to back out. He released Black Hawk's arm and said, "Good luck, and take care. Remember, he's a sneaky bastard."

Black Hawk nodded his head gravely. "Don't worry," he said. "I'll find him. He'll pay."

Evan didn't doubt Black Hawk's word for a moment, and the look in the warrior's dark eyes made a shiver run through him. Red Thunder would not die an easy death.

Then Black Hawk turned and loped away, swallowed by the darkness.

26

Two days later, the rescue party tied up to the pier at Chickasaw Bluffs. Not wanting to stay in enemy territory any longer than necessary lest their presence be discovered by a Choctaw hunting party, they had traveled almost straight through. Their arrival was expected. Black Hawk had reached the settlement that morning, relayed the news of the party's success and Red Thunder's treachery, and learned that the subchief had disappeared shortly after Fire Dancer's abduction was reported, which the vengeful warrior had fully expected. While he pursued Red Thunder, the man's unfortunate kin had been exiled by the furious townspeople, and the smoke from their cabins being burnt to the ground was still curling lazily in the air over the settlement.

Promingo greeted them at the top of the bluffs. It was his practice to do so, but what was surprising was that Eastern Star was also waiting. She embraced Fire Dancer warmly and welcomed her. She even thanked

Evan for his help in bringing her granddaughter back safely.

Other than that, the returning party wasn't detained, and both Fire Dancer and Evan were glad. They were anxious to get to the privacy of their cabin and be alone for the first time since they had openly declared their love. But they didn't fall into each other's arms the minute they stepped into the cabin. Since neither had bathed for several days, they gathered fresh clothing and their bathing supplies and rushed to the stream that was set aside for bathing. He went to the section reserved for men, she to the women's section. It was the quickest bath either had ever taken. With their hair still dripping water, they hurried back toward the village and suddenly came face-to-face in the woods.

Their eyes quickly traveled over each other's length. Since the damp clothing was molded to their bodies like a second skin, every powerful muscle of Evan's body and every soft curve of Fire Dancer's was clearly revealed. They stared in silent admiration at each other, she at his male magnificence and he at her feminine beauty. Then his eyes locked on the two dark circles on the bodice of her toga that marked her nipples. As they hardened and rose and her breasts swelled and strained at the material that covered them, Evan's manhood reacted in the same manner. Fire Dancer watched, mesmerized, as he grew before her very eyes, until the bulge between his legs looked as if it would split his breeches in two. Their eyes met, his blue and hers green, blazing so hot with desire that the sight jolted their senses and fired their blood. Both knew that they couldn't wait until they got back to the cabin. They

wanted each other fiercely, urgently, then and there—
and the world be damned! The clothing and bathing
articles in their arms were dropped heedlessly to the
ground as they crossed the distance between them and
embraced. Their mouths came together with such force
that it bruised their lips, but neither noticed. Their kiss
was long, wild, feverish, bringing Fire Dancer to her
toes and straining against Evan as she silently begged
for more, and more, and more, while his tongue rav-
ished the sweetness of her mouth and his hands rushed
hungrily over her body.

When he finally raised his head, the trees in the forest were spinning around him and his breath was coming in ragged gasps. But he still had the presence of
mind to realize they couldn't make love right there in
the path, where anyone going to the stream might stumble over them. Spying a thick curtain of grapevines a
short distance away, he picked Fire Dancer up in his
arms and quickly carried her there, steeling himself as
she placed hot, feverish kisses on his neck and face. He
bent and shouldered the long strands away, then looked
about. The vines hung from the towering trees all
around him, making the sun-dappled, grassy clearing
where he stood look like a little room. He couldn't have
made a more private place for their lovemaking than
this one nature had provided for him. He set Fire
Dancer on her feet and peeled her arms from around
his neck.

When he tried to separate them, she moaned in objection, not wanting to give him up. Had it been possible, she would have absorbed him, taken him into her
and made him a part of her forever, as she wanted des-

perately to do. Then when he deftly stripped off her toga and placed a trail of searing kisses down her throat and across her shoulders, she did finally step back, and the knowledge of his ultimate destination made goose-flesh break out all over her in anticipation. As he reached his goal, his teeth ever so gently raking the erect nipple before his warm mouth closed over it, she cried out softly and arched her back to give him even better access.

Evan ministered to one swollen breast, then the other. His mouth descended slowly as he traced her rib cage with his tongue, dropping lower and lower while his hands caressed her hips and her thighs. He fell to his knees, and his hands slipped to the backs of her thighs, stroking back and forth, back and forth, before he cupped her buttocks and lifted her. His tongue greedily lapped a drop of moisture left from her bath in the dark curls between her legs, then found her heated, pulsating center with the sureness of a bee drawn to nectar. Fire Dancer cried out again, feeling as if a torch had been set to her there, then gave herself up to sensa-tion, holding tightly to his golden head for support, until the waves of ecstasy washing over her left her so weak that her knees buckled.

Evan caught her before she fell and spread her toga on the ground. From there Fire Dancer watched with dazed eyes as he stripped off his clothing, baring his magnificent male body along with the blatant proof of his desire for her. When he started to lie down beside her, she sat up and said sharply, "No! I want to look at you first."

Evan brought himself back up to his full, impressive

height while Fire Dancer's eyes took in every inch of him. Her warm, hungry look heated his blood to new heights as she devoured him with her eyes. When she muttered in a husky voice, *"A-chookoma,"* a little smile of amusement crossed his lips at her calling him "beautiful warrior."

Fire Dancer had meant what she said. To her, Evan was beautiful, in both body and spirit. Not only was he graced with golden good looks and a splendid physique, he was the strong, courageous, utterly masculine warrior who epitomized everything a man should be, and she could hardly believe he loved her.

Evan watched the hot look of desire in Fire Dancer's eyes turn into the warm, tender look of love. The transformation shook him to his roots and momentarily tempered his raging desire. When she rose and muttered, "Let me love you," he offered no resistance, feeling a strange tightening sensation in his chest and a lump in his throat.

And Fire Dancer did just that—showed Evan her love. She dropped kisses all over his face, neck, and chest while she caressed him, taking special pleasure in running her hands through the mat of golden hair on his chest, then thrilling at his hiss of pleasure when she licked and teased his flat male nipple. Just as he had done earlier, her mouth descended, nipping at the hard planes of his stomach, following the line of golden hair that pointed to his splendid manhood like an arrow. When she dropped to her knees to reciprocate his earlier loving, Evan didn't think he could bear any more of her soft, teasing kisses and tingling caresses, but he had no recourse. He didn't have the will to refuse the delights she was offering him. Every powerful muscle in his body trembled with need, and he broke out in a cold sweat as she ministered to him, her tongue and mouth instruments of exquisite pleasure until he reached an unbearable peak of excitement and *his* knees buckled.

When Evan collapsed, he pushed Fire Dancer back to the toga on the ground. For a moment, he lay weakly over her, drinking in deep breaths and struggling to control his raging desire. Then he propped himself on his elbows and looked down at her. "I love you," he said softly.

"I love you too," Fire Dancer replied, sudden tears springing to her eyes.

With the words spoken and the depth of their mutual emotion so profound in their eyes, their lovemaking took on a deeper meaning. Each tried to give the other the most pleasure and, in giving, received much more in return. Evan kissed and tongued every inch of Fire Dancer's satiny skin, even the soles of her feet, and Fire Dancer adored him in return. Their kisses were deep and sensuous, tongues dancing and intertwining, breaths mingling. Even though they tried to keep their passion at bay so they could enjoy this very special loving to the fullest, their senses were soon spinning, their pulses pounding, their breaths rasping, their blood racing through their veins like liquid fire, every nerve ending in their bodies aflame. Fearing he was about to explode and wanting to be inside her when it happened, Evan rose over Fire Dancer and entered her slowly— ever so slowly—savoring the sensation of her warm, wet velvet surrounding his rigid member inch by inch. Then when he was buried deep inside her, feeling as if he were drowning in her sweet, tight warmth, he sighed. If there had been any doubts in his mind as to what his sentiments for Fire Dancer were, they were firmly put to rest. He felt as if he had come home after a long, tiring journey. A deep contentment washed over him.

Fire Dancer, too, was savoring their joining, not just the feel of his hard muscles pressing against her soft flesh, chest to chest, hip to hip, thigh to thigh, or the tingling sensation of her warmth surrounding him where he lay deep inside her, but their special closeness at that moment, their total oneness in spirit as well as body.

For a long time they lay that way, relishing their union. Then Evan raised his head and looked down at her tenderly, lovingly, and Fire Dancer felt as if her heart were melting. A sob of pure happiness escaped her lips just before he bent his golden head and kissed her. His thrusts were slow, exquisitely sensuous movements that quickly rekindled the fires of their passion. Then Evan increased the tempo, and it seemed to Fire Dancer that he was pouring himself into her, as if he fully intended to crawl into her and claim her body as his. All Fire Dancer could do was cling to him and sob against his sweat-dampened throat, desperately wanting what he was doing to her, giving to her, making her feel with each powerful, magnificent thrust, and feel, and feel, and feel until she thought she would die from the exquisite sensations. Never before had Evan's possession been so intense, so demanding, so wildly exciting as he took her in a sweet fury of loving that quickly led her up those glorious, spine-tingling heights of rapture. He held her on the trembling brink for what seemed an eternity of breathless anticipation, making Fire Dancer squirm beneath him and beg for release. Then twisting his hips and driving into her, Evan brought them to that mindless, searing burst of passion in a violent explosion that rent their souls from their bodies and sent them hurtling among a starburst of flaming, glorious colors.

They drifted on that warm, glorious cloud of utter fulfillment, slowly descending, still locked in that sweet embrace. Then Evan rolled from Fire Dancer and placed her head on his shoulder, dropping a tender kiss on the top of her head as he did so. They lay that way in silence for a long while. They didn't need words to express the deep emotion they both felt. Their mutual happiness was so powerful that it flowed between them like a unseen river, binding them even closer.

It wasn't until much later in the day that they left their secluded private place in the woods. Surprisingly, they didn't make love again. Neither would have thought their passion would be so easily satisfied, particularly in view of their normal hunger for each other and after their long abstinence. But neither felt the urge for another physical joining. Just being together, just knowing how much the other cared was all that mattered. It was a quiet time, a time in which no demands were made on each by the other, and for that reason, it was a special time that they both cherished. Feeling a deep contentment, they walked hand in hand back to the village.

Several mornings later, when Evan and Fire Dancer were eating breakfast, she suddenly announced, "My mare is with foal. I suspect your stallion is responsible. I think it happened when they were on the way back from the Chickasaw village on the Ohio."

Evan looked at Fire Dancer's stern expression. "I take it you're not too happy about it."

"Of course I am not happy! My mare has pure Chickasaw blood in her."

"For your information, my stallion is a Thoroughbred too."

"An English Thoroughbred! They can't compare with a Chickasaw horse!"

Instead of taking offense, Evan chuckled. He was too damn happy to get upset over Fire Dancer scorning his mount again. He'd never known such contentment, such joy as he had the past few days.

"I don't think it's funny!" she said, pouting. "Now I will have to wait until next year to breed her again, if I want a decent foal from her."

"And how do you know you won't get a decent foal?" Evan countered. "Hell, maybe you'll even get a *superior* foal. Introducing new blood has been known to improve an animal, you know. Just look at yourself. You're half Chickasaw and half English." Seeing her about to object, he quickly held up his hand to silence her. "No, don't bother to deny your English blood. I'm not listening to that foolishness anymore. Whether you like it or not, you're half English. Where do you think you get your stubbornness from? I used to think it was the Chickasaw blood in you, but now I know better. Stubbornness, pride, fierce determination are all English traits too. How do you know which parent you inherited them from?"

Fire Dancer was so taken aback by his logic that she

could only stare at him. Then Evan smiled, a devastating smile that tugged at her heartstrings. "Don't be upset about the colt, love," he said softly. "Maybe it will turn out as wonderful and exceptional as you are."

Any displeasure Fire Dancer may have felt disappeared like a puff of smoke in the wind under Evan's warm look and his compliment. As he stretched his hand out to her, she didn't have to ask what he planned. She knew he was inviting her back to bed.

The two were just rising to their feet when a knock sounded at the door. Evan frowned, reluctantly dropped her hand, and walked to the door. Opening it, he saw Josh standing there with Black Hawk at his side.

"Sorry if I'm interruptin' anything, but I figured ye'd want to know that Black Hawk came back," Josh said.

Evan's and Black Hawk's eyes met. The warrior gravely nodded his head, silently but eloquently telling Evan that the deed was done. Evan didn't ask any questions. He didn't want to know any of the gruesome details. "Thank you. I'm glad you have returned safely. Won't you come in?"

"No, I am very tired," Black Hawk answered. "I go to my cabin to sleep now. I will return this evening."

As Black Hawk turned and walked away, Josh said, "I've got some other news for ye. The runner ye sent to Fort Laudoun with that letter to General Amherst is back."

"He delivered it and got back that soon?" Evan asked in surprise.

"He didn't get it delivered. A party of Cherokee caught him a few miles from the fort and took the pouch from him. They destroyed everything in it."

"Even the map?" Evan asked in distress.

"Aye."

"Dammit! I'll never be able to reconstruct that map, at least not with any accuracy."

Josh didn't say so, but he thought it just as well. This way, he'd have the edge on the other traders for a good while. "Well, don't get too upset. The runner did manage to make the return trip, with the packet the general sent you. He was a little miffed at the way the Cherokee had treated him the first time and was determined he'd outsmart 'em on the return trip."

"What packet?"

"This one." Josh reached into his shirt and pulled out an oilskin pouch, then handed it to Evan.

Evan walked across the room and sat down beside Fire Dancer on one of the low couches, as Josh followed. Then he removed two letters from the pouch. "Who is the other letter from?" the Scot asked curiously.

Evan flipped the letter over and looked at the wax seal on the back. "I don't know. I don't recognize the seal," he said.

Evan set the unidentified letter down and opened the missive from General Amherst. After quickly reading it, he looked up and said to Josh, "Quebec has surrendered."

"When?" the Scot asked in surprise.

"In early September, shortly after we left Virginia. General Amherst plans to march on Montreal next spring, but for all practical purposes, he considers the war pretty much over. Montreal isn't much of a military objective. It never has been and never will be the fortress Quebec was."

"So ye'll be joining him up north?"

"Not yet. My enlistment is up next month. He suggests that if I'm going to reenlist, I take a leave and go back home for a visit before rejoining him for the mopping-up phase."

"Then you'll be going back to England?"

For years, Evan had been wanting to go home, but now the prospect didn't excite him in the least. A little baffled by his own reaction, he answered vaguely, "Maybe, maybe not." Then he picked up the second letter, broke the seal, and read it.

A stunned expression came over his face as he scanned the missive. "Who's it from?" Josh asked.

"The barrister who's handling my brother's estate," Evan mumbled.

"Estate?" Josh asked in surprise. "Are ye sayin' yer brother's dead?"

"Yes," Evan answered, clearly shaken by the news.

"Which brother?" Fire Dancer asked. "Your twin, or your younger brother?"

"My twin." Evan looked up at her with a dazed expression on his face. "He, his wife, and son were all killed when a fire destroyed his town house while they were visiting London."

"I'm sorry to hear that," Josh commented. "A fire, ye say? I've heard London has some bad ones, that entire sections of the city are wiped out sometimes."

"Yes, there are a lot of wooden homes built close together. If a fire starts in one, it's almost impossible to keep it from spreading, particularly if it starts at night and gets a head start on the firefighters, as this one did."

"Then you're the earl now?" Fire Dancer asked.

"Yes, the tenth Earl of Linchester."

"Well, I suppose ye'll be going back to England for sure now, and for good," Josh remarked.

Evan was still too shocked by the unexpected news even to know how he felt about it, much less what he was going to do. He rose to his feet. "I don't honestly know what I'm going to do," he said. "I need time to think, to mull this over. If you'll excuse me, I'm going to take a walk by the river."

As Evan walked from the cabin, Fire Dancer felt as if her world were shattering into a million pieces, and her heart was breaking. Since he had told her he loved her, she had begun to hope that he might stay in America. He'd had to give up his home to his brother, but there might be a future for them here. She would even have been willing to accept the role of his mistress, if need be. All that mattered was that she share some part of his life, for without him, her own life would be empty and meaningless. She had already had a taste of that particular hell when they were separated after they had left Virginia. But now Fire Dancer knew her dreams would never materialize, now that Evan had attained what he had wanted for so long. He might say he didn't know what he planned to do, but she knew. Fate had dropped his dream right into his lap—the title, the property, the beloved lands—and he wouldn't turn his back on them. He would go back to England now, to his world, and there was no place in that world for her. Not even his feelings for her could change that. She knew enough of the white man's way to know that a lord of the realm might love a lowly mestizo, but he would never provide a place for her in his life, not even as a mistress. His high position would never allow it.

Yes, what she had dreaded all along had come to pass, Fire Dancer thought sadly as a lone tear trickled down her cheek. Evan would walk out of her life for good now. Their precious time together was over.

27

Evan walked along the top of the lofty cliff that overlooked the Misho Sipokni for a long time, trying to sort out his feelings about his brother's untimely death and his sudden inheritance of everything that he had coveted for so long. He was genuinely saddened by the news of his brother's demise. Evan had never wished him or his family any harm. He had just wanted what his brother had, what Evan had thought should have rightfully been his. But it seemed now that possessing the title and all that it entailed was no longer his primary desire in life. Fire Dancer was. He wanted her more than he had ever dreamed was possible, more than anything on earth. Even more, he wanted her as his wife.

This admission was a revelation to Evan. He had never seriously considered what role he wanted Fire Dancer to play in his life, at least not consciously. For the time being, it had been enough just to know he loved her and that she loved him in return. As long as he couldn't leave because of the Cherokee uprising, he had been perfectly content just to let things drift between them, to bask in his happiness. But the news of his inheritance had changed that and forced him to look at the future. Now, he realized that walking out of her life would be more than just difficult. It would be impossible.

Just the thought of life without Fire Dancer at his side was unbearable. He wanted her there forever, to share all its pleasures and its disappointments with him, to mother his children, to grow old with him, to lie beside him even after death.

A thought came to Evan that put a chill on the warm glow he had been feeling. What if Fire Dancer refused to marry him and go to England with him? It would mean giving up the high Chickasaw position she was destined to inherit and the land that she loved so much. And fast on its heels came another disturbing question: Did he really want to take her to England and possibly subject her to being scorned again?

Evan scowled deeply; then his active mind took yet another twist. Maybe she wouldn't be scorned, he mused, not if she stayed on his country estate and if those who lived there came to know and respect her as he had. They were simple people, good at heart, much more fair-minded than their so-called "betters," and he'd be perfectly content to spend most of his time on his beloved land with his Chickasaw princess.

The reminder that Fire Dancer was a princess made Evan think of another Indian princess. Pocahontas had been taken to England by her husband, too, and she had died there of the plague several years later. Fire

Dancer had no more resistance to that horror than she did to any of the other diseases that scourged his country. Why, even a common childhood disease such as measles could kill her. Evan remembered the terror he had felt fearing for Fire Dancer's life when she was a Choctaw captive, and he knew, if he took her to England, he would always live in fear of losing her. It was a risk he could not, would not, take, even if it meant giving up his inheritance.

The last thought took Evan aback, but he found the idea of relinquishing his inheritance not in the least disturbing. Considering how long he had yearned for it, that was surprising. But sometime during the past few months, he had come to realize that titles and worldly possessions couldn't bring real happiness. Only a special person could do that. And for him, that special person was Fire Dancer. Still, a question remained to be answered, one of paramount importance. Would Fire Dancer be willing to give up her inheritance for him? Just because she loved him didn't necessarily mean she would. He had learned the hard way that Fire Dancer wasn't a woman to take for granted.

Evan spun around and strode rapidly back to the settlement, a determined look on his face.

When Evan entered the cabin a short while later, he found Fire Dancer sitting on one of the low couches beading a pair of moccasins. He frowned when she didn't even lift her eyes or acknowledge his presence in any manner. "There is something I need to discuss with you," he said.

Fire Dancer knew what Evan was going to say. That

he was leaving her. She couldn't bear to look at him, for fear she would burst into tears, and her fierce pride would never allow her to do that. Nor could she speak. There was a huge knot in her throat. Keeping her eyes glued to the beads in her fingers, she nodded.

Fire Dancer's attitude made Evan feel awkward and insecure, feelings he had never experienced in his entire life. It made asking her the most important question he had ever asked all the harder. He cleared his throat nervously, summoned his courage. "Will you marry me?" he asked.

Fire Dancer's breath caught at Evan's surprising, totally unexpected question. Dumbfounded, she looked up at him, wondering if her ears were playing tricks on her.

Her mute staring only increased Evan's discomfiture. "I know I'm asking a lot, for you to give up your inheritance for me, but I thought—"

Before Evan could tell her his decision to relinquish his inheritance, she regained her composure. "I had already decided to give up my inheritance," she said, "since I could never fulfill my obligations to the tribe. I could never lie with another man after loving you. It would be a"—Fire Dancer paused, looking for the right word—"a sacrilege."

Evan knew Fire Dancer spoke the truth. There was a world of difference between loving someone and making love. Making love had no heart and soul to it, and once you had experienced the sublime beauty of the combined emotion and the act, just making love was a mockery, a cheap imitation of what it should be, of what God had meant it to be. "Then you'll marry me?"

Fire Dancer knew what marriage to Evan would entail. She would have to give up her home and her people and live in his world—that cold, alien world that she disliked so much and where she was so disliked. But when she considered her alternative—going through life without him—there really was no choice. If need be, she'd go to the ends of the earth for the man she loved. No, she amended fervently—she'd go to hell for him!

Once she had made her decision, Fire Dancer allowed her steely control over her emotions to relax. A profound happiness came surging to the surface like a monumental tidal wave. "Yes!" she cried out joyously. "Yes, I'll marry you!"

To Evan, Fire Dancer's brief hesitation had seemed like an eternity, and he had been filled with dread that she would refuse him. When she finally gave him the answer he wanted, he was so relieved, his knees almost buckled. Caught up in the emotion of the moment, he swept her into his arms and embraced her, then kissed her long and fiercely, putting a firm seal on their commitment to each other.

When he finally broke the kiss and drew back, he was stunned to see tears streaming down her cheeks. "You're crying!" he said in amazement.

"Yes," she answered irritably, furiously swiping at the tears. "It must be that weak English blood in me. Chickasaw women don't cry, particularly not from happiness."

It was the first time that she had admitted to her English blood, and even if she did call herself weak, it pleased Evan. He smiled warmly and gently wiped a tear from her cheek with his thumb. "You can cry from happiness anytime, but not for any other reason, not if I can help it," he said softly.

Evan lowered himself to the couch and pulled Fire Dancer down beside him. "Now that you've agreed to marry me, there are some things we need to discuss. We need to decide where we're going to live."

"You mean, which of your estates in England?"

"We're not going to England. I've decided to pass my inheritance down to my younger brother."

Fire Dancer was so stunned that she could only stare at him for a moment. Then, her eyes narrowed suspiciously. "Why are you doing this?" she asked.

"I've decided I no longer want it."

Fire Dancer strongly suspected that Evan was giving up the earldom for her sake. "You must not do this," she objected. "You will regret it someday."

"No, I won't. The more I think about it, the more convinced I am. I'm not the same man who left England four years ago. I've changed. My values have changed. I'd be bored to tears sitting in Parliament listening to a bunch of pompous nobles argue about things they don't know anything about. And I'd have to do a certain amount of that, you know. And even when I was on my country estate, I'd be tied down to conformity. If I wanted to get out and dig in the dirt with my serfs like I did with you and the other Chickasaw, I couldn't, not without creating a certain amount of scandal. But I like being outdoors in the wide open, not for just a daily ride, as I'd do back in England, but working outdoors. That title would be like a stone around my neck, holding me back from doing what I really want to do. Here, in this country, I can do what I damn well please. I've had a taste of freedom of choice, and I like it."

"Then we'll go back east, to one of the colonies?

Evan remembered all too well how badly Fire Dancer had been treated there. "No."

"The frontier?"

That would be a little better, Evan thought. There was considerable prejudice against the Indians on the frontier, but a lot of mestizos had successfully blended in. But still . . . a glimmer of an idea came to Evan, one that had been playing around in the corners of his mind for months without his knowing.

"Do you remember that prairie we passed through on our way to the Chickasaw village on the Ohio? The place Black Hawk said was God's country?"

Fire Dancer had never forgotten the beautiful place or its breathtaking expanse of blue sky. Every time she looked into Evan's eyes, she thought of it. "Yes, I remember."

"Do you think God would mind if we used it for a while, perhaps a lifetime?"

"What are you talking about?"

"I thought maybe we could settle there. It wouldn't be all that isolated, certainly no more so than many of the colonists' homes on the frontier. We could build a cabin, a barn, some outhouses, clear some land for an orchard and a garden, and raise horses."

"Horses?" Fire Dancer asked in surprise.

"Yes. That land would make excellent pasturage with its lush native grass, and we'd need only a part of it. You have a herd of Chickasaw horses, and I have enough in savings to buy several more Thoroughbred breeding stallions, besides my own horse."

"You are planning on contaminating my entire herd by breeding them with English horses?" Fire Dancer asked in horror.

"Have you forgotten what I said this morning, how introducing new blood can produce a superior animal? Stop and think, Fire Dancer. Imagine a horse with my Thoroughbred's size and good looks and the Chickasaw mount's speed, endurance, and hardiness. A horse like that would bring top money anywhere in the colonies and on the frontier, and the way this country is going to grow, there's going to be a big demand for horses—and not just from the colonists, but from the other Indian tribes. Travel by boat will never be as important here as it is in Europe. We're going to be a mounted country, because horses can go where there aren't any rivers, and the more horse-conscious the people in this country become, the more particular they're going to be about what they're riding. A Chickasaw horse won't be enough. They're going to want a good-looking Chickasaw horse. Now *that* will be prime horseflesh."

Despite her earlier objections, Fire Dancer found the idea of a horse with the characteristics Evan had described not only intriguing but exciting. But she still had reservations. "I have never sold my horses. I don't know if I want to."

"I have to have some means of making a living, love," Evan answered patiently. "Let's face it. I don't mind digging in the dirt every now and then, but I'd never be a really successful farmer if I had only myself to depend upon, nor would I make a good trader, like Josh. But I do know about horse breeding. I dabbled in it a bit back in England. It's outdoor work. I think it's the perfect solution."

"You don't have to make a living. We can plant a garden, you can hunt, and we can live off of the land."

"And exist like some of those poor settlers we saw when we traveled back east, just barely getting by? No, Fire Dancer. I intend to give you more than that. We'll have a nice home, one we can really be proud of, one with some of the comforts of life in it."

"Are you thinking of a feather bed?" Fire Dancer asked, frowning her disapproval.

Evan chuckled. "Only if you want one. But I still think it's just a matter of getting used to it."

Perhaps it was, Fire Dancer conceded silently. She wouldn't mind having one those spinets, or one of those desks for Evan, or . . .

Seeing the smile spread across Fire Dancer's lips, Evan asked, "What are you thinking?"

"I just thought of what I want. A brass bathtub."

"Agreed." A wide grin spread across Evan's face. "But one with no feet on it," he added.

Their eyes met, and each knew the other was remembering that day in Williamsburg and looking forward to their next bath together. Then Evan said, "I'll send a letter back to the barrister telling him of my decision as soon as this mess with the Cherokee is settled."

"Then you won't be going back at all?" Fire Dancer asked in surprise.

"I don't know why I should. In a month, my enlistment will expire, and I'll be a civilian. Then I can do what I want." He paused. "How soon can we marry?" he asked.

"The Chickasaw do not have a marriage ceremony. As soon as the families of the couple come to an agreement, the two are married."

Evan frowned. "Then you'll have to get your grandmother's permission."

"No. I already told her I would not accept my inheritance, that the only person I could ever marry would be you, although I never dreamed that might actually happen. She understood and released me from my obligations to the tribe. She's been an entirely different person since I returned from the Choctaw. She said she had always loved me, but she didn't realize how much until she thought she had lost me. All she wants for me is my happiness, so I'm perfectly free to make my own decisions."

Evan's heart raced. "You've agreed, and I've agreed. Does that mean we're married?"

"Yes. All that is left is . . ." Fire Dancer's voice drifted off as she glanced at their bed.

"Consummation," Evan finished for her in a husky voice. He rose, swept her up in his powerful arms, and carried her swiftly to the bed. "That can be arranged, love. I can't wait to make you my wife, to make you mine for eternity."

As Evan carried her across the cabin, Fire Dancer snuggled closer, pressing her face into the warm crook of his neck and breathing in his heady masculine essence. She knew he had spoken the truth when he said he wanted to stay in this country. She had seen the change in him herself and had hoped that he would do just that. But she had never dreamed that he would turn his back on his world completely and walk with her in her own. That he loved her so much touched her deeply, and she fervently vowed he would never regret it. She would love her arrogant Englishman, her fierce golden warrior, with her whole heart and soul and every ounce of her being. And she would bring him untold happiness and strong, beautiful children. They would have a long, wonderful life together.

This was just the beginning, and it would last forever.

JOANNE REDD is a native Texan currently living in Missouri City. A retired obstetrics nurse, Joanne is the author of many critically acclaimed historical romances, including STEAL THE FLAME, APACHE BRIDE, DESERT BRIDE, CHASING A DREAM, and TO LOVE AN EAGLE, which won the *Romantic Times* award for Best Western Historical Romance.